Critical acclaim for David Baldacci's novels

'Skilfully constructed . . . Difficult to put down . . .
Another winner'
Booklist

'Brilliant plotting, heart-grabbing action and
characters to die for'
Daily Mail

'Baldacci inhabits the skin of his creations –
tripping us up with unexpected empathy
and subtle identification'
Sunday Express

'As expertly plotted as all Baldacci's work'
Sunday Times

'Baldacci cuts everyone's grass – Grisham's, Ludlum's, even
Patricia Cornwell's – and more than gets away with it'
People

'A plot strong enough to make the bath go
cold around you'
Independent on Sunday

'Yet another winner . . . The excitement builds . . .
The plot's many planted bombs explode unpredictably'
New York Times

Memory Man

David Baldacci is a worldwide bestselling novelist. With his books published in over 45 different languages and in more than 80 countries, and with over 110 million copies in print, he is one of the world's favourite storytellers. David is also the co-founder, along with his wife, of the Wish You Well Foundation, a non-profit organization dedicated to eliminating illiteracy across America. Still a resident of his native Virginia, he invites you to visit him at www.DavidBaldacci.com.

Also by David Baldacci

The Camel Club series

The Camel Club • The Collectors
Stone Cold • Divine Justice
Hell's Corner

Sean King and Michelle Maxwell series

Split Second • Hour Game
Simple Genius • First Family
The Sixth Man • King and Maxwell

Shaw series

The Whole Truth • Deliver Us From Evil

John Puller series

Zero Day • The Forgotten • The Escape

Will Robie series

The Innocent • The Hit • The Target

Other novels

True Blue • Absolute Power
Total Control • The Winner
The Simple Truth • Saving Faith
Wish You Well • Last Man Standing
The Christmas Train • One Summer
The Finisher • The Keeper

DAVID BALDACCI

Memory Man

PAN BOOKS

First published 2015 by Grand Central Publishing, USA

First published in the UK 2015 by Macmillan

This edition published 2015 by Pan Books
an imprint of Pan Macmillan
20 New Wharf Road, London N1 9RR
Associated companies throughout the world
www.panmacmillan.com

ISBN 978-1-4472-8796-4

1 3 5 7 9 8 6 4 2

A CIP catalogue record for this book is available from the British Library.

Typeset by Ellipsis Digital Limited, Glasgow
Printed and bound by CPI Group (UK) Ltd, Croydon, CR0 4YY

Visit **www.panmacmillan.com** to read more about all our books
and to buy them. You will also find features, author interviews and
news of any author events, and you can sign up for e-newsletters
so that you're always first to hear about our new releases.

To Tom and Patti Maciag:
Go forth and have fun.
You've earned it!

Memory Man

1

Amos Decker would forever remember all three of their violent deaths in the most paralyzing shade of blue. It would cut into him at unpredictable moments, like a gutting knife made of colored light. He would never be free from it.

The stakeout had been long and ultimately unproductive. Driving home, he had been looking forward to catching a few hours of sleep before hitting the streets once more. He'd pulled into the driveway of the modest two-story vinyl-sider that was twenty-five years old and would take at least that long to pay off. The rain had slicked the pavement, and as his size fourteen boots made contact, he slipped a bit before traction was gained. He closed the car door quietly, certain that all inside would be asleep at this late hour. He trudged to the screen door leading into the kitchen and let himself in.

The quiet was to be expected. But the *too* quiet nature of the setting was not. He had not sensed that then and later wondered why not. It was one of many failures on his part that night. He had paused in the kitchen to pour a glass of water from the tap. He chugged it, set the glass in the sink, wiped his chin dry, and headed to the next room.

He slipped on the floor and this time his big body tumbled. It was slick herringbone-patterned parquet and he had fallen before. Yet this time would be far different because of what he was about to observe. The moonlight had shafted in through the front window enough that he could see clearly.

When he held up his hand it was a different color.

Red. Blood.

It had come from somewhere. And he picked himself up to find out where.

He discovered the source in the next room. Johnny Sacks. His brother-in-law. A big, burly fellow like him, laid low. He bent closer, got on his knees, his face an inch or so from Johnny's. His throat had been slit from ear to ear. There was no need to check for a pulse; there could be none. Most of his blood was on the floor.

He should have pulled his phone and hit 911 at that very moment. He knew better. He knew not to stampede around a crime scene, for that was what his home had become by virtue of the dead man, killed by violent means. It was now a museum; you didn't touch anything. His professional side screamed this at him.

But this was only *one* body. His gaze jerked to the stairs and his mind suddenly disengaged as total panic seized every bit of him—the gut feeling that life had just robbed Decker of everything he would ever have.

So he ran, his boots pushing coagulating pools of blood outward like an incoming tide.

He was destroying vital evidence, royally screwing up what should have been kept pristine. Right now he didn't give a damn.

He tracked Johnny's blood right up the stairs, taking the treads three at a time. His breaths were gasps and his heart was pumping so fast and feeling so bloated it was a wonder his chest wall could contain it. His mind seemed paralyzed, but his limbs were somehow still moving of their own accord.

He hit the hallway, bounced off one wall and then its twin as he rocketed down to the first door on the right. He never took out his gun, not even bothering to think that the killer could still be there. Waiting for him to come home.

He smashed open the door with his shoulder and looked wildly around.

Nothing.

No, not true.

He froze in the doorway as the light on the night-stand dimly illuminated the bare foot that protruded above the mattress on the far side.

He knew that foot. He had held it, massaged it, and kissed it on occasion over many years. It was long, narrow, but somehow still dainty, the toe next to the big one slightly longer than it should have been. The veins on the side, the calluses underneath, the nails painted red, it was all as it should be, except it should not be poking above the mattress at this time of night. That meant the rest of her was down on the floor and why would that be, unless . . .

He edged to that side of the bed and looked down.

Cassandra Decker, Cassie to all including and most importantly him, stared up from her position on the floor. Well, staring was beyond her now. He stumbled forward, stopped next to her, and then slowly knelt, his blue jean knees coming to rest in the patch of blood that had collected next to her.

Her blood.

Her neck was clean, no wound there. That was not the source of the blood. Her forehead was.

Single-entry gunshot. He knew he shouldn't, but he used his arm to scoop her head off the floor, cradled it next to his heaving chest. Her long dark hair splayed out over his arm like frozen spray from a hard breaker. The dot on her forehead was blackened and blistered from the heat of the bullet.

A contact wound preceded by a muzzle's kiss, lasting only a second before the projectile ended her life. Had she been asleep? Had she awoken? Would she have endured the terror of seeing her killer standing over her? He wondered all this as he held his wife for what would be the last time.

He put her back where he had found her. Decker stared down at the face that was white and lifeless, the blackened dot in the middle of her forehead to be his

final memory of her, a grammatical period at the very
end.

Of everything.

He rose, his legs feeling numb as he staggered out of
the room and down the hall to the only other bedroom
up here.

He did not force this door open. He was in no hurry
now. He knew what he was going to find. He just didn't
know what the killer's method would have been.

First, a knife. Second, a gun.

She wasn't in the bedroom, which left the adjoining
bath.

The overhead light was on in there, burning brightly.
The killer had obviously wanted him to see the last one
clearly.

There she sat, on the toilet. Held there with the sash
from her robe wrapped around the water tank, for
otherwise she would have fallen over. He drew close.

His feet didn't slip. There was no blood. His little girl
had no obvious wounds that he could see. But then he
drew closer and saw the ligature marks on her neck, ugly
and blotchy like someone had burned her there. Maybe
the robe sash had been used. Maybe the guy's hands.
Decker didn't know, didn't care. Death by strangulation
was not painless. It was excruciating. And terrifying.
And she would have been staring right up at him while
he slowly compressed her life away.

Molly would have been ten in three days. A party
had been planned, guests invited, presents bought, and

a sheet cake with chocolate inside ordered. He had gotten time off to help Cassie, who worked full-time and also did pretty much everything here because his job was not a nine-to-fiver, not even close. They had joked about it. What did he know about real life? Grocery shopping? Paying the bills? Taking Molly to the doctor?

Nothing, as it turned out. Not a damn thing. Clueless.

He sat down on the floor in front of his dead child, crossing his long legs like his little girl liked to do, so the bottom of each foot was wedged against the inner thigh of the opposite leg. He was flexible for a big man. The lotus position, he dimly thought. Or something like that. He didn't even know why he was thinking this. He realized he must be in shock.

Her eyes were wide and open, staring back at him, but not seeing him. Like Mom. She would never see him again.

Decker just sat there, rocking back and forth, looking at her but not really seeing her, and his baby girl sure as heaven not seeing her daddy either.

This is it. Nothing left. I'm not staying by myself. Can't do it.

He slipped the compact nine-mil from his belt holster and made sure a round was chambered by racking the slide. He cupped it in his hands. Nice little piece. It was accurate, with enough stopping power. He'd never shot anyone with it. But he'd wanted to.

He stared down at the muzzle with the iron sights. How many rounds fired at the police range? A thousand? Ten thousand? Well, he couldn't miss tonight.

He opened his mouth and swallowed the muzzle, angling it upward so the bullet would hit the brain and make the end quick. His finger came to rest on the trigger guard. He looked up at Molly. Suddenly embarrassed, he slipped the gun out and put it against his right temple and closed his eyes so he couldn't see her. Again, his index finger slipped to the trigger guard. Once past it, to the trigger, then the slow, steady pull until the point of no return. He'd never feel anything. His brain dead before it could tell the rest of his body that he'd jacked himself.

He just had to pull. *Just pull, Amos. You got nothing to lose because you got nothing left. They're gone. They're . . . gone.*

He held the gun there, wondering what he would say to his family once they were all reunited.

I'm sorry?

Forgive me?

I wish I'd been here to protect you from whoever did this? I should have been here to protect you?

He held the gun tighter, digging the metal against his temple so hard he felt the smooth barrel cut into his skin. A drop of blood appeared and then was wicked into his graying hair, which, he was fairly certain, had become even grayer over the last few minutes.

He wasn't seeking the courage to do it.

7

He was desperately searching for the right balance. Yet could there ever be balance in taking one's own life?

Still holding the gun in place, he slid out his phone, dialed 911, identified himself by name and badge number, and in two concise sentences described the slaughter of a trio of people. He dropped the phone on the floor.

Down below was Johnny.

Down the hall was Cassie.

Here, on the toilet, was Molly.

And suddenly, without warning, he was seeing all of this outlined in the most *terrifying* shade of blue. The bodies, the house, the whole night. This bubble of blue; it was everywhere. And he tilted his gaze to the ceiling and screamed out a curse, fueling it with all the rage and loss he was right now feeling. The damn colors, intruding even on this. Why could he not be normal, for just this one time, in his complete misery? He lowered his head and sat there on the floor with a gun to his head and absolutely nothing left in the rest of him. He was ready to die, ready to join them.

But for some reason unknown even to him, Amos Decker didn't pull the trigger.

And so that was exactly how the cops found him when they showed up four minutes later.

2

A park bench painted red.

The unsettling knifelike chill of fall draining to winter.

Amos Decker sat on the bench, waiting.

A sparrow zipped across in front of him, narrowly dodged a passing car before soaring upward, catching a breeze, and drifting away. He noted the make, model, plate number, and physical descriptions of all in the car before it left him. Husband and wife in the front, and a kid in the back in a booster seat. Another one next to him, older. About ten. The rear bumper had a sticker. It read, MY KID IS AN HONOR ROLL STUDENT AT THORNCREST ELEMENTARY.

Congrats, you've just told a psycho exactly where to snatch your very smart kid.

Then a bus rolled to a near stop. He ran his gaze over it, making the same observations. Fourteen passengers, most looking depressed and tired though it was still only midday. One was energetic, a child. He bebopped next to his exhausted mother, who sat slumped over, a fat bag perched in her lap. The driver was a newbie, her face a sheet of nervousness. Even with the power steering she fought the wheel and took the next turn so slowly it looked like the bus's engine had died.

A plane soared overhead, low enough for him to ID it as a United 737, a later model because of the winglets. With the number 737, for him the color silver popped out. The number 737 was, in his mind, a beautiful concoction. Sleek, silver, fast, bulletlike. Anything beginning with a seven gave him that reaction. He appreciated that Boeing numbered all its aircraft beginning with seven.

Two young men walked past. Observed, recorded. One was older, bigger, the alpha, the other was the sidekick, only there for laughs and to push around. Then he noted the four kids playing in the park cross the street. Age, rank, serial number, pecking order, and hierarchy established before age six, like a pack of wolves. Done.

Next, a woman with a dog. A German shepherd. Not that old but with bad hips. Probably dysplasia, common in the breed. Cataloged. A man jabbering away on his smartphone. Zegna suit, the G for Gucci on the slick shoes, quarter-sized rock set in a gold band on his left hand, like a Super Bowl ring. Four-thousand-dollar Zenith watch on his right wrist. He was too small and the wrong build for a pro athlete. Dressed far too nicely for a typical drug dealer. Maybe a hedge fund manager, malpractice lawyer, or real estate developer. Memory socked away.

On the other side of the street an old woman in a

wheelchair was being rolled out of a medical transport van. Her left side was useless, facial paralysis on the same side. Stroke. Documented. Her caregiver had mild scoliosis with a clubfoot. Imprinted.

Amos Decker noted all of this and more as his mind sorted through everything that was in front of him. Deducing here and there. Speculating sometimes. Guessing other times. None of it meant anything other than it was just what he did to pass the time while he was waiting. Just like counting in color. Just what he did to pass the time.

He had lost the house to foreclosure. They were barely making the payments with his and Cassie's salary. On his paycheck alone it was a no-go. He had tried to sell it, but who wanted to live in a house covered in blood?

He'd lived in an apartment for several months. Then a motel room. Then, when his job situation changed, he had relocated to a friend's couch. After the friend became less friendly he had opted for a homeless shelter. When funding ran out for the place and it was closed, he "downsized" to a sleeping bag in the park. Then a cardboard box in a parking lot when the sleeping bag wore out and the cops rousted the homeless from the park.

He had hit rock bottom. Bloated, dirty, wild-haired, bushy-bearded, he looked like he should be living in a cave somewhere attempting to conspire with aliens. And he pretty much was until he woke up in a Walmart

David Baldacci

parking lot one morning staring at a Georgia-Pacific logo on the inside of his corrugated box and had the churning epiphany that Cassie and Molly would have been deeply ashamed of what he had become.

So he had cleaned himself up, worked a bunch of odd jobs, saved some dollars, and moved into a room at the Residence Inn and hung out his PI shingle. He took whatever cases came his way; they were mostly lowball, low pay, but they were something. And he didn't need more than something.

It was a meaningless existence, really, just like he was, meaningless. His beard was still bushy, his hair still pretty wild, and he was still way overweight, but his clothes were reasonably clean and he showered, some-times more than twice a week. And he no longer lived in a box. In his mind progress was always to be meas-ured in inches, especially when you didn't have yards or even feet of success to show off.

He closed his eyes to block out his recent street observations, though it was all still there, like a cinema screen on the inside of his eyeballs. It would always still be there. He often wanted to forget what he had just seen. But everything in his head was recorded in per-manent marker. He either dialed it up when needed or it popped up of its own accord. The former was help-ful, the latter infinitely frustrating.

That night the cops had talked him out of eating a round from his pistol. He had thought many times since of killing himself. So much so that, while still on the police force, he'd gone to therapy to work around that little issue. He'd even stood in front of a circle of like-minded suicidals.

I am Amos Decker. I want to kill myself. Period. End of story.

He opened his eyes.

Fifteen months, twenty-one days, twelve hours, fourteen minutes. Because of what he was, the clock was spinning in the forefront of his mind. That was the span of time that had passed since he had discovered the three bodies in his home, his family wiped out. And in sixty seconds it would be fifteen minutes plus the year, months, and days. And on and on it would go.

He looked down at himself. A four-year college football player and a professional for an extraordinarily short stint, he had kept fit as a cop and later a detective. But he had not bothered with any of that after officially identifying the bodies of his wife, brother-in-law, and daughter. He was fifty pounds overweight, probably more. Probably a lot more. Six-five and a blimp with bum knees. His gut was soft and pushed out, his arms and chest flabby, his legs two meat sticks. He could no longer see even his overly long feet.

His hair was also long, peppered liberally with gray, and not very clean. It seemed perfectly suited to conceal a mind that by forgetting nothing managed to let him down all the time. His beard was startling both for its bulk and for its chaotic appearance, wisps and curls and stray strands meandering everywhere like vines searching for purchase on something. But he told himself it was good for his line of work. He had to go chase scum, and scum, by definition, did not often look mainstream. Indeed, they often ran from it.

He touched the threadbare patch on his jeans and then looked down at the knees where the bloodstains were still visible.

Her blood. Cassie's blood. Morbid to still have it there.

Burn the pants, Amos. Most normal people would have done that.

But I'm not normal. I haven't been normal since I stepped on that field and took that hit.

The hit was the only thing he had never remembered. Ironic, since it was the catalyst for his never forgetting anything else. But it had been played relentlessly on the sports shows at the time. And even the national news felt the need to document the violence done to him to their countrywide audience. Someone told him the snippet had even been uploaded to YouTube a few years ago and had over eight million views. And yet he had never seen it. He didn't have to. He'd been there. He'd *felt* it. That was enough.

And all he had done to deserve the folderol of attention was to die on a football field, not once, but twice.

He ran a furtive, mostly embarrassed glance down at his jeans. His gut hung over the waistband because he'd been far thinner back then. He had washed them, but the bloodstains had not come out. Why should they be different from his brain? The pants could have, should have been evidence. Let the cops take them, but they hadn't, and he hadn't offered. He kept them, wore them still. Stupid way of remembering. Asinine, really. Horribly macabre way of keeping Cassie with him. Like toting her ashes in a Scooby-Doo lunchbox. But then again, he wasn't really okay. Even though he had a place to live, held a job, and was functioning, for the most part. He really wasn't okay. He would never be okay in any way.

He technically had been a suspect in the case, because husbands always were. But not for long. The timing of the deaths cleared him. He had an alibi. He didn't care about alibis. He knew he hadn't touched one hair on their heads, and didn't give a damn if no one else thought the same.

The real issue was that no one had ever been arrested for the murders. There hadn't even been any suspects, not a lead to come by. Nothing.

The working-class neighborhood they had lived in was quiet and the folks friendly, always offering a helping hand to others because nobody had much and everybody needed some assistance from time to time. Fixing a car or a furnace, or hammering a nail into a board, or cooking a meal because a mom was sick, or shepherding kids in a communal transportation system based on trust and need.

There were some tough nuts who lived there, for sure, but he hadn't spotted a homicidal one in the bunch. Mostly bikers and pot-heads. He had looked. He had done nothing else except investigate the crimes, even though officially they had told him to stay away from it all. But no clues presented themselves, even with his obsessively running everything down.

There were opportunities and obstacles for a crime such as this. Doors were left unlocked; folks came and went. So access was clearly there. But the houses were close together, so something should have been heard. But no sounds were ever heard from 4305 Boston Avenue that night. How could three people have died so quietly? Didn't violent death provoke outrage? Screams? A struggle? Something? Apparently not. The gunshot? Like a ghost whispering. Or else the whole neighborhood had gone deaf that night. And blind. And mute.

And months later there was still nothing, long after the trail had grown cold and the odds of solving the case and catching the killer had dropped to near zero. He had left the police force then because he could no longer push paper and run down other cases and bother with precinct drama. The upper management said they were sorry to see him go, but no one asked him to stay either. The truth was, he was becoming disruptive, unmanageable. And he was all of those things. Because he no longer cared about anything.

Well, except for one thing.

He had visited their graves all the time. They were buried in plots he had hastily purchased, because who would buy a plot for a man and a woman in their early forties and a grave for a ten-year-old? But then he had stopped going because he could not face them lying there in the dirt. He had not avenged them. He had done nothing except identify their bodies. A pitiful penance for letting his family die. God would hardly be impressed.

Their deaths *had* to be connected with what he did. He had put lots of people away over the years. Some were out now. Others had friends. Just before the murders at 4305 Boston Avenue, he had helped break up a local meth ring that was doing its best to make everybody in the metro area an addict and thus a good customer, young, old, and every demographic in between. These dudes were bad, evil, kill you to look at you. They could've found out where he lived. Easy enough. He wasn't undercover. And they might've taken out their revenge on his wife and child, and her brother who had picked the wrong time to visit from out of town. But there was not a scrap of evidence against this group. And without that, no arrests. No trial. No judgment. No execution.

His fault. His guilt. Maybe led them right to his family, and now he had no family.

The community had held a fund-raiser for him. Collected a few thousand bucks. It was all sitting in a bank account untouched. Taking the money would have seemed to him to be an act of betrayal for those he had lost, so the money sat, though he certainly could have used it. He was getting by, barely. But barely was all he needed. Because *barely* was all he was now.

He settled back against the wood of the bench and shrugged his coat closer around him. He was not here by accident.

He was here on a job.

And as he looked to his left, he saw that it was time to get to work.

He rose and headed after the two people he'd been waiting for.

3

The bar was much like every other bar Decker had ever been in.

Dark, cool, musty, smoky, where light fell funny and everyone looked like someone you knew or wanted to know. Or, more likely, wanted to forget. Where everyone was your friend until he was your enemy and cracked a pool stick over your skull. Where things were quiet until they weren't. Where you could drink away anything that life threw at you. Where a thousand Billy Joel wannabes would serenade you into the wee hours.

Only I could drink a thousand drinks and never forget a damn thing. I would just remember every detail of the thousand drinks down to the shapes of the ice cubes.

Decker took a seat at the bar where he could see himself in the reflection of the big mirror behind the stacked rows of Beam and Beef, Glen and Sapphire.

He ordered a dollar draft, clutched the mug between his hammy hands, and studied the mirror. Back corner and to the right. They had sat down there, the couple he'd followed into the place.

The gent was late fortyish, the girl half that. The

man was dressed in the best he had. A pinstripe wool three-piece, yellow tie dotted with blue flecks in the shape of what looked to be sperms on their way to fertilize an egg, and a dandy pocket handkerchief to match. Hair swept back revealed a lined, mature brow—attractive on a man, less so on a woman, but then life had always been unfair that way. Impressive diamond rings on the manicured fingers. Probably stolen. Or fakes. Like he was. His toenails were probably clipped too. His shoes were polished, but he'd missed the backs. They were scuffed, which came much closer to the man's actual nature. He was scuffed too. And he only wanted to impress on the way in, not on the way out. After the way out, you'd never see the prick again.

She was doe-eyed and dough-brained. Pretty in a vacuous, seen-it-a-thousand-times sort of way. Like watching a 3-D movie without the requisite glasses; something was just off. The lady was so blindly faithful and oblivious that part of you just wanted to walk away and leave her to her fate.

But Decker was being paid *not* to do that. In fact, he was being paid to do the opposite.

She was dressed in a skirt and jacket and blouse that probably cost more than Decker's car. Or the car he'd once had. The bank had gotten that too, as banks often did.

She came from old money. She was so used to the privileged life that was attached to such status that it made her incapable of understanding why someone would work so hard to snatch from her things she simply took for granted. That made her a potential victim every minute of every day of her life.

Such was the current moment: the shark and the dummy. Decker saw him as a six, a dirty number in his mind. She was a four, innocuous and uninteresting.

They touched hands and then lips. They shared drinks—he a whiskey sour, she a pink martini.

Figured.

Decker nursed his beer and bided his time. He looked at them without seeming to. In addition to the number tag, to him she was outlined in orange, the guy in purple, the same color he associated with zero, an unwelcome digit. So the guy really represented two numbers to him—six and zero. It seemed complicated, he knew, but he had no difficulty keeping it straight because it was just there in his head as clear as an image in a mirror.

And it wasn't that he saw them exactly in those colors. It was the *perception* of those colors. That was the best and only way he could explain the sensation. It wasn't like they taught a class on this. And he had come to it relatively late in the game. He was just doing the best he could. After all, he thought he'd left the world of Crayola back in kindergarten.

They continued with their lovey-dovey, hand-holding, foot-rubbing, heavy-petting afternoon fun and games. She obviously wanted more. He was unwilling to give it, because you teased a mark. Rushing could only mean bad things. And this guy was good. Not the best Decker had seen, but serviceable. He probably made a decent living.

For a purple zero.

Decker knew the guy was waiting to make an ask. A loan for a business prospect that couldn't miss. Some tragedy in his extended family that needed financial remedy. He wouldn't want to do it. Hated himself for it. But this was his last resort. She was his last chance. And he didn't expect her to understand. Or say yes. The debate framed that way, what other answer could she give? Except, "Yes, my darling. Take double. Triple even. Daddy will never miss it. It's only money, after all. *His* money."

An hour and two more pink martinis later, she left him there. Her parting kiss was tender and moving, and he reacted in just the right way, until she turned away and his expression changed. From one of reciprocal tenderness and love to one of triumph and some might even say cruelty. At least that's what Decker would say.

Decker did not like interacting with people. He preferred his own company. He hated idle conversation because he no longer understood its point. But this was part of what he did. This was how he paid the bills. So he told himself to get over it. At least for now.

Because it was time to punch the clock.

He carried his beer over to the table in time to put a massive hand on the man's shoulder and push him back into the seat he was just about to vacate.

Decker sat across from him, eyed the man's untouched whiskey sour—predators didn't drink on the job—and then raised his own beer in praise.

"Nice work. I like to see a real pro on the job."

The man said nothing at first. He eyed Decker, sizing up his unkempt appearance and looking unfavorably impressed.

"Do I know you?" he said at last, his tone snarky. "Because I don't see how that's possible."

Decker sighed. He had expected something a bit original. It was apparently not to be. "No, and you don't have to know me. All you have to do is look at these."

He pulled the manila envelope from his coat pocket and passed it across.

The man hesitated but then picked it up.

Decker took a drink of his beer and said, "Open it."

"Why should I?"

"Fine, then don't open it. No sweat off here."

He went to take the envelope, but the man jerked it out of reach. He undid the binding and slid out the half dozen photos.

"First rule of a con, Slick," said Decker. "Don't play on the sidelines while you're on a job. And when I said you were a pro I was being charitable."

His hand reached out and he tapped the photo on top. "She doesn't have enough clothes on and neither do you. And by the way, that particular act is illegal in pretty much all states south of the Mason-Dixon."

The man glanced up, his look one of caution. "How did you get these?"

Again, Decker felt disappointed by the query. "So now it's just a matter of negotiation. I'm authorized to give you fifty thousand bucks. In return, you write this one off and move on to someone else. In another state."

The man smiled, slid the photos back, and said, "If you thought these were a real problem for me, why not just show them to her? Why come here and offer me a way out with cash?"

Decker sighed once more and for the third time felt disappointed. This guy was just not a challenge. He collected the photos and put them back neatly in the envelope.

"You read my mind, Slick. Exactly what I told her old man. Thanks for validating my opinion. The girl's very religious, by the way. What you're doing to the lady in that third picture is a deal killer, in addition to the fact that she's your *wife*. Have a good one."

He rose to leave, but the man clutched at his arm. "I can hurt you," he said.

Decker took the man's fingers and bent them back until he gasped, and then and only then did Decker let go.

He said, "I'm fat, but I'm two of you and a whole lot meaner. I don't have to have a pretty face to do what I do. But you do. So if I take you out back and smash it in, what does that do for your future cash flow? You see my point?"

The man held his injured hand and paled. "I'll take the money."

"Great. I have the check for twenty-five grand right here."

"You said it was fifty thousand!"

"That was only if you pulled the trigger when I asked. You didn't. The consequences are your return goes down by half."

"You son of a bitch."

Decker sat back down and slipped a piece of paper from his pocket. "Plane ticket. One-way. For as far away from here as you can get without leaving the lower forty-eight. Leaves in three hours. A condition of the check clearing is you being on it. They'll have people there to confirm, so don't do anything stupid."

"Where's the check?" demanded the man.

Decker pulled out another piece of paper. "You need to sign this first."

He handed the paper across. The man ran his gaze down it. "But this—"

"This ensures the lady will never think of you again, except in a very bad way. Which means even if you try to slink back here it'll be a no-go."

The man's brain ran through what was happening, what this all really meant. "So you're blackmailing me with the photos and the fact that I'm married to get me to sign this? And if I don't sign you'll show her the photos and tell her I'm married and trust that will be enough to get me off her?"

"What a genius you are."

The man sneered. "I have a dozen more just like her. And far better-looking. She wanted me to sleep with her. I kept putting it off. You saw the photos. I have filet mignon at home. Why would I settle for hamburger, even if it does come with a trust fund? She's a dumb shit. And she's only fair-looking on a good day, even with all of *Daddy's* money."

"Mr. Marks saw you coming from a mile away, even if his little girl didn't. But then again, Jenny's been taken in before by scum like you. She deserves better."

Decker didn't know Jenny Marks and could not have cared less about her romantic entanglements. He had made these comments because he needed Slick to keep going. Keep talking. Get it all off his chest.

"*She* deserves better? Shit, I don't know why I even bothered. I could get better ass than Jenny Marks without even trying. And I wouldn't have to listen to her baby talk."

"Dumb shit? Baby talk? Really? Lady has a college degree." Decker already had more than he needed, but he was starting to enjoy this.

"Actually, she's not a dumb shit. She's a freaking moron."

Okay, fun is over.

Decker took the unsigned piece of paper and slid it into the envelope with the photos. He put them all away in his coat pocket.

"What the hell are you doing?" the man said incredulously.

In answer Decker pulled out a miniature digital recorder and hit play.

"I'm sure she'll enjoy your description of her," said Decker. "What kind of hamburger by the way? All beef? Organic? Or just freaking moronic?"

The man sat there looking stunned.

Decker put the recorder away and pushed the one-way ticket toward the guy. "We'll let you keep this. Be sure your butt is on the plane. The next guy they send out will be even bigger than me, and it won't just be your fingers he cracks. It'll be you."

The man said pitifully, "Are you telling me I get none of the money?"

Decker stood. "Like I said, what a genius you are."

4

Decker sat on his bed in his one room about the size of a prison cell. For dealing with clients he used a table in the dining room of the Residence Inn, where his monthly payment included a daily buffet breakfast. They were definitely losing money on him with that arrangement. He would just pick up entire plates of food from the buffet and carry them to his table. He could have used a backhoe instead of a fork.

He had gotten his check from Mr. Marks's emissary. A buddy on the police force had recommended Decker to the rich guy to handle this delicate matter concerning his vapid daughter who was always falling in love with the wrong guy. He'd never met with the old man, only his reps. That was okay; he doubted Marks would have wanted him soiling his fancy furniture. They had met at the breakfast bar—two young jerks in thousand-dollar suits who declined to even sample the coffee. They were probably more into double espressos spit out from those shiny little machines manned by a barista. He could tell from their expressions that they knew exactly how good they had it and how not good Decker had it. He'd worn his best shirt to the meeting, meaning the other one.

Daddy Marks had authorized up to a hundred grand to get rid of the albatross around his little girl's neck. After sizing up the con, Decker had told the reps he could get it done for a lot less. And he had. For the price of a one-way ticket, in fact. Chump change. You'd think Daddy Warbucks would have bonused him at least a percentage of the six-figure savings. But he stuck to the letter of their agreement and Decker just got his flat hourly rate, though he'd padded that considerably and made a nice payday for himself. Yet a percentage would have been good. Probably how the rich stayed rich. But it had been worth it, to see a con conned. And he figured Jenny Marks would be in the same boat in a few more months and he'd get called up again. Maybe he should ask Daddy Warbucks for a retainer.

He left his room and made his way to the dining area right off the inn's lobby. It was early and he was the only one there other than eighty-year-old June, who was enjoying her golden years by shoveling greasy home fries onto a platter at the buffet stand.

After loading up his plate he sat down to eat at his usual table.

His first forkful was halfway to his mouth when he saw her come in.

She would be forty-two now, same age as he was. She looked older. Her job just did that to a person. It had done so to him.

He lowered his gaze and his fork and salted every-thing on his plate four times over, including the pan-cakes. He was hoping that a man of his considerable size could shrink to invisibility behind a wall of protein and carbs.

"Hello, Amos."

Well, apparently not.

He shoved a forkful of congealed eggs, grits, bacon, home fries, and ketchup down his throat. He chewed with his mouth open, hoping that the sight would prompt her to hit a U-turn and go back to where she came from.

No such luck.

She sat down across from him. The table was small and she was small as well. But he was not. He was huge. He took up most of the table just by being there.

"How're you doing?" she asked.

He stuffed more food into his mouth and smacked his lips together. He didn't look up. What would have been the point? There was nothing that she could possibly say that he would want to hear.

She said, "I can wait this out, if that's how you want to play it. I've got all the time in the world."

He finally looked at her. She was stick-thin because of the cigarettes and the gum, which she always substi-tuted for food and drink. He was probably having more food at this one meal than she put away in a month.

Her hair was a pasty blonde, her skin wrinkled and splotchy. Her nose was crooked—some said from an encounter with a mean drunk when she was a beat cop. Her small, pointy chin seemed overwhelmed by her disproportionately large mouth where uneven and nicotine-stained teeth lurked like bats hanging in a cave.

She was not pretty. Her looks were not what made her memorable. What made her remarkable was that she had been the first female detective in the Burlington Police Department. As far as he knew she was still the only one. And she had been his partner. They had made more arrests leading to more convictions than anyone in the history of the department. Some on the force thought that was just great. Others thought they were full of themselves. Starsky and Hutch, one rival had called them. Decker never knew which one he was supposed to be, the blond or the brunet.

"Hello, Mary Suzanne Lancaster," he said, because he somehow couldn't *not* say it.

She smiled, reached over, and poked his shoulder. He winced slightly and drew back a bit, but she didn't seem to notice. "I didn't know you even knew my middle name."

He looked down at his food, his limited chitchat quota exhausted.

She ran her gaze over him, and when she was done Lancaster seemed to silently acknowledge that all reports of Decker having hit rock bottom were spot on.

"I won't ask how you've been, Amos. I can see not too good."

"I live here instead of in a box," he said bluntly.

Startled, she said, "I'm sorry, I didn't mean it that way."

"You need something?" he asked. "I have a schedule."

She nodded. "I'm sure. Well, I came by to talk to you."

"Who did *you* talk to?"

"You mean how did I know you were here?"

His look told her that was obviously his question.

"Friend of a friend."

"Didn't think you had that many friends," said Decker. It wasn't a funny line, really, and he certainly didn't smile. But she forced a chuckle as a potential ice-breaker, but then caught herself, realizing, probably, that it was stupid to do so.

"Well, I'm also a detective. I *can* find out things. And Burlington isn't *that* big. It's not New York. Or L.A."

He smacked his lips, shoveled in some more food, and his mind started to wander back to colored numbers and things that could tell time in his head.

She seemed to sense his withdrawal. "I'm sorry for everything that's happened to you. You lost a lot, Amos. You didn't deserve this, not that anyone does."

He glanced at her with not a single emotion evident in the look. Sympathy was not going to hold his attention. He had never sought sympathy, mainly because his mind didn't really get that particular sensation. At least not anymore. He could be caring. He *had* been caring and loving with his family. But sympathy and its even more irritating cousin, empathy, were no longer in his wheelhouse.

Perhaps sensing that she was losing him again, she quickly said, "I also came to tell you something."

He ran his gaze up and down her. He couldn't help himself, so he said, "You've lost weight. About five pounds you couldn't afford to lose. And you might have a vitamin D deficiency."

"How do you figure?"

"You were walking stiffly when you came in. Bone ache is a classic symptom." He pointed to her forehead. "And it's cold outside but your head is sweating. Another classic. And you've crossed and uncrossed your legs five times in the brief time you've been sitting there. Bladder problems. Another symptom."

She frowned at this very personal appraisal. "What, did you start medical school or something?" she said crossly.

"I read an article four years ago while I was waiting at the dentist's office."

She touched her forehead. "I guess I don't get out in the sun much."

"And you smoke like a rocket, which doesn't help anything. Try a supplement. Vit D deficiencies lead to bad stuff. And quit the cigarettes. Try a patch." He glanced down and saw what he had seen when she first sat down. He said, "You also have a tremor in your left hand."

She held it with her right, unconsciously rubbing at the spot. "I think it's just a nerve thing."

"But you shoot left-handed. So you might want to check it out."

She glanced down at the slight bulge on the right side of her jacket at the waistband where her pistol rode in a belt holster.

She smiled. "You have any more Sherlock Holmes stuff to throw at me? Want to check out my knees? Look at my fingertips? Tell me what I had for breakfast?"

He took a prolonged sip of coffee. "Just have it checked out. Could be something else. More than a tremor. Bad stuff starts in the hands and the eyes. It's an early warning, like a canary in a coal mine. And departmental firearms recert comes up next month. Doubt you'll pass with your grip hand going wacky on you."

Her smile faded. "I hadn't thought about that. I will, thanks, Amos."

He looked down at his food and drew a deep breath. He was done, just waiting for her to leave. He closed his eyes. He might just go to sleep right here.

She idly played with the button of her jacket, shooting glances at him. Preparing for what she had really come here to do. To say.

"We made an arrest, Amos. In *your* case."

Amos Decker opened his eyes. And kept them open.

5

Decker placed his hands on the table.

Lancaster noted the hands turning to fists and the thumb rubbing against the forefinger so hard it was leaving a mark.

"His name?" asked Decker, staring at a mound of uneaten scrambled eggs.

"Sebastian Leopold. Unusual one. But that's what he said."

Decker once more closed his eyes and turned on what he liked to call his DVR. This was one of the positives of being what he was. The frames flew past his eyes so fast it was hard to see, but he could still see everything in there. He came out the other end of this mental exercise with not a single hit.

He opened his eyes and shook his head. "Never heard of him. You?"

"No. And again, that's just what he told us. It might not be his real name."

"No ID, then?"

"No, nothing. Empty pockets. I believe he's homeless."

"Run his prints?"

"As we speak. No hits yet."

"How'd you get onto him?"

"That was the easy part. He walked into the precinct at two o'clock this morning and turned himself in. Easiest collar we've ever made. I've just come from interviewing him."

Decker shot her a penetrating look. "After nearly sixteen months the guy walks in and cops to a triple homicide?"

"I know. Certainly doesn't happen every day."

"Motive?"

She looked uncomfortable. "I just came here to give you a courtesy heads-up, Amos. It's an ongoing police investigation. You know the drill."

He leaned forward, nearly clearing the width of the table. In a level voice as though he were staring at her across the distance of their slung-together desks back at the police station he said, "Motive?"

She sighed, pulled a stick of gum from her pocket, bent it in half, and popped it into her mouth. Three quick chews and she said, "Leopold said you dissed him once. Pissed him off."

"Where and when?"

"At the 7-Eleven. About a month before, well, before he did what he did. Man apparently holds a grudge. Between you and me, I don't think the guy is all there."

"Which 7-Eleven?"

"What?"

"Which 7-Eleven?"

"Um, the one near your house, I believe."

"On DeSalle at Fourteenth, then?"

"He said he followed you home. That's how he knew where you lived."

"So he's homeless but has a car? Because I never walked to that 7-Eleven in my life."

"He's homeless *now*. I don't know what his status was back then. He just walked into the precinct, Amos. There's a lot we still don't know."

"Mug shot." It wasn't a question. If he had been arrested they had to take his picture and his prints.

She held up her phone and showed it to him. On the small screen was the face of a man. It was sunburned and grimy. His hair was wild and he was crazy-bearded. And, well, in that way, Leopold looked like Decker.

He closed his eyes and his internal DVR turned back on, but at the other end there were, again, no hits.

"I've never seen him."

"Well, he might look different now."

He shook his head and said, "How old?"

"Hard to say and he didn't. Maybe early forties, maybe."

"How big is he?"

"Six feet and about one-seventy."

"Lean or flabby?"

"Lean. Pretty wiry, from what I could tell."

"My brother-in-law was my size, construction worker,

and he could bench-press a truck. How'd Leopold manage it in a hand-to-hand confrontation?"

"That's part of the investigation, Amos. I can't say."

He looked directly at her again but this time let his silence speak for him.

She sighed, chewed her gum ferociously, and said, "He told us your brother-in-law was drunk at the kitchen table. Never saw it coming. He said he thought he was you, in fact. At least from behind."

He thought he was killing me when he was slitting my brother-in-law's throat?

"I don't look anything like my brother-in-law."

"From the back, Amos. And I'm telling you, this Leopold is a whack job. His elevator doesn't leave the basement."

Decker closed his eyes.

So then this whack job with the broken elevator for a brain next went upstairs and shot my wife and strangled my daughter?

He opened his eyes when Lancaster rose from her seat.

"I have more questions," he said.

"Well, I have no more answers. I could lose my badge for coming here and telling you what I just did. You know that, Amos."

He rose too, towering over her, a great big blob of a man who could cause little children to run screaming away in fear just by . . . being.

"I need to get in to see this guy."

"Impossible." Lancaster was already backing away. Then she noticed the bulge at his waistband.

"Are you carrying?" she said incredulously.

He didn't glance to where she was staring.

"I turned in my weapon when I left the force."

"Not what I asked. Anybody can buy a gun. One more time. Are you carrying?"

"If I were, there's no law against it here."

"Open carry," she corrected. "But there is a law against carrying one concealed unless you're a police officer."

"It's not concealed. You *can* see it, can't you? From where you're standing?"

"That's not the same thing, Amos, and you know it."

He held out his hands one next to the other. "Then cuff me. Take me in and put me in the same holding cell as Sebastian Leopold. You can take my gun. I won't need it."

She backed away some more. "Just don't push this. Let us do our job. We've got the guy. Let it run fair and square. We have the death penalty here. He could get the needle for what he did."

"Yeah, ten years from now, maybe. And so for a decade he gets a home with a bed and three squares. And if he *is* crazy and his lawyer papers it just the right way, he goes away for life to a nice comfy psych ward to read books, work puzzles, go to counseling, and get free meds that make him feel no pain. From where he's looking, not bad. I'd take that deal right now, in fact."

"He confessed to three murders, Amos."

"Let me see him."

She had already turned away and was fast-walking back to probably where she had parked her car.

She turned back around once and snarled, "By the way, you're welcome, you prick!"

He watched until she was gone from the lobby.

He sat back down at his table. He considered it *his* because everyone needed someplace to call his own. And this spot was it for him.

He had woken up this morning with not a single purpose in life, other than to live until the next morning.

Now that had all changed.

6

Decker went back to his room and pulled out his phone. He didn't like having to pay for a phone that had Internet access, but it was like having a huge library and an army of research assistants on the cheap. He checked the news feeds. They must have a lockdown on the Leopold arrest, because he found nothing. When he searched the name online he got a few hits but obviously it was other people only with the same name.

The guy had walked in and copped to three homicides. Even if he did plead insanity, he was looking at a lifetime inside. Was he the real deal? Had he done it? The cops should be able to tell pretty easily. Decker knew they had held back many details from the public about the crimes. They would interrogate Leopold, if that was his real name, and quickly determine if he was the guy or lying for some reason.

If he was the guy what would Decker do? Try to thwart the criminal justice system and kill him? And then end up in prison himself? But if he wasn't the guy, well, that offered up possibilities too.

Right now he could do nothing. Nothing construct-ive, at least. Leopold would be arraigned and formally charged, or let go, depending on the outcome of the interrogation. If he were kept locked up there would be a trial, or maybe not if the guy pled, which most defend-ants did, either because they were poor and had no money for a decent attorney or they were guilty or they were both. Rich guys always fought it out, especially with jail time in the equation. They had a lot to lose.

But the prosecution wouldn't have to offer a plea. They might want to try this sucker for their own pro-fessional gain. If so, Decker would be in the courtroom every day. Every minute. He wanted to see this guy. Smell this guy. Size him up.

He lay back on the bed. He looked like he was sleep-ing, but he was far from it. He was remembering. He was thinking back to what he once was. And what he was now. He thought about this often, even when he didn't want to. Sometimes, most of the time, the de-cision wasn't up to him. It was up to his brain, which, ironically enough, seemed to have a mind of its own.

I am Amos Decker. I'm forty-two years old and look at least ten years older (on a good day, of which I haven't had one in four hundred and seventy-nine days), and feel at least a century older than that. I used to be a cop and then a detective but am no longer gainfully employed in either occupation. I have hyper-thymesia, which means I never forget anything. I'm not talking about memory techniques where you can teach yourself to

42

remember things better, like the order of a pack of cards using association tricks. No, with me it's just a turbocharged brain that has somehow unlocked what we all have but never use. There aren't many hyper-Ts—my shorthand—in the world. But I'm officially one of them.

And it seems my sensory pathways have also crossed streams so that I count in colors and see time as pictures in my head. In fact, colors intrude on my thoughts at the most random times. We're called synesthetes. So I count in color and I "see" time and sometimes I also associate color with people or objects.

Many people with synesthesia are also autistic or have Asperger's syndrome. Not me. But I no longer like to be touched. And jokes don't really register with me anymore. But that may be because I don't ever intend to laugh again.

I was once normal, or as close as humans get to that state.

And now I'm not.

His phone buzzed. He looked at the screen. He didn't recognize the number, but that meant nothing. In drumming up PI work he had left his phone number a lot of places. He didn't want to focus on work right now, but then again, he couldn't ignore paying clients either. If he got kicked out of this dump for non-payment it was back to cardboard. And winter was coming. And while he had a lot of fat on him to keep warm, he would always take a firm roof over paper products.

"Decker," he answered.

"Mr. Decker, I'm Alexandra Jamison with the *News Leader*. Can I ask you some questions about the recent development in the case involving your family?"

"How'd you get this number?"

"Friend of a friend."

"Second time I've heard that phrase today. Don't like it any better this go-round."

"Mr. Decker, it's been sixteen months. You must be feeling something knowing that the police have finally made an arrest."

"How do you know they have?"

"I work the police beat. I have contacts. Solid ones that told me a suspect is in custody. Do you know any more than that? If you do—"

Decker hit the end button and her voice was cut off. The phone immediately rang again, and he turned it off completely.

He hadn't liked the press when he was a detective, though they could be useful in small measures. However, as a PI he had no use for them at all. And they would get no story or help from him about the case "involving" his family.

He left his room and caught a bus at the corner and rode it to a second bus, which he took all the way downtown. There were a few skyscrapers mixed in with a bunch of other buildings of low and medium height, some in good shape, others not. The streets were well laid out on a tight grid of right angles and straight thoroughfares. He hadn't spent much time downtown.

Crime, the serious crime at least, was either on the north side of town or in the suburbs. But the precinct where he had worked, and where the holding cell was for arrestees, was right here, smack in the center.

He stood on the street and stared across at a building he had walked into every day for a very long time: Precinct Number 2. It was actually Precinct Number 1, because the old number 1 had burned down. But no one had taken the time to redo the numbers. Probably not in the budget.

It was named after Walter James O'Malley, a chief of distinction some forty years ago. He'd dropped dead outside a bar with his mistress clinging to his arm. But that had not stopped them from naming a building after him, which proved conclusively that adultery did not really harm one's legacy. Even if it killed you.

His old digs were on the third floor. He could see the one window he would stare out, when he wasn't looking at Lancaster, who sat directly opposite him in the cramped quarters. The holding cells were in the basement and on the side facing this street, which meant that Sebastian Leopold was barely fifty feet away from him.

He had never been this close to his family's alleged killer. Yet maybe he had, when he'd apparently dissed this guy at the 7-Eleven.

He turned away when he saw two plainclothes and a uniform that he knew. Though he had changed a lot since he'd left the force, he doubted they could miss him. Stepping into an alley, he leaned against the wall. His anxiety level was riding high. Headaches came and went. His brain grew tired because it just never stopped. Not even when he was asleep. It was as though his subconscious was actually his conscious. For a man who never forgot anything it was difficult for him to remember who he used to be. And how he had gotten to be what he was now.

He closed his eyes.

This "gift" came to me when I was all of twenty-two years old. I was a middling college football player who walked on to an NFL team carrying only fair ability, but a ferocious chip on my shoulder. I stepped on the field for the first game of the season after playing my butt off during the preseason and surviving the final cut. I'm on the kickoff team. My job is simple: Sacrifice my body to create mayhem and holes in the return team so other guys can make the stop. I run my ass down the field. I'm about to make mayhem. I'm running so hard that snot is flying from my nose and spit from my mouth. I'm being paid more money than I've ever made in my life. I aim to earn it. I'm about to lay some dude out, stone cold out.

And that's all I remember. Dwayne LeCroix, a rookie out of LSU, was five inches shorter and fifty pounds lighter than me but apparently a force to be reckoned with, because he laid me out on that field with a hit I never saw coming. The dude blew me up, as they say in the NFL. He would be out of the league in four years with both knees devoid of cartilage, his left shoulder pared down to nothing but bone on bone, and his bank account overdrawn. *He was currently residing in a max prison in Shreveport for crimes committed against his fellow humans, and he would die there one day either soon or distant. But on that day he walked away, fist pumping and sauntering like the cock over the hens, while I lay on the field unconscious.*

And after that collision nothing for me would ever be the same.

Not a damn thing.

7

Decker opened his eyes when he heard the commotion across the street. Doors were being thrown open. Cars were squealing as rubber kissed pavement way too hard. Sirens sounded. Raised voices, metal clattering on metal. Heavy boots on concrete.

He stepped clear of the alley and looked across the street as patrol cars, sirens wailing, poured out of the precinct's underground garage. More officers and plainclothes had burst out of the front door of the precinct and raced to cruisers and unmarked cars parked on the street.

He continued to watch as a bulky SWAT truck lumbered down a side alley on the precinct side of the street, made its turn, and then the driver slammed his foot on the gas and the metal rhino charged down the road.

Decker inched closer to the street, joining a bunch of citizens who had appeared from the crevices of their lives to watch this disturbing spectacle. He listened to the others to see if they knew what was happening, but everyone there seemed to be stunned by what they were seeing.

Decker hurried across the street when he saw the man emerge from the precinct.

"Pete?" said Decker.

The man was dressed in a suit with stains on the sleeve. He was in his early sixties, very near retirement, slightly stooped and with comb-over gray hair. He stopped and looked up at him. Decker could see that Pete Rourke had his service weapon out and was checking the mag.

"Amos? What the hell are you doing here?"

"I was just passing by. What's going on?"

Pete turned pale and looked ready to collapse on the pavement. "Got some sicko at Mansfield High School. Walked in loaded for war and started shooting up the place. Lots of bodies, Decker. Mostly kids. I gotta go." He let out a quick sob. "Shit, my grandson goes there. He's just a freshman. Don't know if he . . ."

He turned and stumbled toward his car, a light tan Malibu, fell inside, started it up, and left tire rubber on the street.

Decker watched him go. An army of cops heading to a shot-up high school? Mansfield High. Where Decker had gone, a thousand years ago.

He looked around as the sounds of the sirens dissipated. The folks across the street were dispersing, returning to their slivers of existence. Many were checking their phones for news. Decker did the same, but there was nothing as yet. It was all still just happening. However, the news *would* pick it up and then not let it go.

Until the next shooting came along. Then they would rush headlong that way.

Until the next one.

Decker stared up at the door to the precinct. He wondered how many personnel would be left in the building. Surely they would have kept some behind. They had a high-profile prisoner in a cage there.

He touched the bulge of the gun at his waistband. That would be a problem. A magnetometer was right inside the front door. He looked around and spotted the trash can next to the building. He walked over and lifted the top. It was barely a quarter full. Trash pickup wasn't until the end of the week, he recalled. There was a rag on top of the trash pile. He slipped out his gun, wrapped it in the rag, and set it down in the can.

He looked down at his clothes. Another problem. He glanced around and saw the storefront. He had bought some things there before. A long time before.

Grady's Big and Tall Shop.

Well, I'm big and I'm tall. Right now I'm bigger than I am tall.

He slid out his credit card. It had a limit. A pretty low limit. But it might just be enough.

He went to the shop and the doorbell tinkled when he walked in.

A well-dressed, rotund man came over to him and then just as quickly took a step back.

"Can I help you?" he said from a respectful distance.

He probably thought Decker was homeless and looking to rob him.

Decker took out his wallet and flashed his PI badge. He did it fast so it looked like something else. He glanced down the street toward the precinct to add another layer to this subterfuge. Lying did not come naturally to him. And after the hit on the gridiron his filter had been vastly reduced, so it was even harder for him not to always tell the literal truth. He instinctively craved precision and was reluctant to accept anything less than that. Yet as a policeman who often moved in the underbelly of the criminal world, he had had to prevaricate. As a detective and now a PI, he had to be able to bullshit, otherwise his job would have been impossible. He had finally struck on a method that had seemed to work.

I will lie, perfectly.

He said to the man, "I've been working an assignment for too long. Let myself go. Chase rats you have to look like one. Gotta get back to civilization. Understand?"

The man had followed Decker's gaze to the precinct and nodded. His manner relaxed. He even smiled.

"You're not the first," he said encouragingly. "We get lots of customers from the Burlington Police Department."

"I've shopped here before," said Decker.

"Sure, I remember you," lied the man.

Decker shopped fast. Jacket, size fifty-four extra

long. Pants, size forty-eight, which were still snug, and he let his belly droop over the waistband as many out-of-shape men did. He opted against purchasing a belt. His pants were definitely not going to fall down. Luckily his legs were long and he could get a pair already hemmed that fit. Shirt, mammoth. Tie, cheap but effective. Shoes, size fourteens. He opted for the faux leather. They pinched his feet. He didn't care.

"Wouldn't happen to have a brush and an electric razor?" asked Decker, looking in the mirror.

"In our toiletries section over here."

"Briefcase?"

"Accessories, over here."

He paid for everything on credit. When Decker asked, the clerk threw in a legal pad and some pens that he had behind the counter in a box of office supplies.

"They keep cutting our budget," Decker explained. "How do we protect people if we can't even afford pens?"

"It's a crying shame," said the man. "World's going to hell. You interested in a tie clip or pocket square?"

Decker took everything to the restroom, rinsed off in the sink, rolled on antiperspirant he had purchased, buzzed off much of his beard, leaving only a shallow layer of fuzz over his chin, jaw, and upper lip, trimmed and tidied his hair, dressed in his new clothes and shoes, and put the old ones in the store's bag.

He walked out carrying the bag and headed back to the precinct. The tie cut into his throat, and despite the deodorant, he already felt a bit sweaty under the arm-pits, though the air was cool. But he didn't look like he had looked before. He hadn't looked this respectable even when he'd *been* a cop.

He added the bag of clothes to the gun in the trash can and marched up the steps of the precinct. He knew this was stupid. Insane. He hadn't been gone that long from the force. He could be recognized at any moment, like with Pete Rourke. But he didn't care. He really didn't. This was his shot. Maybe his only one. He was taking it.

He cleared the magnetometer. There was one young cop in the lobby manning the entrance. Decker didn't know him and he didn't know Decker.

Good and good.

He walked over to the information desk. The elderly woman sitting there was obviously not in uniform. She must be a civilian. Having a uniformed officer sitting at the front desk was not a smart deployment of resources.

His cover story formed in his head, Decker looked down at her. She looked up at him. Her eyes widened, perhaps simply to take in the whole of him.

"Can I help you?" she asked.

"You have a prisoner in the holding cell, Sebastian Leopold?"

She blinked in confusion. "I'm not sure what you—"

"I'd like to talk to him."

"And who are—"

"He needs counsel. I don't think anyone has been appointed to rep him yet."

"I'm not sure—"

"Sixth Amendment, right to counsel. Can't be denied. Just need a few minutes with him."

"I'll have to phone—"

"If you have to you have to. But I know things are pretty hairy around here right now. So if you don't get an answer, I just need a few minutes with him."

Decker lifted up his briefcase so she could see it and patted the side. "His arraignment is coming up. He'll need to be prepped for the plea. I've got some ideas."

"If you could have a seat."

Decker looked around at the police officer manning the magnetometer. He was staring at Decker, which was not good.

Realizing he might have just blown a bunch of money he didn't have on lawyer-looking attire, Decker sat down in a chair bolted to the wall and waited. The old woman picked up her phone and slowly, ever so slowly, punched in numbers.

Numbers. Always numbers.

They had a hypnotic effect on him, sending him to places he didn't always want to go.

Decker closed his eyes and his mind began to whir, back . . . back to the day, no, to the exact *moment* when his life changed forever.

8

The crowd went berserk every time the hit was replayed on the megatron, and that was often, I was told later. My helmet flew five feet and rolled another six, ending at the feet of a zebra who picked it up and maybe checked inside to see if my head was still in there.

I think my brain bounced against my skull multiple times like a bird trying to introduce itself to a window until its neck snaps.

Yep, the crowd cheered and whooped whenever the megatron belched out the replay.

Then I was told that they stopped cheering. Because I didn't get up. Because I didn't move a muscle. And then someone noticed I had stopped breathing and had also turned blue. They told me the head trainer was alternating pounding on my chest like a punch press attacking metal slabs and blowing air into my mouth. Later, they told me I died on the field twice but he brought me back both times from the hereafter. They told me he was screaming in my ear, "Hang on, ninety-five. Hang the hell on." I was such a nobody that he knew my jersey number but not my name. My professional football player identity was a nine and a five printed on my chest. Nine and five. Violet and *brown in my counting colors mind. I never consciously assigned colors to numbers. My brain did it for me without my permission.*

The collision changed everything about me, because it essentially rewired my brain. So I died, twice, and then came back, essentially as someone else. And for the longest time I thought that would be the most awful thing that would ever happen to me. And then came that night and those three bodies in neon blue, and the gridiron blindside dropped to a distant number two on the list of my personal devastations.

"Excuse me, sir? Sir?"

Decker opened his eyes to see the woman staring down at him. Not the old lady from behind the desk. She was far younger, maybe in her late twenties, dressed in black slacks and a light blue blouse with the two top buttons undone. She had a fresh complexion and an optimistic, efficient air about her. She must be very new, he thought. She wouldn't look this way in a year. Or maybe even in six months. Dealing with scumballs all day aged you faster than the sun.

He eyed the lanyard ID riding on her hip.

Sally Brimmer. Public Affairs. She must have come on after he left. His luck was running great right now.

Lie perfectly, Amos. You can do this. You have to do this. Every word counts. Because there will be blowback on this. Every word . . . So hit it.

He stood and held out his hand. "Yes, Ms. Brimmer?"

They shook hands. Hers was swallowed by his and he hoped she didn't interpret his sweaty palm as evidence of his deceit.

She said, "I was told you wanted to meet with Sebastian Leopold?"

"That's right. I understand he needs legal counsel."

"And who do you understand that from?"

Decker fought back the anxiety building in his chest, fast-framed through his mental DVR, formulated his response, and out came the words.

"I have a contact at the *News Leader*, Alex Jamison. Heard of her?"

"Yeah, I have. She's good. She probably does know. And you're a lawyer?"

He showed her a business card with an office address on the other side of the city that was actually the address of a law firm.

She stared down at this and then handed it back. "We've got an emergency going down," she said.

"I heard. Pete Rourke told me on the way in. Mansfield High School. His grandson goes there. I hope he's okay."

"So you know Pete?"

"We go way back, Ms. Brimmer."

She sighed and looked around. "I'm not really the one who should be making this decision."

"I could come back." Before she could react to this offer he quickly added, "But Leopold has to be arraigned in forty-eight hours or else he gets released. I doubt anyone here wants that."

"No, no they don't. It's just that—"

The right words flashed through Decker's mind. It was like he was reading off a teleprompter. "And sending him to an arraignment without counsel or with ill-prepared counsel could create a legal snafu that could come back to bite the department in the ass, pardon the French. I know you don't want that either. No law-abiding citizen would."

She started to nod halfway through his spiel.

"You'll only need a few minutes?"

"All I'll need," he said.

She hesitated and he could read the vacillation in her eyes.

She wanted no part of this and was feeling boxed into making a decision.

The farther he got into this lie the more anxiety he started to feel. He drew a long breath, pushing the bile back down his throat with the exhalation. "Just a few minutes," he said. "Then I'll be out of here. And he won't be able to complain later."

Decker truly meant this last part.

"You know what he's accused of?" she asked.

"Yes, I know it pretty well, actually. But regardless of these heinous acts, he is entitled to counsel. And if he's found guilty they can lethal-inject him without one complaint from yours truly. That I promise."

The truth will surely set you free, Amos.

Her vacillation finally broke, like water from a womb.

"Okay, follow me."

And Amos Decker followed her.

9

They rounded the corner of the hall and there he was, a rat in a cage, at least to Decker's thinking. But that wasn't enough. He needed to be sure.

Brimmer looked at Decker and then Leopold.

"There he is. I can give you fifteen minutes, max."

"All I'll need," replied Decker.

There was a jailer there, again a guy that Decker didn't recognize. As a detective for ten years he hadn't mixed that much with the uniforms.

"Open it up, please," said Brimmer to the jailer.

Keys came out and the door slid back and Decker walked into the cell and stared down at the man, who sat perched like a cat on the bunk bed.

Brimmer said, "Fifteen minutes, okay?"

Decker nodded but didn't look at her. Her heels tap-tapped away. Decker waited until the jailer went back to his desk at the end of the corridor before moving forward and fully focusing on the prisoner.

Sebastian Leopold wasn't as big as he would have thought from Lancaster's description.

Or maybe I've just gotten a lot bigger.

They'd put him in an orange prison jumpsuit. His hands and feet were manacled and the waist chain bolted to the wall. Which was a pity because if he tried to attack Decker, Decker could just kill him in self-defense.

The head turned to Decker and he braced for some sort of recognition from Leopold. But none came. Strange, since he'd apparently dissed this guy so badly he'd taken his revenge in the slaughter of Decker's family.

The eyes were bloodshot, the pupils dilated. Decker figured the cops had given him a drug test, made him pee into a bottle, taken a cheek swab for DNA and breathalyzed him for booze. The jumpsuit had short sleeves, so the man's forearms were revealed. There was a tattoo of twin dolphins on his right arm. That was interesting.

There were also drug tracks. And they looked relatively new. He wondered if the man had taken a pop before waltzing in here and copping to three murders. You'd need some extra juice to do something like that, Decker thought.

Part of one finger on his left hand was gone, cut off at the first section. There was a scar on his face. A busted nose that slid ten degrees to the left. Hands heavily callused and strong-looking. He had done manual labor.

And are those the hands that took Molly from me?

"Mr. Leopold?" he said.

61

Leopold continued to look at him without really seeing anything. At least it seemed that way to Decker.

Still no recognition. And with the cleanup and cutting of beard and hair, Decker looked closer to the cop he'd been seventeen months ago when he'd allegedly dissed Leopold at the 7-Eleven.

He stared into the man's face and turned on his DVR. Frame after frame raced through his mind, going back to the precise time period when he had supposedly run into the man. The date flashed up in his head so close that it seemed to be on the other side of his eyeballs. One month before the murders, that's what Lancaster had said. Decker tacked on one week on either side of that date just to be sure.

His DVR whirred and frames flew past by the hour, by the minute. Decker had been to that 7-Eleven three times during that period.

Sebastian Leopold was simply not in there.

Decker shut off his DVR and sat down in a chair built into the wall.

"Mr. Leopold," he said in a low voice. "Do you recognize me?"

Leopold seemed to be listening but not actually hearing.

"Do you recognize me?"

Leopold gave a shake of the head.

He moved his hands in odd ways in front of him. Decker observed the precise patterns the man was making.

"You need an attorney," said Decker, and he patted his briefcase.

Leopold stopped moving his hands and nodded at this.

Decker took out his pad and pen.

"Can you tell me what happened that night?"

"Why?"

There was a sudden caginess in the voice that slightly surprised Decker. He had interviewed many prisoners, many accused. Many were dumb as dirt and had committed crimes for reasons stupider than they were. But some were a lot smarter than folks gave them credit for. And maybe Leopold was one of those.

"You need a defense. You've confessed to three murders."

"I'm guilty. I done it."

"You still need legal representation."

"Why?"

"It's just how the legal system works. So I need to know the facts."

"They're going to execute me." The tone was of a child confessing his expected punishment. The cagey prisoner had transformed into a little boy. Decker wondered if it were the drugs doing this to him, making a pinball game out of his thought process.

"Is that what you want?"

"Not up to me."

"You're right. It's largely up to a judge and a jury.

But you still have input. So, you want to tell me what happened?"

Decker checked his watch. Four minutes had passed. And at any moment someone might walk by who knew him. He turned so that his back was to the cell door.

"I killed them," said Leopold simply. He was staring dead at Decker now, and Decker was looking for any hint of recognition in the other man's eyes. If he saw it, what would he do? Strangle the man like he might have done to his daughter?

Leopold started moving his hands again. He looked like a conductor leading an orchestra that didn't exist. Decker watched for a few moments, then refocused.

"And why did you do that?"

"Dude pissed me off."

"What dude?"

"The dude. Dude that lived there."

"How'd he piss you off?"

"Just pissed me off."

"But how?"

"Didn't show me no respect."

"You worked there? You were a customer there? At the 7-Eleven on DeSalle?"

Leopold ignored this and said, "Well, I got him, didn't I?"

"How'd you do that?"

"Killed his family."

"No, I mean how did you know where he lived?"

"Followed him."

"How?"

Now there came a caution in the man's eyes that Decker had not seen before.

"I don't need to tell you shit. You a cop? Trying to trick me?"

"You confessed, Mr. Leopold. There's nothing left to trick. Do you see that?"

Leopold blinked and rubbed at his neck. "Yeah, I guess I see that."

"And, no, I'm not a cop. So you followed him. How?"

"What do you mean, how?"

"Car, foot, bike?"

"Ain't got no damn bike."

"So a car?"

"If I ain't got a bike, I ain't got no car."

"So on foot, then?"

Leopold nodded slowly and then studied Decker closely, perhaps to see his reaction to this.

Decker wrote something down on his pad. He wiped a bead of sweat off his brow even though it was cold in the basement cell. If he was discovered here, *he* could go to jail. And he didn't actually like talking to people, so the briefer the better. But he had to do this. This might be his only chance.

"So you found out where this 'dude' lived and then you planned to kill his family. But you waited a month or so. Why?"

"Who said I waited a month?"

"That's what you told the police."

Leopold hunkered back down, the rat hiding among the crevices. Only there was no place to hide in here.

"Okay, that's right. I had to plan it out. Watch the place, see what the lay of the land was, so to speak."

Decker glanced down at the tattoo. "When were you in the Navy?"

Leopold's eyes flashed for just a second. "Who says I was?"

Decker pointed at the tat. "Two dolphins. Sailors often have those. You have it positioned so it won't show from under your uniform sleeve, per regulations."

Leopold looked down at the tat as though it had betrayed him.

"I'm not in the Navy."

"So you got the lay of the land and then went there that night. Take me through it."

Decker glanced over his shoulder at a sound. But it was only the jailer walking down the corridor. He rubbed another bead of sweat off his cheek.

"Take you through it?" parroted Leopold.

"From the moment you got there to the moment you left. Let's start with how you got there."

"Walked."

"House address?"

Leopold hesitated. "It was a two-story, yellow siding, carport on the side."

"How'd you get in?"

"Side screen door into the kitchen."

"Remember any details of the room?"

"It was a damn kitchen, man. Stove, dishwasher, table, and chairs."

"Remember the color of the walls?"

"No."

Decker glanced at his watch again. He had to speed this up, and his anxiety at being here was growing by the second.

"Who'd you kill first?"

"The dude. Thought it was the guy that dissed me. But I guess it wasn't."

"How do you know that?"

"Pictures in the paper. After."

"Go on."

"He was at the kitchen table. Been drinking."

"How do you know that?"

Leopold looked up, obviously irritated. "Why you keep asking me that?"

"Because the cops will. The court will. The jury will want to know these things."

"Hell, I confessed."

"They can still try you."

Leopold looked shocked by this. "Why?"

"To make themselves look good. How do you know he'd been drinking?"

"Beer bottles on the table."

"How'd you kill him? He was a lot bigger than you."

"He was drunk. I took my knife and cut him, right here." He pointed at his neck.

"He was found in the adjoining room."

"Yeah, yeah, that's right. But, see, he crawled in there, after I cut him. Bleeding like a bitch. Then he, hell, he just didn't move again."

"Did he make any sounds?"

Leopold said, "Yeah, but not no loud ones." He pointed to his neck again. "Got him here. Couldn't make much noise."

"Remember what he was wearing?"

Leopold looked blankly at him. "Long time ago. Pants? Shirt?"

"What next?"

"Knew he had a family. Went to go kill them too."

"Take me through it," Decker said calmly, though he was feeling the opposite. His heart was beating so fast he could feel the pulses in every part of his body, like he had a thousand tiny hearts pumping madly.

Almost there, just hang on, Amos, just hang on.

"I went up the stairs. First room on, on—"

"The left?" suggested Decker.

Leopold pointed at him. "Yep. The left."

"And?"

"And I went in. She was in the bath—no, she was on the bed. That's right, on the bed. Pretty little thing. She had a nightie on. See right through it. Damn, the bitch looked good."

Decker gripped the edge of his chair and kept his

eyes on Leopold. His wife had not been raped. That had been confirmed. But there had been something else.

"So the light was on?" Decker asked.

"What?"

"You said you could see right through her nightie. I was assuming the light was on."

Leopold looked unsure. "No, I don't think it was."

"Then what?"

"I stood over her."

"While she was lying in the bed?"

Leopold looked crossly at him. "Shit, man, can you let me tell it?"

"Sorry, go ahead."

"I had my gun. I put it against her forehead and I shot her."

"What kind of gun?"

Leopold answered right away. "Forty-five. Smith and Wesson."

"Where'd you get it?"

"Stole it off some guy."

"Guy have a name?"

Leopold just shrugged.

"Keep going."

Overhead Decker could hear doors opening and feet trooping around. It seemed some of the cops were returning from the high school.

"So I shot her. No, wait a minute. She did wake up, come to think. She sat up, she was starting to scream.

That's right. And I shot her. Then the bitch fell off the bed."

"Flat on the floor? Her whole body?"

Leopold looked at him warily. "Maybe parta her got hung up. Foot or arm or something."

"What then?"

This was the critical point. The one that had not made it into the papers. The wound to her head was not the only one Cassie had suffered. It had been discovered during the autopsy.

She had not been raped. But the outside of her genitals had been mutilated.

"Knew he had a daughter. I went down the hall to her room. She was sleeping."

"So you were done with the woman. Nothing else with her?"

Leopold just stared up at him. "I told you what I done. I *shot* her. Dead!"

"Okay."

"Then I went down the hall to the kid."

"Wait a minute, the shot didn't wake the girl up?"

Leopold looked puzzled again. "I, no, don't think so. She was sleeping."

"Then what?"

"I took her outta the bed."

"Why?"

"I just did. Wasn't thinking too clearly then. Took her to the bathroom."

"Again, why? Not thinking too clearly?"

"That's right. Maybe I had to take a leak and didn't want her getting away."

"Did you take a leak?"

"Don't remember."

"And she didn't scream when she saw you?"

"No. She was scared, I guess. And . . . and I told her to be quiet."

"Then?"

"Then I strangled her. Put my hands around her neck and just squeezed tight as—"

Decker put up a hand for him to stop. He looked away for a moment, the most brilliant blue blinding him. The color was so bright he thought he might be sick. It was like he was suffocating in sapphire.

"Hey, man, you okay?" asked Leopold with genuine concern on his face.

Decker's forehead was drenched in perspiration. He slowly wiped it off. "Okay, you killed her, then what?"

Leopold looked unsure again.

Decker said, "Did you do anything with the body? Do something with her clothing?"

Leopold snapped his fingers. "That's right," he said, his face beaming like he'd just got the answer right in algebra class. "I sat her up on the toilet and I tied her, uh, whatchamacallit."

"Her robe belt?" prompted Decker.

"Right, her robe belt around her and the toilet."

"Why?"

Leopold just stared at him. "'Cause . . . 'cause that's what I thought to do at the time."

"How'd you get away?"

"I went out the way I came in."

"Did you have a car?"

"No, I *told* you I walked!"

"Anybody see you?"

"Not that I know of."

"What'd you do with the gun?"

"Trash."

"Where?"

"Don't remember."

"The knife?"

Leopold shrugged. "The same."

"You tell anybody what you did?" asked Decker.

"Not till now."

"So why now?"

Leopold shrugged again. "They gonna fry my ass?"

"Lethal injection. Frying comes later."

"Huh?"

"In hell."

"Oh, yeah." Leopold chuckled like he thought Decker was making a joke. "That's a good one."

"So why come forward now?" asked Decker.

Leopold said, "Seemed as good a time as any. Ain't had nothing else going on."

Decker eyed a lump on the side of Leopold's neck. "What's that lump? You sick?"

Leopold reached up and gingerly touched it. "Ain't nothing."

"You have it checked out?"

Leopold snorted. "Yeah. I went to the Mayo Clinic on my jet. Paid in cash."

Sarcasm. Interesting.

"If you were in the Navy you might have health coverage."

Leopold shook his head. "DD. Dishonorable discharge."

"So you *were* in the Navy?"

"Yeah," conceded Leopold.

The sounds from above were getting louder. Decker checked his watch. Two minutes left and Brimmer seemed like the type who would show up right on time to escort him out.

"Any PTSD?"

"Any what?"

"Head problems? Depression? From combat?"

"I was never in combat."

"So you're just a sick son of a bitch who wipes out a family because somebody dissed you?" Decker kept his voice level and calm.

Leopold attempted a grin. "I guess so. I'm bad news, man. Always have been. If my momma were alive she could tell you. I'm just a shit. Screwed up every damn thing I ever touched in my whole life. No lie."

"And when we check your military records it'll show you were in the Navy as Sebastian Leopold?"

Leopold nodded, but absently, as though he weren't really agreeing with the statement.

Decker leaned closer. "Let me ask it clearer. Is Sebastian Leopold your real name?"

"One I been using."

"Since birth or more recently?"

"Not since birth, no."

"So why use that name, then, if it's not yours?"

"What's in a name, man? Just letters stuck together."

Decker pulled out his phone and, pointing it at Leopold, said, "Say cheese."

He took Leopold's picture and then put his phone away.

Then he held out a pen and a piece of paper. "Can you write down your name for me?"

"Why?"

"It's just for my records."

Leopold took the pen and slowly wrote out his name.

Decker took back the paper and the pen, stood, and said, "I'll be in touch."

He went to the door and called for the jailer. When the man came and unlocked the door Decker said, "Memory serves, there's a bathroom right down there, right?" He pointed the opposite way he had come in.

The jailer nodded. "Yep, men's room is the first door."

Decker stuffed his pad and pen back into the briefcase and moved swiftly down the hall toward the john. His change in plan had been prompted by the footsteps he'd heard clattering down the steps. More than one pair, which meant that Brimmer had reinforcements. Which meant they knew something was up.

Decker walked past the door to the toilet and hung a left and then a right and hit another corridor. He was as familiar with the layout here as anyone.

The hall ended in a door. He opened it and stepped out onto the loading dock. There was no one there. And only one truck backed up to the dock, its overhead door open, revealing the trailer to be empty.

Decker skittered down a short stack of steps and his new, tight shoes hit asphalt. He turned left down an alley and emerged on the main street ten seconds later. He hung another right and then a left at the next inter-section. There was a hotel there and a cabstand.

He told the lead cabbie, "Head north as far as five bucks will take me."

The cab dropped him off a while later. He hoofed it to a bus stop, and two rides later he was back at the Residence Inn. As he stepped off the bus he noted there were two police cars parked out front and an official departmental car he knew had to belong to someone other than a street cop.

Well, shit.

10

The only good thing, figured Decker, was that he hadn't gotten the chance to retrieve his gun from the trash can along with his other clothes. Walking in armed to the situation that was probably awaiting him would not be smart. He could run for it, he supposed, but that was probably what they were expecting. And he didn't like running. He just wasn't built for it anymore.

So he loosened his tie, undid his top shirt button, let out a sigh of relief as his thick neck was freed from this glorified noose, and walked into the lobby of the Residence Inn. There he was immediately surrounded by four police officers.

Decker studied them calmly. "With what's going down at Mansfield I didn't think you'd be able to spare the manpower."

"Cut the shit, Decker," said a familiar voice.

Decker slid his gaze to the side. "Hello, Mac."

"That's Captain Miller to you."

"I'm no longer on the force."

"Show some respect or you might be in a jail cell before I'm done with you."

MacKenzie Miller was in his late fifties, puffy as a bullfrog and with similar coloring. He was as wide as he was tall, Decker in miniature. He was dressed in a suit, and when his coat moved open as Miller strode across the lobby, Decker could see the ubiquitous braces that held up the man's pants, though his substantial waistline, like Decker's, did that job fine all by itself.

"And why would that be?"

Miller gave him a patronizing look and then snapped, "Brimmer!"

An embarrassed-looking Sally Brimmer hurried over from where she had been standing next to a fake ficus plant with a thick coating of dust on the leaves.

"Is this the man, Ms. Brimmer?"

"That is undoubtedly *him*, sir," she said quickly, narrowing her eyes and giving Decker a venomous look.

"Thank you," said Miller with an undertone of triumph. He turned back to Decker. "You came into the precinct today while we were undermanned because of the horrific situation at Mansfield, and using this situation to your advantage you misrepresented yourself as a lawyer and gained admittance to Sebastian Leopold's jail cell."

"Well, that's *one* version," said Decker.

Brimmer exclaimed, "That is the *only* version."

"No, it's actually not," said Decker calmly.

Miller spread his pudgy hands wide. "Then lay another on me, Decker. This has to be good."

"I came into the precinct and asked to see Sebastian Leopold. I said he needed a lawyer. I never said *I* was a lawyer."

"You gave me your card," pointed out Brimmer.

Decker's mind had already flown forward six moves. It was like he was playing chess and they were playing checkers. "I gave you *a* card. It was Harvey Watkins's. He's a member of the bar. I've done PI work for him. He handles criminal cases. And he's good. I've sniffed out work for him before. No law against it."

"But you represented yourself as this Watkins person," exclaimed Brimmer.

"Maybe you took it that way. But I never provided ID that said I was Harvey. And you never asked for my ID. I just gave you his card when you asked if I was an attorney."

"But you said you knew Pete Rourke," said Brimmer in an exasperated tone.

"I *do* know Pete. Worked with him for years. Again, no law against telling the truth."

"But you . . . you . . ." Brimmer faltered and looked at Miller for help. But the captain kept his gaze on Decker. He obviously wanted to see this play out.

Decker continued, "I guess since I had on a suit and tie and carried a briefcase you just assumed I was a lawyer. I asked you for an interview with Leopold. You said I had fifteen minutes. I took my allotted fifteen minutes, and then I left Leopold sitting in his cell." He looked around at the cops. "So I'm not sure why the cavalry is here."

Brimmer looked stunned. The cops looked unsure. Miller clapped his hands in appreciation and then pointed at the uniforms. "You boys can head on." He hooked a thumb at Brimmer. "And give the lady a ride back, will ya?"

"Captain Miller," Brimmer began, but he waved her off.

"Later, Brimmer. Just go with the fellas."

They trooped out, leaving Miller and Decker staring at each other.

Miller said, "Can we talk about this?"

"You need to focus on Mansfield, Mac. You want to come back and arrest me, I'll be right here."

Miller nodded and an appreciative smile broke over his features before disappearing. "Let's sit for a few. Can I get a decent cup of coffee in this place?"

Decker led him over to his table in the restaurant off the lobby. Then he poured out two cups of coffee from a beverage stand set up against one wall and brought them back over, sitting down across from his former boss.

"How's Mansfield?" asked Decker.

"Catastrophic. We're still finding . . . stuff. Bodies. The death count will go higher, no question."

"What about Pete's grandson?"

Miller shook his head. "I don't know, Amos. I don't have names yet. A bunch of cops' kids go there. It's the biggest high school we have."

"And the shooter?"

Miller ground his teeth. "He got away."

"How?"

"Don't know yet. Everything is still . . . developing."

"Usually they eat their own bullet on site."

"But not this time. It's like a school shooting a week now across the country. When's it going to end, Amos? You're a smart guy. When?"

"I'm not that smart."

Miller slowly nodded while drumming his fingers on the fake wood tabletop. In several quick bursts he drank down his coffee. Rubbing his lips, he said, "Why'd you do it, Amos? Talking your way in to see that son of a bitch?"

"Wanted to eyeball him for myself."

"Lot of ways to do that without doing what you did."

"Brimmer shouldn't get in trouble."

"Well, you taught her a very valuable lesson. Don't trust anybody." He eyed Decker's suit and tie. "I heard you'd gone down in the world. Was my info wrong?"

"I was a lot farther down than this."

"You and Mary were a great team. Damn shame."

"It's *all* a damn shame, isn't it?"

Miller crumpled up his empty paper cup. "What'd you talk to Leopold about?"

"I have notes, if you want to see them."

Miller loosened his tie. "I'd rather *hear* them, from you."

"He's a strange guy."

"If he killed three people in cold blood, I'd say he's very strange. I hope someone like that is always considered 'very strange' no matter how screwed-up the world becomes."

"He had some knowledge of the crime, but nothing he couldn't have gleaned from the papers. Or—"

"Or what?" Miller said quickly, his light blue eyes holding steadily on Decker's face.

"Been told by someone who had *more* detailed knowledge of the crime."

"As in the person or persons who actually did it?"

"Do you see Leopold as our guy?"

"I don't see him one way or another. All I know is he walked in early this morning and confessed. What else?"

Decker said, "He was in the Navy. I noted the tat and he finally admitted that he was. Sebastian is probably not his real name. Checking with DoD should tell us who he is. Guy has a lump on his neck. It doesn't seem to be causing him pain. But it might be cancerous. He was confused on some of the major details at the scene."

"For example?"

"For example, he couldn't seem to remember which side of the hall the first bedroom was on. I suggested left. He agreed. When it's actually on the right. That's probably not that big of a deal. But then he said he shot Cassie while she was sleeping and then changed his story to shooting her after she woke up. The wound

81

was a contact. I don't see how he does that if she's awake and screaming and maybe fighting him. And she was found on the floor. I think he remembered that and changed his story to reflect it. And he didn't mention what else was done to her."

Miller nodded. He obviously knew what Decker was referring to. "Go on."

"The guy is a little cagey, but not all there. He sort of comes and goes. I don't think his memory is that good. Also, he's a druggie. Needle tracks on his arm are fresh."

"Go on."

Decker had already decided not to tell him everything he had discovered or thought about. His gut told him to hold things back, see how it all played out. "He said I dissed him at my neighborhood 7-Eleven. He didn't say if he worked there or not. Apparently he told you guys the same thing. The 7-Eleven. Now, that store? I only ever drove there. Never walked. He doesn't have a car. But he said he followed me back to my house. So how did he do it? And I've never seen the guy before. I would have remembered if someone had a problem with me."

Miller considered all this while he rubbed one hand down his tie and fiddled with his tie clip. "You never forget anything, do you?"

Decker had never told anyone about what had happened to him. When his condition had been diagnosed he'd been sent to a research facility outside of Chicago for additional testing. He had spent months there meeting others with similar abilities, both men and women. They had done numerous group sessions together. Some had been better adjusted than others. Some had really deep problems adjusting to what they were. Some may never have adjusted. To his knowledge, Decker had been the only one not born with his condition. The others in the group seemed to have lived with it much longer than he had, which was both a positive and a negative, he supposed.

"Everyone forgets stuff," he said.

"I had you checked out. I ever tell you that?"

Decker shook his head.

"Knew you were a jock. Saw that play on TV."

"You mean on YouTube?"

"No, I mean I was watching the *game* when you got laid out. Hardest hit I've ever seen. I don't know how you survived it, Amos, I really don't."

"Why'd you watch the game?"

"You were a damn good player for Mansfield. Best QB we've ever had, kickass of a linebacker on the D side. You were fast for your size. You were a good college player. And far as I know you were the only person from the humble town of Burlington to ever play in the NFL. So, yeah, I watched the game. Would've gone to it if I could have."

"Well, good thing you did watch, since that play was my only one in the NFL."

Miller continued, "And I checked your scores at the police academy. And your tests for detective grade."

"Why'd you do that?"

"Because I was curious about you, Amos. Don't think the department didn't notice your success rate as a cop and then a detective. You had something extra that the others didn't have."

"Mary is a good cop."

"Yes, she is. Good, but not great. Good, but not perfect. But, see, your scores at the academy and later the detective's exams *were* perfect. You didn't miss a single question. They tell me it's the first time in the history of the state. Then I went back to your college days. You were a good student, but a B student. Nothing perfect about your record back then."

"Football didn't leave a lot of time for studying."

Miller rubbed his chin and looked thoughtful. "Let's get back to it. What else you got?"

Decker could feel the migraine marching up the back of his neck. The lights in the room were dim, but right now they felt like three-ring circus illumination. The color blue, terrifyingly electric, was starting to seep out of all corners of life with the goal of converging on his very soul. He could sense it all building.

"I don't think Leopold is our guy," he managed to say.

"I already knew that before I sat down across from you."

"How's that?" Decker asked.

84

"You didn't kill him before you left the precinct. Because that's why you went in there, right? Size the guy up, ask your questions, stare him down, read his mind, see if he was the guy? And if you decided he was, no more Leopold." He looked Decker over. "Easy enough. Football player, strong as a horse. You might be way out of shape now, but you are still one big dude. Leopold wouldn't have had a chance."

"You can't arrest someone for thinking about committing a crime."

"No, and sometimes that's more a curse than a blessing."

"So why the riot act with the cops and Brimmer here?"

"I'm the captain, but I have bosses too."

"So this was a CYA visit?"

Miller surged to his feet and adjusted his tie, sliding the knot back up to his Adam's apple.

Decker looked up at him, the migraine starting to beat against all sides of his brain. He half closed his eyes to keep out even the dim light that felt like a million incandescent bulbs. "So what are you going to do?"

"With you, nothing. Now Leopold will be arraigned based on his confession. After that we either confirm his story or we prove it false. I'll seriously consider all that you've told me. At the end of the investigation he either stays locked up, goes to trial or cops a plea, or he goes free."

"And if someone got him to do this?"

"Might give us an opportunity. I'm sure you thought of that already."

"Will you let me know what you decide with Leopold?"

"You're no longer on the force. I wish you were, but you're not."

"It was the choice I had to make at the time."

Miller rubbed his nose and buttoned his jacket. "Well, different times call for different choices."

He started to leave but turned back. He held up one finger. "Today was your freebie, Amos. You only get one, so you have none left. Don't forget that. And forget Sebastian Leopold is even on the same planet as you. We'll take it from here. You screw me over on that, I'm no longer your ally. I will crucify you. Have a good one."

Amos Decker sat there for a minute and then rushed back to his room, locked the door, closed all the curtains, lay on the bed with the pillow over his face to block out all the remaining light, and succumbed to the beast devouring his vastly altered mind.

11

The heavy clouds ate away at the fragile sky until there was no significant light left, although the sun was up there somewhere, diminished and vacant. It was akin to staring at a forty-watt light bulb while wearing a gauzy blindfold. For Decker, who was deeply influenced by color in everything, it seemed the only one left in the world right now was gray.

He had his hands in his pockets as the chilly wind bit into him. He had recovered from the migraine, gone to a local Wendy's, and gulped down a Coke, letting the sugar drain the last vestiges of the discomfort away—an acid wash on dreary, stained metal—and allowing the sweat to dry off his pores. He had then bused back downtown and retrieved his gun and clothes from the trash can. Fortunately, they had not been discovered. He could not afford to lose his only other set of work clothes any more than he could his only weapon.

Now he was standing there in his old clothes, braced against a stiff wind and staring over at Mansfield High. It had been built, along with thousands of other schools across the country, in a postwar construction boom.

The birth rate had spiked in 1946 and those kids would need to go to high school at some point. That's what being away from home fighting a war for four years did to a man. It made him horny as hell. The wives of America's returning veterans probably hadn't slept for an entire year.

Mansfield was three stories high, all brick, and time had not been kind to it. Windows were boarded up or broken. Mortar had leached out from the neat lines around the rectangular bricks and mottled the school's façade like meaningless graffiti. The grounds were full of chickweed and dirt patches, the asphalt cracked and the chain-link fences mangled, with gates hanging off twisted, rusted hinges. The place now looked more like an abandoned state mental asylum than a high school.

It had been built principally as a school for children of the military personnel who worked at the Army base right next door. The base had been one of the biggest employers in Burlington, and servicing all those soldiers was an economic boost to the area. And then the Pentagon downsized and the base in Burlington was one of the first to go. Now the defunct Army base just sat there a hundred yards from Mansfield High behind high chain-link fences and walls of vegetation that had partially reclaimed the land it was on. Burlington had never recovered from the soldiers pulling out, and the later economic downturn was the last nail in the town's coffin.

Today, like many other schools, Mansfield was

underfunded, beaten down, discipline was hard to find, teachers didn't stay long, and drug and alcohol abuse was rampant. The student population was less than half of what it had once been, and graduation rates were heading south as fast as snowbirds fleeing to Florida before winter set in.

Burlington, even without the military base, had once been a prosperous manufacturing town, like thousands of other communities dotted across the middle of the country building what America and the rest of the world needed. Now, with all the manufacturing out-sourced overseas, the only thing one could build here was misery. There were two grocery store chains here. From what Decker had seen, the two most popular food items purchased there were Hamburger Helper by the kilo and sugary orange pop by the barrel. And the fast-food places also did brisk business, fattening both the young and old to impossible degrees and foretelling diabetes, cancer, stroke, and heart disease stats blowing right through the roof.

And didn't he know that firsthand?

In Burlington, the few rich lived in gated communities on the west side of town and pretty much never strayed from there. Everybody else lived on the three other compass points. The homeless lived on the streets in ratty sleeping bags, old blankets, and cardboard condos.

Just like I did.

Decker had attended school at Mansfield over twenty-five years ago. Some of the trophies bearing his name were still in the gym's locked glass cabinet. He had been an outstanding high school athlete, lettering in three different sports. He was simply bigger, faster, and stronger than anybody else. He had been popular, dated all the hot girls, slept with a number of them, done okay in the classroom, and everyone had thought him a lock for a pro career.

How wrong they had been.

He had been a good, but far from great, college player. And then the funnel narrowed even more. He had gone undrafted on pro draft day because there were hundreds of prospects far better than he was. He had taken that as a personal attack. Decker had worked his way onto the Cleveland Browns by busting his ass on the practice field, sacrificing his body in idiotic ways that had come back to haunt him in his forties, and being the last to leave the film room. For all that effort his career had lasted one regular-season play and had left him with a brain permanently changed.

Something good had come out of it, at least. He had met Cassie while he was rehabbing his "other" injuries. Because, as it turned out, the hit had not only addled his brain. Both cleats had stuck in the turf as Dwayne LeCroix leveled him. The result was a broken right femur, a blown-out ACL on his left knee, and a torn MCL on his right. Pretty much the whole package, the surgeon had told him. Well, in for a dime, in for a dollar.

Cassie had been a newly minted physical therapist attending him. He had worked his butt off to get back right. His leg and knees eventually healed. His brain was what it was. But she had been with him every step of the way, encouraging when necessary and bullying her patient when encouragement failed to motivate.

During that time he and Cassie had fallen as deeply in love as he imagined anyone could. After his stint at the institute outside Chicago where they studied people who had extraordinary mental abilities, he and Cassie had gotten engaged and then married and moved back to his hometown. He had previously given a lot of thought to what he would do in the future, and had come back here with the express purpose of enrolling in the police academy. The classwork was a cakewalk with his new and improved and utterly infallible memory. His physical skills, though somewhat diminished by his injuries, were still far superior to almost all in his academy class. He had sailed through the process, was sworn in, and got his badge and gun. Nine years later he was promoted to detective. For nearly ten years he had investigated major crimes against the good citizens of Burlington—although most of the crimes had also been committed by the not so good citizens of Burlington, with the occasional outsider thrown into the mix.

They had wanted a large family but had struggled to conceive a child. They spent money they didn't have on specialists, and at long last Cassie had become pregnant. And they had Molly. She would be their only child.

The pregnancy had nearly killed Cassie, and a compli-
cation had required surgery that had rendered her incapable of conceiving again.

They had named her after Decker's mother. His
parents had both perished in a car crash while Decker
was in college, so Molly didn't have paternal grand-
parents. But she had carried her grandma's name. Carried it all the way to her premature death at the hands
of, perhaps, Sebastian Leopold.

He stared up at the brick fortress that Mansfield had
become. Crazy-angled police tape was everywhere, like
a spider's yellow web looking venomous and terrifying. There were cop cars and forensic trucks, and black
trucks with no windows standing ready for the body
bags. For Decker was certain the corpses were still in
the school. Except for those injured and needing medical attention, you didn't subtract anything from a crime
scene until it was thoroughly gone over, photographed,
measured, and adequately poked, prodded, and ana-
lyzed. It wouldn't matter to the dead how long they lay
on the floor in pools of their own blood, their lives
ripped away by some psycho with unfettered firepower.
Forever was forever, after all.

If Decker had still been on the force he would be in
there right now. From where he was standing, he had
already seen Mary Lancaster come and go twice. She
looked haggard and repulsed and depressed. She glanced
his way once but it didn't seem to register. He knew she
had other things on her mind. She probably had forgot-

ten that a man named Sebastian Leopold was sitting in a holding cell. That he had confessed to murdering three people, two of whom had meant everything to Decker. Lancaster had a pile of fresh bodies to work on right now. And with it a criminal out there walking free to possibly kill again, as opposed to one sitting placidly in a holding cell.

The school story had of course hit the national pipeline. The town was the number one headline on every media platform. The names of the dead had still not been released. Decker had been checking on his phone. "Pending notification of next of kin" was the standard catchphrase. He had heard from a friend on the force that Pete Rourke's grandson was okay. But a son of a beat cop had not been so lucky. And a police dispatcher's husband, Andy Jackson, an English teacher at Mansfield, was in the hospital in critical condition with multiple gunshot wounds.

Decker began to walk, choosing his path with care as he made his way in a long loop around the grounds of the high school and outside the investigative barriers. Miller had said the shooter had escaped. The entire city of Burlington was up in arms about this development. Wasn't it enough that they had lost their loved ones? But to have the killer walking free right now, perhaps ready to murder again? It made the already horrible completely unbearable.

Yet how *had* the man escaped? It was personally and professionally offensive to Decker that any criminal should just walk away from an Armageddon of his own creation.

And then there was the complex reason. Decker could do nothing more with Leopold. He could either sit powerless and run through endless and ultimately pointless speculation. Or he could think about Mansfield and who had done it. And where that person was now. He chose the latter.

He kept walking, toward the football field, where he'd enjoyed some of his greatest glories. Football season was over halfway done, and the grass was beaten down. The home game scheduled for this Friday would not be played. They might not play another game this year. Maybe not another game here ever.

He went up into the stands and took a seat near the fifty-yard line. It was a labor getting his obese body up the steps, and he told himself once again that he needed to lose the weight, get back in some semblance of shape. At this rate, at forty-two, he might not make it to fifty-two. Hell, he might not make it to forty-three.

As he stared down at the field he ran back in his mind pretty much every play he had been involved in as a high school player. They must have been in his brain somewhere, but he had been incapable of digging through the gray matter to reach them. Now it was effortless. The DVR just went back to the date of his choosing and the game film ran.

It was both exciting and a bit disturbing to see himself as a young man running over and through other young men. He could throw the ball a mile and with accuracy. In college he had quickly learned that his arm wasn't strong enough to make all the throws required of a college QB. He had switched to defense full-time, and discovered that the guys on that side of the ball were bigger, stronger, and faster than he was. It was a rude awakening for a guy used to effortless success. He could have given up, but he had chosen to simply work harder than his more gifted teammates.

In the end it had been for naught. His playing days long over, his law enforcement career also in the toilet, he sat on the hard aluminum bleacher with the row of ridges that guaranteed your butt would be rubbed raw after only one half of a football game. And in doing so decided that he could not look any farther ahead in his life than the next morning. But he had the rest of the day to think about things. And what he was thinking about were ways for a killer to escape from this place.

There were exit doors all over Mansfield, front, rear, left, and right sides. The place was built long enough ago that people did not walk in with AK-47s and open fire, and thus the original builders had never considered that possibility. But over the years, as the number of school shootings multiplied, many of the doors had been locked down or could only be opened from the inside. Visitors were now supposed to go to the front entrance and check in at the office. There had been talk of putting in metal detectors, but the cost was prohibitive for a nearly bankrupt school system. The school did have an automatic alert mechanism that would be sent out to folks' emails in the event of an emergency. Presumably that had been deployed today in what was by far the worst emergency the city had ever suffered.

Outside the ring of police vehicles and media trucks stood the families. When he had passed them earlier Decker saw as much pain in those faces as he was ever likely to see in another human being.

Molly would have gone to Mansfield when she entered the ninth grade. He could have been one of the parents standing out there, feet stamping lightly on the ground, hands in pockets, faces looking at shoes, a few murmurs between grieving folks. It was all horrible, and Decker felt his gut clench.

He reached into his pocket and pulled out his wallet. Inside was a fading photo of his daughter on her ninth birthday—as it turned out, the last one she would ever celebrate. He traced the line of her impish smile and then the curls of her hair. Her eyes were her mother's, hazel and sprightly. He remembered, of course, exactly when the picture was taken and precisely what he was doing when the camera had flashed. It had been early summer, so he'd been barbecuing in the backyard, grilling two of his daughter's favorite foods: ribs from Kansas City and water-soaked corn on the cob still in their husks.

He looked back at the school and wondered again how the person had done it. First, gotten into the school with weaponry. Second, committed the murders. Third, managed the exit. That was the crux of the thing, really. Point number three: the exit. With all those people around, many of them still alive, how did you get away with no one seeing you?

"Dollar for your thoughts?"

He looked down on the ground near the crushed gravel path that ran around the football field, which itself was enclosed by a waist-high chain-link fence.

Mary Lancaster was staring up at him, a cigarette perched in her right hand, while the left one rode on her hip trembling away.

She slowly made her way up the steps and sat down next to him. She had looked pale and uncomfortable this morning. Now she looked crushed and even disoriented. It was amazing what life could do to you in less than a day.

She puffed on her smoke, said nothing, but gazed out onto the empty field.

"Shitty time," noted Decker quietly.

She nodded but didn't answer.

"What's the situation?" he asked.

"You want to come and see for yourself?"

He turned to stare at her. Before he could speak she said, "I heard what you did with Leopold."

"I never mentioned you coming to tell me."

"If it was me, I probably would have just shot him."

He knew that Lancaster had one child, Sandy, who had Down syndrome. Her husband, Earl, was in construction, which meant right now he was probably not working very much. They subsisted mostly on Lancaster's salary, which wasn't that large, but did come with good health benefits at least.

"You don't think he's good for it, do you?" she asked.

"I'd have to know a lot more."

"He'll get arraigned in the morning. With the confession we can hold him. They're asking for no bail because he has no known address, no ties to the community, and thus is a decent flight risk. They'll set it for trial once he lawyers up."

"PD?" asked Decker, referring to a public defender.

"Looks that way. So, the Mansfield crime scene? You want to see?"

"I can't go in there, Mary, you know that."

"You can, if Mac says it's okay. As an official consultant to the Burlington Police Department. A *paid* consultant. You won't get rich off it, but it's probably more than your PI gig is paying you."

"He really said it was okay?"

She held out her phone. "Want to read the email yourself? Or let me do it for you." She turned the screen back to her and read, 'Get Decker on Mansfield. See what he sees. We need help and him sitting on his fat ass feeling sorry for himself or obsessing over Leopold or playing private dick for lowlifes is not a good use of his time.'"

"I see he's been following my recent career."

"I guess so." She rose, puffed her smoke nearly all the way down, and then flicked the butt away. Decker watched as it dropped down to the crushed gravel, flamed for a sec, and then went out.

Like all those dead in the school, thought Decker as he rose and followed his old partner down the steps.

12

Schools should never be this quiet. That was Decker's first thought as he walked down the hall next to Lancaster. His second thought was that this was the grimmest place he would ever visit.

He passed pictures on the wall of long-ago principals of Mansfield, including the man who had headed up the school when he was there. He glanced at rooms where he had sat in class, sometimes listening, sometimes taking notes, and sometimes sleeping while pretending to listen and take notes.

He forgot about the past when he saw the leg right at the juncture of two halls. It was a bare calf, which told Decker the body probably would be female.

As they made the turn, his deduction was confirmed. She was sprawled on the linoleum that looked old enough to have been there when Decker had trod these halls.

Photos and measurements had already been taken, and forensics gathered or nearly so, Lancaster had told him. The girl seemed posed, one hand out like she had been waving to a friend when someone had violently stolen the remainder of her life.

"Debbie Watson," said Lancaster as Decker stared down at the girl. "Senior. Just turned eighteen. Her parents have been notified."

Decker looked around. He had been working crime scenes for twenty years as a beat cop and then a detective. He should feel perfectly natural here looking for things he had looked for a thousand times before. But he did not feel natural. He felt like an outsider. He felt like all the air in the school was being sucked away from him.

He fought hard against this inner turmoil and said, "But they haven't seen her?"

She shook her head. "You know the drill. Crime scene. No one gets in, including parents. Besides, why would they want to see her . . . like this?"

Decker had put on plastic booties and gloves Lancaster had given him. He knelt down next to Debbie Watson. As he did so his head started to spin. He cleared his throat and focused on her body.

She had taken what looked to be a round of buckshot full in the face. The result was she no longer had a face. He glanced at the wall behind her. It was splattered with bits of her. Books lay beside her; a notebook was soaked in blood. He looked down at a piece of paper that apparently had fallen out of a book. If these were the girl's doodles she had been a good artist, thought Decker.

"You have the order of shootings yet?" he asked.

"From everything so far, it seems she might have been the first one killed."

"Shooter's entry?"

"This way."

Lancaster led him a short distance away to what he recognized as the rear of the school. She pointed at the rack of doors. "They're kept locked during the school day." She pointed at a camera attached to the upper corner of a wall. "That camera gave us a nice view of the ingress."

"Description?"

"I've got the image loaded on my laptop in the command center we set up in the library. But it was a big guy in full camouflage gear. Face completely obstructed by a mask and a face shield."

"Belts and suspenders," commented Decker. "Methodical."

Lancaster continued, "We believe he walked in this way, turned the corner, encountered Debbie Watson, and shot her."

"Wouldn't there have been other people in the halls?"

"At that time of morning everyone was in their classes."

"So why wasn't Debbie?"

"She was going to the nurse's office. She had an upset stomach. That's according to the teacher who gave her permission to leave class."

Decker looked around again. "Everyone was in class. So either the shooter was lucky or he knew the routine of the school."

"That thought struck me too."

"And after Debbie went down?"

"He went to the gym, killed Joe Kramer, the teacher there, reversed course, passed Debbie's body, and headed toward the front of the school. By then the shots had alerted everyone, but people were more or less trapped in their classrooms. He shot one more student dead in a classroom. He went into a second classroom and opened fire. One more dead and one wounded, a teacher."

"Andy Jackson? English? I heard it on the news."

"Yes. Then he walked to the opposite corridor and entered another classroom. Another dead. Another classroom on the same corridor, a sixth person shot dead. He headed to the school office, where he shot and killed the assistant principal. He then shot and killed one more student in another classroom. All told we have eight dead. And Jackson's in critical condition, so the death count could go up by one."

"So six students and two adults?"

"Yes. And one critically wounded."

"You said the shooter was dressed in cammies, mask, and face shield?"

"Right."

"What else? Type of footwear?"

"The video shot is from the waist up. No one we

interviewed noted his footwear. He was wearing gloves. Weapons were a shotgun and handgun. Ballistics guys are still searching and spreadsheeting all of it. A lot of the ordnance is still in the victims. When he used the handgun he fired multiple rounds into his victims."

"To make sure they were dead," said Decker. "Don't really have that concern with a shotgun."

"No, you don't."

"So hood plus a face shield?"

She nodded.

"Concealment was important for him. He might have been afraid he would be recognized. You said big guy. How big?"

She pulled her notebook. "Our video shot framed him with a poster hanging on the wall. We did some measurements. We're looking at a guy at least six-two with very broad shoulders. Like yours. Strong. Definitely male. Over two hundred pounds."

"So he walks all over the school and we only get one video shot of him?"

"Maybe he knew where the cameras were and avoided them," said Lancaster. "Maybe he's been here before doing some recon for this massacre."

"But in one instance he didn't avoid the camera," rejoined Decker.

"Why do you think? Inconsistency? Mistake?"

"Too early to tell, but if it was deliberate, we need to find out why."

Lancaster wrote down some notes.

"You said he entered classrooms?"

She nodded.

"But only killed one person in each before heading on?"

"That's right. Except he wounded the teacher in one of them."

"These people have anything in common?"

"You think he might have been specifically targeting folks?"

"Can't rule it out yet."

"He'd have to know what classrooms they'd be in at that time of the morning."

"And he might have found out somehow."

"I'll check into that," said Lancaster. "But it strikes me as doubtful with all the chaos going on that the guy would be able to run down a tally sheet of targets."

"Maybe it was chaotic for everybody else. But not him. He had the guns."

"But still, Amos," she said doubtfully.

"And the exit?" he asked, ignoring her last comment.

"We haven't nailed that down yet."

He studied her. "By the time the guy was finished shooting, how much time had passed?"

"The prelim time frame we pieced together is ten minutes, maybe a bit more."

Decker glanced out a window. The front of the school was set far back from the road, within its own grounds. Across the street were residential properties.

"Nobody over there heard anything? Shots, screams?"

"Still canvassing. He might have used a suppressor."

"Not on a shotgun he didn't. But my point is, how does a guy in cammies, hood, and face shield with at least two different weapons, and one of them a long barrel, walk out of here and nobody eyeball him? For that matter, how did he walk *in* and no one see him?"

The air was starting to feel close again. Sweat sprouted on his forehead. He put a gloved hand out to the wall. If Lancaster noticed his distress, she said nothing.

"The video shows him entering on the rear side. There's really nothing back there except the old Army base. He might have slipped in unseen. Maybe he hid in the Dumpster back there and popped out."

Decker rubbed at his belly.

"You okay, Amos?"

"My diet is for shit. Did you check the Dumpster?"

"We checked everything and found nothing. We even checked the fence around the base. Nothing had been disturbed. And it's so overgrown that there probably would have been some indication of someone having come that way."

"So he shot his way from the rear of the school to the front. Presumably he left that way. How did no one see him then? There are houses across the street. And cars going up and down the road."

"Well, the homes directly across the street are empty because of foreclosures. And it's a working-class neighborhood. There might not have been many people at the other homes at that time of the morning. And the school is set far enough back that the sounds might not have carried."

"But presumably you had traffic along the street. And kids and teachers at the windows probably screaming their heads off. Cell phones hitting 911. Cruisers rolling. I was at Precinct Two when the guys started pouring out of the place. What is the time to the school from there by car? Fifteen minutes?"

"About that, yeah."

"And even if nobody on the outside saw him leave, there had to be eyeballs at the school windows. Kids using phones as cameras. From what I remember, there's not an exit in this building that's not visible from some classroom window."

"And you knew this because you, what, snuck out a lot?"

"All the time."

"Well, you got me there. I went to high school in the next county. This is your turf, not mine."

"And that still doesn't cover his ingress. How did he walk in here and no one see him? Even if it was in the rear. There are windows overlooking it."

"Yeah, but the second and third floors are unused."

"But the first floor has windows looking out over the rear of the school."

Lancaster could only shake her head.

"Has the school been searched?"

"It's being searched right now."

"And the teachers, admin, and students?"

"Evacuated to safety."

"To safety?" said Decker, ignoring now the pains in his head and belly.

"We weren't sure whether the shooter was still here, Amos. The first priority on something like this is to get the innocent to a safe place and secure the area."

"Well, to state the obvious, if no one saw him leave, how do you know you also didn't evacuate the *shooter* to a *safe* place?"

"No one was allowed to leave the area until we got descriptions of the shooter. The women were obviously above suspicion. All witnesses said it was a man. And there's not one guy in the building who fit his description."

"Not even the students? They're growing kids pretty big these days."

"All the male students who were of that size had alibis. Most of them are on the football team and are well known. They were all in their classrooms with thirty other kids. They couldn't have been the shooter. There were four male students who were out of class for various reasons. Not one of them is taller than five-nine and weighs more than a buck fifty. All witnesses said the shooter was easily two-hundred-plus pounds in addition to the height. And jacked, like an athlete."

"How about guys who were absent from school that day?"

"Still checking on that. It might turn up something. But my gut tells me this is a stranger."

"And none of the male teachers is that size?"

"The gym teacher was. But he's dead. So was the assistant principal. He's dead too. Everybody else was under six feet and no more than one-seventy. And not one of them is what you would call broad-shouldered. The only living teacher approaching the requisite weight was the chemistry guy, and he's five-seven and a heart attack waiting to happen."

"So where did the guy go? Did he drive up here?"

Lancaster shook her head. "Don't think so. No one saw any vehicles come or leave at the requisite times."

"According to you, no one saw *anyone* come or go at those times, Mary."

"It's problematic, I know," she admitted. "Look, if the guy *is* hiding in the building still, we'll get him. The place is surrounded by cops. Nobody is getting out of here."

"You said a search is being conducted?"

"We've been going through the school one inch at a time as soon as we got the place emptied out. Nobody could have gotten out unseen, Amos."

"Then you're walking right into a dead-end maze."

She cocked her head and chewed her gum. "Come again?"

"If the place turns up empty and nobody saw the guy leave, then the shooter has to be someone who was in the school. A teacher or a student or an admin. All custodial folks accounted for?"

She nodded. "They're older and all have big guts. But I see your point."

"Can I see the video footage of the guy?"

He followed her to the library. After they passed through the double wooden doors, Decker could see that the library had become the opposite of a quiet sanctum. The FBI had their corner, the state police their spot, and Lancaster and her crew were relegated to the far back left slice of the place.

Lancaster started walking to where her colleagues had set up shop, but Decker just stood there at the entrance to the library. He had been away from this world for a while now, but it suddenly felt like forever. He did not like crowds. He did not care to walk in here and join this large group of investigators even if they all had the same goal. Part of him wanted to slink back to the Residence Inn, close his door, shut his eyes, and let his cast of colors envelop him. And what good would he be anyway? He couldn't find his family's killers. How would he have a shot to find this one? He eyed the door. He could still escape.

"Amos!"

He looked over and watched in silence as Captain Miller headed his way. He had on his police uniform this evening. He held out a hand, which Decker shook unwillingly.

"Thank you for helping us, Amos," said Miller. "We can use it."

Decker eyed the manpower in the library. "Looks like you have all the help you need."

He tried to pull his hand away, but Miller kept hold of it, his gaze locked on his former detective.

"Looks can be deceiving. And I want you involved. You see things. I mean, you *see* things, Amos. And we have to catch this guy. We have to make this right. We have to give closure." He continued to keep his gaze directly on Decker's face until the latter looked back at him. "Amos, we need closure. You understand that. I know you do."

"I do," said Decker. "I understand it, if only because I never got it."

Miller let his hand go. "Why don't you go over and join your 'partner'? Good to see you two together again."

Decker said nothing. He just turned and walked over to where Lancaster was waiting for him.

His opportunity for escape was now gone. And more than a part of him believed that Miller knew exactly what he was thinking when he'd been standing over by the door. And the police captain had decisively cut off his retreat.

Decker settled his large bulk next to Lancaster at a table in the middle of the local cops' command center. Laptops were set up across the length of the table. Multiport outlets littered the floor connected to extension cords, and computers, printers, and scanners were plugged into them. People moved around with files, papers, electronic tablets, all bearing an air of quiet desperation, Decker noted. He also knew that many of the cops had kids in the school. Not that they needed any extra incentive to nail the shooter.

After Miller had called out his name, several suits and a couple of uniforms had recognized Decker and given him nods or grim looks, but none had spoken to him. He had not left the department under the best of circumstances, yet he doubted anyone really held it against him.

But he was here now, and so he might as well get to work.

He looked at Lancaster. "The video?"

Lancaster hit the requisite keys, and a few seconds later Decker was staring at the grainy footage.

"There's the son of a bitch," said Lancaster.

He glanced at the time stamp. "Eight-forty-one. When did classes start?"

"Eight-thirty sharp. Everyone needs to be in their class by then."

"You said he came in through the rear doors? That's where this image is from, right?"

"Yes."

"Aren't the exit doors kept locked?"

"They're supposed to be. But they're also not hard to jimmy open."

"Did you find signs of forced entry?"

"Those doors haven't been replaced since the seventies, Amos. They're beat to hell. It was really impossible to tell if they'd been forced or not."

She hit some more keys and zoomed in on the corridor. "Now we've identified this as the hall bleeding off . . ." She faltered. "Sorry, poor choice of words. As the hall *coming* off the ingress we've already identified. He would have made his turn, and that's where he would have encountered Debbie Watson, say maybe a minute later."

"So first shot at eight-forty-*two* or thereabouts, allowing one minute from the video stamp and him encountering Watson?"

"Pretty much. And shotgun blasts folks remember. In fact, a bunch of people looked at the time when they heard it. So eight-forty-two is a good number for the first shot."

"Okay." Decker thought about what his next question should be. It should have come automatically, but it didn't. He was definitely rusty. He looked around at all the seasoned investigators toiling away. He used to be one of them. The fact was, he had checked out of his professional life as soon as he'd found his family dead. Actually, he might be, he had to admit, more of a hindrance here than a help.

He looked down at Lancaster, who was staring up at him, a sympathetic expression on her face.

"It's like riding a bike, Amos," she said, apparently reading the self-doubt on his face.

"Maybe not, Mary. I guess I'll find out. But if I can't carry my weight, I shouldn't be here."

She looked back at the screen. "Okay, the camera doesn't have audio, so you can't hear it. And there was no camera on the next hall."

"Why not?"

"Why else? No money in the budget. We're lucky to have any functioning cameras at all."

He thought for a moment. "But they keep them up as a deterrent?"

"Right. Because people didn't know they weren't operational."

"But our guy was able to avoid all of them except this one."

"It really didn't matter whether he did or not. He was completely covered, Amos. No way to recognize any feature."

Decker slowly nodded, feeling once more slow and reactive in his mental process.

He looked back at the image on the screen. Hood and face shield. And the camera shot was reflecting off the glare from the shield. He edged closer to the screen, like a scent hound ferreting prey.

"There's no direct hit even on his hooded face. He knew where the camera was and avoided it, even though he's covered."

"You think that's important?" she asked.

"At this point in the investigation, there isn't anything that's not important."

Lancaster nodded. "I think that was the second rule you ever taught me."

"The first being to suspect everybody," Decker added absently, his gaze still squarely on the shooter.

She said nothing to this and he finally looked at her.

"Like riding a bike, Amos. You were the best I've ever seen. I think you still can be."

He looked away, not really feeling better from her praise, because his altered mind didn't respond to that anymore either. "Can you run the feed all the way until he turns the corner?"

Lancaster did so, and then, at Decker's request, did it three more times.

He finally sat back, lost in thought, his gaze still on the screen, though.

She stared over at him. "You see anything that hits you?"

"I see lots of things that hit me. But none more than a guy dressed like that, carrying weapons, who can apparently vanish into thin air."

"I don't believe in ghosts or magic."

"I don't either, Mary. But I do know one thing."

"What's that?"

"That this guy is not going to get away."

She kept her gaze on him, her expression becoming concerned. "You sure you're not talking about Leopold?"

He shrugged, his eyes seeming to stare at somewhere a million miles from here. "In a way, they're all fucking Leopolds."

13

With Captain Miller's blessing, Lancaster had arranged temporary credentials and an access badge for Decker. He had worked enough crime scenes to watch where he walked and not disturb or corrupt potential evidence. He looked over reports, studied the video some more, chatted briefly with department folks he knew, nodded to some he didn't. While he was a long way from feeling comfortable working a crime scene again, he was starting to feel certain things coming back to him. His chief strength had always been observation. Looking around and seeing things, but not the way most people did. He had built convictions from small details that most overlooked, including, most significantly, the ones who had committed the crimes.

And he had observed a lot here so far, and not all of it connected to the shootings.

Principally he noted that the FBI was playing the usual peacock game. Strutting around and overwhelming everyone with their resources. But then again, he knew the police wouldn't mind the help. The goal was the same. Get the guy who did this.

He fell back into the routine that he had employed in countless other investigations. He walked and observed and asked questions and read more reports. His travels took him around the entire perimeter of the school several times. He looked at it from every possible vantage point. Then he went back inside the school and looked out of every window in the place. It was the darkest moments before dawn broke. He had been here for hours. It felt like ten minutes, because he really hadn't come up with anything. But that was okay. Miracles and epiphanies rarely happened in the middle of criminal investigations. If you wanted something like that you needed to turn on the TV. Results in the real world came from slow, dogged work, compiling facts and building conclusions and deductions based on those facts. And a little luck never hurt either.

A few minutes before dawn broke the transports were called up to start taking the bodies to the morgue. There was a loading dock in the rear of the school. The police had shielded it from view with a tarp and steel support poles. The vehicles drove one by one through a gap in this wall. Behind the tarp Decker knew the bodies were coming out, housed in black sturdy bags. The bodies had names but also numbers. They weren't human beings anymore. They were pieces in a criminal investigation. Debbie Watson would be Vic-1. Her body had been the starting point in numbering everybody else who had fallen. Joe Kramer, the gym teacher, had been labeled Vic-2. And on the numbering went, down the list of dead.

Decker leaned against the outside wall of the school near the loading dock and studied the blue tarp. And then he closed his eyes, because he equated the color blue with the slaughter of his family. He didn't need to see color in the outside world. He had enough of it going on inside his head.

Get back to basics, Amos. Slow and easy. You know how to do this. This was all you did for so many years. Mary is right. You can do this.

Motive.

It always began with that, because motive was just another way of saying, *Why would you do something like this?* Greed, jealousy, kicks, personal vendetta, perceived slight, insanity? The last was always tough to decipher, because how did you read a mind that was deranged?

But this guy had method. This guy had some inside knowledge of the school. This guy had taken great care to not allow even a piece of his skin to be observed. They didn't even know if he was black or white. Although most mass murderers were white. And male. And with this shooter's size and shape, he was most definitely a male.

The face shield was an unusual step. It was not for defense. It couldn't have stopped a bullet. It was for concealment.

He watched as the last of the transport vehicles

pulled away, rack lights on but no sirens engaged. The dead were in no hurry. Each body would be cut up as the medical examiner looked for clues. But the best they could hope for here would be ballistics. What type of bullet had killed them? He doubted the shooter had laid a finger on any of his victims. If you didn't touch, you didn't leave any usable trace behind. With the bullets they could at least, one day, match them to the guns that had been used. And if the guns had an owner, the chain of title to this horrific event possibly could be traced.

He walked back to the library, where Lancaster was sitting and going over case notes. She looked up as he approached.

"I'm surprised you're still here," she said, stifling a yawn.

"I have nowhere else I have to be," said Decker.

He sat next to her.

"Did you do your normal walk-around?" she asked.

He nodded. "But I didn't really see anything."

"You will, Amos. Give it time."

"Earl with Sandy?"

She nodded. "He's used to it. Been a lot of long nights lately." She glanced around the room. "But nothing like this."

Decker nodded slowly. Again, his chitchat component was at an end. "Do you have completed witness statements yet?"

"I've been putting some of them on the computer.

There's not much there. But I haven't talked to the wounded teacher yet. Odds are he won't make it. And if he dies that'll make nine vics total."

"Andy Jackson. How was he shot?"

"Students in the class said he tried to stop the shooter."

"How?" asked Decker.

"Ran at him. Put himself between the shooter and the students."

"Before or after he shot one of them?"

"After."

Decker settled back and thought about this as Lancaster watched him.

"Pretty brave of the guy," said Lancaster.

Decker didn't respond to the statement.

"I need to see the witness statements." His tone was now brisk, confident.

Lancaster noted this and allowed a tiny smile to escape her lips as she pulled them out for him.

He went through each page of the statements. When he was done he flipped back to page two and then over to page ten of the witness statements before putting aside the notebook.

"See anything?" asked Lancaster, who had been watching him off and on as she worked away.

He rose. "I'll be back."

"Decker!"

But for a large man carrying a lot of extra weight, he could move faster than one would have expected.

Perhaps a little of the freewheeling football player was left inside him. He closed the library door behind him and set off down the hall.

Lancaster hadn't followed him. Being his partner for ten years, she was well used to his doing this. Some bee would get in his bonnet and off he would go without a word to her or anyone else. She went back to her work.

Decker had gone ten paces when he stopped and glanced out a window overlooking the front parking area. It was starting to rain, he could see. He could also see a large group of candles seemingly floating in midair. They weren't candles, of course. The rain would have doused them. They were cell phone lights. It was a vigil group out front. It seemed like the whole town of Burlington was out there, and maybe it was. And after what had happened here, maybe it should be.

There had been a vigil outside his house the night after the murders. They had been real candles then. Plus a pile of flowers, signs, and stuffed animals. It had been meant as signs of support, love, solidarity, caring. That was all good. But the sight of that pile had left him sickened and disoriented. And mad with something even beyond grief.

He turned away from the window and kept walking as the rain started to hammer down on the school's roof.

He could imagine the cell phones winking off as the group hastily put them away. Or maybe they would keep them out in the rain. Let them die too, as a sign of solidarity to those who had been lost inside this place.

Decker passed a detective he knew in the hall. He was talking to someone in a suit whom Decker had seen before in the library; the man was FBI. The detective nodded at Decker.

"Hear you're consulting on the case, Amos. Good to see you."

Decker nodded hesitantly as he glanced at the FBI agent. The man was giving Decker the once-over, and the appraisal, Decker could tell from the man's expression, did not turn out favorably.

"Yeah," was all Decker could manage in a gruff voice, before he hurried on.

But then he put aside the awkward encounter, which his mind allowed him to do quite easily. He could compartmentalize at an astonishing level. It came from not giving a shit.

And something did not make sense. That was the reason for his abrupt departure from the library.

Page two of the witness statements.

Melissa Dalton, aged seventeen and a junior, had been putting books away in her locker. The time had been early, 7:28, more than an hour before school officially began. She was here to take a makeup test she had missed due to an illness.

Dalton had known the exact time because she had glanced at the clock on the wall above her locker, afraid that she would be late. She had perfect attendance throughout high school, with not even a tardy to mar her record. This was important to her, since her parents had said four years of such perfection would merit a hand-me-down car all her own when Dalton graduated.

So 7:28.

That's when Melissa Dalton had heard something. And she had told Lancaster when Mary interviewed her.

She had heard something one hour and two minutes before the bell would ring. Maybe twelve minutes *after* the bell rang, or at approximately 8:42, Debbie Watson would lose her face and her life when the shooter turned the corner and raised his shotgun. All because she had an upset stomach.

But how could Melissa Dalton have heard what she did?

Small observations can lead to large breakthroughs.

He kept going.

14

Decker stopped and looked around. The gym was to the far left on the last hall on the first floor. Then classrooms, then the rear entrance. On the other side of the main corridor were more classrooms, the custodial space, and the rear loading dock off that. The main corridor ran front to back, splitting the first floor exactly in half, with three corridors running off that to the left and right, like straight branches off a tree trunk.

Since only the middle hallway had exits on either end, that meant there were four sets of entry and exit doors, situated at all four points of the compass.

He headed to the rear entrance and peered up at the camera. Then he walked to different spots along the rear doorway and checked the camera each time he did so.

Interesting.

He reversed course and walked down the main hall until he neared the front entrance. Then he veered to the left, down the hall where the cafeteria was located on his left and the library on the right.

This was where Melissa Dalton's locker was located,

directly across from the cafeteria. He looked at the locker. Just behind it was the library where Lancaster was toiling away. On the opposite side, next to the sprinkling of classrooms, was the large cafeteria.

Decker recalled from his school days that there was a storage and prep area at the end of the cafeteria with an exterior door leading to a small concrete porch area where shipments of food would be stacked. So that actually made *six* doors. Four main ones off the halls, one off the rear loading dock, and one here off the cafeteria.

At 7:28 Melissa Dalton had heard a door open and close. It was not an interior classroom door, because there had been a whooshing sound associated with it, she had said. Like a vacuum closing.

Like a vacuum closing. Those had been Dalton's words. Lancaster had noted in the statement that Dalton had told her she loved science and the class had just gone over vacuums, which was no doubt why that term was fresh in her mind. Lancaster had put multiple question marks next to this statement, plus a large asterisk. She was no doubt planning to check that out later. Decker couldn't blame her for marking the statement so. It didn't seem to make sense.

So that was page two of the statements.

On page ten of the witness statements was a little nugget. It was the counterpart information that had really caused Decker to come here.

The cafeteria workers came in at 8:45 sharp. Not

before, not after. That had been verified from multiple sources as being the case yesterday as well. All the cafeteria workers were female. There was simply not a six-two, two-hundred-plus-pound, broad-shouldered male among them.

And since the shooting had started at 8:42, none of the cafeteria workers had actually made it into the school. Four of them were getting out of their cars in the parking lot and another was waiting to turn into the lot when all hell had broken loose.

Decker stepped into the cafeteria and looked around. His hand instinctively went to the butt of his pistol, which was wedged in his waistband and hidden under his jacket. He nudged the safety off with his thumb. He already had a round chambered. The lights were off in here. Decker found the switches and flicked them on using his elbow.

He walked across the main space, passing tables with chairs stacked neatly on top of them. At the end of the room were the serving counters, all stainless steel and glass. The serving tubs were all empty. Everything was clean, dishes stacked neatly, all ready to go except for the absence of any hungry students and folks ready to serve them.

His gaze was roaming to the floor as he stepped. But there wasn't a discernible footprint there. Decker stepped through the opening into the rear space. There were portable shelving units here used to carry food from this area to the serving area. They were parked against the walls. There were mops and buckets and other cleaning tools.

That was of no interest to Decker.

What *was* of interest to him was the built-in freezer located at the far end of the storage room.

A whooshing sound. A vacuum. A freezer door closing.

Or *opening*.

He pulled out his pistol. He wasn't actually expecting to find the shooter in full cammies inside the freezer. They had to have searched back here and of course opened the freezer. But he had seen enough weird shit in his life not to discount the possibility. And to take anything for granted at this point could mean he too might leave the school in a body bag in the back of a silent transport.

He aimed his pistol at the door, stepped to the side, gripped the handle with his coat sleeve, jerked it upward, and tugged it hard. The door opened cleanly.

With a *whoosh*, he noted, as the air seal was broken. He imagined in the early morning hours it would have echoed right out into the empty, silent hall and into Melissa Dalton's ears. Well, this had been his little experiment, and it seemed to corroborate what the girl had said.

Decker backed away and took up position behind a worktable. He edged around it until he could see fully into the freezer. It was empty, except for food. But had it been empty at 7:28 the morning of the rampage?

Decker stepped inside the freezer and looked around. He noted that the door had a safety mechanism that allowed anyone inside to open it. That way one couldn't become trapped inside and freeze to death.

Then he noticed it. Or *felt* it, rather.

Freezers were supposed to be really cold, set at zero, in fact. This freezer was merely cold. Maybe not as cold as even the temperature outside.

He checked the temperature gauge. No wonder. It read forty-five. He opened up some of the containers in the freezer and saw what he expected to see. The meat and other perishables had defrosted and were beginning to go bad. They would have to throw them out.

So the guy had upped the temperature in the freezer and used it as his hiding place. And Melissa Dalton had heard exactly what she thought she had. A whooshing sound as the guy emerged at 7:28. But why hide in the freezer? And how did he get in the school to begin with? Presumably the freezer was used during the day, so he had to have come in after hours. And he had to have come in the night before the shooting. Otherwise he would have been discovered when the freezer door was opened by the kitchen staff when they began their duties.

Next question: What would coming in here gain him?

And the mother of all questions: How could he have walked from the cafeteria at the front of the school all the way to the back to commence his rampage and no one see him? It was like he'd teleported in from a space-ship.

Fresh questions started coming in waves to Decker as the potential suspect pool morphed.

What about visitors? Parents? Outside service people? Lancaster hadn't mentioned anyone like that. But he presumed that anyone in the school at the time would have been held for questioning. That was the most basic rule of a criminal investigation. No one got to simply walk away. But there had been a gap between the shoot-ings and the police shutting down ingress and egress. The shooter had to have made his escape then. But how had he done it without being seen?

Decker came out of the freezer and closed it behind him. He walked a few paces and looked up. The freezer did not have a hiding place. But here was something.

He grabbed one of the chairs and planted it in the middle of the room. He heaved himself up onto the chair. With his height he bumped his head against the tile ceiling. A drop-down ceiling, what people also called a floating ceiling, since the light tiles rode on metal racks that hung down about two feet from the actual perma-nent ceiling. It had been a retrofit, he knew, done long after the school was originally built. No one was install-ing drop ceilings in the 1940s.

He lifted one of the ceiling tiles and poked his head through. Using his phone as a flashlight, he shone it around the darkened interior of the space. There was a lot of crap up here, including electrical lines, pipes for the sprinkler system, and HVAC ductwork. There was no way a guy that big could fit up here. And even if he had managed it, the light supports wouldn't have held his weight. He repositioned the chair three more times until he found something. Not up top, on the floor. A bit of ceiling tile dust. He looked at the spots that he had already examined. There was a bit of such dust now under each because he had lifted the tiles there and dislodged the grainy material. But he hadn't touched the tiles at this spot.

He took pictures of everything from different angles. Then he positioned his chair and hoisted himself up once more. He used his hand, covered with the sleeve of his jacket so as to not smear or add to any fingerprints already there, to push the tile gently up. He poked his head through and looked around. The space was empty here. No pipes or electrical lines or ductwork. What *was* here was space to hide something. Like cammie gear and perhaps even weapons.

He looked over every inch of space and then hit pay dirt.

Snagged on a metal support was a thread. He shone his light on it. It looked beige. At another support point there was a smudge in the dust. And a third spot might just be oil residue from maybe a shotgun wedged there.

He touched nothing, climbed down, and texted Lancaster. The forensics team would have to come down here and tear this place apart. While he was waiting for them, he walked to the exterior door opening onto the small loading dock.

"Shit."

It had looked locked, but when he had leaned his bulk against the door it had fallen open, prompting his expletive. He stepped out onto the small loading dock. It was surrounded by a six-foot-tall wooden fence. With his height he could see over. Some garbage cans were located here, as well as a small Dumpster. And wooden crates were stacked in one corner. Decker nudged open the fence gate and peered out.

Two parking spaces, both empty now. Off that, a short strip of cracked asphalt and then a chain-link fence that led to a long row of ten-foot-tall bushes and other shrubbery that had grown up right next to the fence. He walked quickly over to the fence. At the spot opposite from the kitchen entrance he pushed his way through the bushes. The chain-link fence here was split right down the middle. He shone his cell phone light over it. Rusted. It had been this way for a while. He continued through the bushes and came out on the other side. Here was a path that led down into the woods that had been next to the school since forever.

Easy come, easy go.

15

Lancaster whittled down her gum while a tech team scoured the cafeteria and kitchen area. Outside, teams of police and FBI agents were following the trail that Decker had showed them.

Decker leaned against one wall of the cafeteria, his hands in his pockets, and took in all that was going on. Lancaster walked over to him.

"We had looked in the freezer before," she said. "But we didn't check the food or the temperature gauge. That was an oversight. I'm sure we would have noticed it later."

"You were looking for a shooter, clearing rooms," Decker said. "Not worrying about spoiled hamburger. I didn't have to worry about that. I was just nosing around."

"Right, after you took off from the library without a word. I called after you, you know. I could have come with you, Amos."

He noted her hurt look and then gazed around. It had not occurred to him at the time. She was still on the police force, so her and Decker finding this new line of investigation together would have helped her career. As it was, it had been Decker's discovery, which helped Lancaster not at all.

"I . . . I didn't—"

"Forget it," she said abruptly. "You did the same thing when we *officially* worked together."

"I did?"

"I guess it's just a quirk of yours. Although for a guy who has this great memory, I would have expected you to remember doing it. At least to me."

"I'm a little out of sorts here, Mary."

Her irritation seemed to lift. "No, I think you're getting your mojo back. I knew you would. That's the important thing."

"It's not like you need me to solve this case. You have a lot of resources."

"The thing is, Amos." She looked down for a moment, chewing her gum. Then she gazed up at him and said, "Truth is, I miss working with you. I think we made a good team."

Decker nodded but said nothing.

As the moments went by, Lancaster evidently realized he was not going to comment on this admission. She said, "But what I don't get is, if he was in here, how did the video camera capture him at the rear entrance? It doesn't jibe."

Decker pushed off the wall. "I'll show you."

He led her to the rear of the school and pointed at

the camera that had captured the image of the gunman. "Check the angle."

She stared up at the lens. "Okay."

Keeping to one side of the rear foyer, Decker circled around so that his back was to the rear door. Then he stepped to his left. "This is the spot where the camera picks up an image. I could see it on the feed. That middle door behind me is the only one in the frame."

"So the shooter could have done what you just did? Come in from the side and then gotten picked up by the camera."

"And made it *appear* that he had come in the rear entrance when he really hadn't."

"I wonder why the camera is positioned that way?"

"Well, it could have been moved."

Decker went over to the camera, extended his arm, and touched it. "I can reach it, but I'm tall. Yet someone shorter using a stick or a broom or something like that could have repositioned it. Probably no one would notice. It's not like someone is monitoring this full-time, right?"

"Damn, this thing keeps getting more and more complicated."

"No, it's getting more and more *premeditated*, Mary."

"You want to go outside and smoke with me?" she asked.

He looked at her funny. "I don't smoke."

"I thought this might make you start."

"I can be fat or I can smoke. I can't be both."

They walked back to the cafeteria.

When they reached it Lancaster popped another stick of gum in her mouth and started chewing. "Captain Miller's calling you in paid dividends."

Decker looked at her. "What dividends?"

She pointed at the room they were in. "This, Decker. Jesus. For a smart guy you can be obtuse at times."

"I found this, so what? Not really a clue to the shooter."

"He was hiding in the freezer with the temp turned way up. It looks like he hid his weapons and maybe his cammie gear in the ceiling. So he was already here, which is why no one saw him come in."

"But have you found any other trace?"

"Oil mark on a ceiling tile support. Could be from a gun. The thread you found. Looks to be cammie fiber. The FBI is verifying. So that's something."

He drew his hands from his pockets and placed his index finger a half inch from his thumb. "This is how much I found. Nothing to cheer about."

"Well, it's more than we had."

"I saw the control panel. When does the security system get turned on here?"

"Normally ten p.m. But there was an event that night. A school play that ran late. Lots of people. So the system wasn't turned on until midnight so everyone could get out of the building."

"And no activity on the alarm log?"

She shook her head. "None. First thing we did was check with the monitoring company. The log is clear."

"So the shooter has to get in before midnight. Did this play involve refreshments in the cafeteria?"

"No. A friend of mine went because her kid was in it. She told me everyone left right after the play was over."

"So he comes in during the gap before the alarm system was set and takes up his hidey-hole."

"Why put his guns in the ceiling, then, Amos? Why not just have them in the freezer with him?"

"You're assuming he came in with them and then took up his hiding spot. What if he brought the weapons in at another time and hid them? Then the freezer wouldn't work. Someone would spot them. The ceiling would work just fine. If he *did* hide them up there."

She shook her head stubbornly. "Why not do it all at once? It was pretty risky to get the guns in and hidden. And then sneak in again and hide in the freezer? Another risk that someone might have seen him."

"Agreed. But if that's the way it happened, then there must be an explanation for it. This guy strikes me as being methodical and thoughtful."

"I can see that," said Lancaster.

Decker continued to ruminate, seemingly talking to himself. "Guns and gear first. Then the shooter. He might have come in for the school play along with everyone else. Or appeared to do so. The auditorium is across the main hall from the cafeteria. Entering the main entrance, you turn left for the auditorium. Maybe this guy hung a right and went to the cafeteria. Or if folks came in the back entrance too from the parking lot out there, the right and left are reversed. He stays all night and starts his rampage the next morning. So you need to check if anyone saw someone they didn't recognize at the school last night." He paused. "But there's the same old hitch."

"What?" asked Lancaster as she popped another stick of gum in her mouth after wadding up the old one in a tissue and throwing it into the trash can.

"If your theory holds that Debbie Watson was the first vic, she was on the hall next to the rear entrance. That would mean that if our guy was hiding in the freezer overnight he would have had to walk down the hall between the cafeteria and the library, turn right down the main hall, pass two more corridors on both sides, past classrooms and presumably people, to take out first Watson and then, at the other end of the hall, the gym teacher Kramer. Then he reverses his path and starts mowing folks down as he moves back to the front of the school." Decker looked at her skeptically. "That doesn't seem plausible. Why not just start shooting on the front half of the school and work your way to the back? Which would mean Watson would be one of the last vics, not the first."

"But the time stamp on the video?"

"That's the real hitch in all this. That tells us he *did* begin his shooting at the rear part of the school. And he wanted us to see him on that camera for some reason. Now that we know he might have been hiding in the cafeteria, the video image looks like misdirection. So that means we have one proven point—the video camera time stamp, and one almost proven point—the shooter was hiding in the cafeteria. If they're both true, neither makes sense as a whole. One plus one does not equal three."

"You're starting to lose me, Amos."

"You have the school interior laid out with your prelim shot register?"

She nodded.

"Let's take a look. Because it might just be this guy did the reverse of what we think he did."

"But if you're right about what you found, and he did go front to back to front, he would have made his escape out through the storage area off the cafeteria and then through the path to the woods. That's the easiest egress. It would all fit."

Decker took a breath, let it out, and stared at the ceiling.

"And maybe that's exactly what the son of a bitch wants us to think."

16

His confidence in his ability to perform as a detective growing, Decker spent another hour going over and over the preliminary shot registry. It was based on witness accounts, which Decker knew were unreliable; forensic evidence, which he knew was not nearly as flawless as TV made it seem; hunches, which were just that and nothing more; and, lastly, common sense, which might just be the most accurate and helpful of the bunch.

Lancaster looked away from her laptop screen and studied him.

"So what do you think?"

Decker absently stroked his shortened beard, his belly rumbling. It was now light outside. And it had been a long time in between meals for him. But he could stand to miss a few meals. A few hundred of them, in fact. He was like a polar bear. He could live off his accumulated fat all winter.

"Point one. I think he originated from the cafeteria."

"Okay."

"Point two. I think Debbie Watson *was* the first vic."

"So we're back to your dilemma. One plus one equals three. How did a big guy in cammies, hood, and face shield walk the length of the school with weapons totally unseen? And then where did he go? He can't just vanish."

"There's no way there could be two shooters?" he said. "One coming out of the freezer and one coming in the rear?"

She shook her head. "Impossible. There was only one shooter. Same description. Unless you think identically shaped men did this together."

"Okay, one shooter. The pistol is easily hidden. The shotgun could be stowed down a pants leg."

"But the clothing. The shield?"

Decker thought some more about this. "Who's to say he put that on in the cafeteria?"

"We found a fiber in the ceiling."

"Still doesn't mean he had all the stuff on in there."

"So he carries it down the hall with him? In what? And the guns? The guy must have been so bulky that someone would have noticed. Especially if he was a stranger. And then where does he change?"

"You're sure no one was seen walking the halls at that time?"

"Yes."

"No one? Really? In a busy school?"

"Everyone was in class, both students and teachers. The folks in the office were working. Most had not been at their desks long. The gym teacher was in his office where he was shot. There was a half-eaten Egg McMuffin on his desk and a nearly full cup of coffee. Custodians were in their part of the school going over the schedule for the day."

"But if no one was in the halls, there was no one to see a stranger roaming." But then Decker immediately corrected himself. "Only all the doors have windows. He would have had to pass by numerous ones."

"Exactly," agreed Lancaster.

"No visitors?"

"None logged in and no one remembered any. That's not to say someone didn't slip in. That's always possible. And like you said, he could have come in the night before during the play. The school was wide open then."

"But why would the guy hide in the freezer?" said Decker. "Is there security here at night?"

Lancaster shook her head. "No, but if he came in during the school play, he would want to be out of sight. He couldn't know someone wouldn't come into the cafeteria that night for some reason."

"Okay, that makes sense. Let's move to Debbie Watson. She was heading to the nurse's station?"

Lancaster nodded. "Yes. She had stopped, apparently, to get something from her locker. It was right near where she was found. The locker door was still open."

"And the nurse's room is in the office section?"

Lancaster nodded again. "She would have had to walk along the main corridor from the rear to the front."

"What class was she coming out of to go to the nurse?"

"Math. Classroom 144."

"Same hall as custodial?"

"That's right," said Lancaster. "Which has a loading dock. And thus an exit."

"So if we're right and the guy came through the cafeteria, here's what his route looks like. He went from the front to the back of the school on the first floor. I'm assuming the second and third floors were clear?"

"We're searching them, of course. But the enrollment at Mansfield has steadily gone down over the years. There are enough kids to fill out the first floor and that's it. They have a hard enough time finding bodies to fill out the football team. The upper floors are used for storage and such. And they're locked and barred off. And they were still secure when we checked them, with no sign of tampering."

"Then for some reason he waited to start shooting until he got to the rear of the school. Then he starts popping people, going down halls, entering classrooms, shooting as he goes. He reaches the office at the front, kills the assistant principal. And then he escapes through the cafeteria's loading dock and takes the footpath to the woods. How likely is that?"

"You mean why didn't he just start shooting in the front, work his way to the back, and then escape out the rear?"

Decker was studying the ceiling. "Let's put means

aside and look at motive. Mansfield has its share of violence. Gangs, drugs, assaults. Kids mature a lot faster."

"No argument there."

"So is this a Columbine? A kid with a grudge? Maybe not even a student. Either from another school or he graduated, or he dropped out."

Lancaster said, "We're compiling a database with all that info. The FBI is helping."

"When will they have an answer?"

Lancaster rubbed her eyes and checked her watch. "I'm not sure. Look, I've got to get home, grab an hour's sleep, and change my clothes. And I need to give Earl a little break. Sandy hasn't been sleeping very well lately."

Decker knew Sandy Lancaster as gentle, funny, bubbly, and wildly enthusiastic about everything and everyone. But he knew she could also become depressed and anxious over something relatively trivial. And then she wouldn't sleep. Which meant no one else in the Lancaster household did either.

"You need any help with that?" asked Decker.

She looked surprised. "Are you offering to babysit?"

"I don't know. I'm just . . . asking," he finished awkwardly. He had never done much with Molly when she had been really little. He was so big and she was so tiny he'd been terrified he'd break her.

She smiled. "I'm good, Amos. But thanks. I'll be back at the station later this morning. We can grab a cup of coffee and go over things. You need a ride back to your place?"

"No, I'll hang out here for a while."

"Suit yourself. You want to talk, about anything, give me a ring."

She gathered up her things and started to leave. But she stopped and looked at him. "It really feels like old times."

Decker said nothing, but he gave her a slight nod, which made her smile. She turned and walked out.

He sat in the chair in the library. He'd spent more time in here now than he probably had in his four years as a student. It wasn't that the schoolwork had come easily to him; it hadn't. But he was not the type to sit and read. That had changed. Now he devoured prodigious amounts of information. Now that he could remember it all, it was like he couldn't get enough of it. He wondered if his brain had a capacity limit. If so, he hoped it was as big as he was.

He watched the FBI suits doing their thing at a table across the library's main area. They all looked clean-cut, on the younger side, inexhaustibly professional, starched shirts, ties no doubt as straight as their spines. A few of them looked up occasionally at him, no doubt wondering what a fat weirdo dressed like a homeless person was doing in the middle of *their* investigation.

Well, at least I trimmed my beard and cut my hair. Or else they'd probably arrest me for looking like a big-ass version of Charlie Manson.

And then the next moment he forgot all about the FBI. He was really no longer in the library at Mansfield. He was no longer looking into the mass shooting here. It was something Lancaster had said.

I'll be back at the station later this morning. We can grab a cup of coffee and go over things.

Decker would not be at the station later this morning. He had somewhere else to be.

I'll be at an arraignment.

Sebastian Leopold took solid form in Decker's thoughts. He went back over every second of their conversation. Every word, every look, every mannerism. Something seemed off, but he couldn't pinpoint what, when he almost always could. Orphan facts, he liked to call them. There was no one to claim ownership because they were lies.

Yet not with Leopold for some reason. And that was cause for concern but also hope. The reason for hope? Simply Leopold's existence. Before, Decker had nothing to go on. Now, in the form of the prisoner, he had a layer that had been partially peeled back. And when that happened it couldn't help but reveal what was underneath.

He left the library and made his way outside.

It was still raining. If anything it was raining harder. The body bag wagons had all gone, and with them the crowd had drained away. No more cell phone candles.

But in front of the school was a mountain of flowers, hand-painted signs, Teddy bears.

All drenched and soggy. But the intent was still clear. Still powerful.

He read some of the signs.

RIP Mr. Kramer.

Miss you, Debbie.

Never going to forget you, Eddie.

The town knew who the dead were for a very simple reason, though no names had been officially released. Those people hadn't come home.

Cammie man had seen to that. Cammie man with no face and the ability to leap long school halls effortlessly. Because that's what he must have done, to get from point A to the kill zone with "Miss you, Debbie."

Decker went back to the bleachers and sat there under an overhang to keep dry, though he was pretty much already soaked.

Sebastian Leopold was going to be arraigned in a few hours. Decker planned to be there when he was. Arraignments were typically boring, mechanical stages of the law. Yet there was one important bit of information Decker wanted to see in person.

He sat there for a few minutes more, then, when the rain slowed, he rose and walked back to the Residence Inn. It took him a while because he didn't move as swiftly as he used to. But it gave him time to think. And he arrived in time for breakfast. He absorbed half the buffet, catnapped for exactly one hour, showered, combed his hair, put his "lawyer" clothes back on, and headed to the courthouse to see exactly what Sebastian Leopold was going to say to the most critical question the judge would ask him today.

17

Normally, the courthouse would be packed for something like this. A triple homicide and a guy saying he was good for it. Two days ago, it would have been the biggest story in Burlington, maybe the whole state.

But after the slaughter at Mansfield, nobody gave a damn.

Well, one person did.

Decker knew the drill, having testified in the court building countless times during the course of prosecuting folks he'd helped apprehend. He passed through security, nodded to a couple of county sheriffs he knew, and checked the court docket posted on a board near the information desk. Then he headed to the courtroom, where in about twenty minutes Sebastian Leopold would make his first court appearance after walking into the police station and giving himself up.

Decker swung open the heavy oak door and took a seat in the middle of the large room. He was the only one there. No bailiff. No court reporter. No lawyers. The press was covering Mansfield, he reckoned. Part of him would have preferred to be at Mansfield too. But the most important part of him wanted to be right where he was.

A minute later the prosecuting attorney, a woman in her forties, came into the courtroom, passed by Decker, and took her seat at the counsel table. Decker knew Sheila Lynch, but she had not made eye contact. She opened her briefcase, took out a file, and read through it. Decker stared at the back of her neck, which was exposed because her hair was up in a tight, professional bun. Lynch's skirt and jacket were black and already showing traces of grime. The back of her right shoe had a gouge out of it and her nylons were a bit ragged where the shoe met the stocking.

At five minutes to ten the same door Decker had passed through opened again. He glanced back. Lancaster gave him a tiny wave. Behind her was Captain Miller. He was in uniform today.

They took seats on either side of him.

Lancaster said, "Don't know what I was thinking about when I said I'd meet you at the station. Of course you'd be here."

"Why aren't you at Mansfield?" Decker asked.

Miller answered, "I have been. Since six-thirty this morning. Now we're here. After this, Lancaster is heading there while I go sit my fat ass behind my desk and deal with crap I don't want to deal with."

"Doesn't answer why you're here," said Decker.

"No, I guess it doesn't."

Decker continued to eyeball Miller. "I don't have a

gun. I passed through the magnos at the entrance. I can't shoot the guy."

"Never doubted that for an instant," said Miller, smoothing out a wrinkle on his dark blue jacket. "But this is an important case, and so here we are."

"Were you able to trace Leopold's real identity? Was he in the Navy?"

"We sent his prints through the FBI's IAFIS database. No hits."

Decker said, "He told me he was in the Navy. He had the tat. But maybe he wasn't in *our* Navy."

"Foreigner?" said Miller in a thoughtful tone. "That might explain it."

"Do you think Sebastian Leopold is his real name?" asked Lancaster.

"I didn't," answered Decker. "But I'm not sure now."

"Well, we can have the Bureau make international inquiries for us," said Miller. "They can go through overseas databases a lot easier than we can."

At the stroke of ten the rear door leading into the judge's chambers opened and the bailiff, a portly man with a handlebar mustache, stepped through. He told them to rise and all four of them did. Decker heard the door creak open and turned to see a young woman dash in and take a seat at the rear. She held a notepad in one hand and a tiny digital recorder in the other.

The press. All *one* of them. She must be very junior, thought Decker. Or else she would be over covering

Mansfield. His brain dug into the big pile of stuff inside his head and pulled out the name.

Alex Jamison.

The woman who'd called him about Leopold. She worked for the *News Leader*. He'd hung up on her. He turned back around before she could focus on him.

It was at this moment that the black-robed Judge Christian Abernathy stepped into the courtroom. He was old, bespectacled, and frail, and his white hair, what was left of it, sprouted all over his head like bits of fading cotton taped to pink wax paper masquerading as skin. The running bet among the police was how long it would be before Abernathy croaked on the bench, toppling over onto the marble floor. Decker remembered that the man never made it easy for the police to convict anyone, but maybe that was as it should be, he thought.

Abernathy sat and so did they.

The door to the right opened. The holding cell was kept there, Decker knew.

Out stepped Sebastian Leopold in his bright orange jumpsuit, his hands and feet chained, with two burly uniforms on either side of him. He performed the shackle shuffle as he walked. He looked around the large high-ceilinged courtroom as though he was not fully cognizant of where he was or what he was doing here.

He was escorted to the counsel table, although there was no counsel there.

Decker leaned in to Miller. "PD?"

Miller shook his head and mouthed, "Apparently not." He did not look happy about this. Not happy at all.

The uniforms removed the shackles and stepped back.

The bailiff rose, picked up a docket sheet, and called the case and read out the charges that Leopold was facing. Then, his duty completed, he stepped back with the mechanical movement of a cuckoo clock figure returning to its hiding place.

Abernathy adjusted his glasses and peered down at the prosecuting attorney.

"Ms. Lynch?"

Lynch rose, adjusted her shirt cuffs, and said, "Mr. Leopold has been charged with three counts of murder in the first, Your Honor. He has no known address and his ties to the community are apparently nonexistent. In light of the serious charges, we request no bail be set and that he be remanded to the county jail until trial."

Well, thought Decker, that was all to be expected. They weren't about to cut the man loose.

Abernathy turned to Leopold and peered down at him from his high perch. Then he shot a glance back at Lynch.

"Where is Mr. Leopold's counsel, Ms. Lynch?"

Lynch cleared her throat and said, "He was not able to afford counsel and a public defender was appointed to represent him. However, Mr. Leopold refused those services. Numerous times, I might add."

Abernathy's gaze swiveled back to the accused. "Mr. Leopold, do you understand the charges that have been read to you?"

Leopold looked around as though he was wondering to whom Abernathy was speaking.

"Mr. Leopold, do you not want counsel?" asked Abernathy sharply.

Leopold turned to face him, shook his head, and said, "I got no money."

"That's why we have *public* defenders, Mr. Leopold," Abernathy said testily. "They're *free*. You can thank the Supreme Court's interpretation of our Constitution for that. I will set this arraignment aside for now until one is provided for—"

"I did it, sir," said Leopold, interrupting.

Abernathy gazed down at him as though the defendant were a mildly interesting bug lying on the sidewalk. "Excuse me?"

"I done it, so I don't need a lawyer."

"Are you telling me that you're pleading guilty to three homicides in the first degree?"

"I killed them, so yes sir, I guess I am."

Abernathy took a moment to clean his glasses, as though that would make what was happening a bit clearer. After settling them on his long, crooked nose, he said, "This is hardly the time for *guessing*, Mr. Leopold. These are serious charges, indeed the most serious of all. Are you aware that not only your freedom is at risk here, but also your life? This is a capital case."

"You mean the death penalty?"

Abernathy looked like he might stroke. "Yes. Of *course* that's what I mean, Mr. Leopold!"

"Well, I'm pleading guilty 'cause I done it. So I guess we don't need no trial."

Abernathy looked back at Lynch and said in an admonishing tone, "Ms. Lynch, I find this reprehensible."

"Judge Abernathy, we tried our best. Mr. Leopold refused all entreaties to—"

Abernathy looked over Lynch's shoulder and spotted Miller. With a slow wave of his hand he beckoned the police chief forward.

"Shit," muttered Miller.

He stood, passed in front of Decker and Lancaster, and hurried up to the bench along with Lynch.

Decker watched as the police captain, prosecutor, and judge engaged in a heated discussion. Well, actually Abernathy was doing most of the talking. It seemed the judge was quite animated, and gesticulated twice at Leopold.

Miller nodded and said something. Lynch did the same and they hastily returned to their seats, each looking upset.

When Decker looked at him questioningly, Miller shook his head and said, "Later."

Abernathy said to Leopold, "I'm ordering you to be returned to your cell for now. A public defender will be appointed to represent you. You will then be returned to this court for your arraignment tomorrow morning." He glanced at Lynch. "And get the psych eval done promptly, Ms. Lynch. Understood?" She nodded, her gaze refusing to meet his. Abernathy said, "Officers, please remove the defendant."

He rapped his gavel down. The two uniforms immediately came forward, shackled a confused looking Leopold, and led him back out.

Abernathy said to the bailiff, "Call the next case, please. And I trust *he* will have counsel." As he said this he shot first Lynch and then Miller a withering look.

Decker, Lancaster, and Miller rose and headed out as the second prisoner was led in for his hearing.

The reporter had already left.

Out in the hall a scowling Lynch came over to Miller.

She said, "I don't like getting my ass handed to me in court, Mac."

"We couldn't force him to accept a lawyer, Sheila. You were in the middle of it. You know."

"Well, he's getting one whether he likes it or not, if only to enter a guilty plea." She shot Lancaster and then Decker a glance. "Hello, Amos, I guess I'm not surprised to see you here."

"I guess not," replied Decker.

Lynch turned back to Miller. "Since Abernathy's ordered a psych eval, I'm not sure he'll be able to plead to anything if the eval comes back like I think it might."

"You mean mentally unfit," said Lancaster.

"You've seen the guy. You think he's all there?"

"Maybe he was sixteen months ago," said Decker.

"Doesn't matter if he's not legally competent to stand trial now."

She turned and hurried off, her briefcase banging against her thigh.

Decker turned to Miller. "So?"

"So we got read the riot act by Abernathy. He was pissed that Leopold had no PD, and he's right. Death penalty case with no lawyer? Whatever happened at this level would get overturned on appeal automatically. And Abernathy does not like to get overturned by the appellate court. That's why he was ticked off. I think he thought we were setting him up. As if."

"So why wasn't a PD appointed?" asked Decker.

"Like Lynch said, Leopold didn't want one. He was totally uncooperative. Kept saying he did it so why did he need a lawyer. We had our hands full with Mansfield or else we would have handled it differently. We basically dropped the ball there."

Decker stuffed his hands into his pockets and let his chin fall to his chest. "So you lawyer him up, he comes back in, pleads guilty, and then what?"

"Well, hopefully his lawyer will convince him to plead *not* guilty just so it looks better. We can talk about a deal and see what comes of it. But we also have to see what the psych eval says. If he's unfit it throws a monkey wrench into things."

"And if he isn't guilty?" asked Decker.

"Do you think he *is*?" asked Miller.

"I met with the guy once. I can't say definitely what I think."

"Well, none of this is going to happen today. So we've got time." Miller glanced at Lancaster. "You better get back to Mansfield. I hear the FBI is working hard to take over the case."

"And if they want to can we really stop them?" asked Lancaster.

"We're not going to roll over and play dead for the Feds, Mary," said Miller sternly. He looked at Decker. "You going to be able to continue helping us on it? Leopold will keep. This prick at Mansfield, the longer it goes, the harder it'll be for us to find him."

Decker looked off. The answer should have been easy. Only it wasn't.

Miller studied him for a few moments. "Well, let me know."

He turned and walked off, leaving Lancaster and Decker standing in the hall. Activity in the courthouse had started to heat up and the corridors were growing full. Moms crying about sons in trouble. Lawyers clustered like chickens in a pen. Cops were coming and going, and folks were wandering around who were already in trouble or about to be.

Lancaster said sharply, "Why the wavering? Last night you said the shooter wasn't going to get away with it."

Decker didn't answer right away. He was watching

the reporter standing next to the entrance to the court-house. She was obviously waiting for him.

"Amos?" said Lancaster.

He glanced back at his former partner. "I'll be at the high school later today."

"Does that mean you're still engaged on it?"

"Later today," said Decker. He headed for the rear exit.

The reporter caught up to him halfway down the hall.

"Mr. Decker? Mr. Decker?"

Decker's first plan was to just keep walking, but the woman gave every indication that she would simply follow him out of the building, down the street, and into his next life if need be. So he stopped at the exit, turned, and looked down at her. His mind automatically collected observations and distilled them into an assortment of deductions.

She was in her late twenties, pretty, tall, slim, and brunette, with her hair cut short around her ears. Ears that weren't pierced even for earrings. He saw tat letters on her left wrist where her cuff rode up.

Iron Butterfly. Well, they did make a comeback after she was born.

Her eyes were a dull blue that clashed with her complexion. One of her incisors was chipped, her nails were bitten down to the rims, her right index finger had once been broken and healed badly with a little bend to it in the middle, and her lips were overly thin and chapped. She didn't smell of smoke, drink, or perfume.

Her clothes were not new, nor overly clean, but they rode well on her tall, slender figure. She had a dark blotch on the inside of her right middle finger where the pen was held. Not just a keyboard clicker, then. She used ink.

Her face held the wonderful enthusiasm of youth as yet unblemished by life. That age was a nice time in anyone's life. And it was necessary. To get through what was coming in later years.

If we all started out cynical, what a shitty world that would be.

"Mr. Decker? I'm Alex Jamison with the *News Leader*."

"You like 'In-A-Gadda-Da-Vida'? It was Butterfly's biggest seller. Thirty million and still counting. In the top forty of all time." Decker had read this in a *Rolling Stone* article three years ago while eating a PBJ and drinking a cup of coffee at a diner downtown while he was a witness in a case involving a burglary ring he and Lancaster had busted. It was on page forty-two of the magazine, lower right-hand corner. He could see the page and the accompanying picture in his head so clearly it was like he was watching high-def TV. At first this total recall had scared the crap out of him. Now it was as natural to him as swallowing.

She seemed surprised by this until she glanced down at her tat. She looked back at him, smiling. "My mom got me into their early music. Then when the band re-formed the last time I became sort of obsessed. I mean, they played with Jimmy Page and Zeppelin. Lot of tragic stuff with them, though."

Decker did not follow this up with anything, because music was not why she was here, and he had places to be. She seemed to get this point by his silence.

"I tried calling you. I don't like to chase people down in the courthouse," she said a bit defensively.

Decker just kept staring at her. All around them the courthouse activity went on, bees in a hive, oblivious to the pair of intruders into their world of legal higgledy-piggledy.

"Sebastian Leopold didn't have counsel."

"That's right," said Decker. "But he will."

"What do you think about all of this?" She held up her recorder. "You mind?"

"I don't have anything to say."

"I'm sure you're going through hell right now. I mean, this guy just pops up out of nowhere and con-fesses. You must be reeling."

"I don't reel," said Decker. He turned to leave.

"But you must be feeling *something*. And how was it facing Leopold in there? It must have brought every-thing back to you."

Decker faced her. "It didn't bring everything back to me."

She looked stunned. "But I thought—"

"Because it never left me. Now, I have someplace to be."

Decker walked out of the courthouse and Jamison did not follow him.

18

Decker caught a bus a block over from the courthouse and rode it to within a half mile of where he was going. As his large feet carried him down the sidewalk, the color blue intensified in his head until it seemed that the entire world had been covered in it. Even the sun seemed to have been transformed into an enormous blueberry so utterly swollen that it seemed it might burst at any moment.

It sickened him but he kept on going, his breath growing heavier and his tread slowing. He was out of shape, but that was not the reason. The reason was just up ahead.

When he turned the corner and saw the house he stopped, but only for a moment. If he didn't pick up his pace, he knew he would turn and run away.

It was still bank-owned. No one had wanted to move in there even at a reduced price. Hell, they probably couldn't give it away. And there were lots of empty houses in Burlington. It was a place one wanted to get away from, not move to. The front door, he knew, was locked. The door off the carport and into the kitchen had always been easy to jimmy. He wondered if the killer had gone in that way. Leopold had said that was his ingress, if he was to be believed.

He passed by the front and opened the chain-link gate to the backyard. The color blue had initially been limited to the bodies. Now the entire property and everything within a half mile of it was blue. He had first experienced this the third time he had returned to the house, and it had been that way ever since. He could never adequately explain to anyone what it felt like to see blue grass, blue trees, blue siding on a house you knew was painted yellow. Even the blue sky felt different because all the clouds were also that color.

He eyed the tree in the back and the swing dangling from it. He'd put that up himself because Molly had wanted one. When she was little Decker would push her. Sometimes he had pushed Cassie and Molly together. It had been cheap entertainment for a young couple with little money.

Now the rope was rotted and the long plank of wood Decker had fashioned for a seat was warped and splintered. The bank was having someone cut the grass, but it was full of weeds.

He turned to look at the rear of the house. The back door led into a small utility room. Had that actually been how the killer had entered?

He jimmied this door easily enough. It seemed none of the locks on the house worked very well, something that, again, caused him enormous guilt. A policeman who couldn't even secure his own house?

He closed the door behind him and looked around. Short flight of steps up to the kitchen. Where his brother-in-law had sat drinking beer until someone had sliced his neck from ear to ear.

He went up the blue steps and stepped into the blue kitchen. It was full of dust and some dead insects were on the floor and on the countertops. He eyed the spot where the kitchen table had been. That's where Johnny Sacks had been attacked.

The blood had long since been cleaned up, but Decker remembered where every drop had been. Not red now, all blue, like the color of blood as seen inside veins through one's skin, only a thousand times more potent.

He passed into the next room and up the stairs. The same stairs he had taken three at a time on that night. Bouncing off walls, oblivious to whoever might have been in here harming his family.

The mattress and box springs were gone from their bedroom. Evidence. They were at a secure storage unit maintained by the Burlington police. They might be there forever.

Still, he clearly saw her bare foot raised up above the bed. He crossed the room and looked down and saw neon-blue Cassie on the floor. The only thing that wasn't blue about her was the single gunshot wound to her head. Even in Decker's altered mind it would forever be just like it actually was: black and blistered.

He turned and left because his resistance was wearing down and he had other rooms to visit.

He opened the bathroom door and looked at the toilet where his child had been seated, the bathrobe cord cruelly holding her dead body in place.

Leopold had not explained that. He had just done it. Didn't really know why. Felt right. *He said*. The man no one could identify. The man who wanted to plead guilty and die.

He looked down at the spot where he had sat crosslegged with the gun first inside his mouth and then pressed against his temple. His dead daughter in front of him. He had wanted to join her, he guessed, in death. But he hadn't pulled the trigger. The cops had come and recognized him and talked him out of the weapon. It was a wonder they hadn't shot him. Maybe it would have been better if they had.

He turned and walked back down the hall to the next door.

Molly's room. He had only been here a few times since cleaning it out after her death.

The noise from inside caused him to stop, his hand halfway to the knob. He looked around. He had left his gun back in his room because he knew he had been going to the courthouse. He listened some more and then his tension eased. It was not human feet he was hearing.

Scampering, tapping, tiny.

He opened the door in time to see a rat disappear into a hole in the drywall.

He could recall every stick of furniture, the placement of every stuffed animal, the location of each book, for Molly had been a voracious reader.

Decker had been about to fully enter the room when he stopped and stiffened. There was something here that his perfect memory did not recall, and with good reason. Because it had not been here the last time Decker had been in this room.

On the wall, written in red block letters.

We are so much alike, Amos. So much. Like brothers. Do you have a brother? Of course you don't. I checked. Sisters, yes, but no brother. So can I be yours? We're really all the other has now. We need each other.

He read through this message three times. He wanted to dig beneath the words and discover the author. But the more he stared at the words, the more unsettled he became. The person had come back here. Had come back here to write this message to him. This was not about some perceived slight at a 7-Eleven. This was deeply personal with Decker.

As the message had said, Decker had no brother. He had two sisters. Long since moved away. One in California with her Army husband and four kids. The other was in Alaska, childless but prospering and enjoying life with her oil executive husband. They had come for the funerals and then had gone back home. He had not spoken to them since. His fault. They had tried. Repeatedly. He had rebuffed. Repeatedly.

But still, he had to make sure. Whoever had written this message had done his homework. *Sisters.*

He slowly pulled his phone from his pocket and texted each of them. He waited, waited, waited. Then a pop on his phone. California sister was fine and happy to hear from him.

Two minutes later he hadn't moved. It was even earlier in Alaska. Maybe she wasn't up—

Another pop. His sister from Fairbanks had texted. She was fine. To please call when he got a chance.

He punched in another number and waited for the person to answer.

"Lancaster," the voice said.

Decker said, "Mary, you need to see something. And you need to see it now."

19

Lancaster had come. Then Captain Miller. Then the uniforms. Then the forensics team with all its bags of gadgets. It was like that night all over again, only he wasn't staring at his dead daughter while holding a gun against his head.

The message had been written with a red Sharpie. The ink dried almost immediately, and there was no telling how long it had been there. Thus Leopold was not in the clear. He had only been locked up since very early yesterday morning.

Miller had wanted to know how the killer would have known Decker would come back here, enter this room, and see this message.

"I've been back here before," admitted Decker.

"And you went inside each time," said Lancaster.

"Not every time, no. I couldn't . . . every time."

"When was the last time you were in this room?" asked Lancaster.

"Four weeks and three days ago, right about this time."

"So at least we have a time window to work with," noted Lancaster.

"Maybe this guy has been following you and knows you come here," said Miller. "That's why he put this message up."

"We can canvass the neighborhood, see if anyone saw something," said Lancaster.

"They didn't see who murdered three people," countered Decker. "I don't see why they would have seen the person who did this."

"But still," replied Miller. "We're going to do it."

"Brothers?" said Lancaster curiously as a police photographer took shots of the message. "We might want to get a shrink in on this to analyze what's going on inside the dude's head."

"So you think this is Leopold's work?" asked Miller. He was staring at the graffiti like it was part of an inscription on the doorway to hell.

Decker said nothing because he had nothing to say. In his head the words were indeed a flaming red, thus not so far away from hell. Whoever had written this was either being straightforward, at least in a deranged way, or else he was playing head games with him. Decker turned and left, ignoring Lancaster's calling after him.

He never saw Miller grab Lancaster by the arm. He didn't hear his old captain tell her to let him be. He didn't hear Lancaster's retort, and then Miller's request sharpen into a direct order for her to stand down.

They both watched him from the window striding down the sidewalk with a purpose. He soon turned the corner and was gone from their sight.

Decker didn't stop walking until he reached the 7-Eleven on DeSalle at Fourteenth. This marked the first time in his life he had not traveled there by car.

There were no cars parked in front. He opened the door, heard the bell tinkle, and then let it close behind him.

There was a woman behind the counter. She was short but looked taller because of the elevated floor there. Her hair was dark and straight, falling to her shoulders. She looked Latina. She had on a beige long-sleeved blouse with a bra strap showing on one side. She was around fifty and her eye sockets were starting to recede into her face like a pond starting to dry up. A large dark mole was on her left cheek. She had some sheets of paper in front of her and was studying them and then counting off packs of cigarettes shelved in slots overhead.

A man appeared from down one aisle. He had a mop in hand and was using it to steer a bucket with soapy water in it. Decker ran his gaze over him, his police training guiding his eye to certain vital statistics. He was white, midthirties, an inch under six feet, very lean and wiry, with narrow shoulders. His short-sleeved shirt showed off the veins in his arms. His hair was brown and curly and fell like apple peelings across his head.

The woman looked up at him just standing there in the doorway. "Can I help you?" she asked. She had no accent.

He came forward and took his phone from his pocket. He hit a couple buttons and held it up.

"You ever see this guy before?"

She looked at the photo of Sebastian Leopold. "Who is he?" she asked.

"Some guy that either might have worked here once or hung around here at some point."

She shook her head. "I don't remember seeing him. Why you want to know?" Decker fished out his PI license and flashed it in front of her. "I'm trying to find him. He might be due some money. Got a line on him that brought me here. How about your friend over there?"

He looked at the man who was leaning on his mop and studying him quizzically.

The woman said, "Billy, you want to look at this picture?"

Billy parked his mop and bucket against a rack of candy bars, wiped his hands on his faded jeans, and ambled over. He looked pleased to have an excuse to stop cleaning the linoleum.

He looked at the photo and then shook his head. "Nope. Don't look familiar to me. Weird-looking dude. Spacey."

Decker lowered the phone. "How long have you two been here?"

The woman said, "Nearly six months for me. Billy came just a few weeks ago."

Decker nodded. *Too recent, then.* "And the people here before you?"

She shrugged. "I don't know. There was a woman, a couple of men. Turnover is high here. The pay is not very good. And the hours are long. I wouldn't be here if I could find something better. But the job market sucks," she added bluntly.

Decker looked at Billy. "You?"

Billy grinned. "I don't know nuthin' 'bout this place. Just drawing a paycheck, man. Beer money on the weekends. Looking to have a good time with the ladies. Need cash for all that."

He went back to his mopping.

"I'm sorry we can't help you," said the woman.

"Part of the job," said Decker. "Thanks."

He turned and left.

His phone buzzed. He looked at it.

Lancaster.

He put it away without answering.

It rang again.

He looked at it again.

Lancaster.

He sighed, hit the answer button.

"Yeah?"

"Amos?"

Decker immediately went rigid. Lancaster sounded nearly hysterical. And she wasn't the type ever to do so.

"Mary, what is it? Not another shooting?" Decker had been worried about this from the start. Things about the attack at Mansfield had made him believe that the guy was—

"No," she said breathlessly. "But, but there's some-something—"

"Where are you?" he interrupted.

"At Mansfield."

"So it has to do with Mansfield? You found some—"

"Amos!" she shrieked. "Just let me finish."

Decker fell silent, waited. It was as though he could hear her heart beating from across the digital ether.

"We ran ballistics on the pistol used at Mansfield."

"And what did—"

Interrupting, she said, "And we found a match."

His grip tightened around the phone. "A match? To what?"

"To the gun that killed your wife."

20

A .45 round.

Semi-jacketed. Hollow-point.

An SJH, in ballistics shorthand.

It was a brutally efficient piece of ordnance. Not exactly a dumdum, named after Dum-Dum, India, where a British army officer had invented a bullet that mushroomed out on impact and acted as a miniature wrecking ball inside the body.

Innovation wasn't always good for you.

The .45 SJH had blown right through the front of Cassie Decker's skull and ended up lodged deep in her brain. It had been dug out of her during the autopsy and the slug preserved as evidence in her murder investigation. It had retained enough of its shape and lands and grooves to one day be matched to the weapon that had fired it. Well, they didn't have the weapon, but they had something else.

Now they knew that the very same pistol that had fired *the* bullet ending Cassie Decker's life had also terminated the lives of half the victims at Mansfield. The other half had endured the blunt force of the shotgun.

The medical examiner had removed the matched round from Kramer, the gym teacher and, per normal protocol, run it through the department's database. The hit had been immediate.

Because of the magnitude of the finding, the FBI had run its own tests on the slug and came back with the same conclusion.

Same gun. Ballistics didn't lie. The grooves and lands on the bullets' respective hides had matched like a fingerprint. And that wasn't all. They had recovered the single bullet casing from the Deckers' bedroom. They had compared it with several of the casings found at the school. The pinprick on the bottom of the casing where the firing pin strikes was nearly as good as a fingerprint. And it too had matched on all salient points.

The murders of Decker's family and the massacre at Mansfield were now inextricably connected.

Decker huddled in his coat as he stood outside the darkened façade of the school, enduring the driving rain pinging off his hair and burly shoulders. The case had mushroomed from Mansfield High to his home on a quiet street with symbolically an ocean's distance in between. He had never given any thought to a connection between the two crimes. Now that fact dominated him.

There was a chance that there were different killers. Since the shooting at his house, the gun could have been lost by, taken from, or sold by the original killer. The same gun was often used in different crimes by different perps. But Decker believed it was the same shooter in both instances. And if that was the case, it let Leopold out. So Leopold was lying. Yet it was possible he had been told facts of the Decker case by the real killer. And if that were so, then Leopold was the best hope he had to find the person who had murdered his family. And all these others.

Despite the recent writing on the bedroom wall, the case was cold on the Decker family end. Conversely, it was red hot on the Mansfield High School end. So the Mansfield end was where he would focus—that and on Sebastian Leopold. If Leopold knew who the Decker killer was, then he knew who was behind the Mansfield crimes too.

He flashed his credentials at the perimeter security and walked through the front entrance. Yesterday had been disjointed and confusing for him in all respects. He didn't know if he belonged in the middle of all this. He felt cut off from everyone and everything going on around him. But with the possible connection to the murders of his family, Decker knew that he *did* belong. He would be on this case for as long as it took. They would have to dynamite him out of here.

He didn't head to the command center in the library. He went to the cafeteria and stared at the freezer. Then he looked at the ceiling tiles.

Cammie fiber, possible gun oil. Maybe all bullshit. Maybe.

He looked at the exit door. False lead too, or so he now believed.

He left the cafeteria, walked down the hall fronting the library, turned right onto the main corridor that bisected the first floor, and counted his steps off as he made his way to the rear of the school.

At each intersection with another hall he studied the lay of the land, first left, then right. Classrooms on both sides. The last corridor was where Debbie Watson had died. And where, to the left, so had Kramer the gym teacher over his breakfast sandwich and coffee. The rear entrance with the camera faced him. The angle of the camera still intrigued him. That had been deliberate. And deliberate action always had a deliberate motivation.

Then he looked at the classroom to the right of where Debbie had perished. ROOM 141 was stenciled on the glass.

He tried the door but it was locked. He pulled a pick set from his pocket and unlocked it. He stepped inside and turned on the light. He was surprised to see that it was set up as a shop class. They had had shop class back when Decker attended here. But he had thought it now a thing of the past. He looked around at the work places, table and miter saws, planers, drills, buckets of tools, vises clamped to wood, shelves on the walls holding metal tubing, nuts, bolts, wood, more power tools, extension cords, work lights, pretty much anything someone would need to build something. There were three doors at the back of this room. He opened two of them. Storage. He saw stacks of what looked to be old school projects: jumbles of half-finished furniture, metal twisted into various shapes, wire cages, part of a roof section, sawhorses, plywood sheets, stacks of wood, lots of dust, and lots of nothing.

The last door would not open. He took out his lock-pick set again and used it to open the door. He peered in. There was an old boiler in the far corner, now connected to nothing. Some window air-conditioning units were stacked on the floor against one wall up to about ten feet.

Again, a lot of nothing. He closed the door, walked back through the shop class, snapped off the light, and shut the door behind him. Down the hall from the shop class was Classroom 144, the one Debbie Watson had been coming from when she had been shot.

Decker looked over at the open locker on the wall. That was Debbie's. She had been at her locker when she'd been murdered. Probably getting something to take with her to the nurse's office. That might explain the detour here. Or it might not. Teenagers were unpredictable. They could be sick as dogs and stop at their locker to look for some gum. *Or* examine her face for zits in the mirror that hung on the inside of Debbie's locker. He noted the tube of pimple cream standing up on her locker shelf next to a small opened pack of breath mints.

Blood splatters showed that she had been standing in

front of her locker when she'd been shot. She had turned around to face her assailant, because she'd taken the blast from the shotgun directly to her face.

She had died at 8:42.

Decker had concluded that Watson was indeed the first victim. Which made him wonder what the shooter was doing between the whooshing sound at 7:28 on the front hall that Melissa Dalton had heard and Debbie losing her face on the rear hall one hour and fourteen minutes later.

Decker closed his eyes and thought this through.

It took me sixty-four steps and not even two minutes to go from front to back. The shooter appeared on the video at 8:41. But when did he leave the cafeteria? There is no way to be sure. And the biggest question of all: How did he go sight unseen from front to rear? I answer that, I answer everything. I don't answer it, the case goes nowhere.

At least six-two, thick broad shoulders, over two hundred pounds. Decker had looked at the video footage of the shooter and did not dispute those physical estimates. Yet there was no male of that size and height at the school, other than the dead gym teacher and assistant principal, or a bunch of football-playing students hunkered in classrooms with a hundred alibis attached to them. And two of the players who were that size had been killed during the shootings.

It was as though the guy had appeared, done his killing, and then vanished into thin air. Since that was not a possibility, Decker had to be looking at this wrong somehow.

He went into Room 144 and sat down at the teacher's desk. He surveyed the classroom. Twenty-one empty seats arranged in three rows front to back. One of them had been occupied by Debbie Watson. The last moments of her life were clear enough: an upset stomach; a trip to the nurse's office authorized; a detour to her locker. And she was dead minutes later.

She'd been in the third row, fourth seat. He imagined her raising her hand, looking and feeling ill, getting permission to leave, walking out the door, never to walk in it again.

He rose and walked out the door, stopped, and turned. He was facing Debbie's open locker. The mirror on the inside of the door reflected his image back. For some reason Decker didn't recognize himself. This big fat bearded dude, drenched with rain, looking like hell.

But then he looked past the reflection and to something else in Debbie's locker: a stack of textbooks and notebooks.

Decker looked back at Classroom 144 and then at the locker.

Life had coincidences. Serendipity abounded. Wrong place, wrong time. It came as the result of seven billion people jostling each other within the span of a single planet.

But there was an unwritten rule in police work: There are no coincidences. All you needed was more in-depth investigation to show that there are no coincidences.

He phoned Lancaster. She was in the library.

"Did you talk to Debbie Watson's parents?"

"Yes."

"Did they mention that she felt ill when she came to school?"

"No. I asked her that. The mom said she seemed fine. Might've been a bug that came on fast, though."

"And what about the teacher? When Watson asked to leave?"

Decker could hear the woman flipping through her notebook.

"She said Debbie had looked fine but then raised her hand, said she felt nauseous, and asked to be excused."

"Did she make out a note or—"

"They have them preprinted. The teacher filled in Debbie's name and gave it to her."

"So just thirty seconds from start to finish before Debbie left the room?"

"I guess about that."

"What time did she actually leave the classroom?"

"The teacher thought maybe a few minutes before. Maybe five before the shot was heard."

"That's a big gap. Her locker is seconds away from her class. And I walked from the front of the school to the back in less than two minutes."

"Maybe she lingered there for a few minutes. Maybe

she thought she was going to throw up and was trying to collect herself. Look, why are—"

"I'll explain later. It may be nothing."

Decker clicked off and put his phone away. He was just about to have a very radical thought that might potentially crush certain people. He didn't do this lightly. He did this only to get to the truth. The truth was worth everything to him. But he needed something concrete to go on before he could move forward on this.

Fate for Debbie was 8:42 outside this door. After that she would be no more, her life over. How would it run? Debbie raises her hand, gets permission to leave. She exits the class, but doesn't go to the nurse directly. She heads to her locker and opens it. Another minute burned. But Lancaster had said the teacher thought it was several minutes, maybe as many as five. What had Debbie been doing all that time? Maybe she had been lingering or trying to steady herself, like Lancaster had said. But maybe there was something else.

He stared once more at the locker's contents.

The bloody notebook and other items that had been on the floor next to Watson's body had been taken by the police along with her remains. But not the stuff in the locker. No, not that. That was all still there. And it was in decent shape because her body had mostly shielded the contents from the shotgun blast.

He grabbed the stack of items, went back to Classroom 144, and sat down. He opened the first book and went through it page by page. He went through all the textbooks, looking for marginalia, notes, sketches, anything.

He had gone through three of her lined notebooks and had reached the nineteenth page of the fourth when he stopped looking.

Debbie had drawn a picture on this page. It was a good sketch, actually. The girl had possessed talent.

But Decker was far more focused on the *subject* of the drawing.

It was a man in full camouflage gear.

With a big heart drawn right next to it.

21

Decker had showered, changed his clothes, carefully combed his hair, and put on his most professional expression. He believed that the folks sitting opposite him deserved nothing less than that.

Debbie Watson's mother and father stared back at him. The dad was a small, mousy man in his midforties, with a little scrap of mustache above his thin top lip. He had a stunted right arm, the malformed hand hanging from the elbow.

He looked like a freight train was bearing down on him.

Debbie's mom was chain-smoking. The ashtray in front of her was filled with butts. Nicotine's ability to rob the blood of oxygen had whittled fine lines prematurely around her mouth and deeply and unflatteringly chiseled a face that had probably not been pretty even in youth. Her forearms were veiny and darkened and spotted, probably from lying out during the summer in the hammock Decker had seen strung between two trees in the small side yard. The mom didn't look like she'd seen a freight train. She looked as though someone had sucked her soul out. And the smell of the liquor easily crossed the width of the scarred coffee table set between them.

On Decker's right, Lancaster was perched on the couch like a cat on a ledge. Her features were tight and serious and hunkered down and had been ever since Decker had showed her the drawing of cammie man in Debbie's notebook. She occasionally looked lustfully at Beth's cigarette, as if waiting for an invitation to pull out her own smokes.

They had not shown the sketch to the FBI or anyone else. They had decided to keep it to themselves for now. Decker had said, and Lancaster had agreed, that before anything was released publicly they needed to talk to the parents. If the sketch was unconnected to the murders, then they didn't want Debbie's family to suffer unnecessarily. In the world of the twenty-four-hour news cycle, the Watson family would be sliced and diced to such a degree that no matter what exculpatory facts were revealed later, the truth would never be able to rise above the earlier electronic tsunami.

Decker had prefaced his questions with a lot of disclaimers. He had waited until the Watsons were fully prepped before showing them the sketch. When their gazes had held on the image, both had recoiled and then stiffened like they'd been electrocuted.

Decker saw them both outlined in a creamy white. For him death was blue, while white represented despair. When he looked at himself in the mirror for a full year after his family's murders, he had figured he was the whitest white man in the whole world.

"Can you think of a reason why Debbie would have drawn these images?" asked Decker quietly. He pointed first to the cammie figure and then the heart. "Was she seeing anyone?" he added. The heart seemed to indicate this was a possibility. Even in the twenty-first century a heart drawn by a young woman next to the image of a man probably meant exactly what it had always meant throughout time.

George Watson shook his head, his mustache trembling along with the rest of him. His stunted arm swung next to his torso. Decker wondered how many jibes the man had endured over his life for his unusual appendage. That abnormality had probably defined everything about him, not because it should but because sometimes the world and the people in it could be so cruel.

Beth Watson didn't shake her head. She nodded slightly and both Decker and Lancaster immediately focused on her.

"Who was he?" asked Lancaster.

"Never knew," said Beth haltingly. "I mean, she never brought anyone home that we didn't know."

"We're interested in *anyone* she might have brought home," said Decker.

"No, I mean those were boys. You said this person was big. The paper said six-two, couple hundred pounds or more. Debbie never brought anyone home bigger than her father."

George cleared his throat and said ruefully, "And I'm not even five-eight. Had my first growth spurt in tenth grade and never had another." Then he fell silent, looking perplexed and a bit appalled that he had bothered to offer up triviality in the face of such tragedy.

"And they were all boys from school," said Beth. "One of them's dead too, in fact. Like my poor Debbie."

"Which one?" asked Lancaster, her pen poised over her pad.

"Jimmy Schikel. Nice kid, played on the football team. Very popular. We've known them for years. Debbie and Jimmy went to elementary school together. He took Debbie to the junior prom, but they were just friends." She bowed her head and said, "You just can't imagine what it's like to lose your child." She picked up a paper towel off the coffee table and dabbed at her eyes while her husband awkwardly rubbed her shoulder.

At the woman's words, Lancaster had shot Decker a glance, but he didn't return it. He kept his gaze on Beth. He knew exactly what it was like to lose a child. And that fact wouldn't matter in the least in this circumstance. There could be no commiseration among such people despite the seeming commonality of loss, because it was actually each parent's totally unique hell.

"But there was someone else?" prompted Decker. "Someone you didn't know but that Debbie also didn't bring here? That's what you mean, right?"

Beth balled up the paper towel and dropped it on the carpet. Her husband picked it up and placed it on the coffee table. She flicked him an annoyed look, and in observing that, Decker wondered how bad the marriage was. Just the little paper cuts that added up over the long term and that most unions survived? Or was it more than that? Enough to bring them to the point where losing Debbie might become the irreparable crack? Then again, it could cause them to circle the wagons. He had seen that happen too.

"She'd post stuff online about him. But she never talked directly about him. Even so, I picked up the signs here and there. A mom just does."

"So you read the online posts?"

"I had her password for a while. When she found out, she changed it. She never named him. But she did have a pet name for him."

"What was that?" asked Lancaster.

"Jesus."

"How do you know that? Was it in one of the posts?"

"No. I saw it on the chalkboard that's in her room. She had done some little poem about Jesus. Debbie wasn't religious. I mean, we don't go to church or anything, so it wasn't that. It was a guy. The poem . . . was a little personal. It was definitely about a guy. When I went to ask her about it, she ran to her room and erased it."

Decker and Lancaster exchanged a glance. He said, "But do you know if it was biblical or a Latino reference?"

When she looked at him puzzled, he added, "I mean Jesus or Hey-soos."

"Oh, well hell, I never thought about that. I just . . . I just thought she had some sort of God complex with the guy. But I don't think my Debbie would have been hanging out with some Hey-soos Mexican," she added in an offended tone. She wiped her nose and smoked her cigarette. "I mean, moms always know, even if their daughters don't believe they can know stuff. Debbie certainly thought we were clueless." She gave a sideways glance at her husband. "And some *are* clueless. Really clueless."

Hubby removed his hand from her shoulder and dropped it between his legs, like a dog doing the same with its tail. He might have trousers on, thought Decker, but he clearly didn't wear the pants in this family.

Decker flicked a glance at Lancaster. "Online posts?"

She nodded. "We'll get all of it."

"So she never said anything about this person? Nothing?"

"I asked. More than once. But she didn't bite." She paused. "Well, she did slip and say that I wouldn't understand him. He was so . . . mature."

"Meaning older. Not in high school?" said Decker.

"That's what I took it to mean, yes. I mean, she was a senior. She sure as hell wasn't talking about any of her classmates. And she didn't bother with the juniors. And Debbie was a real looker. All developed and everything.

Lots of boys had their eyes on her. I tried to give her advice, but girls don't listen. I didn't listen when my mom tried to tell me. I always went for the bad boys."

Her husband looked at the detectives almost apologetically. "And then she married me."

"*Had* to marry you, George. We had Debbie on the way. My mother almost had a heart attack anyway. By far the best thing to come out of our marriage was Debbie. And now *I* don't even have *her*. Which means I've got *nothing*."

Lancaster looked away at this and George Watson bit down on his lip and decided to focus on an old water ring mark on the coffee table.

Decker studied the pair of them. In the wake of such tragedy all other societal rules within a marriage tended to give way. What was never spoken about was now easily and readily revealed. It was as though the dam holding it all back had failed. Debbie might have been the dam. And now her death represented the breach.

"Why the sketch of the cammie gear?" asked Lancaster. She looked at George. "Do you hunt? Do you have camouflage gear here?"

He shook his head forcefully. "I couldn't shoot an animal. I don't even own a gun."

Decker said, "I guess your condition would make it difficult to hold a weapon properly."

George looked down at his malformed arm. "I was born with it." He paused. "It's made lots of things difficult," he added resignedly.

"So the cammie gear might be a reference to this guy Jesus?" said Decker.

"It might be," said George cautiously.

"It *had* to be," snapped Beth. "She had a *heart* next to it." She glanced at Lancaster with a knowing, exasperated look. "Guys don't get it, do they? Never set foot in a damn Hallmark store."

Decker said, "I saw the laptop on the kitchen counter. Did Debbie use that?"

"No, she had her own. It's in her room."

"Can we take a look at her room now?"

They were led down the hall by Beth. Before she turned away she took a last drag on her smoke and said, "However this comes out, there is no way my baby would have had anything to do with something like this, drawing of this asshole or not. No way. Do you hear me? Both of you?"

"Loud and clear," said Decker. But he thought if Debbie were involved she had already paid the ultimate price anyway. The state couldn't exactly kill her again.

Beth casually flicked the cigarette down the hall, where it sparked and then died out on the faded runner. Then she walked off.

They opened the door and went into Debbie's room. Decker stood in the middle of the tiny space and looked around.

Lancaster said, "We'll have the tech guys go through her online stuff. Photos on her phone, her laptop over there, the cloud, whatever. Instagram. Twitter.

Facebook. Tumblr. Wherever else the kids do their electronic preening. Keeps changing. But our guys will know where to look."

Decker didn't answer her. He just kept looking around, taking the room in, fitting things in little niches in his memory and then pulling them back out if something didn't seem right as weighed against something else.

"I just see a typical teenage girl's room. But what do you see?" asked Lancaster finally.

He didn't look at her but said, "Same things you're seeing. Give me a minute."

Decker walked around the small space, looked under piles of papers, in the young woman's closet, knelt down to see under her bed, scrutinized the wall art that hung everywhere, including a whole section of *People* magazine covers. She also had chalkboard squares affixed to one wall. On them was a musical score and short snatches of poetry and personal messages to herself:

Deb, Wake up each day with something to prove.

"Pretty busy room," noted Lancaster, who had perched on the edge of the girl's desk. "We'll have forensics come and bag it all."

She looked at Decker, obviously waiting for him to react to this, but instead he walked out of the room.

"Decker!"

"I'll be back," he called over his shoulder.

She watched him go and then muttered, "Of all the

partners I could have had, I got Rain Man, only giant size."

She pulled a stick of gum out of her bag, unwrapped it, and popped it into her mouth. Over the next several minutes she strolled the room and then came to the mirror on the back of the closet door. She appraised her appearance and ended it with the resigned sigh of a person who knows their best days physically are well in the past. She automatically reached for her smokes but then decided against it. Debbie's room could be part of a criminal investigation. Her ash and smoke could only taint that investigation.

She whirled around when Decker came back into the room.

"Where'd you go?" she asked.

"Had some questions for the parents, and I wanted to take a look around the rest of the house."

"And?"

He walked over to the musical score written on the chalkboard wall and pointed to it.

"Debbie didn't do this."

Lancaster gazed at the symbols. "How do you know that?"

"She doesn't play an instrument. I checked her school record earlier. She's never been in the band. I asked her mother. She's never played an instrument and there are none in the house. Second, there are no sheets of music in this room. Even if you didn't play an instrument and just composed music, I think you'd have some sheet music or more likely blank score sheets in your room. Third, that's not Debbie's handwriting."

Lancaster drew closer to the wall and studied the marks there and then compared them with the other writing on the wall.

"But how can you really tell?" she asked. "I mean, musical scores aren't like other writing. They're symbols, not letters."

"Because Debbie is right-handed. Whoever wrote this was *left*-handed. Even though it's not letters you can still tell by the sweeps, flourishes, and general flow of the marks." He picked up some chalk and wrote on a different section of the board some of the musical symbols. "I'm right-handed and you can see the difference."

He pointed to some smudges on the board. "And that's where the person's left sleeve smeared some of the score. For a righty it would be in the opposite place. Like mine." He pointed to where his sleeve had brushed against some of the chalk marks. "And Leopold is right-handed."

"How do you know that?"

"He signed a paper I gave him when I saw him in his prison cell."

"Okay, but maybe a friend of hers who *is* a musician did it."

But Decker was already shaking his head. "No."

"Why not? I could see a buddy of hers writing out a tune or something on here. Maybe inspirational, to match some of Debbie's writing."

"Because those notes make no sense at all. You couldn't play it with any instrument of which I'm aware. From a music composition perspective, it's gibberish."

"How do you know? Did you play music?"

Decker nodded. "In high school, guitar and drums. I know my way around scores. And not just the ones on the football field."

Lancaster glanced back at the symbols. "So what is it, then?"

"I think it's a code," said Decker. "And if I'm right about that, it means Jesus *was* in this house."

22

Decker and Lancaster had sealed off Debbie's bedroom and called in the forensics team, which had gone over the room and the house in meticulous detail. Burlington had never suffered a crime such as this one, and everyone, from the rookie on the team to the most senior departmental official, was bringing his A-game.

The Watsons said they knew nothing of the musical score. Decker tended to believe them. After the forensics team finished, Decker and Lancaster sat down with the Watsons once more.

"If the guy came to this house to write the score on the wall, could he do so without your knowledge?" Decker asked them.

"Well, we do have to sleep," said a defensive Beth. "But the house isn't that big. And our room is right next to Debbie's. George and I are both light sleepers. I don't see how she could have had a guy in her room and we not know about it."

"What about during the day?" said Lancaster.

"I'm a stay-at-home mom. George is a nine-to-fiver. I'm here a lot more than Debbie, actually."

"How long ago do you remember seeing the musical score on the chalkboard?" asked Decker.

"It wasn't there two weeks ago, I can tell you that," she replied.

"How do you know that?" asked Decker.

"Because I wiped the whole thing clean." She paused. "We'd had an argument and I just, well, I lost it and wiped all that crap off." She let out a little sob. "And now I'll never see her again."

"Argument about what?" asked Decker, ignoring her distress. He needed answers. And he needed them now. She could grieve later.

Beth composed herself. "Debbie was a senior. She took the SAT and did okay, but she hadn't applied to one damn college. She made excuses about cost. And it's true that we can't really help her out. But I kept telling her there's financial aid out there. And without a degree what was she going to do? Be me?" She paused again as her husband looked away. "So I lost it and wiped her damn board clean. All those messages she had on there about changing the world and having a purpose. It was bullshit! She was doing nothing and going nowhere. So I wiped it clean. Clean slate. Hoped she'd get the point. Guess she didn't. Guess she never will now. Not now. Oh, shit, my baby. My baby."

Beth dissolved into tears and started writhing uncontrollably on the couch. With Decker's help her husband managed to get her into the bedroom to lie down. Decker could hear her calling out to her dead daughter the whole way as he walked back down the hall to join Lancaster.

George Watson came back out a few minutes later and said, "I think we're done for now, if that's all right."

Decker said, "Have you and your wife gone away on a trip recently?"

George looked at him in some amazement. "How did you know that?"

"The guy came here and wrote what he wrote. If you had been here you probably would have seen him. And he wouldn't take that kind of chance. So you were gone at some point?"

"A week ago we drove to Indiana to be with Beth's sister. She was ill. We were there two days and then drove back."

"And Debbie stayed here?"

"Yes, we couldn't take her out of school."

"So that's probably when he came," said Decker.

George began to shake, wrapping his arms around himself. "Do you really think that animal was in our house? In our daughter's *bedroom*?"

Decker gave the man with the wrecked arm the once-over. "I think it's highly possible, yes."

Lancaster gave Decker a fierce stare and said quickly, "Well, thanks for your help, Mr. Watson. We'll be going now. And we're very sorry for your loss."

George walked them to the door. As he opened it he

said, "Debbie wouldn't have helped anyone kill people at Mansfield. They were her friends."

"I can appreciate that," said Decker. "I hope it turns out you're right."

George blinked rapidly, as though he had never considered that he might be wrong. He shut the door behind them.

Decker and Lancaster walked down the sidewalk.

"Your bedside manner is as terrific as always," said Lancaster sarcastically.

"I'm not here to be his friend and hold his hand, Mary. I'm here to catch whoever killed his daughter."

"Okay, okay," she said. "I got an email from forensics. They found nothing pertinent on Debbie's phone or laptop. No photos, emails, texts, voicemails. And there are no online postings on any site they could think of or which Debbie had access to. Her mom said she had seen some alluding to this guy, but Debbie must've deleted them. But maybe our guys can still dig them up somehow."

"This guy would never have let her take his picture. No electronic trails either. Far too easy. Our guy may not even have Web access."

"How do you figure?"

"I'm seeing someone outside the mainstream. No ties. A loner. He floats from place to place."

"Based on what? Something you saw?"

"No, something I felt. But one thing has me puzzled."

"Just one, you're lucky then," she said, smiling grimly. "My list is six pages long."

He went on as though he hadn't heard her. "Why Debbie? Why pick her to team with?"

"Team with? What exactly did she do? I thought she was just his girlfriend."

"She gave him something he needed."

"Something he needed? At the school? You don't mean the guns? There's no way she's lugging in a pistol and a shotgun."

"I don't necessarily mean the guns, no."

"But why would he need her to bring him anything?"

"That's what's puzzling me too. Why her and why the meeting at the school on that day?"

"Whoa, Decker, you're pulling way ahead of me. What meeting?"

"She *pretended* to be sick. She got out of class, met this guy, probably gave him something, and then he killed her. But there's a time gap that I can't figure right now."

She asked him another question, only Decker wasn't listening. His gaze was moving down the street, to his left. It was dark, the night air chilly with mist rising from both their mouths as they exhaled. There seemed to be nothing good out in that blackness. But to Decker the night was suddenly full of threes, his least favorite number.

It had first happened when he was a rookie cop. Thankfully he'd been out on patrol alone. He'd been sitting in his squad car sipping coffee when out of the darkness came movement. At first he thought it was some people trying to sneak up on him. Back then Burlington had a big gang problem, mostly consisting of young men with no jobs and no hope, too much testosterone, and access to too many guns.

He'd thrown his coffee out the window, his hand had gone to his gun, and his other hand to his radio. He'd been about to step out of the vehicle and give a warning to whoever was out there. That's when the figures appeared clearly in front of him. Giant, towering number threes.

It was like he'd been suddenly propelled into a bad sci-fi novel.

He thought he was going mad. But something coalesced in the middle of his brain. A small scrap of memory from one of the doctors at the institute outside Chicago where he'd gone after his injury and all the weird things had started happening to him.

The doctor had said, "Amos, for you, a new day can mean new things. The brain never stops. It is relentless. It is constantly configuring and reconfiguring. I'm trying to tell you that what has happened to you so far may not be the only change you experience with your mind. Tomorrow, next month, next year, a decade hence, you may wake up and discover it is doing something else. There is no way for us to predict it, unfortunately. And it may be terrifying when it does happen.

But just know that it's *your* mind. It's just all in your head. It's not real."

With that remembrance, Decker turned back to face the army of numbers, his initial fear receding, but it was replaced with a fresh one.

What new stuff will tomorrow bring?

He had gotten off duty, gone home, dropped into bed, and wept quietly so that he wouldn't awaken Cassie. In the morning he told her what had happened. She was predictably supportive and encouraging. And Decker was predictably upbeat, blowing it off as something that was actually funny. But it wasn't funny. It wasn't funny at all. The threes had been gone for a while. In fact, he hadn't seen them coming out of the darkness since Cassie and Molly died. But now they were back.

Wonderful.

And the threes had added a new dimension. A trio of knives was coming off each of the digits' stems. No, not funny at all.

"Let me know if they crack the code," he said as the threes charged forward, knives at the ready.

Then he turned left and headed down the street.

"Don't you want a ride home?" asked Lancaster.

Decker kept walking, his hands shoved deeply into his coat pockets.

He didn't need a ride. He needed to think.

He looked at his feet to avoid staring into the faces of

the legions of numbers coming at him from out of the gloom.

What did Debbie Watson have that their shooter needed? Guns? No. Cammie gear? Maybe. But why couldn't he have brought that on his own? He didn't need her for that.

The heart and the picture. She was in love. She had a crush on the guy. Would do anything for him. But would she sacrifice her classmates? The picture of the cammie man had not included any weapons. Had Debbie not known what the actual plan was to be? So why had she come out of her classroom to meet the guy?

He lifted his eyes, saw the threes flying head-on at him, and lowered his gaze once more. When he had done stakeouts or pulled shifts at night he had worn special glasses that tinted the darkness into a golden color. Gold for him was a sky full of geese. No threes to bother him. He had lost the glasses a long time ago. Now the threes were back and they were armed. He would need to get new glasses.

He stopped walking, leaned against a tree, closed his eyes, dialed up his mental DVR, and replayed everything he had seen in the Watsons' house. The spool unwound in his head and then he slowed the pace of the mental frames. And then he stopped his DVR and a row of images stared at him like figurines on a fireplace mantel. Actually, the image was quite literal.

They *were* on the fireplace mantel.

Decker turned around and walked quickly back to the Watsons' house. He knocked and George answered.

"Did you forget something?" George asked, sounding a little annoyed.

"Pictures on your mantel. I saw them earlier. Can you walk me through them?"

"Pictures on the mantel?" said George with a perplexed look. "Walk you through them?"

Decker stepped inside the house, forcing the much smaller man to step back quickly.

"I'm assuming they're family members?"

"Yes. But what does that have to do with anything?"

"I've worked cases long enough to know that it's the one thing you let pass that ends up holding the answer you need. We can't afford any lapses here, Mr. Watson, I'm sure you can understand that. If we're going to find whoever killed Debbie and the others."

What can the man say to that other than agree?

Watson slowly nodded, though he still looked unconvinced. "Okay, sure, follow me."

He led Decker into the small living room and over to the mantel that topped an old brick fireplace that had mortar leaching from the seams.

"Where do you want to start?"

Decker pointed to the picture on the far left. "With him."

"Okay, that was my wife's father, Ted Knolls. He died about two years ago. Heart attack."

"What did he do for a living?"

"What the hell does that have to—"

Decker cut him off. "Just tell me what he did for a living."

Decker looked menacingly down at the smaller man. He was a grizzly against a chipmunk, which was exactly how he wanted Watson to see it.

Watson took a step back, changed color, and looked at the photo. "He was a long-haul trucker. Bad diet, no exercise. He was as big as a house when he collapsed on his front lawn picking up the newspaper. He was dead before he hit the grass." He eyed Decker's massive frame when he said this. "But that's all he did, he drove a truck back and forth across the Midwest and down to Texas and back."

"Was he close to Debbie?"

Watson self-consciously rubbed at his malformed arm. "No, not really. I mean, we saw them at holidays. But, to tell the truth, things weren't good between us and them. My mother-in-law never warmed to me."

"And the man next to him? That picture looks pretty old."

"That's my grandfather, Simon Watson. He's been gone, oh, a good six years. He was a young man in that picture."

"So Debbie's great-grandfather," said Decker, and Watson nodded.

"He lived to over ninety years old. Smoked and drank and didn't give a damn, as he liked to say."

"But Debbie knew him if he's only been gone six years?"

"Oh, yes. In fact he lived with us the last five years of his life."

"So she would have spent time with him?"

"I'm sure she did. Debbie was still a kid then and Gramps had had a pretty interesting life. Fought in World War II and then the Korean War. Then he left the service and went to work for the civilian side of the Defense Department."

"Doing what?"

"Well, he worked at the military base here when it was open."

"The one next to Mansfield High School? McDonald Army Base?"

"That's right."

"What did he do there?"

"He had a series of jobs. His training was in engineering and construction. So he worked on the facilities and plant side."

"Do you know the dates?"

"Come on, what does this have to do with anything?"

"I'm just looking for leads, Mr. Watson. The dates?"

"I can't tell you for certain." He paused and thought about it. "He left the regular Army in the sixties. Then he went to McDonald probably around 1968 or '69. It must have been '69. I remember associating it with the astronauts walking on the moon. Then he worked there until he retired. About twenty years later."

"And the base closed eight years ago."

"That sounds about right."

"That wasn't a question, Mr. Watson, it *did* close eight years ago, on a Monday. There was sleet that day."

Watson looked at him strangely and then coughed. "If you say so. I can't remember what I was doing last week. Anyway, it was part of a Pentagon base realignment and Burlington lost out. I heard tell most of the operations moved east, maybe to Virginia. Closer to Uncle Sam and his dollars in D.C."

"So, presumably Simon talked about his work at the base with you, with Debbie?"

"Oh, yes, I mean the parts he could talk about. Some of it was classified, I guess you'd call it."

"Classified?"

George's features eased to a grin. "Well, I don't think they did nukes or anything there. But the military always has its share of secrets."

"So what *did* Simon talk to you about? I mean with the base?"

"Some of the history of it. People he met. Some of the work he did. They kept adding on to the base for years. Building, building, building. All the people who worked there sent their kids to Mansfield for high school. His son—my father—went there. So did I. So did my wife for that matter."

"Did Debbie ever mention to you some of the things she and her great-grandfather talked about?"

"Nothing that I really recall. As Debbie got older she didn't spend as much time with him. Old people, young kids, oil and water. Gramps wasn't as much fun, I guess." He looked down. "And I guess neither was I."

"Okay, take me through the other pictures."

A half hour later Decker was on his way through the dark streets once more.

Cammie man had gone to the Watsons' house and written on that wall in code disguised as a musical score. That he was sure of. He didn't know what the message said, and he didn't know what the man had needed from Debbie. Yet out of all the students at Mansfield, why ally himself with her? There must be a reason. A good one.

His phone buzzed. It was Lancaster.

"The Bureau think they broke the code. It *was* some sort of substitution cipher. Pretty simple actually. Well, actually, they're certain they did crack it."

"How can they be *certain* they did?"

"Because of what the message said."

"Don't keep me in suspense, Mary. What did it say?"

He heard her release a long breath that seemed filled with apprehension.

"It said, 'Good job, Amos. But in the end it won't get you where you want to go, bro.'"

23

I'm an "acquired savant."

More precisely, I'm a high-functioning acquired savant.

Decker was lying in his bed in his one-room home at the Residence Inn. He was not sleeping. He could not sleep.

Orlando Serrell.

Orlando Serrell was also an acquired savant, having been hit on the head by a baseball when he was ten. Ever since, he had come to possess extraordinary abilities in calendrical calculations, precise memories of weather on any particular day, as well as the near-total recall of where he was and what he was doing on any given day.

Daniel Tammet.

Daniel Tammet had suffered a series of epileptic seizures as a small child. He came out of that nearly fatal experience with one of the greatest minds of the century, able to recite pi out to over twenty-two thousand places and learn entire languages in a week. He had been diagnosed with Asperger's syndrome and also saw numbers and other things in color, as Decker did.

Decker had studied everything he could find about

savants who had not been born with their abilities but had acquired them after some event, whether an injury in Serrell's case or a prior medical condition in Tammet's.

There weren't many savants in the world, and Decker had been totally unprepared to join their ranks. When LeCroix leveled him on that football field, the doctors who had extensively examined him later came away with the conclusion that the injury had done two things to his brain.

First, it had opened up channels in his mind, like unclogging a drain, which allowed information to flow far more efficiently. Second, it had caused other circuitry in his mind to intersect, providing him the ability to see numbers in color.

But this was only speculation. Decker had come to believe that doctors today knew only a bit more about how the brain really worked than doctors a hundred years ago.

Decker had woken up in the hospital after the hit and looked over at his vitals monitor with all the numbers skipping across it. He had seen his heart rate, 95—the same number on his football jersey—represented as violet for the nine and brown for the 5. Before his injury he didn't even know what the color violet was. And the numbers had swelled huge in his head, tall and massive. He could see every detail of them. They were like living things.

He remembered sitting up in bed, the sweat pouring

off him. He thought he was going insane. He had rung the nurse's bell. A doctor was called and Decker had stammered out what he was experiencing. Specialists were called in. Many months later, and after his lengthy stint at the research facility outside Chicago, the consensus was that he was now officially an acquired savant with hyperthymesia and synesthesia abilities. The injury on the field had ended forever his football career, but had given him one of the most exceptional brains in the world. All these years later he recalled the names and backgrounds of every doctor, nurse, scientist, technician, and other practitioner who had seen him, and there were over a hundred of them.

He could have been written up in scholarly journals and there could have been a great deal of media attention surrounding what had happened to him, the odds being somewhere around one in a billion. But he had not allowed any of that to happen. He had not seen himself as a prodigy. He had seen himself as a freak. For twenty-two years of his life he had been one sort of person. He had been ill-prepared in the span of a few minutes to involuntarily become someone else entirely. To become the person he would one day die as. It was like a stranger had stepped into his body and taken it over, and he could do nothing to get him out.

A squatter for life is inhabiting my mind. And he happens to be me.

For every action, there was an equal and opposite reaction. Well, in his case the outgoing, gregarious, prankish but driven young football player had become reserved, withdrawn, and socially awkward. He no longer related to the great many things that human beings spent a good deal of time over: small talk, little white lies, emotionally nuanced venting, gossip. He could not understand sympathy or empathy. He was not concerned with others' feelings. Their pain and their grief. It was like these things bounced off his new and improved brain, never making a dent. By making him much smarter, the hit had robbed him of the things that made everyone human. It was as though that was the payment demanded. He'd had no choice in accepting or not.

He did not even care to watch sports anymore. He had not seen a football game since his injury.

Marrying Cassie had really saved him. She knew his secret. She shared his anxieties. Without her, Decker doubted he could have turned his life around, found a new career as a policeman, and then thrived as a detective, turning to the pursuit of justice his new and vastly improved mind. And though he had never been able to be as affectionate with Cassie as he would have before the hit, he cared for her, deeply. He would have done anything for her. They even laughed about his inability to connect more as a human than as a machine. But Decker knew that both of them wished he could.

Whenever he held his daughter, Decker could think of nothing but her, as though his monster of a mind was mesmerized by this little person who liked to cuddle with her huge father—a bear and its cub. He would stroke her hair and rub her cheek, and though the recollection was fuzzy, like watching an old TV with a coat hanger for an antenna, it was like he could remember being what he used to be more vividly than at any other time.

It was as though his new mind had allowed an exception for these two people, enabling him to be a bit closer to what he once was.

But only for those two.

Now he was alone.

And just a machine forevermore.

And he had some prick taunting him. Some sick monster who had killed his family and then turned his sights on Mansfield High School. And if the graffiti on the wall of his house had not convinced him, the coded message had put all doubt to rest.

The shooters were one and the same.

And his family had died because of him. He had known all along that this was possible, even probable. But that little bit of uncertainty had actually been a good thing, allowing him to believe there was a chance that he had not been the motive in their slaughter.

Now the uncertainty was gone. And with absolute clarity came terrible, demoralizing resignation. And a sense of guilt that had hit him harder than even Dwayne LeCroix had.

At 5 a.m. he rose, showered, dressed in his suit, and stood in front of the small mirror in a bathroom that was about the same size as he was. In the reflection he saw pops of light and colors, numbers soaring across the glass. He closed his eyes and the picture did not change. It was not on the glass, it was all inside his head. It was said that savants, particularly those diagnosed with Asperger's syndrome, were drawn to very narrow slices of interest: numbers, history, a certain field of science, or languages. Decker did not know what his narrow slice was supposed to be. He didn't know if the hit by LeCroix had given him Asperger's. He didn't know if that was even possible, and he had never been officially diagnosed with the condition.

All he knew was that he could never forget anything. His mind attached colors to things that were not supposed to have them. He could remember what day of the week a particular date in the last hundred years fell on. His mind was a puzzle all put together, but somehow still jumbled, because he understood none of it. It was just who he was now. And it had scared the hell out of him from day one.

Yet with Cassie next to him, he had managed it. Without her, without Molly who had given him something to think about beyond his own lifetime, Amos Decker had become once more a freak. A Jekyll and Hyde. Only Jekyll was gone and would not be coming back.

The army of threes awaited him as he trudged through the darkness to the breakfast buffet that opened at six on the dot. He collected his plate brimming with food and went to his little table/office and then just sat there staring at the mounds of stuff on his plate and not electing to eat a single bite.

June, the buffet attendant, hurried up to him.

"Amos, are you okay?" she said, her old face creased with concern. He had never failed to devour his food.

When he said nothing she held up a pot of coffee. "Can I pour you a cup? Lots of problems get solved by a hot cup of coffee."

Taking his silence for assent, she poured the steaming coffee into a cup, left it on his table, and walked away.

Decker had not acknowledged her because he had not even been aware she was there. His mind was a long way from the restaurant at the Residence Inn.

He didn't need to look at his watch. It was now 6:23. A part of his mind kept this internal clock at all times, a better timekeeper than anything you could buy.

At ten o'clock Sebastian Leopold would be arraigned, this time with counsel attached. Decker intended to be there.

He walked. He preferred to walk, even in the dark. The army of threes was there so he kept his head tilted downward.

Decker had read that other savants felt comforted by the oceans and skies of numbers that routinely enveloped them. To Decker numbers represented a means to an end. They gave him no real happiness. Perhaps because he had experienced happiness in being a husband and father. Numbers simply could not compete with that, even for a savant.

He sat on a bench outside the courthouse and watched the sun drift into the sky, the dawn breaking and wreaking havoc with the black, smearing it with tendrils of red, gold, and pink. Or in Decker's mind a slew of related numbers.

At 9:45 he watched the police van pull into the side alley of the courthouse. The prison transport had arrived. He wondered how many other defendants had ridden across with Leopold or whether the alleged triple murderer had come alone.

Decker heaved himself to his feet and walked slowly across the street to the courthouse entrance. A few minutes later he was seated in the second row. He noted the PD sitting at the counsel table going over the file. The guy looked to be in his early forties, with gray just starting to creep into his hair. His brown two-piece suit was nicely tailored and had a colorful pocket square. The guy looked confident and, well, veteran. Decker doubted anyone wanted a rookie on this case.

The same bailiff stood next to the door to the judge's chambers chatting with Sheila Lynch, who seemed to be wearing the same skirt and jacket from yesterday.

Decker heard the door to the courtroom open and turned to look.

It wasn't Lancaster or Miller.

It was Alex Jamison the reporter. She saw Decker, nodded, smiled, and then took a seat near the back.

Decker turned back around without acknowledging her.

The bailiff had disappeared into the judge's chambers. Lynch had gone back over to the counsel table, spoken a few words with the PD, and then taken her seat.

The door through which prisoners were led opened and there was Sebastian Leopold, looking much as he had yesterday.

He was escorted over to his lawyer, the shackles were removed, and the officers stepped back.

The bailiff opened the door, made his announcement, everyone rose, and Abernathy stepped through and took his seat behind the bench.

He took a moment to look over the courtroom and smiled in a satisfied way when he saw the lawyer sitting next to Leopold.

Then he eyed Lynch.

"Has the psych evaluation been completed?"

It had, Lynch told him. And it stated that Leopold was fit to stand trial.

This surprised Decker.

"Mr. Leopold, how do you plead?"

His attorney gripped his client's arm and together they stood.

"I plead not guilty," said Leopold firmly.

Decker listened to his statement but did not seem to be able to process it.

His attorney said, "Your Honor, I move that all

charges against my client be dismissed. The state has no evidence of his involvement in the three murders."

Lynch jumped to her feet. "You mean other than his *confession*."

The PD said smoothly, "A confession that he is now recanting. Mr. Leopold is bipolar, went off his medications, which resulted in some unfortunate emotional distress. He is now back on his meds and his reason has returned, hence his passing the psych exam." The lawyer held up some documents stapled together. "And then there's this. Permission to approach?"

Abernathy waved him forward. Lynch hurried after opposing counsel.

The PD said in a voice loud enough for Decker to hear, "This is an authenticated arrest report complete with mug shot and fingerprints showing conclusively that Mr. Leopold was in a lockup in Cranston, two towns over from here, on the night the murders in question were committed. I also have a copy of Mr. Leopold's arrest record from Burlington. They've been independently evaluated and the picture and the prints match perfectly. It is undoubtedly him, as I'm sure Ms. Lynch will agree."

Lynch said furiously, "Your Honor, defense counsel did not share this with me."

Abernathy looked at her with disdain. "You can pull an arrest record faster than defense counsel can, Ms. Lynch. If he found it you should have too."

Lynch flushed. "What was he arrested for?" she said in a snarky tone.

"Vagrancy," said the PD. "He was released the following morning. Cranston is seventy miles from here and Mr. Leopold has no means of transportation. But more to the point, the police report shows that Mr. Leopold was arrested at six in the evening and released at nine the next morning. Thus he could not have committed the murders, which occurred around midnight." He handed the papers across to Lynch, who looked down them, her spirits and confidence ebbing completely away as she reached the bottom of the last page.

"He could have had an accomplice," she said weakly.

"Well, if you can prove that, more power to you," said the PD. "But so far you haven't proven anything. My client went off his meds and involuntarily lied about committing a crime he could not have committed. That is your entire case in a nutshell, which means you have no case."

"We can charge him with wasting police time, obstruction of justice."

"As I said, he was off his meds. He could not form the intent necessary for either of those two crimes."

Lynch said, "I believe that given time—"

Abernathy cut her off. "Do you have any evidence other than the recanted confession tying the defendant to the crimes alleged against him?"

Obviously flustered, Lynch said, "Your Honor, the

defendant turned himself in to the police and confessed to the crime. Thus we have not attempted to build a forensic case against him."

"Did he sign the confession?"

"Yes," she said firmly.

"Did it include details that only the actual perpetrator of this crime would know?"

Lynch was again caught off guard. "I . . . I don't believe so, no. I'm sure that additional questioning was going to take place, but—"

Interrupting, Abernathy said, "So with the confession off the table you have no evidence?"

"No," Lynch admitted, her anger evident but restrained.

"And now we know for certain that Mr. Leopold was seventy miles away in jail when the murders were committed."

"Yes, we do," said the PD, barely able to hide a smile.

"Please step back," said Abernathy pleasantly.

The counsels returned to their respective corners.

Abernathy peered down from the bench. "The charges against the defendant Sebastian Leopold are dismissed without prejudice. Mr. Leopold, you are free to go. And stay on your meds."

He smacked his gavel.

His lawyer turned to Leopold to shake his hand, but Leopold was looking around the courtroom as though he was still unsure of where he was. When his gaze fell on Decker, he smiled weakly and gave a tiny, shy wave.

Decker didn't smile or wave back as the officers took Leopold out of the room.

As Abernathy disappeared back into chambers, Decker watched as Lynch and the PD exchanged sharp words. Then Decker rose and headed out of the courtroom.

Alex Jamison walked out with him.

"Did Leopold wave to you, Mr. Decker?" she asked, her tone curious, and in its undertones, a trace of suspicion seemed to percolate.

"I don't know what he did."

"Have you met him before?"

Decker kept walking.

She called after him. "People would like to hear your side of things."

He turned and walked back to her. "My side of things on what?"

"Do you know Leopold, because I think he made eye contact with you. He smiled and waved. You were the only one sitting there."

"I don't know him."

"But you two *did* talk before, didn't you? In his prison cell?"

Decker made the connection instantly. *Brimmer.* This was her way of getting back at him for juking her at the jail. She had leaked his meeting with Leopold to Jamison.

"Why did you meet with the man accused of killing your family?"

Decker turned and walked away. And this time he kept going.

24

Decker had taken a bus directly over because he didn't want to miss the man.

As he waited, he watched folks walking and driving past. Burlington had a deeply wounded look to it, as though an evil had stolen into town and taken its most valuable possessions. Which was exactly what had happened.

Twenty minutes later Decker stiffened slightly as the door to the facility opened and Sebastian Leopold stepped out dressed in the clothes he had walked in with, the orange prison jumpsuit and shackles stripped off him along with the murder charges.

He looked around for a few moments as though orienting himself to his surroundings. Then he turned right and started walking north.

Decker waited about twenty seconds and then followed him, staying on the other side of the street. Paralleling the man, he kept his gaze forward but his peripheral on Leopold.

Fifteen minutes later they had reached an area of

Burlington that Decker knew well—seedy, disreputable, and known to harbor criminal elements with relish.

A dive bar was on the right. Leopold walked down the short set of wobbly brick steps and went inside.

Decker looked from side to side and then hustled across the street and down the same steps. He had been in this bar during a couple of stakeouts years ago and had come away empty each time. Maybe the third crack would be the charm.

Leopold was seated at the center of the bar. The interior was dark and dreary, the lights turned down low. Decker knew this was primarily because everything in the place was filthy and the owner probably thought that would be a turnoff to business. Decker doubted the patrons cared, though. When he had been here they were mostly stoned on liquor, drugs, or both.

He settled into a table at the back with a chest-high partition that he could see over but that provided him with some cover. He was hard to miss, and even though he had only met Leopold once, he had to assume the man would remember him. He had seemed to recognize Decker in the courtroom.

But that's not right. We've met twice, according to Leopold. When I dissed him at that 7-Eleven. So why can't I remember that when I can remember everything?

Leopold ordered a drink, and when the bartender delivered it he just stared at the glass for a long minute before raising it to his lips and taking a small sip before replacing it exactly in the same spot. He maneuvered the glass a bit, apparently to match the water ring on the bar.

This did not escape Decker's notice.

Possibly OCD.

During his earlier meeting with the man Decker had noted the constant movement of Leopold's hands. Was he really not all there? The PD said he was bipolar but was now back on his meds. Maybe they could finally have a cogent conversation.

A waitress came over to Decker. She was tall and thin with a sea of bleached blonde hair all done up in curls that nearly covered her face. The smell of the chemically treated hair wafted over him, sweet and slightly nauseating. He ordered a beer, which she brought to him a minute later.

He took a drink, wiped his mouth, and waited. There was no mirror behind the bar, so Leopold had no way to spot Decker behind him unless he turned around.

Twenty minutes passed and no one had approached Leopold. The man had taken exactly two more sips of his drink and was staring down at it as though he was unaware of how it had gotten there.

Decker left two bucks on his table, picked up his beer, walked up to the bar, and sat down next to him.

Leopold didn't look over. He was still staring at his drink.

"Feel good to be out?" asked Decker. "Celebrating?"

Leopold looked at him. "You were in the courtroom. I saw you."

"I was also in your jail cell."

Leopold nodded, but the statement had not really seemed to register with him. He mumbled something Decker did not catch.

Decker's gaze ran swiftly over the man. They had cleaned him up for his two court appearances and his clothes had been laundered, probably because the cops couldn't stand the stink.

Leopold said in a louder voice, "In my jail cell. That's right. We talked."

"Yes, we did. So you recanted?"

Leopold looked alarmed. "I did what?"

"Took back your confession."

Leopold picked up his drink and took another sip. "I don't really drink. But this is good."

"Celebrating, like I said."

"What do I have to celebrate?" Leopold asked curiously.

"Not being charged with a triple homicide. Not being in jail. Both good things, wouldn't you say?"

Leopold shrugged. "They fed me. I had a bed."

"Is that why you confessed to the murders? For a bed and three squares?"

Leopold shrugged again.

"So you were in jail in Cranston on the night of the murders?"

"I guess I was. It was a long time ago. I don't remember. There are lots of things I don't remember."

"Like your real name?"

Leopold glanced at him but didn't really seem to register what Decker had said.

"Well, the judge wouldn't have let you off if there was any doubt. It had to be your picture and prints on that arrest record."

"The lawyer was very happy," said Leopold, staring down at his drink.

"How did you even know about the murders?" Decker asked.

"I . . . I killed those people, didn't I?" said Leopold in a timid voice that carried with it not a trace of conviction, or even, it seemed, understanding.

The bartender, a man in his fifties with a gut nearly the size of Decker's though he was six inches shorter, looked up from the glass he was wiping and stared at Leopold for a long moment before looking away.

"That's not what you told the judge this morning. You said the opposite of that. Did your lawyer tell you to say that?"

"He said I shouldn't talk about any of this with anybody."

Decker stared curiously at the man.

A glimmer of lucidity, of self-preservation amid a sea of insanity? Is it the meds talking?

"Well, then I guess you shouldn't, unless you want to. But I don't see a problem for you. Cops have zip.

You were in jail at the time. The judge dismissed the case without prejudice, but they can't re-charge you unless they have some evidence tying you to the crime. Now, they may go out and get some. Find an accomplice who did the killings for you for some reason. They may even make something up."

"Can they do that?" asked Leopold in childlike wonder.

"Sure. They do it all the time. If they think you're a bad guy they'll do anything to nail you, get you off the streets. They're sworn to protect and defend. You can see that, right?"

Leopold bent down and took another sip of his drink without lifting up the glass, like a dog lapping from its bowl.

"So *are* you, Sebastian?"

"Am I what?"

"A bad guy they need to get off the streets?"

"I don't know."

Decker felt his irritation start to rise. What had happened to his head might have rerouted his brain functions and caused other features to mentally intersect, but it had also robbed him of his ability to deal with bullshit, deceit, and generally squirrelly behavior. He liked straight lines, A to B, 1 to 2. He did not like back-and-forth that got one nowhere except riled up. This had been both a blessing and a curse as a cop.

"You said you killed those people. You told me you did. Told the cops you did. And this morning you said you didn't. But sitting here at this bar you said you probably did even though you were in jail two towns over and couldn't have even been at that house. So you can understand my confusion, can't you? And the cops'? Where does the truth lie? That's what we need to determine."

Leopold turned to him and seemed to really see Decker for the first time.

"Why do you care?"

If Decker had dissed this guy at the 7-Eleven seventeen months ago, Decker hadn't changed so much that Leopold wouldn't recognize him. He was just fatter and uglier now. So either the guy was innocent or the asshole was lying. And Decker had no clear indication of which answer was correct.

"I took an interest in the case. Never thought they'd arrest somebody after all this time."

"It was a cold case."

The phrase caught Decker's attention. "You know about cold cases?"

"I like the TV show. I watch it at the shelter sometimes."

"Homeless shelter?"

Leopold nodded. "I'm homeless, so I got to go somewhere. Sometimes I sleep outside. Most times I sleep outside," he added in a tired voice.

"Why's that?"

"'Cause it's safer. There are guys in the shelter who aren't . . . nice."

"Is that what got you interested in the murders here? Because it was a cold case?"

"I think so, yeah."

"Why that case in particular, though? It's not the only cold case. Somebody talk to you about it?"

Leopold was nodding. He looked down at his drink, took another sip without using his hands.

"What'd you order?" asked Decker, glancing at the glass, concealing his disgust with how the other man was drinking his liquor.

Leopold smiled. "Kamikaze. I like them."

"You said you didn't really drink."

"I don't because I never have any money. But I found a five-dollar bill I didn't know I had. When I do drink I order Kamikazes because I like them."

"The drink I take it, and not the Japanese suicide pilots?"

Leopold shrugged noncommittally. "I wanted to be a pilot when I was a kid."

"But not one who crashes the plane on purpose?"

"No, not one like that."

"So you talked to somebody? They told you about this case? Maybe got you excited. So you decided to use it to get a warm bed and three squares? Is that what somebody told you that you could get with a confession? Food and a bed?"

"Who would tell me that?"

Decker finished his beer and slammed the mug down on the bar with a sharp rap that made Leopold jump, which was what Decker wanted. He wanted this weasely son of a bitch to wake the hell up.

"I don't know, Leopold. That's why I'm asking you. Does this person have a name?"

"I gotta go."

He started to rise, but Decker put a hand on his shoulder and held him in his seat. "Speaking of three squares, how about some food? You look hungry. And the cops didn't feed you, did they?"

"How'd you know that?"

"You walked on a murder rap. They're pissed. They were giving you nothing. So let's order some food and kick this around."

"I really do need to go."

"Go where? You got somebody to meet? Maybe I'll tag along."

"Why would you want to do that?"

"I got nowhere to be and you look like an interesting guy. I like interesting people. There aren't enough of them in this town."

"This town is full of dicks."

"Dicks? Full of 'em, you're right. Anybody in particular dickish to you?"

Leopold rose and this time Decker let him go. The bartender was staring at him. The last thing he needed was for the man to call the cops on him.

"See you around, then," said Decker.

You can count on it.

Leopold walked out of the bar. Decker waited about

fifteen seconds and then followed him out. He would trail Leopold right to wherever he called home.

The only problem was that when Decker got outside Sebastian Leopold was gone.

25

Decker walked up and down the street in both directions for a hundred yards. There was one alleyway next to the bar, but it was a dead end and no doors opened off it other than the bar's side entrance and a door to an adjacent pharmacy that was both barred and bolted shut. There were no other side streets that Leopold could have reached in fifteen seconds if he'd been flat-out sprinting. Decker ducked back into the bar to see if maybe Leopold had circled back in there through the side door in the alley, but he hadn't.

There were a few shops that were open, but Leopold was in none of them and no one in any of those places remembered seeing him pass by. There were no people on the street who might have witnessed anything.

There could be only one answer: Someone had picked up Leopold in a car and they had driven off. And that pickup, however absurd it sounded, might have been prearranged. This of course deepened Decker's suspicion of the man. And made him doubly upset that he had managed to lose him.

Yet there was nothing more to be done here, so he set off for Mansfield High.

The mourners had gone and had been replaced by two groups of protestors stationed just outside the yellow police tape. One group was pro-gun, the other on the flip side of the debate. They chanted and screamed and occasionally briefly skirmished with each other.

More guns! No guns! Second Amendment! Guns kill! No, people kill! Where does the slaughter end! Go to hell!

Decker bypassed all this and used his new credentials to get past the security perimeter. He met up with Lancaster at the command center in the library.

When he told her what had happened at the arraignment she appeared dumbfounded.

"He just walked?"

Decker nodded.

"Mac is gonna be pissed about that. And I would have expected better from Sheila Lynch. Looks like she got blindsided by the PD."

"He was just doing his job. Truth and justice don't necessarily enter the equation. The fact was, Abernathy probably made the right decision. With the confession recanted there was no evidence to hold him. And Abernathy was already ticked at the prosecution. He was probably looking for a way to drop the hammer. And he did. We've both seen that before."

Decker had participated in so many trials over the

years that he felt he was a lawyer in every way except as a holder of the official sheepskin and bar card.

"I'm glad you can look at it in such a coldly efficient way, Amos," she said, a distinct frostiness in her own tone.

"How else do you want me to look at it?" he said just as bluntly. "Otherwise I've got my head in my ass, and where does that get us?"

She looked away and chewed her gum. "Forget it," she said. "I'm just having a shitty day."

Decker didn't tell her about his tailing and then losing Leopold at the bar. He didn't think it would add anything to the scenario, and he felt like an idiot for having let it happen. And even with an altered brain, who wanted to look like an idiot?

"The FBI seems excited," he observed. The suits were running around with an even greater degree of energy than they normally exhibited.

"Mass murderer, connected cases, the stuff you found with Debbie Watson. It's definitely upped the stakes." She paused and fiddled with some pages in front of her. "And they want to talk to you, Amos. The FBI, I mean."

He looked mildly surprised. "Why is that?"

"Foremost, because you're the one discovering all the fresh clues. But it's also clear that the killer has a personal thing with you. The message at your old home was directed at you. The coded note at Debbie's house was about you too. So the FBI wants to basically question you to see if they can get any leads from whoever might have a vendetta against you."

"And when do they want to do this?"

"Now would be a good time, actually."

Decker looked up to see a six-foot-tall, broadshouldered man in his forties standing next to him. His suit was impeccable down to the yellow pocket square that neatly matched the tie. He was clean-shaven and fit. He seemed to be the leader of the pack, if the way the other agents were anxiously staring at him was any indication.

Decker had never seen him before. He must have just arrived on the scene, perhaps from Washington. A heavy gun brought in for a heavy case that was gaining widespread attention across the country. It just seemed like the federal way. Leave the chickenshit cases to the local chickens while they grabbed the glory on the ones destined for the national pipeline.

The man put out a hand and smiled, revealing a slight gap between his very white front teeth. "Special Agent Ross Bogart. I'm a little late to the party. I was finishing up some things in D.C. Mr. Decker, let's find a quiet place to go over some things, if you don't mind."

"Would it matter if I did mind?"

"We all have the same goal. I know you were a cop and then a detective. You know the drill, nothing too small. Nothing too obscure to follow up. Shall we?" He pointed to a door at the back of the library that Decker had previously discovered was used as a reading class-room for ESL students.

He rose and followed the man back. Another agent joined them, a woman Decker had seen before. She was blonde, in her thirties, with muscled calves and a jaw that jutted out like a slab of stone. She had a recorder in one hand and a notebook and pen in the other. A federal shield rode on her hip.

"Special Agent Lafferty will be joining us," said Bogart.

"How about Detective Lancaster joining us, then?" suggested Decker. "She's been right in the middle of this too."

"Maybe later," Bogart said with a smile, as he held open the door and flicked on the light.

They all sat around a small table, Decker on one side, the two special agents on the other. Lafferty turned on her recorder and held her notebook open, looking ready to write down everything that was said in the room.

"Do they still teach shorthand with all the digital stuff they have these days?" asked Decker, looking at her. "It seems that a recording would be one hundred percent accurate, whereas your shorthand might contain interpretations and selective nuances, of which you might not be even consciously aware, instead of what was actually said. Just a thought."

She did not seem to know how to respond to this, so she glanced at her boss.

Bogart said, "Let's start at the beginning, if you will, to help me come up to speed."

"Why don't you just let me summarize so we don't waste time?" said Decker. He didn't wait for an assent from Bogart but plunged ahead. "My family was killed sixteen months ago. The case is unsolved." He then told the FBI agents about Sebastian Leopold's confessing to the crime, being jailed, recanting, and then being released because there was no evidence to hold him. "As you know, ballistics has tied that case and this one together."

"And you're sure he couldn't have been the school shooter?" asked Bogart.

"Impossible. He was in jail at the time. Hours before the guy started his rampage."

"You figured out where he might have been hiding," said Bogart. "In the cafeteria. The food locker."

"I tied some witness statements together and made an educated guess."

"Then you found the notebook in Debbie Watson's locker with the picture of the shooter."

"Another educated guess."

Bogart went on, seeming not to have heard him. "Then you went to Watson's house and made the discovery of the coded message held in the musical score. And then there was the earlier message, or taunt really, that someone left on the wall of your old house, where your family was murdered. You spotted that too."

Bogart paused for a moment and then said, "Aren't you going to say, 'Another educated guess'?"

"I *guess* I don't have to now, seeing as you said it for me."

"You seem to be taking this all rather lightly. Can I ask why?"

"I'm not taking any of this lightly. That's why I'm working the case even though I'm not on the police force."

Bogart glanced at a file in front of him. "*Cases*, really, isn't it? Separated by sixteen months."

"Actually sixteen months, two days, twelve hours, and six minutes."

"And how do you know that so precisely? You didn't even look at your watch."

"There's a clock on the wall behind you."

Bogart didn't turn and look but Lafferty did and she wrote something down.

Decker hadn't needed to look at the wall clock. He had his internal timer that kept that count faithfully. Better than a Rolex and a lot cheaper.

"Still," said Bogart. "To the minute?"

"To the *second* in case you're interested," replied Decker evenly. "And if you're wondering where I was when the school shooting was happening, I was at the Second Precinct."

Bogart's brow furrowed and he looked bemusedly at Decker. "Why would you offer up an alibi in the first place? Do you think you're under suspicion somehow?"

"If you really *think* about it, everybody's under suspicion *somehow*."

Decker watched as Lafferty wrote this down word for word.

"Are you being deliberately antagonistic, Mr. Decker?" asked Bogart politely.

"No, this is just my personality. Ask anyone who knows me. I have no filters. I lost them years ago and never found them again."

"You had an outstanding record in the police force. You and your partner."

"Former partner," Decker corrected, for he had a need for things to be precise, especially right now.

"Former partner," conceded Bogart. "But in talks with people it seems that you were the clear leader of the pair. I won't say you were the brains, because I have no desire to minimize Detective Lancaster's contributions to your casework."

"That's very nice to hear," said Decker. "Because Mary is a good detective and works her ass off." He looked at Lafferty. "And if you work hard too, you might become more than a note taker for your boss. I'm sure you have the ability if you're ever given the chance to use it."

Lafferty flushed and set her pen down.

Bogart leaned forward. "This person seems to have a vendetta against you. Any idea who that could be?"

"If I did I would have already provided the information to the *Burlington Police Department*."

"We're all in this together," said Bogart, who was no longer smiling politely.

"I'm glad that you think so."

"So no one comes to mind?"

"When I talked with Leopold he said I had dissed him at the 7-Eleven. This was about a month before my family was killed. Only I never dissed anyone there. And if someone had a problem with me I would've remembered."

"Are you saying your memory is infallible?"

"I'm saying I would have remembered if someone had a problem with me."

"But all that time ago, you could have forgotten. And it might have been something slight, or seemingly innocuous. It might not have even registered with you. We all miss things. And memories are inherently fallible."

"When were you born?"

"What?" asked Bogart sharply.

"Tell me when you were born, month, day, year."

Bogart glanced at Lafferty and then said, "June 2, 1968."

Decker blinked five times and said, "Then you were born on a Sunday."

Bogart sat back. "That's right. I of course didn't know it at the time. How did you know? Did you look up my personnel file?"

"I wouldn't have had access. And until five minutes ago I didn't even know you existed. If you want more proof I can do the same thing for your colleague."

"And your point?"

"I would've remembered dissing someone at the 7-Eleven whether it was seventeen months or seventeen years ago."

"You think Leopold was lying, then?"

"I think Sebastian Leopold is not what he wants us to think he is."

"And what exactly is that?"

"Homeless and more than slightly out of his mind."

"So you're saying he's neither homeless nor out of his mind?"

"I'm saying that I think he's dangerous."

"But you said he couldn't have been the school shooter. Do you think he killed your family?"

"He couldn't personally have done it. He has an alibi for that too. But I'm rethinking whether he was still involved somehow."

"Why?"

"Because he walked on a murder charge he confessed to. And now he's disappeared. You don't luck yourself into either one of those results."

"So you *do* think he's involved somehow. And now he's disappeared?"

"I have no proof. And even if we find him we can't charge him with what we have, which is basically nothing."

"So why do you think he's involved?"

This came from Agent Lafferty.

Bogart turned to her, seemingly surprised that she had uttered actual words.

Decker stared dead at her. "Because he's inexplicable. And I don't like people who are inexplicable."

26

Decker left Bogart and Lafferty in the little reading room and walked across the hall to the cafeteria. This was where it all started, and it seemed that the old checkerboard linoleum-floored space kept calling out to him.

Maybe like a Siren serenades a sailor to his doom.

He walked around the perimeter of the space, looked in the freezer, turned the corner, and checked the kitchen area, then the outdoor loading dock, which led off into the woods. Initially they thought the shooter had escaped that way. Well, many of them still thought that, which was why a forensics team had been scouring the entire path and its environs ever since Decker had discovered what he had in the cafeteria.

But Decker no longer believed it.

He came back in and parked himself in one of the chairs the kids used. His wide butt hung off both sides of it and he could almost hear the scream of the seat's spindly legs as it supported a bulk not usually seen in a high school.

So why had the shooter really been in the cafeteria?

It was far from where the shooting spree started. The farthest possible spot except for the office and the library, places that would have had people in them at that time of the morning.

7:28—Melissa Dalton heard the whooshing sound as the freezer door opened.

8:41—Cammie Man was caught on video.

8:42—Debbie Watson lost her face and her life.

Basically one hour and thirteen minutes were unaccounted for. What took all that time? If he was already dressed and gunned up? Why had he waited? Or had he waited at all? Perhaps he was *doing* something. Perhaps he was doing something critical to his plan that took some time.

Decker sat there for a few minutes while his mind chewed on this.

No one had been seen walking from the cafeteria to the far hallway where Debbie Watson had died. They had identified and interviewed two people—both teachers—who most likely would have seen someone walk that route at that time. It was not guaranteed, because a minute off here or there or a head turning to the right instead of the left and there would have been a blind spot.

But if the killer started in the cafeteria, he had to get to the other end of the school unseen. That was point A.

He *had* done it. That was point B.

Point C would be *how* he had done it. Point C was what Decker desperately needed to understand.

And then something trickled into the back of his head, was run through the meticulous filter that his mind had become because of a hellacious hit by a Bayou boy, and the trickle came out the other end reformulated into something.

Decker rose and hurried outside. He hustled over to the cornerstone of the school and read off the date.

1946.

He already knew this, but looking at the numbers seemed to bolster his confidence in the theory forming in his head. Colors had flashed in his mind when his gaze fell on some of the numbers, but colors did not interest him right now.

1946.

A year after the big war ended.

And a new one had almost immediately begun.

The Cold War.

Nuclear war threats. Armageddon. Kids huddling under their flimsy desks as part of emergency drills in case a hydrogen bomb was coming their way. As though an inch-thick laminate shield would protect them from the equivalent of a million tons of TNT.

Decker hustled back to the cafeteria, passing several suspicious-looking Bureau agents in the hall as he did so. He didn't acknowledge them. He barely noticed them. He was on the scent. He had formed walls in his head that had compartmentalized everything down to this one line of inquiry that might answer the one question that seemed unanswerable.

He stood in the middle of the room and looked in all four corners, then pulled his gaze back. He went into the kitchen and did the same thing. Then the loading platform.

He didn't see anything remotely close to what he was looking for. The problem was, he didn't know enough. That was always the damn problem with police work.

I don't know enough. The man who can't forget anything doesn't know enough. How ironic is that?

But if Decker didn't know enough, then maybe the shooter didn't either. Maybe the shooter had had to turn to someone who *did* know enough.

Or who knew someone who knew enough.

Now, that theory, if played out, might answer several questions.

The school was a facility, a building. Changes could be made. Changes undoubtedly *were* made here over the decades. The drop ceiling over his head had assuredly not been here in 1946. What else had been added or taken away?

Or covered up? Because it was no longer necessary? And then forgotten?

Decker slipped into the library and motioned for Lancaster to join him. She finished up a phone call and then hurried over to the entrance to the library where Decker was standing. Decker was acutely aware that Special Agent Bogart and his special agent note taker

Lafferty were both watching him from a distant corner of the space.

He spoke to Lancaster in a low voice, his features relaxed. He might just be shooting the breeze with her. They turned and left together.

Once outside in the hall, Lancaster said, "Do you really think it's possible? I mean, I never heard of such a thing."

"Just because you haven't heard of it, doesn't mean it doesn't exist."

"You went here. Did you ever hear talk of something like that?"

"No. But then again I never thought to ask, either. And it might've been from a long time ago. In fact, it probably was."

"But who would know for sure? From what you said, it could have been put in over sixty years ago. And maybe never used. Anybody who might have known about it is probably dead or nearly so."

"How about students from back then?"

"Well, they'd be pretty elderly too. And the teachers are almost certainly all dead."

"There has to be a way, Mary. Records have to be kept—"

They had walked outside, and Decker broke off his sentence as he looked to his left, where the old military base was.

"The Army might have record of it," he noted.

"The Army! Why them?"

"That base has been here since, what, the thirties?"

"That's right. My grandfather worked there along with half the other people in Burlington. They had a big buildup during World War II, like every other military installation in the country."

"So clearly it was there before the school was built. And lots of parents who worked at the base sent their kids to Mansfield."

Lancaster appeared to understand where he was going with this. "So you think they might have initiated it?"

"And what if Debbie Watson's great-grandfather, who worked at the base starting in the late sixties, knew all about it, and told little Debbie when he went to live with them?"

"And you think she might have told the shooter?"

"I can't think of another reason why he would have needed her."

"But how would he have found out that Debbie would know something like that?"

"It could have been any number of ways. That's not important. But if I'm right, we'll know how the shooter got from the cafeteria to the back hall unseen. And if we can nail that down we might be able to work backward to where the son of a bitch came from."

They hurried off to Lancaster's car.

At the window watching them was Special Agent

Bogart. And the man from Washington did not look pleased.

Next to him Special Agent Lafferty was busily writing down notes.

27

George Watson answered their knock. He looked disheveled and there was a yellow and purplish bruise on his right cheek.

"Are you okay?" asked Lancaster.

Watson leaned against the doorjamb seemingly more for support than anything else. "I'm f-fine. My . . . my w-wife i-is leavin' me, but I'm f-fine. Hell, why w-wouldn't I b-be?"

Decker drew a foot closer and sniffed while Lancaster held Watson's gaze.

Decker looked at her and nodded his head slightly. They had done this same routine when they had been partners. A nod for drunk, a shake of the head for sober or near enough to it. Actually, he hadn't needed to do the smell test. The man's slurred speech, inability to stand without aid of a wall, and blurry eyes were signs enough.

"Is your wife here?" asked Decker.

George pointed inside the house. "P-packin'. Th-the b-bitch!"

"These are very tough times for you both," commented Decker.

"Lo-lost my little girl and . . . and n-now my wife. But you kn-know w-what?"

"No sir, what?" asked Decker.

"Screw 'em." He waggled his deformed arm. "S-screw 'em."

"You might want to lie down, sir," said Lancaster. "And lay off the drink."

George looked affronted. "I . . . haven't b-been drinkin'." He let out a loud belch and looked like he might be sick.

"Good to know. But you need to sleep it off anyway."

Decker took the man's good arm and guided him into the front room and over to the couch. "Just have a lie-down right there while we have a word with your wife."

As George sank down onto the couch he said, "She's n-not m-my w-wife. Not an-any-anymore. B-b-bitch!"

He closed his eyes and grew silent except for his breathing.

Decker led Lancaster down the hall and to a door behind which they heard noise.

Decker rapped on the wood. "Mrs. Watson?"

They heard something fall and hit the floor. "Who's there?" Beth Watson barked.

"Police," said Lancaster.

Beth Watson screamed, "That little son of a bitch

called the police? Just because I hit him? Well, he hit me first, the one-armed prick."

"It's not about that. It's about your daughter."

The door was wrenched open and Beth Watson stood there in heels and a white slip and nothing else. Her pale flesh seemed even paler with that backdrop. The skin around her arms was sagging. One of her cheeks was red and swollen. Decker did not have to take a step closer to sniff out her sobriety status. But apparently, she could be drunk, stand erectly, and talk coherently at the same time. At least she hoped she was coherent.

"What about her?" Beth demanded.

"I asked your husband when we were here last time about his grandfather."

Her brows knitted in confusion. "Simon? Why?"

"He worked at McDonald Army Base before he retired?"

"That's right. So what? He's been dead for years."

"But he lived here with you and your husband. And Debbie."

"Yeah, again, so what?" Unlike her husband, Beth didn't find it necessary to lean against the doorjamb to steady herself. She obviously handled the booze better than her husband. Perhaps she had more practice, Decker thought.

"Did he ever talk to you about his work there?" he asked.

"He was at the age where he *only* talked about the

past. World War II. The Korean War. Working for the government. Blah-blah-blah. All day and all night. Sickening after a while. Who the hell wants to live in the past?"

She pushed past Decker and shouted down the hall. "Who the hell wants to live in the past, George? Not me! I'm all about the future now! *My* future! The past can kiss my ass. *You* can kiss my ass, you ball-less cripple!"

Decker used his massive arm to gently guide her back into the room.

"Did he ever mention to you any work done at Mansfield?" he asked.

The woman's eyes seemed to wobble in their sockets. "At Mansfield? He didn't work at Mansfield. He was at the Army base."

"Right. But the base and the school are right next to each other."

She snagged a pack of cigarettes off the nightstand and lit up. She exhaled smoke and glared at Decker. "I don't see what that has to do with a damn thing."

"The school was built right at the start of the Cold War, shortly after World War II ended. People all over the country were putting bomb shelters in their backyards. Well, folks were doing that in buildings too, including schools. Bombproof shelters under them."

A hint of remembrance came into the woman's eyes.

"Wait a minute. A long time ago Simon did say

something about . . . about a whatchamajigger at Mansfield. He didn't build it originally. He just added to it. I'd forgotten all about it."

"What whatchamajigger are we exactly talking about here?" asked Lancaster pointedly.

Beth pointed at Decker. "Like what he said. A place, a safe place under the school in case the Russians attacked us."

"Soviets," corrected Decker. "But close enough. Did he tell you anything about it? Like where it was located?"

"No, nothing like that. It was never used, apparently. And then I guess it got sealed up or something because they didn't want anyone sneaking down there. You know, high schoolers are full of hormones. You could only imagine what would go on down there." She paused and said in a low voice, "Orgies." Then she giggled and hiccuped. "If I'd known about it when I went to school there, I'd been the first one doing it."

Then she screamed down the hall, "Orgies, you prick. That's what I'll be doing tomorrow! Orgies with other men! Lots of 'em!"

Decker once more guided her back into the bedroom.

"So a shelter *is* down there. Fortunate for us that you remembered that," noted Lancaster with a sideways glance at Decker.

Beth gave a lopsided smile. "Actually, my memory sucks. But I remember Simon was talking to me about it while I was making dinner one night. Funny, I never listened to the old fart, and, like I said, my memory is so bad. I never remember birthdays, shit like that. But I was making German chocolate cake when he was telling me about it. Only time I ever tried it. And I guess that's what triggered it."

"What triggered what?" asked a confused Lancaster.

"German chocolate cake. See, Germans and the Russians. They were in Germany, right? I mean the Russians."

"That's right," said Decker. "They were. At least half of it."

She smiled. "Weird how the brain works."

"Tell me about it," said Decker. "Did Simon have any friends in town who might still be around and who might know about this underground place?"

"Not that he ever mentioned. I mean, he was over ninety when he died. Now he'd be close to a hundred. They're all dead, right?" She added quietly, "Like my Debbie."

There was an awkward silence until Decker said, "If you remember anything else, please give Detective Lancaster here a call. It's important. We want to find who did this. Who did this to . . . Debbie."

"You still think she was . . . was in cahoots with whoever did this?"

"No, I really don't."

The woman's lips trembled. "Debbie was a good kid."

"I'm sure she was, which makes it even more important that we find out who did this."

Lancaster glanced at the partially packed suitcase. "Look, it's none of my business, but do you think you should be making that sort of drastic change right after losing your daughter? It might be better for you and your husband to get through this together and then you can make some decisions. Knee-jerk tends to come back to bite you in the butt."

Beth looked at her cross-eyed. "I wanted to leave two years ago, but I stayed for Debbie's sake. Well, Debbie's not here anymore. So I'm not wasting another second of my life in this fucking place. Now, if you'll excuse me, I need to finish packing so I can get the hell out of here."

She slammed the bedroom door in their faces.

"So much for 'for better or worse,'" said Lancaster.

"For some people, the longer the marriage, the worse it gets," said Decker. "But at least we know my theory might work out. Simon *did* know about something at the school. An underground shelter."

"So now what do we do?" asked Lancaster.

"Let's go outside. You can smoke a cigarette and I can make some phone calls."

"You know I can quit anytime I want."

He stared at her. "No you can't, Mary. You're *addicted* to nicotine."

"I was making a joke. Damn, do you have to take everything so literally?"

But Decker was already on his cell.

It took three phone calls and being passed from one person to the next before Decker found someone who sort of knew what he was talking about. He patiently explained who he was and what he wanted.

"Mansfield," said the woman on the other end of the line. "Where the mass shooting took place?"

"That's right," said Decker. "We're trying to figure out how the killer got in and out. Since it was so close to McDonald Army Base, we thought there might be something there. Turns out we learned there is an underground passage or facility of some kind. We'd like confirmation of that and also particulars on how to get in there so we don't have to tear the whole school down looking for it."

"I'm going to need something in writing on the appropriate letterhead to get this request verified and initiated."

"Okay, but once *verified and initiated*, how long will it take? We're looking for a murderer. Someone who killed a bunch of kids. The longer it goes, the farther away he gets."

"I wish I could tell you it would be fast. But this is the United States Army. The only place we move fast is on the battlefield. The stuff behind the lines, not so much."

Decker got the information on where to send the request and clicked off.

He looked over at Lancaster, who had been leaning

against the hood of her car all this time and had whittled down not one but three cigarettes while Decker had been playing Whac-A-Mole with the Army.

Lancaster dropped her last smoke and ground it into the asphalt with the heel of her shoe. "And?"

"And we might all be dead of old age before they get back to us."

"So what now?"

"So it looks like we'll have to find it ourselves."

28

Decker and Lancaster paced the cafeteria, working from opposite ends of the space.

"So it makes sense an entrance would be in here," said Lancaster. "Big room, get lots of students assembled in here and then down into the shelter in the event of an emergency."

Decker nodded but said nothing.

She continued, "If it's here it must be hidden behind something. Maybe the appliances?"

Decker shook his head. "It couldn't be something that involved. With an emergency you have to have fast access."

"But it was probably boarded up," Lancaster pointed out. "Built over."

"But the shooter still couldn't be tearing into walls, floors, or ceilings, because that would also make noise and leave evidence behind of how he went from here to the back hall."

"Well, he did leave evidence he was in here. The spoiled food, remember?"

"He did that on purpose. He could have easily turned

the temp back down once he came out of it. Hell, he didn't have to stay in the freezer all night anyway. He wanted us to know he was here. But he didn't want us to find how he got from the front to the back. At least not right away. That's the reason he left the trace in the ceiling and the tile dust on the floor. Classic misdirection. He's screwing with us. And he's costing us time. All good for him and bad for us."

Lancaster kept glancing around. "So we're looking for an entrance in here that's been sealed up. We just don't know how or where."

"The term 'sealed' can mean a lot of different things. But the point is, our guy befriended Debbie for one reason and one reason only—to learn about this passage."

"Come on, Decker. How would he even know about it to ask her?"

"*I* found out about it based on observations and hunches and a little research. He could have done the same. This is a relatively small town. He could have found out Simon Watson worked at the base any number of ways. He could have learned he once lived with the Watsons. He could have approached Debbie to see if she knew anything about it. And of course she did."

"That takes a lot of planning and forethought."

"And that apparently is a strong suit for our guy."

Decker walked back and forth in front of a section of the wall.

Lancaster noted this and said, "I bet those rules haven't changed in sixty years. I suppose you adhered to all of them when you went here?" she added with a smile tacked on.

The "rules" she was referring to were posted on a large section of the wall that Decker was studying. They included no loud talking, no throwing food, no eating off someone else's plate, no milk cartons left on tables, all trash in the garbage, no running, and on and on.

"Amos, I said—"

He held up his hand for her to stay quiet, while he paced the wall and then looked at the floor.

"What do you see down there, Mary?"

She bent low and looked where he was pointing.

"Some marks. Probably from a student's shoes."

"I don't think so. There's no uniform requirement at Mansfield. Most boys wear sneakers. And from what I've seen, most girls wear sneakers, flats, or chunky heels. That footwear wouldn't leave those sorts of marks. It's actually scraped into the linoleum. And they're not short, like a heel might make. They're long. And they're on a slight curve. Looks to be a few of them."

"Well, what do you think they are?"

He stood closer to the section of wall where the rules were printed on a massive piece of wood painted to match the wall color. The wood ran down to the floor and nearly to the ceiling.

"No hinges evident," he said. "But—"

He dug his fingers under the right section of the wall and tugged at various spots. He did this on the other side. Finally, after ten minutes of probing, tugging, and pushing, there was a little click and the entire section behind the sign opened outward. He pulled on it, opening it farther. Revealed behind it was a pair of old wooden doors painted the color of the wall.

"Look at the floor," said Decker.

Lancaster noted another set of fresh scuff marks where the wood had dragged in one place across the floor when he'd opened the section.

"Damn, Amos. The mark on the floor was from the door swinging open."

"Hinges were placed about a foot in and mounted on a support structure so they wouldn't be visible to anyone. But the hinges have sagged a bit over time, hence the scuffed floor." He ran his finger along one set of hinges and his finger came away darkened.

"Recently oiled," he said.

There was a small knob in the center of the back of the section.

"What do you think that was for?"

Decker thought for a few moments. "You'd use it to pull shut the wall section once you're on that side of it."

"Right. But why even have a door at all? If they wanted to seal it up, why not just seal it up?"

"I don't know, Mary. It must have cost a lot of money to build. Maybe they wanted to have reasonably easy access to it if they ever decided to use it again."

"I guess."

"I don't see any fingerprints, but let's not take chances. They call them latent prints for a reason."

He grabbed a knife from a box of them on one of the kitchen counters to ease open the door by pushing back on the ordinary lock that secured the two doors. The door opened silently, showing that its hinges had been recently oiled too.

There was a long set of steps down into inky darkness.

Decker grabbed an emergency flashlight from a holder on the wall next to the serving counter and came back over to the doorway. "You ready?"

"Shouldn't we alert the others?" said Lancaster nervously.

"We will, after we see where this goes."

"But the FBI?"

"Screw the FBI, Mary. This is *our* case, not theirs." He stared at her. "You with me?"

She finally nodded and followed him down the steps.

They reached the bottom, and here Decker stopped and shone his light around.

"Look there."

They saw that set against one wall were two large sections of painted plywood. Bent nails were sticking out of them.

Decker said, "That's how they really sealed up the passage. I saw nail holes in the perimeter around the double doors. That plywood had been nailed in front of the doors. If anyone figured out the sign opened, all they'd see is a solid wall."

"You think the shooter did that?"

Decker shone his light on the floor. "Had to be. The sawdust on the floor looks relatively fresh. If he pulled out the nails the dust would come out and fall to the floor. Same when he hauled the sections down the steps. And he might've used a saw to cut through the wood too."

"Which means he had to have done this before. No way is he tearing out wood walls during the school day. Too much noise."

"He could have done it the night before. He comes out of the freezer and gets to work. No one here to hear anything. He opens the wall with the sign on it, cuts through the wall, opens the doors, and puts everything down in the passageway."

"If he did all that, Amos, maybe that's why he hid in the freezer."

"Could be," said Decker.

Decker pointed to the floor once more. In the dust were clear sets of shoeprints heading in the direction they were going.

Two clear sets of footprints heading down the passage.

"Walk to the right, Mary, so we preserve them. And take shots of them with your phone camera as we go."

"Okay, but why two sets? Are they two different people?"

Decker bent down and shone the light on them. "No. The prints look to be identical. And it's not two people walking side by side. The spacing of the prints is too close. But two sets make sense."

"Why?"

"Come on."

They continued on, with her taking pictures as they went. They passed through a massive, foot-thick metal door that only opened easily because it was set on hydraulic hinges.

"Some sort of blast door," said Decker.

Now the space opened up into a large room about forty feet across and twice as long. The floors were concrete, the walls and ceiling the same. On the walls were signs that told what to do in the event of an emergency. Several were imprinted with a skull-and-crossbones symbol, the universal sign for danger. Along the walls were old metal lockers on which were bolted signs. One read, GAS MASKS. Another said, FIRST AID. A third said, WATER AND FOOD. The dust and cobwebs were pervasive and the air stale and musty.

"They must have had an independent air supply," said Decker. "If a nuke hit, you couldn't have access to the outside air."

"But it can't be airtight down here. I can breathe okay."

"Which means it might have been vented so workers down here replenishing supplies and the like could breathe, but they close them off when the alarm sounds."

Following the sets of footprints, they traversed the bomb shelter space and passed through another blast door where there was another passageway matching the one on the other side. The darkness was lifted every few seconds by the flash on Lancaster's phone as she took pictures of the sets of shoeprints that had continued on down this passage.

Decker was counting off the steps in his head. Then they ran into another set of steps. These headed up. Decker had been shining his light on the floor at various intervals. The shoeprints they had seen earlier had paralleled them the entire way. They headed up. At the top of the steps was a blank wall.

"Dead end?" said Lancaster.

"Can't be." Decker dug his fingernails around the edges of the wall, working his way up and down both sides. Then he gained a handhold, tugged. The wall started to give, and then it came loose.

"It's balsa wood," he said, hefting it easily and setting it aside. On the other side of the open wall was a small space that was stacked with junk. On the other side of that was a door.

"The government wouldn't have sealed it with balsa wood," observed Lancaster.

"I'm sure they didn't. But unlike the cafeteria where the wall wasn't visible, this wall would have been in case someone opened that door. The shooter must've replaced whatever wall was here with the balsa. It would look solid but would be easily movable."

"You're talking a lot of work, Amos. He couldn't have done all of that in one night."

"But if he could access the school at night, he might've been here a lot doing what he needed to do."

"But how would he do that? He couldn't count on school plays every night? And bringing in saws and other equipment?"

"I'm not sure how he did it." Decker hit the floor with his light. "Check out the patch right in front of the wall. Not much dust. That pile of junk used to be right in front of the wall, but it's been moved so it doesn't block the way."

Decker checked the doorknob for prints, and then used the knife he'd brought with him to try to force the latch open.

"It's locked. Give me a sec." He passed the flashlight to her and pulled from his pocket his lock-picking instruments.

"Standard PI equipment?" she said wryly.

"You never picked a lock as a cop?"

A minute later the door swung open about a foot or so and then hit something.

"What is it?" whispered Lancaster.

Decker noted that she had her gun out. And that her left hand was still trembling.

"Something blocking the door." He poked his head through the opening and recognized where they were.

"This is the storage room off the shop class. I looked in here before. The door's hitting a stack of old window AC units. That's why I didn't see the door before. The units completely hid it from where I was standing on the other side."

"And I bet when we searched this area, no one noticed the door on the other side for the very same reason."

"Sounds right."

Lancaster eyed the gap. "I can get through there."

She turned sideways and passed easily through the narrow space.

She looked around. "If you can push on the door from your end, I'll steady the AC units so they don't fall over."

He pushed on the door with his bulk and the door slid open farther, pushing the units with it, while Lancaster held on to them, keeping them upright.

"Okay, Amos, that's plenty of room for you to get through."

Decker passed through the widened gap, looked at the partially open door and then at the stack of AC units, and then stared down at the floor.

And then he frowned.

"What now?" asked Lancaster.

"There's not a lot of dust in here, so I don't see any more shoeprints."

"But we saw the sets coming up the stairs. He had to come in here."

"Agreed. So let's assume he came through here and out into the shop class."

They left the storage area and walked into the large room with all the tools and work tables.

"But how did the guy know there'd be no one in shop class?" said Decker.

"Oh, didn't you know?" said Lancaster, sounding pleased she knew something Decker didn't.

"Know what?"

"The shop teacher quit at the end of last year. They couldn't find a replacement, so there's been no shop class this year."

"That's why the door to the classroom was locked. And that's also how the shooter knew. Debbie must've told him that there was no shop class."

"But you were right, Amos. This is how he got from the cafeteria to the opposite end of the school unseen."

He nodded. "He actually did it twice that day. He came out of the freezer, walked down the passage, came out into the halls, shot the people on his way to the front. Then he reentered the passage in the cafeteria, closed the wall after him, and walked back down the passage."

"Which was why there were two sets of identical shoeprints," added Lancaster.

"Right. Now, the shop class is also a big space, so maybe they figured to load kids from both ends of the school and down into the shelter in the event of an emergency."

271

"How far underground do you figure that passage was?" she asked.

"Based on the number of risers, about twelve feet."

"Doubt that would protect you from a nuclear bomb blast. Even if it's all concrete with reinforced doors."

He stared at her. "Well, what exactly *would* protect you from a nuke?"

"Good point."

"I came in here the first night I was here looking around. Those are my shoeprints over there." He pointed to the far wall. "I walked around, and then, like I said before, I looked in the storage rooms in the back."

Decker knelt down and studied the floor. "Mary, hit this section with your light. I must have missed it earlier."

Lancaster did so, revealing a long mark that disturbed the light dust, along with the impressions of shoeprints.

"What do you think that is?"

"Point your light about six inches to the left."

She did. There was nothing.

"Try six inches to the right."

She did and they saw an identical mark.

"What is that?" asked Lancaster.

"Marks from Debbie Watson's feet."

"Her feet?"

"Or her heels, rather, as she was being dragged out of here. The shoeprints are the shooter's."

"Out of here? What was she doing *in* here?"

"Meeting her beau. Her Jesus."

"You aren't serious?"

"Debbie was the first vic the ME did a postmortem on. Did you read the autopsy report?"

"Of course I did."

"COD?"

"Why are you wasting time, Amos? Her cause of death was a shotgun blast to the face, as you very well know."

"That was obvious. But did you note what the coroner found in her mouth?"

"You mean aside from shotgun pellets?" Lancaster said sarcastically.

"He found the residue of some breath mints."

"Breath mints? I don't remember reading that."

"It was near the end of the report. I always read to the end."

"But breath mints?"

"*Residue* of breath mints. There was a pack of them in her locker. Two were missing. That's why she went to her locker. To get the mints. To freshen up her breath before meeting her beau. And her killer. And that would explain the time gap. He comes out of the freezer at seven-twenty-eight. He goes down the passage. But he has to wait for Debbie to get out of class. They probably had a prearranged time. She fakes being ill, gets her permission slip, goes to her locker, gets her mints, and then enters the shop class."

"But you said the door was locked?"

"Jesus would have unlocked it from the inside for her."

"Right." She eyed him suspiciously. "Exactly how long have you thought all this?"

"Not that long." Decker closed his eyes and touched the back of his head about halfway down. "And the autopsy revealed that there was a subacute subdural hematoma on the back of her head, right about here. Left side of the occipital bone was cracked, and that's a tough bone to damage like that. That might have killed her if the shotgun hadn't, just from internal bleeding and resulting pressure on the brain. The ME speculated the injury occurred when she fell backward to the floor after being shot." He opened his eyes and looked at his partner. "Left side."

"Meaning the blow came from the left side and behind? A left-handed person? Like you said the guy who wrote the musical score was, left-handed."

"The probabilities lie there, yes."

"So he meets her in here and knocks her out, but why?"

"He needed her out of the way. And he needed to kill her first, before anyone else. He couldn't risk the possibility that she would survive. She could identify him. So he arranges to meet with her, uses the passageway to get across the school unseen. I would imagine this is not the first time they've done this. They might have had sex in shop class during or after school on other occasions. I wonder how often Debbie got permission to go to the nurse's office?"

"Have sex? Are you serious?"

"Their own private space in the middle of the school? What could be cooler for a teenager in love with her *mature* man who doesn't even go here? And the killer would have wanted to know the passage by heart when he was planning this whole thing. He could bring stuff in and store it here. It was perfect."

"So how do you see it playing out from there?"

"He meets in the shop class with her, she thinks to make out, hence the breath mints. He knocks her out, gets his gear, slips out of the room, walks around the corner to the camera, and gets his picture taken." He glanced at Lancaster. "You saw the shoeprints in the passage?"

"You *know* I did."

"I estimate they're a size nine or maybe nine and a half, but no larger."

Lancaster looked confused. "That's not very big for a large guy," she said slowly. "Earl's six feet and he wears an eleven."

"I'm six-five and wear a fourteen shoe, which is not unusual for a man my size. A guy six-two weighing in at two-hundred-plus pounds with a size nine shoe? Not likely. And I couldn't get past the gap in the door with the AC units in the way. I had to push them out farther. And the lack of marks on the floor showed I was the only one who had. You got through easily enough, but you're short and skinny. The guy in the video had a lot smaller waist than I do, but his shoulders and chest were just as broad as mine. So how did he manage to get through that gap without moving the AC units?"

"I don't know. Do you?"

"I've got some ideas."

Lancaster looked around nervously and chewed her gum so ferociously that her teeth were clacking together. "We need to get a forensics team in here. I hope to God we haven't already tainted evidence. The Bureau will rip us a new one, *after* Mac finishes with us." She looked around and then something seemed to strike her.

"Wait a minute. If the guy knocked Debbie out and then dragged her out of here, how did he shoot her standing up out in the hall? The ballistics was clear on that. She was upright. Blood spatters don't lie. And there was only a minute gap between his picture being captured on the video and him killing Debbie."

"There was a hole in the back of her jacket right where it would sit behind her neck," Decker said. "He probably hooked the jacket on her locker door. It could keep her upright for a short time. He slips around the corner, gets his image captured on the video, comes back around the corner, and shoots her. The blast would have knocked her down. That's when the jacket tore, when it was jerked off the locker door when she fell."

Decker shone his light around the room and picked up more shoeprints, including a set leading back into the storage room and then back down to the passage-way. There were also footprints in the shop class, belonging to Debbie Watson. She had worn clunky boots. They had been on her body. In the prints on the floor Decker could see a picture of activity forming. The two sets of footprints had gotten very close together. Probably when they had been kissing. She had been anticipating sex with the man she called Jesus, and instead she'd been thrown right into an early grave.

Decker leaned against the wall and rewound his DVR until he stopped at the point he wanted. "Did you notice something else down in the passageway, Mary?"

"Something else? Like what?"

He opened his eyes. "There were two sets of shoe-prints going up the stairs to the storage room off the shop class."

"Right."

"And there was a set coming back down the stairs."

"Right, again. So?"

"And while there were scuffed prints all over the place showing that he had used this passage before, there were no clear sets of shoeprints going back down the passage to the cafeteria to match the two sets coming from the front of the school to the back."

Lancaster's eyes widened. "Damn, that's right. So how did our guy escape from the school?"

"Now, that's a really good question."

29

While Lancaster hurried off to alert her colleagues to this new development, Decker slipped back down into the passageway and reached the bottom of the stairs.

So if the shooter hadn't gone back down this passage and escaped via the cafeteria or gone out the front or rear doors, where someone surely would have seen him, then where did he go? The school had been searched, including the unused upper floors, and nothing had been discovered. The police hadn't known about this passageway, of course, and thus it had not been searched. But the guy was not down here now. He had walked down the stairs from the shop class storage area and gone . . . where?

Decker hit the area all around the bottom of the stairs with his flashlight.

There were two blank walls on either side of the stairs. There was no dust here and thus the shoeprints had ended at the bottom of the stairs.

He looked at this spot again. But why was there no dust here when it was everywhere else? Had someone cleaned it away? If so, why? He could think of at least one reason.

It was something someone had said to him.

It had been a very recent statement.

Beth Watson.

She was packing up to leave her husband. Her husband's grandfather had told her about the passageway. But she also said something else that Simon had told her.

He didn't build it originally. He just added to it.

Decker stepped closer to the wall on the right and hit the surface from all angles with his light.

Nothing.

He did the same on the left.

Something.

A slight seam where the wall met the stairs. He dug his fingers into this gap and pulled. And the wall opened on hinges, smoothly and without noise, just like the fake wall back in the cafeteria. It had been recently used.

Decker was peering down a long, dark hall.

The air in here was stale and musty as well. But not overly so, which meant fresh air was getting in somehow, somewhere. He moved down the passage, his light hitting the dirty concrete floor. There were the shoeprints, again size nine or so. He took pictures of them with his cell phone camera.

He stopped when he saw the door. Leaning next to this door and against the wall were sections of plywood with bent nails protruding from them. Like back in the cafeteria. They had been used to seal off this end of the passage, but someone had unsealed it.

The shooter.

He pulled his gun, touched the wood of the door, and eased it open. He shone his light ahead. He could hear water dripping, the scurry of what he assumed were rats, and the beating of his own heart.

Decker was a brave man, because you did not go into his line of work without being braver than average. But he was also scared, because you did not go into his line of work, or at least survive very long in it, without a commonsensical understanding of your own mortality.

He moved ahead. The floor sloped upward after a hundred feet. Then he reached a set of steps. He took them up, trying to keep as quiet as possible. There was another door at the top. It was locked. He tried his lock pick. It didn't work.

He tried his shoulder with over three hundred and fifty pounds of bulk behind it.

That *did* work.

He came out into semidarkness and looked around. The room he was in was large, with windows set up high. There was the smell of grease and oil, and as he looked around he saw the skeletons of vehicles scattered here and there.

They were old abandoned Army vehicles. Because he was now standing in one of the buildings of the long-closed McDonald Army Base.

A passage connecting a school with an Army base?

But the more he thought about it, the more it made sense. Lots of kids who went to Mansfield back then had parents who worked at the base. In the event of an emergency, what better place for the kids than either in the "bombproof" shelter underneath the school or at the base with their parents? Or maybe the underground shelter was designed to hold both base personnel *and* the school kids. Whatever the truth, it was also a fact that it had long since been forgotten about. And it was probably never even used.

But he corrected himself. It had been used recently, so it was not forgotten.

The shooter had exited this way; of that he was now certain. The base was a large place to search, and it had been abandoned for years. No witnesses to see anything. Everything was in disrepair and only a chain-link fence overgrown with vines and bushes and trees around the perimeter. Easy to make one's escape completely unseen.

As Decker shone his light around he could see discarded beer cans and liquor bottles, empty condom packs, and cigarette butts littering the floor. The place was a forensic nightmare. There were probably hundreds of DNA samples down there, most of them from bored teens looking for sex, booze, nicotine—his light hit on a discarded syringe and a rubber hose to pop blood vessels—or something stronger.

But he doubted any of them knew that there was a

passage connecting the base to the school. Even if they had explored the place, they would have encountered a locked door. If they had managed to get through that, they would run into a blank wall. End of exploring. And this would be a summer hangout place. Now that it was nearing winter, the unheated space was freezing. Their shooter would not have needed to worry about running into teenagers screwing and boozing here while he planned his massacre.

He walked around the place and found nothing and no one.

He pulled his phone and called the Watsons' house. George answered. Decker wondered if Beth was already gone for good.

"Hello, who is this?" Watson wasn't slurring his words. Maybe he'd slept it off.

"Mr. Watson, Detective Decker again."

"What do you want?" he asked, clearly annoyed.

"Just a quick question. Had Debbie been spending a lot of time after hours at school, or maybe in the morning before classes started?"

"How the hell did you know that? How the hell do you know so much about my family?"

"Just a guess. But I am a detective. It's what I do. And your wife mentioned that she was home a lot more than Debbie. So I assumed she was doing something after school. So what exactly was she doing?"

"She belonged to some clubs. They had meetings.

Sometimes they ran late. She wouldn't get home until well past dark. Why, is that important?"

"It might be. Thanks."

Decker clicked off. He knew Debbie Watson was not going to club meetings. She was hooking up with "Jesus" in their private space.

He next called Lancaster and told her what he'd found.

He put his phone away, sat down on an oil drum, and waited with his eyes closed. He figured he would not have to wait long. He had left the door in the wall open.

He heard the footsteps coming. One would have made him open his eyes. This was about a dozen. So he kept his eyes closed. A killer came alone, not with an army.

He opened his eyes and saw Special Agent Bogart standing there.

"Another educated guess?" asked the man.

"Another educated guess," replied Decker.

Behind Bogart was a group of FBI agents and members of the Burlington Police Department. Lancaster stepped forward.

"I called Mac, he's on his way," she reported, and Decker nodded slowly.

"How did you figure this?" Bogart asked Decker.

Decker gave him the two-minute drill on his deductions.

"If you had briefed us on your meeting with Beth Watson, we might have been able to help you on this,"

Bogart pointed out. "We might have gotten here sooner."

"We might have," agreed Decker.

Bogart ordered a search of the place and the perimeter and then pulled up an old wooden bench and sat down next to Decker while Lancaster hovered nearby.

"So the shooter befriended Debbie Watson, found out about this link with the school, and used it to get away?" said Bogart.

"He used it to both get in *and* get away. With the passage he could come and go as he pleased. He seduced her. He's a grown man. She's an impressionable teenager with not the best of home lives. They must've had a bunch of trysts here that no one else knew about. She must have felt really special. Right up until he discharged a shotgun in her face."

"We'll contact the Army and get all we can on the base."

"Yeah. Good luck with that."

"I'm surprised no one knew about this passage," said Bogart. "Other than the Watsons."

"Well, if it was originally built in 1946 or close to it, most of those folks would be dead. I doubt they would have told the kids about it, so only the school officials would have known. Maybe it was never used. Maybe they never even had a practice drill. I don't know. Even if they did, the students from back then would be fairly elderly now. Maybe they forgot about it."

"But you said Simon Watson had *added* to the passageway?"

"He came to McDonald in the late sixties, and sometime after that the passage from the base was put in. But when the base was closed everybody left. Lots of people who worked here in uniform were probably transferred to other places."

Lancaster interjected, "And even if there were folks left here who knew about the passage, I doubt they'd think about a killer using it to move around the school. They'd assume it was sealed up after all this time. The public probably believes he shot up the place and made a run for it and got away."

Bogart nodded. "But he could have gotten into the school more easily from this way, meaning the Army base end. But he apparently was in the cafeteria and traversed the school that way. Why?"

"I don't know," said Decker. "We thought it might be to allow him time to cut through the wall sealing off the door behind the sign in the cafeteria. But now since I believe he's been in and out of here a lot, he could have done that any time. And he probably wouldn't have waited until the night before the planned attack, in case something went wrong." He paused. "So, bottom line, I don't know."

"I thought you had all the answers."

"Then you thought wrong."

Bogart considered him thoughtfully. "You really don't forget anything, do you?" Decker didn't look at him. Bogart drew closer and said in a low voice that only Decker could hear, "What makes you tick, Decker? What do you have up in your head that allows you to do what you do?"

Decker didn't acknowledge that he had heard the comment.

"You always tune out like this when someone is trying to have a conversation?" Bogart asked.

"My social skills aren't the best," said Decker. "I told you that already."

"But you can walk and chew gum at the same time. So if you have some special mental ability, it hasn't affected your capacity to function out in the world."

Now Decker looked at him. "Why do you say that?"

Bogart said, "My older brother has a form of autism. Brilliant in his field. Positively clueless in interacting with another human being. He can't carry on a conversation beyond a few mumbled words. And he's actually considered high-functioning because he can work at a job."

"What's his field?"

"Physics. Subatomic particles more specifically. He can expound all day about quarks, leptons, and gauge bosons. But he forgets to eat and has no idea how to book a plane ticket or pay the electric bill."

Decker nodded. "I get that."

"You seem to do okay, though."

"It's all degrees, Special Agent Bogart."

"You been this way since birth?"

"Later," Decker said tersely. "Which might be why I can walk and chew gum at the same time," he added in a tight voice before looking away.

Bogart nodded. "You don't want to talk about this, do you?"

"Would you?"

Bogart rubbed his hands along his thighs. "We need to get this guy. And we have one thing that we haven't really broached yet."

Decker looked at him. "His *thing* with me."

Bogart nodded. "He's sent you two messages. One coded, one not. That was a risk for him. He had to go back to the house where he committed the murders of your family to write one of the messages. Someone could have seen him. And he went to Debbie's house. Again, with the risk of being seen. Now, anyone who kills is a risk-taker, by definition. But like you said, it's a matter of degrees. A killer like this may not want to be caught. So he will minimize his risk. But that was outweighed by his desire to communicate with you. That's important. Because it makes me believe that he feels he has a connection with you somehow that is very strong, very deep."

Decker fixed his gaze on the other man. "You were at Quantico? BAU?"

"Behavioral Analysis Unit, yes. I was what the movie and TV folks would call a profiler. And I was pretty good at it."

"There are no profilers in the FBI."

"You're right. Technically, we're referred to as analysts. And sometimes we're right and sometimes we're wrong. Some say psychological profiling lacks empirical validation, and they may be right. But I don't really care. All I care about is catching the bad guys before they can hurt someone else, and I'll use whatever tools I have at my disposal to do so." He peered more closely at Decker. "And I'm considering you to be one of those tools."

"Meaning what exactly?"

"Meaning that I'd like you to work more closely with us. Together we may be able to make headway."

Decker looked over at Lancaster, who had clearly heard this last exchange.

Decker rose. "I've already got a partner. But we break anything we'll let you know."

He walked off. Lancaster waited for a moment, flicked Bogart a tight smile, and scurried after Decker.

Special Agent Bogart remained sitting, staring after them both.

30

Decker opened his eyes. He was lying in bed, but sleep was elusive. It was raining outside his room at the Residence Inn. This time of year—as fall hunkered down before giving way fully to winter—was always loaded with rain, usually with strong winds that beat the moisture right into your brain.

A size nine shoe. They had confirmed the size. On a guy six-two, two hundred or more pounds, with shoulders as wide as his. He closed his eyes and his mind whirred back to the image on the camera. But it only showed the man from the waist up. Decker was now sure that was intentional. Waist up. He had also walked in front of the camera in a way that was designed to hide how he had actually come into the school. Not from the rear doors, but from the cafeteria via an underground passage.

Yet Decker *had* seen something that didn't make sense; he just wasn't sure what or where. He never forgot anything, but that didn't mean everything was always placed in the proper context opposite either a complementary or conflicting fact.

He was just starting to do that when he heard the noise outside his door.

The Residence Inn was set up so that each room opened directly to the outdoors. Decker was on the second story. A catwalk with a wrought iron railing formed the exterior of this floor, with stairs down at each end to the parking lot.

The noise came again. A scraping, it seemed, against the wall outside his door. The rooms on either side of his were empty. The first floor of the inn was mostly full. He sat up in bed and looked at the door. He reached out and his fingers closed around his gun, which he kept on the nightstand.

He chambered a round, moving the slide slowly so the sound of it moving back and forth was diminished. He threw off the covers, pulled on his pants, slipped his phone into his pocket, and skittered over to the door in his bare feet.

He stood to the right of the door, his gun held down with both hands. He listened. There it was again. The scrape.

Something was out there. Maybe *someone* was out there.

He would do this as he had many busts as a cop. Except in reverse. Going out the door instead of in. He slipped off the security chain, stood to the side, gripped the knob, counted to three in his head, and threw the door open. He catapulted through the opening, swinging his gun first left then right.

He stopped and stared up at her. She had been hung on the bracket supporting the exterior light. Her feet hitting against the side of the wall were the source of the scraping he'd heard.

He checked her pulse at the carotid, but did so only mechanically. She was dead, her eyes open, glassed over and fixed in a way the living could never achieve.

FBI Special Agent Lafferty had written down her last note.

He looked over her body but could find no obvious signs of how she had died.

Then he turned and ran down the catwalk, reached the stairs, and hurtled down them. She couldn't have been up there long. Whoever had done it might still be around. He pulled his phone and dialed 911. He told the dispatcher everything she needed to know in three succinct sentences. Then he called Lancaster. She answered on the fourth ring. It was three in the morning. She had no doubt been asleep. After his first sentence she was wide awake. After his second he could hear her fumbling for her clothes. He put his phone away and sprinted around the parking lot in front of the Residence Inn. He was looking and listening. Any vehicles starting up. Any feet running away.

He heard neither, only his own tortured breath. He stopped and bent over, trying to refill his lungs. He felt himself shaking, his stomach churning. When he looked up he saw them. The army of threes was charging him, knives raised, ready to kill. He knew they were not real, but this night the terror seized him, like it had the first time he had seen them.

He bent farther over and threw up on the asphalt, the sick splashing onto his bare and now frozen feet.

When he straightened he heard the first siren, and the army of threes seemed to dissolve with the sound. A minute later the first siren was joined by another. He walked unsteadily back up the steps to his room. He leaned against the catwalk railing facing Lafferty's body. He wanted to close her eyes, lift her off the bracket and set her gently down on the concrete with her hands folded across her stomach. Peaceful. As if he could ever make violent death so. He certainly couldn't do it for his family.

But he could do none of those things without corrupting the crime scene. So he just stood there. When the patrol cars lurched to a stop in the parking lot he slipped into his room and put his gun back in the nightstand. By the time he got back outside the officers had sprinted up the steps and come to a stop a few feet away.

Decker held up his lanyard. He didn't recognize either patrolman and didn't want them to think the wrong thing.

"Amos Decker. I'm the one who called it in. Detective Lancaster is on her way."

The cops had their guns drawn and were scrutinizing him closely. One drew near to him and checked out his lanyard.

He said to his buddy, "I saw him at the school with the detectives yesterday. It's okay."

The cops holstered their weapons and stared up at the dead Lafferty.

"She's FBI Special Agent Lafferty," said Decker. "You might have seen her at the school too."

Both cops shook their heads, but the first one said, "Shit, a Fed? How'd she die?"

"I don't know. Nothing obvious that you can see."

"Okay."

Decker stepped back from the body. "Not telling you anything you don't know, but I was a cop for twenty years. You should go ahead and secure the crime scene and call in the forensics team and the ME. I'm sure Detective Lancaster will also alert the proper people, but it's a Fed like you said, and you need to follow the book tight on this one."

The first cop said, "Good advice. I'll phone it in."

The other cop said, "I'll get the perimeter tape."

Decker pointed to the open door. "This is my room. I heard a noise and came outside to check. That's when I saw her. I went down to the parking lot. But I saw no one. Didn't hear a vehicle either. Or anyone running away. And the puke down in the parking lot belongs to me. I'm not used to running that fast or far anymore."

"Okay, Mr. Decker. I'd like you to go inside your room. I'm sure Detective Lancaster will see you when she gets here." He stared up at the body and suddenly looked uncertain. "We're sure she's dead?"

"No pulse. I checked. And she's already cold. Been dead a while."

Decker went inside his room, closed the door, went to the bathroom, washed his face and his feet, put on his shoes, sat on his bed, and waited.

He knew where Lancaster lived. He figured thirty minutes or so tops. Ten minutes later he heard activity start up outside his door.

Eighteen minutes after that there was a knock on his door. He opened it and there she was.

He looked past her. The body was on the concrete on top of a sheet designed to collect any and all trace evidence. A tech team was swarming the small area, taking pictures and measurements and looking for evidence in all the obvious places.

The ME, a small, bearded man in his sixties, was kneeling next to Lafferty. After doing his TOD test he looked up at Lancaster.

"She's been dead about three hours."

Decker said, "Puts her death at about half past midnight."

"Cause of death?" asked Lancaster.

The ME lifted up her blouse. Underneath was a single stab wound.

"Up and in," he said. "Right to the heart. Dead almost immediately. She obviously bled out somewhere else. But there wouldn't have been much external bleeding. The knife pierced the heart. It would have stopped pumping."

Something occurred to Decker. He said, "Did you check her genital area? Anything there?" Lancaster gave him a sharp glance and then looked at the ME.

The look on the ME's face gave Decker the answer. He showed them the spot. "The killer used a very rough knife to do the mutilation."

Lancaster looked at Decker. "Like before. With . . ."

Decker said, "Yeah. Like before."

Three black SUVs pulled into the parking lot.

"Here come the Feds," said Lancaster nervously. "I called them on the way over."

Bogart headed the pack, taking the steps two at a time. His hair was disheveled and he was dressed in jeans and a pullover with canvas boaters on his feet and no socks. The men behind him were similarly dressed but wore their blue FBI windbreakers.

Bogart walked directly over to the body and looked down. Then he rubbed his eyes, then his chin, and looked away, over the railing at the darkness beyond.

Decker heard him mutter, "Shit."

Then the FBI agent turned to them. "What do we know so far?"

Lancaster told him the time and cause of death. And also about the mutilation the ME had discovered.

"You see or hear anything?" asked an ashen-faced Bogart as he looked at Decker.

Decker told him what he knew. He added, "I was half-asleep. The scraping noise could have been going on for a while before I heard it."

Lancaster said, "Do you know her movements this evening?"

Bogart didn't seem to hear her.

Decker added, "If we can pinpoint her movements we might be able to get a lead on whoever did this."

"I know that!" snapped Bogart.

Lancaster said, "We know this is extremely difficult, Agent Bogart—"

Decker cut her off. "But you know better than most that the sooner we get a lead the better our chances are. And the reverse is also true."

Bogart glanced once more at Lafferty and motioned them down the stairs.

They climbed into one of the black SUVs, Bogart in front and Lancaster and Decker in the back. Bogart drank down a small bottle of water that was sitting in the front console, wiped his mouth with his hand, and turned to look at them.

"Lafferty was a good agent. A protégée of mine, in fact. Not just a note taker," he added with a sharp glance at Decker, who said nothing in reply.

Bogart sat back, let out a long breath, and said, "I've never lost an agent. It's difficult to process."

"I'm sure," said Lancaster.

"But her whereabouts?" said Decker. "Were you all staying at the same place?"

"Yes. The Century Hotel."

"Were you all on the same floor?"

"No, we were spread over three separate floors. But Lafferty was next door to another agent."

"When was the last time anyone saw her?" asked Lancaster.

"I asked everyone that on the way over. It looks like nine-thirty. She was working in Agent Darrow's room going over some files. She said good night and went back to her room."

"But do we know that she actually went to her room?" asked Decker.

"As a matter of fact she mentioned to Darrow that she was running out for some things she needed."

"Did she say what and where?"

"From what she said, he thought it might be stuff at a pharmacy. I don't think it was the first time she'd done it. We were called out on this pretty fast. Agents don't have a lot of time to prepare."

"So she'd gone to get things before?" said Lancaster. "Maybe from the same place?"

"Right. Just travel stuff, probably," said Bogart, staring out the window, his mind evidently a long way away.

Decker sat back, closed his eyes, and thought for a moment. "There's an all-night pharmacy two blocks over from the Century. That's where I would go to pick up stuff I'd need while traveling. And it has video cameras in the parking lot."

"Well, let's go see if it shows anything," said Bogart.

The drive only took about twenty minutes at that

time of the morning and with Bogart exceeding all posted speed limits. It was not yet 4 a.m. and thus Burlington was still very much asleep. Traffic was scant, pedestrians nonexistent.

There were two people in the open-all-night pharmacy. One was behind bulletproof glass with the cash register, the other was stocking deodorant on a shelf. Both had been on duty since 8 p.m. Bogart showed the photograph of Lafferty and asked if either employee had seen her.

"I haven't seen her tonight. But she came in the night before."

Decker said, "Which means she might not have made it here."

They asked for and were given the DVD from the surveillance cameras for the parking lot.

"She would have walked here," said Decker. "It's too close to drive."

"And none of our vehicles are missing," said Bogart.

They loaded the DVD into a laptop Bogart had in the SUV. There was a time stamp on the feed and Bogart fast-forwarded to right before 9:30. The frames ran as they all huddled around the screen watching intently. When they got to 9:58, Decker saw it.

"That's her."

Lafferty had emerged from an alley next to the pharmacy. She had taken two steps when she was abruptly pulled back into the alley.

"Run it again and slow it down," said Decker.

Bogart did so, playing through the scene five more times and enlarging the images as much as he could on the small screen.

Decker stared at the screen intently, every pixel being memorized and placed in his head. "Can't see who it is."

"We can try to enlarge the shots," said Bogart. "My guys can work wonders."

"He knew the camera was there," said Decker. "Just like at the school. He didn't want to be seen. At least certain parts of him."

"How did he overpower her so quickly?" said Bogart. "Lafferty was no weakling."

Decker said, "There was a gloved hand at her throat. There might have been something in it. She seemed to go stiff pretty quickly. I think he injected her with a paralytic."

"Blood test on her body will confirm that," said Lancaster.

"So nine-fifty-eight she was taken," said Decker.

"But her TOD was around midnight," noted Lancaster.

"Which means they had her for two hours before they killed her," completed Decker.

Bogart looked strained. "You said she was mutilated. Do you think they did anything else to her?"

Decker shook his head. "My wife was not raped. But she was mutilated. In that same . . . area," he added.

"So what is this about?" asked Bogart. "Why do that? It makes no sense."

"When I asked Leopold if he'd done anything else to my wife he didn't answer. Now, the mutilation was never made public. He could only know about it if he was there, which we know he wasn't. But someone who was there could have told him about it. But since he didn't answer, I don't know if he didn't know or just didn't want to tell me. Either way, he's still a suspect."

Bogart rubbed his face. "What else?"

"They had her for two hours. Probably some of that time she was conscious before they killed her."

"What would they do to her?" asked Lancaster.

"Try to find out in which direction the investigation is going," said Bogart.

Decker nodded at this. "They would want to know what we know. If we'd gotten to certain points or not."

"Well, Lafferty would tell them nothing," Bogart said sharply.

"No one is invulnerable to interrogation, depending on the tactics they use," said Decker. "She may have talked, against her will. Regardless, to be safe, we should assume they now know what we know. Principally, that we found the underground passage."

Bogart looked at the frozen screen, at the hand around his colleague's neck. "But how could she not know the guy was following her?" he said. "He must have been right behind her."

Lancaster said, "He could have been hiding in the alley."

Bogart shook his head. "What, waiting for her to come along? How would he even know she was going to the pharmacy?"

"He could have been waiting and watching and followed her when she came out. She'd been to the pharmacy before at least once. Maybe they knew this somehow and saw an opportunity if she went there again. And she could have known he was there but for some reason didn't feel threatened," added Decker.

"Not feel threatened?" exclaimed Bogart. "A dark alley? A murderer running around? How would she *not* be on her guard?"

"She might not feel threatened if it was someone she had no reason to suspect," elaborated Decker.

Bogart's face turned crimson and his features ugly. "Are you accusing me or one of my men of her murder?" he snapped. "Because she doesn't know anyone else in this shithole!"

"Not my point really," said Decker calmly.

Bogart pointed a finger in Decker's face. "She was left at your doorstep. Maybe you killed her, you son of a bitch!"

Decker's face remained impassive and his words slow and deliberate. "And left her on my doorstep to incriminate myself? And then called the cops while I just sat there? If I really did something that stupid I could beat the rap on an insanity plea."

Bogart looked like he wanted to punch Decker, but then he mastered his emotions and looked away.

Lancaster said, "Amos, do you mean someone in uniform? A cop? She wouldn't suspect someone like that?"

"Yes," said Decker. "That's exactly what I meant."

Bogart glanced at him sharply and nodded. "Right. Sorry I jumped down your throat." He paused and then declared, "Okay, we're going to tear that damn alley apart." He got on the phone and called in his team. Then he turned to Decker. "We need to work on this *together*. We have got to stop this guy."

Decker shook his head. "Not guy. *Guys*."

"What makes you say that?" asked a startled Lancaster as Bogart stared at him. "The shooter appears to be a loner. You said that."

"And I was wrong," Decker said decisively.

"But what specifically makes you think there could be more than one man involved?" asked Bogart.

"Because no one can be in two places at the same time."

31

Sunrise.

The clouds had gone and with them the rain. So it was a true sunrise, where the colors changed at first subtly and then suddenly transformed the heavens in a way that no other occurrence could. Short of a nuclear bomb and its towering mushroom cloud.

Yet *both* were transformative in their own right. One side of the world was lit, the other enveloped in blackness. The bomb's kiss was for real. The sun's movement was a metaphor for either darkness descending or light arising.

Decker stood there on the pavement and watched this all take place. Despite the coming light his mood remained trapped in the deepest darkness. He had not gone back to sleep after leaving Bogart and Lancaster. There would have been no point.

The 7-Eleven faced him across the width of the asphalt. It was open. It was always open. Through the glass he could see the same woman counting packs of smokes. But a different punk was mopping the floors. Perhaps "Billy" had moved on to another bucket in another town. Or maybe he was recovering from a night out with the ladies.

He didn't know why he had come here after leaving Lancaster and Bogart. But this place kept drawing him back like metal to a magnet.

He stepped through the door, and when the little bell tinkled it felt like a drill bit boring right through his skull.

"Are you all right?"

Decker refocused and found the woman's gaze on him. She looked a bit frightened, and when he caught his reflection in the mirrored door of a chiller cabinet containing soda he could understand why. He looked wild and demented and his clothes were dirty and his hair disheveled.

"You . . . you were in here the other day," she said. "Looking for someone."

Decker nodded and looked around. "Where's Billy? The floor mopper?"

"Today he comes to work in the afternoon. Did you find the man you were looking for?"

Decker shook his head. "But I'll keep looking."

"You look like you could use some coffee. It's fresh. I just made it. In the back there. Only one dollar for a large. It's a good deal. Maybe some food?"

The doorbell tinkled again and two men in dungarees, work boots, and flannel shirts stomped in. One went to the counter for some cigarettes. The other went to the soda fountain and proceeded to fill a giant cup with Coke.

While the woman attended her new customer, Decker drifted to the back of the store, got his coffee, hooked a packaged pastry from a shelf, and went up to the counter. He waited behind the guy ordering smokes, who also wanted lottery tickets with particular numbers. As Decker waited his gaze flicked absently to the newspaper stand next to the counter. The paper lay flat on it, the upper fold of the front page fully exposed. He nearly dropped his coffee and pastry. He set them down, snatched up the paper, and commenced reading.

He unconsciously started to walk out of the store as he did so.

The woman called after him, "Hey, you need to pay for this." She indicated the coffee and pastry. "And the paper."

Decker stuck a hand into his pocket, pulled out a five and dropped it on the counter, and walked out, leaving the coffee and pastry behind. The woman and the two men stared after him.

He stumbled across the street and perched on the edge of a trash can under a flickering streetlight.

The story was long, detailed, and had a picture.

My picture. My story. No, not my story. Someone's version of a story that holds far less truth than blatant speculation. And lies.

He glanced at the byline, though he needn't have bothered. He already knew who it was.

Alexandra Jamison.

He caught a bus to the Residence Inn, hustled to his room, sat on the bed, and read the story three more times. It didn't change, of course. But it beat into his head with a little more force each time, like a knife repeatedly stabbing flesh.

He fell back on the bed and finally slept for a bit. When he woke it was nearly nine in the morning.

He went to the bathroom, splashed water on his face, went down to the buffet, stuffed his plate with food, poured out three cups of black coffee, carried it all to his table, and then sat there staring down at it.

The sun was well up now and light flooded through the front plate glass windows. The illumination seemed to broadcast him in stark relief, like he was an actor performing onstage under the withering heat blast of a spotlight.

He waited, staring at the food. Then his gaze drifted to the newspaper he had set beside his plate.

His phone buzzed. He looked at it, hit the answer button.

Lancaster said, "Shit, Amos, what the hell did you do?"

"Nothing. Apparently that's the problem."

"Anybody reading this story will come away thinking you hired Sebastian Leopold to kill your family."

"That's what I thought, even though I know better."

"Why is she after you?"

"Because I wouldn't talk to her."

"So you left her no option but to make shit up?"

"I *did* meet with Leopold."

"You mean in his cell."

"Afterward."

"What?"

"I followed him after he was released. It's the picture that's in the article. We were at a bar."

"Why in the hell did you follow him?"

"Because I wanted to talk to him. I wanted to understand why he had told the cops and me that he had murdered my family when he couldn't possibly have."

"And did he tell you?'

"No. He disappeared."

"You mean you lost him?"

"I mean he got in a car and disappeared."

"You saw this?"

"No, but it's the only possibility."

He heard her let out a long sigh. He had often heard Lancaster let out long sighs, usually after Decker had done something totally off the wall, even if it had eventually led to the truth in a case they were investigating.

"Amos, I really don't get you sometimes."

He had heard this so many times he knew that she did not expect an answer and thus he didn't bother giving one.

"So Leopold is gone?"

"For now," he said.

"People are going to eat you alive over this article.

And the witch even included the fact of where you're currently living."

"I have an ace in the hole."

"What's that?" she said curiously.

"I don't give a shit."

"Amos, I don't think you understand—"

"I have to go." He hung up on her and put his phone on the table next to the uneaten mound of food. As he stared down at the pile of eggs, sausages, bacon, and roasted potatoes, he saw not food, but the photo of him and Leopold in the bar. He knew it must seem odd to folks that he would be sitting and drinking a beer with the man who had confessed and then recanted to killing his family. But if he was going to solve those murders, he had to go down any path that presented itself. And Leopold was one such path.

He sighed, pushed his plate away, and looked up. June was standing off to the side holding a pan of muffins. She wasn't looking at Decker. She was looking toward the doorway.

Decker followed her gaze. And saw her.

Alex Jamison stood at the door to the breakfast area. She had on black slacks and a frayed black overcoat out of which peeked a turquoise turtleneck. Her hair was pulled back in a ponytail, and she had on heels that kicked her height up several inches.

She walked over to his table and looked down at the paper next to his plate.

"I guess you've read it," she said quietly.

Decker said nothing. He picked up his fork, pulled his plate toward him, and started to eat.

She stood awkwardly next to his table. When he didn't say anything she said, "I gave you an opportunity to talk to me."

Decker kept eating.

She sat down across from him. "It's not like I wanted to do this."

He put his fork down, used a paper napkin to wipe his mouth, and looked at her. "I find that people almost always do exactly what they want to do."

She tapped the paper. "You still have a chance to make it right."

"People who make things right do so because they've done something wrong. I've done nothing wrong."

"You were meeting with a man who allegedly killed your family."

"Allegedly. And now all charges are dropped, which you knew before you wrote this story. And which I knew before I met him in the bar."

"Why did you meet with him?"

"I had questions for him."

"What sorts?" She took out her recorder, pad, and pen, but Decker held up his hand.

"Don't bother."

She sat back. "Don't you want your story to get out?"

Decker shoved the plate of food away, leaned across the table, and said, "I don't have a story to tell." He sat back, pulled the plate toward him again, and resumed eating.

"Okay, fair enough. But do you think Leopold had a hand in the murders? Even if he didn't commit them personally? And then there's the fact that the same gun was used at the high school."

Decker eyed her grimly. "Brimmer could get fired for that one. It's not public knowledge. And you know it's not, or else you would have already written about it. I could call her out on that. You want to see your contact lose her career? Or is that just considered fair game for the story?"

"You're a very unusual man."

"I have no context with which to frame a reply to that observation."

"Sort of proves my point, doesn't it?"

Now Decker sat back and looked at her. "Tell me about yourself," he said abruptly.

"What, why?" she said warily.

"I can find out easily enough. Everyone's life is online. So, to borrow your phrase, I'm giving you the opportunity to tell *your* story."

"Is this where I'm supposed to say, 'Touché'?"

"You have something to hide?"

"Do you?"

"No. But you know all about me." He tapped the paper next to his plate. "Proof is right there. So tell me about yourself."

"What do you want to know?"

"Hometown, family, education, career, life goals."

"Wow, you don't ask for much."

Decker waited. He had no problem with silence, with waiting. His patience, like his mind, had no bounds.

She folded her arms across her chest and said, "I'm from Indiana, Bloomington. I went to Purdue, graduated with a degree in mass comm. Started out at some small papers in the Midwest basically fetching coffee, writing the crap stories no one else wanted to write, and pulling the shifts no one wanted to pull. I tried some online journalism and blogging but hated it."

"Why?"

"I like to talk to people, face-to-face, not through a machine. That's not real journalism. It's data management fed to you by schmucks you don't even know. It's reporting for lazy people who live in their PJs. Not what I wanted. I want a Pulitzer. In fact, I want a shelf of them."

"Then you came here. Why? Burlington is not a rip-roaring metropolis."

"It's bigger than any other town I was in before. It's got crime, interesting politics. Cost of living is low, which is important, because when you add up my hours worked I don't even make minimum wage. And they let me work my own beat and follow up my own stories."

"Family?"

"Large. All back in Bloomington."

"And the other reason you came here?"

"There is no other reason."

He pointed to a finger on her left hand. "There were two rings there. The marks are slight but distinct. Engagement and wedding rings. No longer there."

"So I'm divorced. Big whoop. So are half the people in this country."

"Fresh start away from your ex?"

She rubbed at the spot on her hand. "Something like that. Okay, are we done with me?"

"Do you want to be done?"

"You understand that you're not actually playing me, right? I'm just feeling generous, sort of going along for the ride, seeing where we end up."

"You follow up your own stories, you say?"

"I do."

"Do you intend to try to trace a connection between the killings of my family and the shootings at Mansfield?"

"Of course."

"What do your friends call you?"

"You're assuming I have friends?"

"What does Brimmer call you?"

"Alex."

"Okay, *Alexandra*, let me be as clear about this as I possibly can be."

She did an eye roll and looked at him disdainfully. "Do I sense a patronizing lecture coming?"

"Would you like a scoop?"

Her expression changed. She picked up her recorder. "Is this on the record?"

"So long as your source is anonymous."

"You have my word."

"Do you normally give it that quickly?"

"You have my word," she said tightly.

"An FBI agent was killed last night and her body was left hanging just above our heads on the catwalk up there. She was a skilled, armed federal agent who really can take care of herself. Now she's a murder victim who was dispatched as easily as someone crushing a bug underfoot." He slid the plate out of the way again, reached over, and clicked off her recorder.

She made no move to stop him.

"I've seen a lot in my twenty years on the force, but I have never seen—" He stopped, grappling for the right words. "I have never seen *menace* like this. But it's not just that. It's—" Again he stopped, tapping his fingers on the table and closing his eyes. When he opened them he said, "*Menace* coupled with brains and cunning. It's a very dangerous combination, Alexandra. And I asked about your family only because I wanted to know if you would have anyone to mourn you when you're murdered too. Because please make no mistake, he will kill you as easily as exhaling smoke from a cigarette."

"Look, if you're trying to—"

Decker didn't let her finish. "He could be watching us right now for all I know, and sizing up where and how exactly he plans to take your life. It seems that he likes to screw with me that way. Kill people I'm close to or associated with. You wrote a big story on me. That ties you and me together in just the way this guy seems to love. And I have no doubt he plans to keep killing until he gets down to his last planned victim."

Jamison no longer looked disdainful. She looked frightened, though trying hard not to show it.

"And who would that be?" She tried to say this flippantly but her voice cracked halfway through.

"That would be me."

32

Alexandra scooped up her recorder, pad, and pen and put them back into her bag and rose. She wouldn't look at Decker.

"Okay, if it makes you feel better, you have officially scared the shit out of me," she said.

"Did you see Leopold leave the bar?"

"What?"

He tapped the newspaper. "The bar where this picture was taken?"

Now she looked at him, her features wary. "I'm not going to answer that."

"You just did. Okay, I have one more question for you."

"What?"

He held up the newspaper. "Where did you get this photo of me and Leopold at the bar? There's no attribution for the photographer. I know the profession is a stickler for that, so I'm wondering why there's no name there."

"I took it."

"No you didn't."

"How do you know that?"

"I'm pretty observant. And I happen to *know* you weren't in the bar. Whoever did take the picture was watching Leopold and me. Which means he followed us both there though I was following Leopold too." He paused. "I wouldn't be asking if it weren't important. How did you get the photo?"

"I got it from an anonymous source," she finally admitted.

"And did this anonymous source also supply you with elements of the story you wrote?"

"I really can't get into that."

"If you don't know the name of the source, you don't have to worry about protecting his identity." Decker let the paper fall to the table. "Did it come by email, text? Surely not snail mail. You wouldn't have had time to write the story."

"Email."

"Can you send me the email trail?"

"Why is this so important to you?"

"Because the person who sent you the email is also the person who killed all those people."

"You can't possibly know that."

"I know it absolutely. And I would assume that the email said that you should write this story because things smelled bad on this. That here I was meeting with the man accused of killing my family. There must be more to it, right?"

As he had spoken, Jamison's eyes had continued to widen. "Did you send the email to me?" she hissed.

"You mean so I could see a story plastered in the newspaper basically accusing me of conspiring to murder my own family?"

She bit her lip. "I'm sorry, that was stupid." She swallowed with difficulty. "Do you really think it was him?"

"He was there. He was within ten feet of me and I never saw him. And I'm just not sure how that's possible."

"You said he was cunning."

Decker nodded. "He is. He obviously wants to destroy me professionally before he kills me."

"Can I ask *you* a question?"

Decker looked up at her. "Go ahead."

"Who the hell did you piss off so badly that he's doing all this to you?"

Decker didn't answer, because he had no answer to give. He wrote down his email address on the back of a napkin and slid it across to her.

Jamison pocketed it, turned, and left.

Decker continued to sit there.

A few moments later his phone buzzed. He looked at the screen and allowed himself a brief smile.

Jamison had just forwarded to him the email trail from her anonymous source. Decker knew that the trail would not lead them back to the sender. That was too obvious. But he wanted to study what the man had written.

He pushed his plate aside and stared down at the message. The sender's name was Mallard2000. That meant nothing to him. He read the message. It basically mirrored what Decker had already deduced. The sender wanted Jamison to write a story raising suspicion about Decker and his family's murder. The word choices were simple and direct. In his mind Decker imagined Sebastian Leopold uttering each of those words out loud, trying to match the cadence of his stilted speech to the components of the message. But it was off, at least in his mind. They didn't seem to match.

There were two of them. In this together. One person can't be in two places at the same time. Leopold in jail during both sets of murders. So if he is involved, and I believe he is, there's someone else. Yet there is a problem with that theory.

One man with such a vendetta against him, okay. But *two* of them?

He forwarded the email to Lancaster and asked her to try to track it down. He doubted she or the FBI could, but they had to try. He had no computer, so he walked to the public library and used one there.

He was not very much of a techie, and his ability to track someone from an email address was limited. He soon exhausted his possibilities on that and got up from the computer. He wandered the shelves, arriving at the nonfiction section.

Something had occurred to him on the way over, and

a library was a perfect place to check out a theory forming in his mind.

The Clutter family.

He worked his way to the authors whose last name
ended in C. Not for Clutter, but for the author of their
tragic story.

He found the book and slipped it out.

In Cold Blood, by Truman Capote.

The story was both simple and complex. Decker had
read it years ago and, as with everything else, had every
page of the book neatly stored in his mind.

A guy in prison gets a tip from another inmate that a
farmer named Clutter in rural Kansas keeps a lot of
money in a safe. The guy gets out of prison, hooks up
with a former cellmate, and they head to the farmer's
home. They break into the house, only to find there is
no safe and no money; the tip was bullshit. It should
have ended there, but unfortunately for the Clutter
family, it didn't. The more timid, though unstable, of
the two crooks decides that they must kill the family.
His partner, who had been the leader of the pack and
the one who had gotten the tip, reluctantly goes along.
One by one the family is murdered. The killers are not
smart. They are pursued and caught. After their respective trials and lengthy appeals they are both hanged at
the Kansas death house.

Tragic all around. Both killers had issues in their
backgrounds, problems, troubles, bad stuff. But nothing

to justify what they had done, not that anything could.

That part of the story did not interest Decker very much at the moment. What did interest him was the possibility of two men from very different backgrounds coming together at just the right moment and forming a partnership that would lead to the slaughter of so many people. He didn't know Leopold. He had never met the man until he sat in that prison cell. So it wasn't Leopold who had the vendetta against him. It had to be the person whom Leopold had hooked up with. But who was he?

He put the book back on the shelf and left the library.

As he was walking his phone buzzed again. It was Lancaster.

"Nothing yet on the email," she said. "You really think it was the guy?"

"I do."

"The FBI is checking it out too."

"Anything on Lafferty yet?"

"That was the real reason I was calling. Can you meet me at the morgue?"

"Yes. Why?"

"Just meet me there. You can *see* for yourself."

Decker took a bus over to the morgue, which was on the outskirts of Burlington in an area that, like much of the city, had seen better days. He had pondered Lancaster's words on the ride over but could not make much of them. What did she want him to *see* for himself?

When he arrived at the morgue's front entrance she was waiting for him. Her expression was tight, edgy, her hand tremor even worse.

"What is it?" he asked.

"Come on, Bogart is already back there."

They walked down halls reeking with the smell of antiseptic. And death. The dead had their own aroma that invaded one's eyes, nose, and throat. Morgues were not clean places. In fact, they were extraordinarily dirty. No one had to worry about their patrons dying from infections.

Lancaster led the way and finally pushed through a pair of swinging doors. Decker followed her in. The space was large and filled with shelves and stainless steel autopsy tables, three of which were occupied by corpses draped with sheets. Water wands hung down from the ceiling, and there were cabinets filled with both bottles of liquids and the instruments necessary to cut up bodies. The whir of a Stryker saw sounded from another room. Decker had heard that one before. Someone's skull was being opened up. He wondered if it was a victim from Mansfield about to have his or her brain plucked out for measuring, weighing, and probing.

A group of people was clustered around a table in the far back, Bogart among them. He was once more dressed in a suit, the tie and tie clip just so, the collar tab perfectly horizontal, not a hair out of place, the very picture of professionalism. But in the puffy face, reddened eyes, and slump in posture, Decker read a very different man. There were two other agents with him and a man Decker knew to be the chief medical examiner. They weren't going to put anyone junior on cutting up an FBI agent. Indeed, Decker was surprised the Bureau hadn't flown in its own guy.

Bogart looked up when he heard them approach. He nodded briefly, gave Decker a stiff hello with his eyes, and then looked back down at the body under the sheet.

Lancaster said to the ME, "What do we know so far?"

"As was noted preliminarily at the crime scene, cause of death, stab wound to the heart. The body was moved after death. Livor mortis showed that. Blood pooled into the interstitial tissues in her back, but she was found hanging from a light fixture." He uncovered one of Lafferty's arms. With difficulty he lifted it up because it was still stiff. "She's starting to come out of rigor now, extremities backward to the jaw and neck, which more or less confirms the TOD preliminary at midnight."

"But the ambient temp?" asked Decker. "It was cold."

"My colleague on site made allowances for that. And the deceased was injected with a very powerful sedative. We found traces of it. It would have rendered her unconscious and incapable of defending herself."

"And there was mutilation of the genitals," said Decker.

The ME nodded. But when he started to lower the sheet to reveal this area, Decker stopped him. "We've already seen it."

He looked at Lancaster expectantly. She in turn glanced at Bogart and said, "I haven't told him. Thought he should just see it for himself."

Bogart nodded and then looked at the other two agents, both burly men who looked like they wanted to kill someone, anyone. "Turn her over."

The ME pulled back the sheet, revealing the body of Special Agent Lafferty. Her skin was very pale in front. The ME had of course already cut her open; the Y-incision track sutures across her upper torso looked brutal, menacing, like twin zipper tracks cut into human flesh. Her facial skin drooped a bit because it had been sheared off in one large piece and then put back up. Her skull had been sawed open and her brain taken out before the procedure was reversed and everything was put back together.

When they turned her over the paleness was gone. Her skin there was red, almost burnt-looking from where the blood had pooled.

Decker was not focused on that.

He was looking at what was on her back.

He drew closer because the skin discoloration made it hard to see clearly.

But then he did see it.

Someone had cut something into Lafferty's back.

Someone had carved out words with the blade of a knife using her body as paper. There were two lines of writing, one directly below the other.

When will it end bro
You tell me

33

They all walked outside. Bogart looked at his men and said, "Give us a minute. I'll meet you at the vehicles." They left. Bogart turned to Lancaster. "I'd like a private word with your partner."

Lancaster glanced at Decker, who said, "I'll see you later, Mary."

"You sure?"

"He's sure," said Bogart sharply.

Lancaster stared at Bogart. "I'm sorry about Agent Lafferty."

"*Special* Agent Lafferty. Thanks."

She turned and walked off, glancing back over her shoulder once before she rounded a corner and disappeared from sight.

The next moment Bogart had pushed Decker up against the brick wall of the morgue. He wedged his forearm against his throat.

"Okay, you fat-ass son of a bitch, we're going to have this out right here and now."

Bogart was big, strong, and in far better shape than Decker. And he had a freight train load of hate and frustration fueling his physical side. Still, Decker had him by well over a hundred pounds and had once been a professional football player. After the men struggled for about a minute, each trying to gain the upper hand, Decker bent his knees and pushed off the wall, and that momentum combined with his bulk thrust both men forward, although it was really backward for Bogart. At the same time Decker hooked his left ankle behind the FBI agent's right one and the man went down. Decker landed right on top of him with the impact of a wall collapsing.

While lying flat on his back with over three hundred and fifty pounds wedged on top of him, Bogart still managed to clock Decker in the jaw. Decker tasted his own blood and felt a tooth loosen. He slammed his elbow into the side of Bogart's head and heard the other man groan with the impact as his skull ricocheted off the pavement.

"I will kill you!" screamed Bogart as he continued to kick and punch while Decker tried to subdue the flailing limbs.

Decker rose a few inches off Bogart and then dropped heavily down, driving his massive shoulder right into the man's diaphragm. Then he did it once more. Bogart grunted, gasped, moaned, and then stopped struggling.

Decker rose off him, staggered back, bent over, and tried to regain his own breath, his hands on his shaky knees, his gut heaving, his lungs doing the same.

When he looked over, Bogart had sat up and his gun

was pointed at Decker's head. In obvious pain, the man slowly rose, keeping his pistol aimed at Decker.

"You just assaulted a federal agent," gasped Bogart, holding his injured, bleeding head with his free hand.

Decker looked at the gun and then at Bogart.

"I could arrest you," added the federal agent.

Decker straightened and then collapsed against the brick wall for support. Finally getting his breathing under control, he said, "Didn't you want to tell me something?"

Keeping his gun pointed at Decker, Bogart swiped his hair out of his face and smoothed out his tie. He moved closer. "What?"

"You said you wanted to have it out. I don't think that meant kicking my ass. I think that meant *saying* something."

Bogart pointed at the door of the morgue. "He left a message on . . . on my agent that was directed at *you*."

"I know he did."

"Which means you *must* know this guy. You must have done something to this guy. He calls you *bro*." Bogart shouted out this last part.

Decker gave one last heaving breath and pushed off the wall, standing on his own. "I don't know this guy. And I'm not his bro."

"You say you never forget. Well, apparently neither does this guy. You did something. Maybe you didn't realize what it was, but he's killed . . . he's killed . . ." Bogart's voice trailed off and he lowered his weapon and then stared at the pavement shaking his head, his expression one of complete despair.

Decker rubbed at the cut and bruise on his cheek where Bogart had punched him. His tongue pushed against the loosened tooth.

"He's killed a dozen people, including my family and Special Agent Nora Lafferty," said Decker.

Bogart glanced up at him and nodded slowly. "Including Nora." Bogart put his weapon away. "Look, I'm sorry I . . . If you want to press charges, go ahead. It was indefensible."

Decker said, "I'm not sure what happened, other than I stumbled and fell and took you with me. Pretty clumsy. But then I'm a big, fat, out-of-shape guy. I think you might need to dry-clean your suit and see to that cut on your head."

Bogart rubbed at some dirt on his sleeve and then glanced at Decker. "Where do we go from here?"

"With all we've done we've really gotten nowhere. You find anything useful at the Army base?"

"Nothing. It was a petri dish of crap. All degraded to mush. And the Pentagon has yet to get back to us. Not sure what they could add anyway. What about that story in the paper?"

"I talked to the reporter."

"Lancaster told us. Gave us the IP info. My guys are tracking it, no luck so far."

"I doubt it will lead anywhere. Too obvious."

"So we've still got nothing, then?" said Bogart miserably.

"We have a lot of things, if we can make sense of them. We have Sebastian Leopold."

"But he had alibis for both sets of murders."

"But not Lafferty's."

"So you're saying he's working with someone? That's what you meant when you said no one can be in two places at the same time?"

Decker nodded.

"But how can you be sure he killed Nora?"

"I can't. But I don't think it was Leopold who carved those words in her."

"Why?"

"I met Leopold. I would've remembered this guy if I'd seen him before. But I don't, which means I didn't. That leaves his partner. This guy wouldn't have allowed Leopold to do it. It was personal. I'm his bro. No one else. *He's* the one with the beef against me."

"But Decker, how could you have run across this other guy and not remember him? If he hates you so much that he's slaughtering people?"

"I can't answer that because I have no answer," admitted Decker. "But I promise you that I will."

34

Decker stared up at the front of the bar. Then he looked on the right side of the façade and then on the left. The buildings here were brick and dilapidated.

He walked down the stairs and into the dark, smoky interior.

He gazed around and saw two working-class men at a booth in the back, both hefting beer mugs. There was a woman alone at a counter-height round table with a glass of white wine in one hand and a half-smoked cigarette in the other. As he watched she placed her cigarette in a black plastic ashtray and set her wineglass down, pulled a compact and lipstick from her purse, and redid her mouth.

Decker passed by them all and walked up to the bar. The same barman was there. Decker sat and ordered a Coors. The barman poured out the draft, skimmed off the foam on top with a butter knife, and slid it across, in return for which Decker passed him a fiver and told him to keep the change. This got the man's attention.

"You were in here before," said the barman.

Decker nodded and sipped his beer. "I was. With the other guy."

"Yeah, that other guy. Weirdo."

"Has he been back in?"

"Nah." The man started to wipe down the mahogany bar using a rag with a circular motion briskly applied.

"Had he been in before?"

"Couple times."

"You ever talk to him?'

"He never talked to nobody. Except you."

"He live around here?"

"Don't know. Only saw his back leaving the place. Never saw him past that."

"I don't see that waitress around."

The barman chuckled. "That's right."

"What happened to her?"

"Her?" He chuckled harder and then stopped wiping, put his elbows on the bar, leaned across, and said, "You call *it* a *her*. Maybe I don't."

"Then what do you call *it*?"

The barman pointed a finger at Decker. "Now that's a damn good question. I don't do the hiring here. I just pour the drinks and wipe stuff down and throw the occasional drunk bastard out the door."

"Who hired her?"

"Management, whoever they are. Place has been sold four times in three years. Only constant is yours truly, and I wouldn't be here 'cept I can't find nothing else that pays better."

"So are you saying she was a guy in drag?"

"Or something, yeah. Don't know for sure. And I wasn't about to check to confirm. I don't hit from that side of the plate."

Decker closed his eyes and the frames flipped through his head.

Tall, thin, blonde curls.

That hid pretty much all of her face.

Or *his* face.

And maybe the Adam's apple, the surefire giveaway. Only surgery could take care of that.

"You have any info on the person? Must have given a name, address. Stuff for payroll?"

"Management has all that. And they're not even local. Maybe even another state. Think they rolled up a bunch of businesses and combined it into one entity. Economy of scale or some shit like that. I bet they're making a crapload of money, me not so much."

"So none of those records are kept here?"

"No."

"Who interviewed the person for the job?"

"Came from an agency."

"You know which one?"

The barman looked at Decker. "Why, you hit from that side of the plate?"

Decker pulled out his police credentials. "Working a case. This person might be someone I need to talk to."

The man studied the credentials and said, "Okay. Matter of fact, I don't know which one. *It* just showed up one day and started working."

"And you didn't question that?"

"Hey, we needed a waitress. The other one didn't show. Said she'd been sent by the temp agency that management uses. So I put it to work."

"When was this?"

"Day before you came in with that other guy."

"And if she hadn't been sent by the temp agency?"

"Well, why the hell would it lie about that?"

"You have a restroom here just for employees?"

"Yeah, in the back."

"The person ever use it?"

"I'm sure it did. Everyone has to take a pee or something more, right? Either standing up or sitting down."

"Show me."

The barman led him down a rear hall to a battered door marked RESTROOM.

"You got any duct tape?" Decker asked.

"In the back."

"Get it for me."

The confused barman left and returned a minute later with a roll.

Decker proceeded to tape off the door with long strips crisscrossing the doorway.

"What the hell are you doing?" asked the barman.

"I'll have a forensics team here in five minutes. No one goes in."

"But what if I have to use the facilities?"

"Use the one the paying customers do. And you're going to be asked to give a description of *it*, so start racking your memory for every little detail."

Decker made the call to Lancaster.

She said, "I'll send them right now. How was your talk with Bogart?"

"Predictable."

He clicked off and walked outside.

He had solved two things by coming here.

First, the waitress had taken the photograph of him and Leopold at the bar and sent it and the story elements to Alexandra Jamison. She was the only one who could have done it. The intent had been to ruin Decker's reputation, to the extent he had one. But more than that, they wanted him to maybe even start questioning the truth.

Second, she had left the bar, gotten a car, and picked up Leopold when he left the bar. It must have been a hybrid or electric car, because Decker had not heard a car engine and he would have.

In the frames in his mind there was only the barman left that day when Leopold had exited. The waitress wasn't there. Because she'd gone for the car.

A man in women's clothing.

Or maybe a woman who used to be a man dressed in women's clothing. It was like that movie he'd seen years ago with James Garner and Julie Andrews, *Victor Victoria*.

And maybe the waitress was Sebastian Leopold's partner in crime.

Decker had not looked at the person's feet, but now desperately wished he had. But if he had to guess, she would have been wearing a size nine. He tried to estimate her height in his mind. He had been sitting. She might have been wearing heels. He rolled the frames through.

Maybe five-ten or -eleven. And slim, with narrow shoulders and hips.

A long way from six-two and over two hundred pounds with shoulders as wide as Decker's.

But not inconceivable. When the will was there, anything was possible. And it seemed anything had been possible here.

He waited for the forensics team. When they showed, he told them exactly what he wanted done. Lancaster had instructed them to follow Decker's orders to the letter. A sketch artist sat down with the barman.

Then Decker set off for the next place.

Because something else had just occurred to him.

35

Shop class.

Shop class that never was this year because the teacher had quit before the school year started.

Decker had wondered if there was another reason—other than the passageway coming up in the storage room off the classroom—for the shooter to want access to this particular space.

He stepped through and into the storage room in the rear. He eyed the mounds of junk from old projects left behind like dinosaur bones waiting for an archaeological dig.

Well, Decker intended to dig.

He started at the top of each mound and worked his way to the bottom.

He found nothing useful. So he sat on the floor and thought about it. He went through the possible steps in his head. Up here, he decided, would not be pragmatic. The shooter would need more privacy, more of a buffer zone.

He left the storage room and went down the steps to the other room that had the false wall made of balsa wood. The junk pile here had been moved to the side by the shooter.

Decker didn't have to dig very deeply through all the crap.

He pulled out the object and held it up.

A chicken-wire and leather contraption with padding built into it. The form was instantly recognizable to an old jock like Decker.

Football shoulder pads.

But much more than that. The structure went all the way down to the waist and included supports for the arms, broadening and thickening at every point. It was built on hinges that swung open when he undid two latches, like a shorter version of the Iron Maiden torture device from medieval times. It was like an entire torso that one could strap on and become basically twice one's size.

He opened the contraption fully and tried to put it on. The thing was, though, he was already nearly the same size, so it wouldn't fit him. But it would fit someone half his size. Instant giant. He marveled at how flexible and malleable were the wire and leather and straps holding it all together. It would have to be this flexible, because the person had had to both move and shoot while wearing it.

One-forty became two-hundred-plus pounds. Slim became the build of a defensive tackle.

Next in the mounds of junk he found pads that

strapped onto the legs, adding weight and depth to the lower frame, matching the enhancements to the upper.

Okay, that solved the question of literal bulk.

Now came the question of height.

He kept digging.

And found it wedged between two old lamps and a table made partly from a tree stump.

He held it up, measured it with his eye. It was a boot with no heel, but rather a thickened sole running the length of the footwear. Wearing it would raise a person's height about three or so inches. And he concluded that it would do so more effectively than a heel. Three-inch heels would severely limit one's agility. This was simply like walking on a level raised platform. He placed the boot against his own shoe. Far smaller. Nine or nine and a half.

He found the matching one a few seconds later.

He put the boots on the floor. Even though he couldn't wedge his far larger feet inside them, he was able to stand on top of them.

Six-five instantly became six-eight.

The same way five-ten or five-eleven became six-two.

He doubted that the shooter could have brought this equipment in with him on the night of the school play, stashed it in the cafeteria, and then taken it with him along the passageway. But he didn't have to. He could have snuck all this in anytime he wanted and left it right here.

He found a trash bag and piled all of the items into it.

Okay, that solved the size, and also how the man had gotten through the door from the passageway without moving the AC units. He had been a much thinner man then, perhaps as lean as Lancaster, who'd had no trouble getting through the narrow opening. Lean like the waitress; she could have managed it.

Decker's mind flashed to the camera at the rear entrance to the school. Only from the waist up. The shooter didn't want any possibility that the platform boots would be videotaped.

The shooter wouldn't have worried about eyewitnesses observing his feet. Those who weren't dead surely wouldn't have bothered to notice the footwear, not when someone was shooting at them.

He called Lancaster and told her what he'd found.

Several "holy shits" later she said she would be there in ten minutes to pick up the evidence in the trash bag.

Decker perched on a counter in the middle of the shop class and looked around. He wanted to order this all in his head, putting the puzzle pieces together, if only to see how many empty spots he still had.

Shooter comes into the school the night of the play, holes up in the freezer in the cafeteria. He comes out the next morning, uses the passageway from the cafeteria to get to the back of the school unseen. He'd arranged to meet Debbie Watson in the shop class. He knocks her out, changes into his gear, guns up, walks in front of the camera after dragging Debbie out of the shop class and positioning her next to her locker, and then turns the corner and shoots her. Then he goes on his killing spree. From the back to the front of the school. Then he flees through the passage in the cafeteria that connected to McDonald Army Base, the existence of which he found out from Debbie Watson. He stashes the elements of his disguise in the junk pile, which would account for the second set of shoeprints going up those stairs. After that, he makes his escape through the old Army base after accessing the passageway revealed through the supposedly solid wall Decker had discovered.

Okay, if that's how it went down, Decker had one very important question.

Why Mansfield? Why shoot this place up?

He had one idea.

He had attended school here. But if this really was personal to him, there were things here that were very personal to Amos Decker. They literally had his name on them.

He lowered himself off the counter and strode down the hall.

School had not resumed and there was talk that students would be transported to other high schools in the area to finish out at least the first semester. Then over the holidays the town would figure out what to do about the rest of the year.

Decker was torn about students ever returning here.

Part of him wanted this place demolished and turned into some sort of memorial for the dead.

The other part of him didn't want to give the bastards the satisfaction of having forced the town to take such a drastic step. It would be like giving in to terrorists.

He entered the gymnasium and walked quickly over to a large display cabinet set against one wall. In here were all the trophies and other awards won by Mansfield over the years. They were arranged in chronological order, so it was easy enough for Decker to find what he was looking for.

Only they weren't there.

Every award that he had won, every trophy that had held his name—and there were about a dozen—was gone. He checked and rechecked. They were not there.

He leaned against the case and put his hand up to his mouth.

Someone had come in here and shot up Mansfield High. And the mass murderer had done it because of him. Amos Decker.

Same motivation for his family's being murdered.

Me, Amos Decker.

He suddenly felt like Dwayne LeCroix had leveled him again.

His phone buzzed. He thought it was Lancaster.

It wasn't. It was Bogart.

"Decker, we found something in a Dumpster in the alley where Nora Lafferty was taken. You were right. It was a policeman's uniform."

Decker sensed something else coming, though, from the man's unnerved tone.

"What else?"

"The uniform was authentic. It was a Burlington Police Department standard issue."

"And?"

"And the uniform had a name stitched on it."

"They all do. Whose name was it?"

But somehow Decker already knew the answer.

"It was *your* name," replied Bogart.

36

Decker arrived breathless outside the building. He rushed over to the gate and input the code in the security box. It was not a very secure code. It was Molly's birthday.

The gate clicked open and he walked through. The storage units all had exterior doors, and he hustled over to the one at the very end. He pulled the key from his pocket, but then saw that the lock was gone from his unit.

They had done that intentionally. They had wanted him to know.

He lifted the roll-up door, his gun in hand just in case. But the place was empty. Empty of living things.

In here were the possessions he had taken from his old home, because where he had moved to after that didn't have the room. But he couldn't get rid of them. In here were also his tangible memories of a life spent with the two people he was closest to in the world: Cassie and Molly.

They were all neatly boxed and labeled and placed on sturdy metal shelving. This place was an expense he

couldn't really afford, but he had never missed one payment, going cold and hungry to afford keeping this
place, these memories, intact. This mirrored his mind—
full of things but neatly organized, with everything capable of retrieval with minimal effort.

There was one box in here that he needed to look at.
Only one.

It was in the rear, to the left, second shelf, fourth box
from the right.

He reached that spot and stopped. The box was there
but the top was open. He lifted it off the shelf and set it
down on the concrete floor. This box contained the
remaining items from his career in law enforcement.
And part of that was his old police uniform that he had
kept when moving up to detective. He had done so
because there were times at the department when even
plainclothes were expected to don their uniform. When
he had left the department, technically he should have
turned the uniform in, but it wasn't like it could
have been recycled. There was no one near his size in
the Burlington Police Department.

The uniform was not in the box. Someone had used
it to fool Nora Lafferty into letting down her guard for
a few precious—and ultimately lethal—seconds in that
alley.

*They know where I live. They know I have this storage
unit.*

They had desecrated it.

He clicked back in his mind to the last time he had come here.

Twenty-seven days ago, 1:35 in the afternoon. Had they observed him then? Or was it before that last time?

Then he hurried to the gate, where there was a security camera.

He didn't think it would provide a likely lead and he turned out to be right.

The camera lens had been spray-painted black. Obviously no one had been monitoring this camera if they hadn't noticed it could no longer record anything for at least nearly a month.

He called Bogart.

Fifteen minutes later several SUVs pulled up to the gate. Decker let them in and then led the team back to the storage locker.

He explained as he went along. When they arrived at the locker, Bogart's team went into action, searching for prints or other traces and any leave-behinds.

Bogart and Decker stood side by side and watched.

"Why didn't you turn your uniform back in when you left the force?" the FBI agent asked.

Decker knew exactly where this conversation was going, but there was nothing he could do about it. And, in some ways, Bogart was right.

"I should have," conceded Decker. "But I didn't."

Bogart nodded slowly.

Decker wasn't sure if the guy was going to lose it

again, but he figured probably not, not with his team all around.

"Well," said Bogart, "it would have taken a real police uniform to fool Lafferty anyway. These guys probably understood that."

This made Decker feel even guiltier, which was obviously the other man's intent. A staggering body blow without one physical punch thrown.

"Do you have the uniform?" asked Decker.

"Evidence bag in the truck."

"Can I see it?"

They pulled the bag.

Bogart said, "The uniform and cap have already been examined for traces. There was nothing usable."

But Decker wasn't checking for that. He was probing the pants near the cuff. About six inches from the bottom of the pants he found what he was looking for.

He pointed it out to Bogart.

"Holes?" said the FBI agent.

"From pins. Hemming pins."

"Hemming pins?"

"I'm six-five with exceptionally long legs," explained Decker. "The guy who wore this had to take the pant legs up about half a foot. Otherwise Lafferty would have noticed the uniform was not his. I was slimmer back then, but I'm sure the guy had to cinch the waist tight and maybe pin it in the back. The shirt the same."

He examined the shirt and found two pinholes in the fabric near the center of the back panel. "Here and here.

And the guy could have rolled the cuffs over and buttoned them to account for the difference in arm length. And a strip of padding in the cap makes a large cap fit a medium head."

"So a much smaller man?"

"About five-eleven. And thin."

"Lancaster told me what you found at the school. Platform boots for height and some sort of contraption to make the shooter look big in the upper body."

"Like football shoulder pads and padding for the thighs. Made a five-eleven and lean man look much bigger."

"We found nothing on the email trail. IP went nowhere," Bogart said.

"Not surprised."

Decker looked down at the name on the uniform's chest.

Decker.

The man in blue. The man he used to be.

Then he saw something else. It was faint, but he also knew it was fresh.

"Look at the badge," he said.

Bogart did so. "Is that an . . . ?"

"It's an X. Someone has marked an X on the badge."

"What might that represent? To signify Lafferty's murder?"

"I don't know."

He handed the uniform back to Bogart. The FBI

agent took it and then gazed at the activity going on inside the storage unit.

"How come you kept all this stuff?"

Decker looked up and said slowly, far more to himself than Bogart, "It's all I had left."

Bogart glanced at him, sympathy flitting across his features.

Decker must have noticed this, because he said, "No reason to feel that way. You make choices. And you live with them."

"You didn't *choose* to have your family murdered, Decker."

"I think the man who did it believed the choice was all mine."

"That's truly sick."

"Yes, he is."

37

When Decker got back to the Residence Inn after the search at the storage unit turned up nothing, he found that others had visited him and left very telltale signs behind.

A hatchet was stuck in the wood of the door. Slurs had been spray-painted across the window and brick front. Headless baby dolls lay on the concrete. Copies of the news story that Alex Jamison had written were strewn across the catwalk or else taped to the wall, with venomous words scribbled across them. The photo of Decker had been doctored in several of them to make him look like the devil.

Under it was written, "Child Killer."

Decker pulled the hatchet free, kicked the other items aside, opened his door, and went in, locking the door behind him.

He dropped the hatchet on the bureau, went over to the bed, and lay down. He closed his eyes and tried to think of what he was missing. Because it was there. He knew it was. For the hundredth time he started to go through all the known facts of the case in chronological order.

The knock on his door interrupted these thoughts. He struggled up, crossed the room, and said, "Who is it?"

"Somebody who owes you an apology."

He recognized the voice and opened the door.

Alex Jamison was standing there holding one of the headless dolls.

"I'm really sorry," she said, and she actually looked it.

"What do you have to be sorry for?"

"Shit, Decker, you're making me feel worse than I already do."

She was dressed all in black, tights, long sweater that covered her butt, low boots with chunky heels, and a short jean jacket. A large bag was slung over one shoulder.

"You have time for a cup of coffee?" she asked.

"Why?"

"I'm not here to interview you."

"Why, then?"

"Brimmer told me you've done all the heavy lifting on this case. Found all the leads, even though she wouldn't tell me what they were."

"She's learning, then."

"Coffee? I have some things I want to talk to you about. I'll buy. Please, it's important."

He closed the door behind him and they walked down the steps, across the street, and over a few blocks to a coffee shop that occupied a small niche between two larger stores, one of which was boarded up and the other one not far from that fate.

"Whole town is going down the tubes," observed Jamison as they passed the shuttered store. "Before long I'll have nothing to write about except bankruptcies and foreclosures."

They got their coffees and sat at a small table near the back. Decker watched as she spooned sugar into her cup.

"What do you want to talk about?" he asked bluntly.

"I *am* sorry about the story, Decker. In retrospect you didn't deserve that. I don't think you had anything to do with what happened to your family. Like you said, I think some psychopath is looking to first screw you and then destroy you. And he used me to do that and I jumped at the bait just so I could write a story. But that got me wondering why. I mean, who could have that sort of vendetta against you and you not know it?"

Decker sipped his coffee while eyeing her directly but said nothing.

She added, "And I'm sure you've been racking your brain trying to think of the same thing."

"I have."

"It has to be personal," she said.

"Murder almost always is."

"No, I mean more than that. Brimmer told me there were a couple of communications the killer made.

Again, she wouldn't tell me what they said, but they were apparently directed at you."

Decker said nothing, but his look clearly told her he was interested.

"So I did some digging."

"Into what?"

"Into you."

"How?"

"I'm a reporter. We have ways."

"And what did you find?"

"You're from Burlington. Biggest sports star the town ever had. The young man who made good."

This comment made Decker think of the trophy case at the school. "The shooter took all the trophies with my name on them from the case at Mansfield."

She sat back and looked satisfied and also puzzled by this. "I wonder when he did that. Surely not the day of the shooting. He's not going to be hauling hardware around."

"There are ways," Decker said. "But I can't get into that now. Maybe one day you can write the whole story."

She said, "So the question becomes, is it someone who's from Burlington who had a grudge against you all these years? Big football star versus some nobody in the background who was jealous of your success? The fact that he took the trophies might indicate it is someone local. Who you went to Mansfield with? He might have thought you were gone for good when you went on to college, and then you come back here and become a cop and do all these great things. And all these years the hatred is building and festering until the guy just explodes."

"Guys," said Decker.

"Guys? More than one, you mean?"

"You can't write that." He leaned forward. "You really can't write that, Alexandra. If he reads it, he'll assume you know not only that but more. More that could be dangerous to him. And then dangerous for you."

"I get that, Decker. You thoroughly scared me before. I go nowhere without Mace and my phone on 911 speed dial."

"But you came back. You're here now trying to help me figure this out. They could be watching. Why take the risk?"

"I didn't get into journalism to be safe. I got into this line of work because I *wanted* to take risks. You and I are a lot alike on that score."

"How so?"

"I figure the only job riskier than pro football and police work is being in combat. So you're a risk-taker. So am I. And if we can do a little good in the meantime, why not? So, any guys you remember from here that hated you?"

"I was good at sports, but I wasn't good at anything else. And I wasn't a prick. I had fun. I was a goofball. I made people laugh. I messed up. I was not Mr. Perfect by a long stretch. Aside from what I did on the field, I wasn't that special."

"I have a hard time seeing you as a goofball."

"People change."

"You *did* change, didn't you?"

Decker took another sip of his coffee. "People change. I'm no exception."

"People do change. But I think you changed more than most."

"How do you mean exactly?"

"The hit. I watched it on YouTube."

"Good for you."

"It was horrible watching it. I can't imagine how it was, actually being the recipient of it."

"I don't really remember it. They told me later I shit my pants. Violent collision like that overpowers the central nervous system. During the preseason the equipment guys came in after games to make sure all the girdles with feces in them were hidden from view and never given out to fans. Along with all the blood inside the helmets and on the uniforms. And they kept the reporters out when the guys were in the trainer's room postgame so they wouldn't hear the screams. And they gave players pops of ammonia or painkillers so they could talk to the media and hide the fact that half their brain was gone."

"I'm not a big fan of football. Gladiators of the twenty-first century, wrecking each other for our amusement while we drink beer and eat hot dogs and cheer when a guy gets wiped out. You'd think we would have gotten beyond that. I guess there's too much money in it."

"See, people don't actually change all that much."

"After the hit you just disappeared for a long time. Got cut by the team, went into limbo. I couldn't find anything on you. And then you turned up back here and joined the police academy. A buddy of mine got me your test scores."

"You have a lot of buddies?"

"A good reporter needs all the help she can get. The scores were all perfect."

"A fact my old captain told me too."

"So Captain Miller looked into it as well?"

"Why all the interest in me?"

"Because I figure that to find this guy, or guys, we have to work backward, from the motivation to the source. You're the motivation. So I have to understand you to get to them." She paused and tapped a spoon against her coffee cup. "So where were you during that time?"

"That's my business."

"You don't want to catch these murderers?"

"Didn't say that."

"But you know I'm right. You're the key to what's happening." She leaned forward and tapped his thick hand. "I want to help, Decker."

"What you want is a Pulitzer."

"I tell you what. You let me help and I won't write

any story without your permission. You get to vet and approve the whole thing. Or you get to pull the trigger and it'll never see the light of day."

"You'd agree to that?"

"Yes."

"Why?"

"Andy Jackson. You know him?"

"The English teacher at Mansfield. Last surviving victim of the shooter. He tried to stop the shooter."

"He died an hour ago. Andy didn't always teach at Mansfield. He was a professor at Purdue, where I went. He's the reason I'm a reporter. He came here to take care of his ailing mother. Sort of person he was."

"You never said this before."

"Because that was *my* business. But I'm saying it now." She put out a hand. "So that's my deal. No story if you say so. But in exchange I get to help you track these bastards down. What do you say?"

Decker slowly put out his hand and they shook.

"So where do we start?" she asked.

He rose. "At a storage unit."

38

It was late and they were sitting cross-legged on the concrete floor of the storage unit going through boxes. Jamison had returned a few minutes before with dinner in the form of Chinese takeout. She had laid out napkins, paper plates, and plastic utensils and filled Decker's plate with food before doing her own.

He looked at her in some surprise.

She explained, "I'm not domesticated, but I am the oldest of seven kids. I'm used to playing parent at mealtime."

He nodded and bit off a chunk of a spring roll while Jamison spooned some egg drop soup into her mouth. She had brought them each a beer as well. Decker took a swig of his and then set the bottle down.

Jamison looked around the unit. "You really kept everything, didn't you?"

"Things that were important to me."

"I don't see anything here from your playing days."

He shrugged and stabbed his fork at a piece of shrimp. "Not important to me."

She nodded slowly. "But with what happened to

your family doesn't it hurt to keep all this stuff? Your daughter's clothes? Your wife's cookbooks? Letters? Pictures?"

"The only thing that hurts is not having them here." He looked at her. "How long were you married?"

"Too long."

He looked at her expectantly.

"Two years and three months," she finally said. "I guess not that long, actually."

"What happened?"

"Things just went sideways. He wasn't the guy I thought he was. And I guess I wasn't the woman he thought I was."

"Kids?"

"Thank God, no. That would have made it a lot harder."

"Yeah, it would. Kids make everything better. And harder."

She leaned back against a cardboard box, drew her knees up, and sipped her beer. She tapped her head. "So the hit altered your mind somehow?"

Decker nodded and took a swig of beer.

"I saw some of the reports from that institute place in the box back there. Was it weird?"

He set the beer down and rubbed at his beard. "Do you mean did I feel like a guinea pig? Yes."

"How did the others come by it?"

"None of us were told that officially. I guess patient privacy. But there's always scuttlebutt. Most were probably born with it. A few, like me, suffered a brain trauma. I think some of the folks at the institute knew about me because the hit was on TV."

"Did you all have similar . . . ?"

"Gifts? There was a core part of it. Near-total recall of certain things. Aside from that, it differed quite a bit. One of them could play any musical instrument with pretty much no instruction. Another could divide any prime number in his head no matter how large. There was this other woman who had qualified as a grand master of memory when she was seven."

"Grand master of memory? What did she have to do?"

"Three tasks. The first was to memorize one thousand random numbers in an hour. Next, she had to memorize the order of ten decks of cards in an hour. And lastly, memorize the order of one deck of cards in under two minutes."

"Wow, who knew it would be so easy," said Jamison sarcastically.

"There are around one hundred and fifty people in the world who have successfully performed the three tasks."

"Didn't think it would be that many."

"It's not, in the grand scheme of seven billion people."

"Could you do it?"

"I've never tried. Never saw the point."

They both fell silent.

Jamison watched Decker closely.

"Even though this guy's motivation is you, it's not about you, you realize that, don't you?"

"Now thirteen people have been murdered because somebody has a problem with me. This is *definitely* about me."

"You didn't pull the trigger. Someone else did. And whatever he thinks you did, it doesn't justify what he's done."

"Tell it to the victims' families."

"You *are* the family of victims."

Decker pushed his plate away and struggled up. His knees and back were killing him and he had to take a leak.

He went outside and around the corner, unzipped his pants, and relieved himself.

He was surprised when Jamison spoke. She had apparently followed him.

"You don't need to guilt-trip yourself. That's what he wants. You know that. It's all part of it. He gets inside your head, he wins, on two fronts. One, his brain beats your brain, so he gets personal satisfaction. And if you're not thinking straight you have no shot at tracking him down. Win-win for him. He's counting on that."

Decker zipped his pants back up and turned to her. "I know that."

"So don't let him do it."

"Easier said than done."

"Maybe for someone with an average mind. You don't have one of those."

He advanced on her, backing her up against the wall of the storage unit. "You think having a freak mind means I don't have emotions? That I don't feel anything? Is that what you think? Because you're wrong."

"It's not what I think. I think the *other* guy doesn't feel anything. He's abnormal in that way. You're not."

"Then what the hell are you saying?"

"You can feel anything you want, Decker. You're pissed beyond belief right now. I get that. You think the slaughter begins and ends at your doorstep. Maybe you want to hit somebody or something. Drive your fist through that wall. Okay, but don't let him mess with the part of your brain that you will need to one day put handcuffs on this son of a bitch and then watch him take his last breath in the death chamber. You want to score this game? That's how you score it. Winner lives, loser gets the needle."

Decker took a step back. She didn't move.

He looked away, then down at the asphalt. Then he walked back to the storage unit to keep digging.

Two hours later they had gone through every box and had pretty much nothing.

Decker sat back against a shelving unit. "I've gone back to the first day I put on the uniform to see who I might have dissed that could have pulled this off. Nobody. I didn't piss off anyone at the 7-Eleven. I busted bad guys, sure, but I didn't do anything to give anyone this sort of *personal* vendetta."

He rubbed his face and closed his eyes.

Jamison rubbed a kink out of her neck and looked across at him, suddenly looking puzzled.

"Why did you only go back to when you put on the cop uniform?"

He opened his eyes. "I also went through anybody at Mansfield that might have something against me. There's nothing there, Jamison. Nothing."

"So you covered your growing up in Burlington. And you covered your life after coming back to Burlington. What about in between?"

"What, you think the guy who laid me out on that hit is behind this? After his knees and shoulders gave out, he was cut from his team, went broke, turned to selling drugs, and he's currently in the custody of the Louisiana prison system. And I was never a good enough football player to make anyone jealous of me in college or the pros."

Jamison yawned. "So if Sebastian Leopold is involved, why would he have told the cops you dissed him at the 7-Eleven if you didn't?"

"You mean why would a murderer lie?"

"I mean, how could you not know him if you did something so bad he's doing all this in retaliation? And his crazy act could just be that, an act. But this guy strikes me as literal. Your family, Mansfield High. The communications to you, can you tell me what they were about?"

"One was written on the wall at my old house."

"What did it say?"

He repeated the message to her.

"And the others?"

He told her about the code embedded in the musical score on Debbie Watson's wall. And then the words carved into Lafferty.

"Jesus," she exclaimed. "So he refers to you as 'bro' in each message?"

Decker nodded.

"And he also says you two are a lot alike. That you're all the other has."

"Yes."

"And with the last message he's asserting that you actually have control of this thing. That you can determine when to end it."

Decker looked at her. "Meaning him or me."

"And he obviously wants to be the one left standing."

"I would expect so."

"Okay. But it seems to me that he feels like he's in competition with you. Brothers. Part of something that we're just not seeing."

Decker opened his eyes. "Like a team?"

"You were never in the military?"

He shook his head.

"Then maybe like a team."

"I already told you, I was never good enough to tick someone off in football. I never took somebody's position and along with it a paycheck. Besides, I can't see someone murdering all these people because he was third string to my second string on a college football team. And in the pros I was just a spare piece of meat. I was never missed."

"But you're convinced Leopold is involved in this?"

"Yes."

"Based on your gut?"

"Based on the fact that he's disappeared. I've checked every homeless shelter in town. He's never been to any of them. He played me. He walked out of that bar knowing that he was going to disappear. And the waitress was working with him. The waitress is the other person. The one with the beef against me. *She's* the one I really want."

"But you mentioned that this waitress might be a man."

"Yes. Our shooter, in fact. Leopold was in lockup both times. It had to be the other one."

"And he used the stuff you found at the school to make himself appear bigger."

"Pretty clever since the cops live and die by physical description. Once they get that height and size in their heads they never look at anyone outside that box. It's just beaten into us."

"So Leopold and/or the shooter might know how cops think?"

"Yes."

Jamison mulled this over. "Then the only direct fact he's really told anyone is that you dissed him at your local 7-Eleven. But you're sure he's lying about that. So we have to go back to that and start from there— Decker?"

Decker had lurched to his feet and was looking down at her.

"What is it?" she asked.

"You said it was our only direct fact."

"Right, I know. But—"

"But it's not."

"Not what?"

"A fact."

He hurried from the storage space without another word. She jumped to her feet, grabbed her bag, and followed.

39

Decker and Jamison sat across from Lancaster at police headquarters. Decker had briefly explained how he came to be working with Jamison and also why he was here.

"We've torn apart my storage unit but there was nothing there," he added. "And then it occurred to me that I had made an assumption that was based on something that had not been confirmed. I accepted as a fact something that had not been proven to be a fact. That's why we're here."

"And so you want to hear my interview notes with Leopold after he was taken into custody?" asked Lancaster.

"Yes. As precise as you can make them, Mary. Every word counts. Literally."

Lancaster looked a little apprehensive but then collected her pages and set them in front of her. "Well, to start off, he didn't say much. In fact, he wasn't making much sense. As soon as he finished I thought his best bet would be to plead diminished capacity."

"I don't think his capacity is diminished at all. Quite

the opposite," replied Decker. "Just read me what he said. And if you can remember anything else, that would be helpful too."

"Well, I guess we've got nothing to lose." She looked sternly at Jamison. "But just so we're crystal clear, one word of this ends up in a newspaper or other media outlet, I will lock you up personally and forget you're there. You're on my shit list already for that crap you wrote about Amos."

Jamison held her hands up in mock surrender, but her tone was deadly serious. "It never will, Detective Lancaster. Not from me. And I *am* a shit for what I wrote. I shouldn't have done it, but I did. And now I'm trying to make it right. It's all I can do."

Lancaster ran a critical gaze over her. "And Jackson was really your college professor?"

"He was a lot more than that. He was my mentor. Easily verifiable if you don't believe me."

"I believe you," Lancaster said curtly. "Then I guess we're all on the same page and the same team." She looked down at her notes and started reading. When she got to the part about Decker dissing Leopold at the 7-Eleven, Decker stopped her.

"Those were his exact words? I dissed him at the *7-Eleven*?"

"Yes. I told you that before."

"What did you ask him next?"

"Well, I asked him which 7-Eleven. I was trying to see if his story made any sense. We don't get many folks walking into the precinct and copping to a triple homicide a year and a half after the fact."

"And he said the local 7-Eleven near me?"

Lancaster looked down at her notes again and frowned. "No, he actually said that you'd know which one." She glanced up. "I guess I just assumed that you would know at which 7-Eleven you had dissed the guy. At least dissed him in his mind."

"So he never said the local 7-Eleven? The one near my house at Fourteenth and DeSalle?"

Lancaster paled, and when she spoke her voice was strained. "No, Amos, he didn't. That was a leap of logic for us both, I guess. But I should not have made that assumption. That was a rookie mistake."

"I made it too, Mary."

Lancaster still looked crestfallen.

"Can I see your notes?" he asked.

She handed them across and he started reading through them.

Lancaster glanced at Jamison, leaned forward, and said in a low voice, "So how do you enjoy working with Decker? I did it for about ten years. No two days were ever the same."

Jamison spoke in the same low tone. "It's . . . um, unusual. He just jumped up and walked out of the storage unit. I had to race after him."

Lancaster let out a rare smile. "Story of my life."

The women drew apart when Decker dropped the notes on the table.

He looked sharply at Jamison. "The email address you got the story elements and photo from: Mallard2000 was the handle?"

"You know it was. I sent it to you."

Lancaster said, "The FBI couldn't trace it back, so I don't see how it's helpful."

"It's actually very helpful. And I should have seen it before."

"Seen what before?" asked Jamison.

"That the answer I was looking for wasn't in tracing it back to the sender. It was right there all along in the name."

"In the name?" said Lancaster. "What name?"

Decker stood and looked at Jamison. "You have a car?"

She nodded and rose too. "A subcompact with a hundred thousand miles on it and held together with duct tape. But it gets great gas mileage." She looked him up and down. "It might be kind of tight for you. Where are we going?"

"Chicago."

"Chicago," exclaimed Lancaster. "What the hell's in Chicago?"

"Actually, it's a suburb of Chicago. And what's there is everything, Mary."

"But how do you know where to look in Chicago?"

Decker said impatiently, "He gave me the address, seven-eleven."

Lancaster shook her head and said incredulously,

"Okay, but, Amos, do you know how many 7-Elevens there are in the Chicago metro area?"

"I'm not looking for a convenience store, Mary. I'm looking for the *street number* seven-eleven."

Lancaster stared up at him blankly. "Shit, are you telling me it was never a *7-Eleven*? It was a street number! But he said—"

"He said the numbers seven and eleven. Which can just as easily be seven-one-one. You just wrote it down the way anyone would have who lives in this country. You just assumed he meant the store chain, when he actually didn't."

"But he never corrected me."

"Did you expect him to draw you a map? This is a game to them. Played by their rules."

"Okay, you have the number, but that's pretty useless unless you have a street to go with it."

"I do have a street. That was in the email address."

"Mallard two-thousand? But how do you even know it's in Chicago? How does that city tie in to what happened in Burlington?"

"It doesn't. It ties in to *me*."

"But Amos, what does—"

Lancaster stopped in midsentence, because Decker had already rushed from the room.

"Son of a bitch!" yelled Lancaster.

Jamison shot her an apologetic look. "Story of your life?"

"Just keep me informed, Jamison. And watch him.

He's beyond brilliant, but even brilliant people do stupid things."

"I will."

And then Jamison hurried after Decker.

Lancaster slumped back in her chair and looked down at her notes. Then she balled them up and threw them across the room.

"Screw 7-Eleven!"

40

As it was originally configured, the subcompact had not exactly fit Decker since they were roughly the same size. They had finally taken out the front seat and he had wedged himself into the tiny back with his long legs sticking into the front of the car over the hump where the seat had been.

He sat with his eyes closed and his hands resting over his substantial belly. They had stopped by his room and he had packed a canvas bag with some clean clothes. He had learned that Jamison kept a suitcase packed and in the tiny trunk of her car.

"Standard operating procedure for a reporter," she informed him.

Jamison looked at him anxiously in the rearview mirror as they sped along. "I wish you could make the seat belt reach you back there."

"Just don't have an accident," said Decker, his eyes still closed. "I will make a very large projectile, bigger than your car. You really don't want to find out the mass times velocity of my ass in flight."

She looked back at the road. They had been on the

interstate for over three hours. They were now in Indiana. They had about another four hours to go.

"I got us rooms on Expedia," she said. "At a Comfort Inn outside of Chicago. It won't break my bank account." She turned to look at him. "You still haven't told me where we're going."

"I *did* tell you. Brockton, Illinois. It's a suburb twenty miles south of Chicago. Not to be confused with Brocton, Illinois, which is a village in Embarrass Township outside of Champaign with a population of about three hundred."

"Embarrass Township? Seriously?"

"I didn't name it."

"Okay, but you haven't told me where in Brockton we're going."

"To the street address Leopold left for me to find."

"Seven-one-one *what*?"

"Mallard two thousand is the street name."

"There's not a street with that name in Illinois. I checked."

"There is a street with that name, but it goes by something else."

"I don't understand."

"It was a thinly veiled code, Jamison. Try to figure it out."

Minutes went by. "Okay, I give. I suck at crosswords."

"The street is Duckton Avenue."

"Duckton?"

"Now try to figure it out in reverse. It won't take you long. I have faith."

She focused back on the road. "Shit," she said a few moments later. "A mallard is a duck and two thousand pounds equals a ton. Duckton."

"Congratulations, you just made junior detective grade."

"But what is at seven-one-one Duckton Avenue?"

"It's a place I used to call home."

She jerked around to look at him, but he was now gazing out the side window.

"Your home?"

"Later, Jamison. For now, just drive. No seat belt, *remember*?"

She angrily turned back around, popped the accelerator, and smiled appreciatively when she heard his head clunk against the back of the car's interior from the sudden uptick in speed.

They stopped at a truck diner off the interstate for a bathroom break, a refueling, and a bite to eat.

Jamison ordered a cheeseburger, fries, and a Corona. Decker had a large pizza and a Coke.

He eyed her food. "Despite the Chinese last night, I had measured you up as a health nut."

She bit into the burger and let fatty juice roll down her chin before wiping it away. "I could probably eat you under the table."

"Maybe in another life."

"What do you expect to find out at this Duckton place?"

"If it's still there. I tried to call the number I used to have, but it's been changed. And the place's number is not listed."

"But what *is* the place, Decker? You called it home."

"It was where people like me were poked, prodded, and tested."

Jamison lowered her burger. "With all the memory geniuses? The . . . the institute?"

"Savants, autistics, Asperger's, synesthesia, and hyperthymesia."

"Hyper what?"

"Thymesia. In Greek, *hyper* means 'excessive,' and *thymesia* translates to 'memory.' Put 'em together and you get me. True hyperthymesia really relates to near-perfect recall of one's personal or autobiographical past. I have that, but I also can't forget anything I see, read, or hear. Perfect recall of, well, everything. I had no idea my brain was that big. But I apparently use more of it than most, but only because I got my ass handed to me on a football field."

"And synesthesia?"

"I see colors where others don't. In numbers, in places and objects. My cognitive sensory pathways apparently also got melded from the hit I took."

"I appreciate your telling me all this. But I'm surprised too. You strike me as a private guy."

"I *am* a private guy. I've never told anyone about this, except for my wife."

"Then why tell me? We don't really know each other."

Before answering Decker ate a bite of pepperoni pizza, followed by a long swig of Coke. "We're tracking down killers together, Jamison. They've murdered a lot of people, including an FBI agent. I figure I owe you the whole story because you're putting your life on the line."

She put her burger down and took a small drink of her beer. "You're making me sound a lot braver than I am," she said softly.

He ate another few bites of pizza and slurped down his Coke. "Let's hope you're wrong about that."

41

They had checked in to their motel, grabbed some sleep, washed up, and changed their clothes. Now they were standing in front of an eight-story brick building with small windows that looked about sixty years old.

Jamison glanced at Decker and then over at the building's address represented by metal numbers bolted to the façade. "Seven one-one Duckton. So this was *home*?"

Decker nodded but kept his eyes on the building. "It's changed a little. It's been two decades."

"Was this a true research facility?"

"For the most part. They were basically trying to understand how the brain works. They were one of the first to approach the field in a multipronged, multi-disciplinary methodological manner."

"Meaning what exactly?"

"Meaning that they didn't just hook electrodes up to your head and measure brain activity that way. They did all the physiological things you would expect—the brain is an organ, after all, and it basically works on electrical impulses. But they also did counseling sessions and group and one-on-ones. They dug deeply into our lives. They wanted to know the science of folks like us, but they also wanted to know, well, *us*. What having an exceptional mind was like, how it had impacted, or changed, our lives."

"Sounds pretty thorough."

"They were."

"But what was the result of all that?"

Decker shrugged. "I was never told. I was here for months and then was told I could go. There was never any follow-up. At least not with me."

"Wait a minute, you were *told* you could go? Were you here involuntarily?"

"No, I volunteered."

"Why?"

He turned to look at her. "Because I was scared, Jamison. My *brain* had changed, which meant pretty much everything about me had changed. My emotions, my personality, my social skills. I wanted to find out why. I wanted to find out . . . what my future might be like. I guess I wanted to find out what I would become, for the long term."

"But I guess there were a lot of positives. I mean, a perfect memory makes school and work pretty easy."

He looked back up at the building. "Do you like yourself?"

"What?"

"Do you like the person you are?"

"Well, yes. I mean, I could exercise more and I have yet to find the right guy, but yeah, I like who I am."

"Well, I liked who I was too. And now that person is gone. Only I didn't have a choice in the matter."

Her face fell. "Right. I didn't really think about that."

"And it would be nice to be able to forget some things. People *do*, you know. Want to forget some things."

"Decker, even someone with a normal mind would never be able to forget something like what happened to your family."

"But I remember every single detail of it, in the color blue. I will never forget any of it, even exactly how I felt when I found the bodies. Not until the day I die. For me time does not heal, because my mind no longer allows for the passage of time to dull my memories. They are as vivid today as the day it happened. It's like a picture that never, ever fades. Some people can't go back? I really can't go forward."

"I'm sorry."

He turned to look down at her. "I can't process sympathy anymore," he said. "I used to. But not anymore." He walked into the building and Jamison hurried after him.

The building directory did not contain the name of the research facility. Decker went over to a reception desk set up in one corner and flashed his temporary police credentials, but the woman there could not help him. She had never heard of the place Decker named.

Decker and Jamison walked around the large lobby. Decker was peering everywhere, taking it all in.

"Going for a trip down *memory* lane?" said Jamison impishly.

He looked down at her with raised eyebrows.

She blushed. "Sorry, I was just trying to lighten the mood. I guess humor doesn't really work with you either."

But Decker had hurried across the lobby to a small flower shop in the corner of the floor. Jamison caught up to him as he approached the counter inside.

A woman in her late forties was behind the counter. She had light brown hair cut short and her build was blocky. Black slacks and a long-sleeved white blouse constituted her work clothes.

"Can I help you?" she asked Decker.

"This place has been here a long time," Decker began. "I remember it."

She smiled. "Dora's Floras. It's been here ever since the building opened in 1955. My mother was Dora. She started it."

"I remember her too. You look like her."

The woman smiled more broadly. "I took over the shop ten years ago. She and my father had built up a great business. When I was in college I'd come here and help them. My only job now is not to screw it up. I'm Daisy, by the way. What else would I be named, right? I'm the youngest of four girls and we're all named after flowers."

"So you've been here ten years, Daisy?"

"Yes." The woman's brow creased with a frown.

"Why do I think you're not interested in purchasing a flower arrangement?"

"I'm not," Decker said bluntly. He showed her his credentials.

"Out of state," she said. "Must be important."

"It is. There was a research facility in the building. Well, it was here twenty years ago. The Cognitive Research Institute?"

Daisy smiled. "Oh sure, I remember them. They were a good customer."

"Were? So they're no longer here?"

"No, they moved out. It was, let me think—oh, probably seven or eight years ago. I remember the big trucks out front. As a general rule most businesses here stay here. It's a great location, beautiful old building that's been meticulously maintained, really prime real estate. And it's just a hop, skip, and a jump to Chicago."

"I suppose you don't know where they went?"

"No, I don't. Did you try looking them up in the phone book? Well, I guess online these days."

"I did. There was no listing."

"Oh, well, I'm sorry."

Decker said, "Thank you anyway." He started to turn away.

She said, "But there is old Dr. Rabinowitz."

Decker turned back. "Harold Rabinowitz?"

"Yes, how'd you know his first name?"

"I did some research before I came," he said quickly.

"Oh, well, yes. He's still around, and if you can

believe it, he still orders flowers from us. You know, the Coggers—that's what we used to call them—were some of our best customers. My mother used to tell me, fresh flowers every week they ordered. And they sent a lot of flowers to folks, too. It was really nice. Nice for them, nice for our bottom line."

"So you have his address?"

Her expression changed. "I'm really not supposed to give that sort of information out," she said doubtfully.

"Can you give me his phone number?"

"I'm really uncomfortable with that too. You seem nice enough, but it's against our policy."

Decker said, "How about you call Dr. Rabinowitz and tell him that Amos Decker would like to see him. If he says it's okay you can give me his address. If not, no harm done."

"Well, I guess that makes sense. So you know him? I saw on your card that you're Amos Decker."

"Yes, I know him."

"Well, why didn't you say so? Hold on."

She went to a phone, looked up the number on her computer, and punched it in. She turned her back to them as she spoke. A minute later she put down the phone and came back to them. She wrote something down on a slip of paper and handed it to Decker.

"Bingo. He said he would be delighted to see you."

Decker looked down at the paper and then back up at her. "Are your parents still alive?"

Daisy looked mildly surprised by the query. "My

mom is at an assisted living center and loving it. Big surprise, she does all their flower arrangements."

"Well, tell her that Amos Decker remembers her flowers. And . . . that they helped a lot."

"I sure will. She'll be glad to hear that. The way Mother sees it, the more flowers we have the better world we'd have."

Outside, Jamison looked at Decker. "Nicely done."

He didn't respond.

"So the flowers helped, huh?"

He shot her a glance. "Yeah, they did actually. So?"

"So maybe you haven't changed as much as you think."

42

On the drive over to Rabinowitz's, Jamison glanced at Decker in the rear of her car. "One question," she said.

"Just one?"

"Maybe not. So to be straight about this, it wasn't Leopold you dissed. It was his partner. The waitress. Leopold simply delivered the message."

"Right."

"Presumably because you would have recognized this person?"

"I'm sure I would have."

"And that person was with you at the institute?"

"It would be the only reason for the Mallard2000 reference. I don't believe in coincidences, especially ones that large."

"Okay. So our shooter was a male. Well, at least the probabilities lie there. Although the barman very crudely called the person an 'it.' He seemed to think she was a man dressed up as a woman. Or maybe a transsexual. Given that sort of radical change, you might not recognize the person."

"Maybe not."

"And she might have been a man at the institute and is a woman now. Or vice versa."

"Could be."

"So you dissed that person while you were at the institute?"

Decker's phone buzzed. It was Lancaster.

She said, "We found a lot of usable prints and DNA in the restroom at the bar. We did basic eliminations and then ran them through the perp databases. FBI did the same."

"And nothing?"

"Couple of druggies and a convicted rapist. They're all doing time now, but at some point they used that restroom."

"So not our waitress?"

"No. How goes it on your end?"

"I'll let you know in a couple hours. Following a lead."

He clicked off and settled back in the rear of the Suzuki.

Jamison gave him a searching glance. "Nothing?"

"Nothing. Let's hope Rabinowitz proves more helpful."

Dr. Harold Rabinowitz lived in an apartment in an old building on the other side of town. When Decker knocked on the door he heard footfalls heading his way.

A voice said, "Who is it?"

"Amos Decker."

The door opened and Decker was looking down at a small, balding man with a gray beard and wearing dark glasses. He was well into his seventies. He had on a worn cardigan, dress slacks, and a collared white shirt.

"Hello, Amos." The man gazed at Decker's belly.

It took Decker a moment to process it.

"When did you lose your eyesight, Dr. Rabinowitz?"

"Fully? Seven years ago. Macular degeneration. A very nasty disease. You're not alone. I can hear someone else."

"My friend, Alex Jamison."

"Hello, Dr. Rabinowitz. Please call me Alex."

"I like your perfume. Vanilla and coconut, very nice. Am I right?"

"You are. Very good."

He smiled, satisfied. "Other senses are heightened to compensate, you know. Please come in."

They settled down in chairs in the small living room. Decker looked around and took in the neat surroundings, the carefully constructed walking paths. He also saw the guide stick for the visually impaired hanging from a peg next to the door.

"I was surprised to hear that you wanted to see me," began Rabinowitz.

"I won't take up too much of your time."

"I've gotten to the point in my life, Amos, where all I have is time. My professional work is done. My wife is deceased. My health is declining. My old friends are dead. My children have their own health problems. My grandchildren are graduating from college and starting their own careers. So your visit is very welcome to me."

Decker settled back and kept his gaze on the man while Jamison shot glances between them.

Decker said, "How long have you been gone from the Cognitive Institute?"

"They put me out to pasture ten years ago. I would have stayed longer, but my eyes were starting to go even then."

"They've moved."

"I know. I keep in touch. The institute has grown, you know."

"No, I didn't."

"Hence the move. They needed more space. We've come light-years since you were with us. We know so much more."

"And you obviously remember me."

"You would be hard to forget. Our only professional football player. It was quite unusual."

"I went into law enforcement when I left here. First as a cop. Then a detective."

"You mentioned that was your ambition when you were here."

"Yes, I did."

"Good for you. And have you had a productive career?"

"It's had its ups and downs, like most careers."

"Hopefully more ups than downs."

"You may be able to help with that."

Rabinowitz frowned. "I don't understand."

Decker mentioned the Mansfield case.

Rabinowitz said, "I heard about that, along with the rest of the country. So tragic. So awful. So many lives just . . . ended. For no reason."

"I'm working that case. And there *is* a reason. In fact, it might have a personal connection to me."

"How so?" Rabinowitz said sharply.

"I think someone at the institute while I was there is involved with the massacre at the high school."

Rabinowitz gripped the edge of his armchair. "What!?"

"I can't give you specifics, but the killer communicated the old address of the institute to me. He said that I had dissed him. He indicated that was why he killed all those people."

"Oh my God!" Rabinowitz nearly toppled from his chair, but, moving fast for a big man, Decker managed to snag his arm and hold him in his seat.

Decker looked at Jamison. "Water?"

She jumped up and hurried into the next room. She was back in less than a minute with a glass of water. Decker gave it to Rabinowitz, and he drank down a bit before carefully placing it on the table next to him.

"I'm sorry," said Decker. "I shouldn't have just dropped that on you. Sometimes . . . sometimes I just don't realize . . ."

Rabinowitz wiped his lips with a trembling hand and then settled back in his chair. "Your neurological switches were set awry, Amos, for want of a better term. I know that certain societal parameters and cues are difficult for you, as they were for many of the folks who passed through our doors. It just goes with the territory. Parts of the brain become extraordinary in what they can do, while other parts, well, other parts regress a bit, at least from a societal perspective. It's all a question of priorities for the mind."

"That's why I'm here. The folks who passed through your doors. One of them could be our killer."

Rabinowitz shook his head, his brow scrunched up in distress. "I find that so very . . . terrible. And unlikely."

"Damaged minds, Dr. Rabinowitz."

"I think you can call me Harold now, Amos. We no longer have a doctor-patient relationship."

"Okay, Harold. Damaged minds, even turned exceptional in some ways, are capable of many things. Some good, some bad."

"But surely you remember quite vividly the people you met at the institute. Did you see a callous murderer among them?"

"Honestly, no. And I can't remember ever 'dissing' any of them. I can't recall insulting anyone while I was there."

"But you say the . . . the man responsible for these terrible acts gave you the address of the institute?"

"The old address, on Duckton. He did it in code, but it was clearly his intent."

Rabinowitz rubbed his mouth. "I'm not sure what I can add to what you already know."

Jamison spoke up. "You've focused on *patients* who were there with you. But what about doctors, psychologists, or other health care professionals you met while you were there?"

Decker nodded slowly. "I hadn't thought about that."

Rabinowitz said firmly, "I can't believe anyone who *worked* at the institute would ever commit such vile acts."

"I don't want to think it either," said Jamison hurriedly. "But in an investigation like this you really can't discount any possibility. It would be irresponsible."

Decker said, "Chris Sizemore."

Jamison said, "Who?"

Rabinowitz said, "He was a psychologist who worked at the institute. I was told he left there several years ago."

"Why do you mention him, Decker?" asked Jamison.

"Because he and I did not get along. We had words. Nothing that would have led me to believe he could be our guy. But we didn't get along."

"Could he be Leopold twenty years later?" she asked.

Decker closed his eyes and clicked through the appropriate frames in his head. "Right height and build. Facial features similar. But it was hard to tell Leopold's age. Sizemore would be in his early fifties now. Bottom line, while doubtful, I can't be certain that Sizemore and Leopold aren't the same person. The tats on his arm could have come later. He could have lied about being in the Navy. His voice could have changed over the years. A lot of things about him could have changed over two decades. But the police have Leopold's prints and DNA from when he was arrested. Presumably Sizemore's prints are available in some professional database. It should be fairly straightforward to see if the two are one and the same."

He had a photo of Leopold on his phone, but of course he couldn't show it to Rabinowitz to see if it might be Sizemore.

He looked at Rabinowitz. "Do you know what happened to Sizemore? Why did he leave the institute?"

The older man was nervously tapping his fingers against his thigh. "As I said, I was gone long before he left."

"But you also said you keep in touch with former colleagues."

"Yes, well, he had some professional issues."

"What sort?"

"I really can't get into that. But I can tell you that they were serious enough for him to be asked to leave."

Jamison said, "What sort of problems did you have with him, Decker?"

"He had his protégés, and I wasn't one of them."

Rabinowitz said, "Chris *did* have his favorites. I would like to think that *I* treated all of our patients with the same level of courtesy, respect, and thoroughness.

But I'm also human, and I of course would have certain cases that interested me more than others. There are very few blunt-force brain trauma cases where the patient actually died before being resuscitated that result in the sort of cognitive rerouting that took place with you, Amos." Rabinowitz paused to smile. "And I've been a Bears fan for over sixty years, and though you played for Cleveland, you were the only NFL player to ever come through our door. Now that you mention it, I do remember Chris having issues with that. Whether it was from a genuine dislike of you, or rather from the effects of his personal issues that later led him to leave the institute, I don't know. But he seemed to think that with you our priorities were off."

"I don't get that," said Jamison. "What would he base that on?"

Decker answered, "Sizemore thought that, being a football player, I had accepted the risk of getting my brain destroyed. I guess he thought I was taking up the space of someone who deserved to be there more."

Rabinowitz said, "Now, that I didn't know."

"That's because I never told anyone. He let that slip during a 'conversation' we had one day in the hallway."

"That was highly unprofessional of him," said Rabinowitz sharply.

"Perhaps. But I also never considered that it *might* be the motivation for what happened at Mansfield."

Jamison said, "So the million-dollar question: Where is Dr. Sizemore now?"

Rabinowitz said, "I don't know. I haven't heard from him since I left the institute."

"Maybe he moved to the Burlington area?" commented Jamison.

Decker said, "If he's still in the profession he has to be on a database somewhere for licensing purposes. We should start there."

"I can call the institute and get whatever information I can," offered Rabinowitz. "Since it doesn't involve a patient, I think they would be more forthcoming. Some of them might know where Chris is now."

Decker gave him their contact information.

"We'll be in town for a day or so." Decker rose and said, "Thank you, Harold, you've been a big help."

Rabinowitz stood too. "I pray that Chris is not your man, but if he is I pray even harder that you will be able to catch him and stop him from harming anyone else."

"Then let's hope that God is listening," said Decker.

"So you think the person might kill again?" said Rabinowitz.

"I know he'll *try*."

43

After they left Rabinowitz, Jamison and Decker stopped to grab some lunch. While they were at a café, Decker called Lancaster and filled her in.

She said, "Okay, we'll track down this Sizemore guy if we can. And if his prints are online somewhere we'll subpoena them and compare them to Leopold's. As soon as we find out anything I'll call you." She paused. "So, back at your old stomping grounds. I never knew you were at this institute place."

"No one knew, other than Cassie."

"We were partners for a long time, Amos."

"It never occurred to me that you would be interested in my past, Mary."

"Well, that goes to show, even people with big brains make mistakes," she said curtly, her frustration and disappointment evident.

She clicked off and Decker set his phone down next to his plate containing a half-eaten cheeseburger and a small mound of fries.

"Everything okay?" asked Jamison.

"Yeah," said Decker as he picked at a fry.

Jamison said, "If it turns out Sizemore is Leopold, he must be one sick dude."

"If he killed thirteen people he *is* one sick dude."

"That's not what I mean."

"So explain."

She slid her plate aside and leaned in. "The 'diss' was you got more attention than some of *his* protégés? Like it was a beauty pageant for brains? Really? So in retaliation he kills all those people?"

"Correction, if he *is* Leopold, he killed no one. Well, we don't know who killed Agent Lafferty. But Leopold was in jail when my family was killed and also when the shootings at Mansfield happened. He has a rock-solid alibi. And it seems that both incarcerations were planned."

"Meaning he knew your family was going to be killed *and* he knew the shooter was going to attack Mansfield?"

"The timing of his coming in to confess to the Burlington police was a little too coincidental. And I checked on the arrest record from Cranston. Disorderly conduct. He spent one night in jail and that was it. They didn't even bother arraigning him. They just let him go the next morning. But that unequivocally proved he could not have committed the murders of my family."

"Right, so he's partnered with someone, our five-foot-eleven skinny dude turned broad-shouldered maniac, to do the actual murdering."

"And there is no way that person is Sizemore."

"So if Sizemore *is* the one you dissed, he's partnered with this person who impersonated a waitress at the bar. I wonder who that person is that kills so readily?"

"I wonder too."

"But still, if Sizemore is behind this, how does someone that effed up become a psychologist?"

"Something in his mind could have snapped. He could be bipolar and the meds aren't working anymore. Leopold apparently told his lawyer he was bipolar and had gone off his meds, or at least that's what the PD told the judge. Or he could have had some sort of trauma, either physical or emotional, that changed him. He had a lump on his neck and drug tracks on his arm. Could be a lot of stuff going on inside him. A lot can happen to someone in twenty years. If it is Sizemore, he took a risk in letting me confront him. He knows how my mind works. I don't forget anything. If it is him, I *could* have recognized him."

"But you didn't. So maybe it's not him."

"Maybe."

"It's still all so scary."

"Of course it's scary. Because something like that could happen to any of us."

"Or he could be just plain evil."

"Or he could be," agreed Decker. "Does that make you feel better?"

She shivered. "I don't think anything about this case could make me feel better."

Decker's phone buzzed. He answered it.

Rabinowitz said, "Amos, I don't know if this is good or bad news, but the institute has been forwarding professional mail to Chris since he left. Enough time has passed that it's slowed to a trickle, but they did have an address."

Decker wrote it down, thanked Rabinowitz, and then looked up the address on his phone.

He said, "It's halfway between Chicago and Burlington. We passed it coming up here."

"Meaning if he still lives there he could get to Burlington and back relatively easily."

"Let's go."

"Decker, shouldn't we call in the police on this?"

"On what? We have no proof that he's done anything wrong. Not a shred. We can track this down. And if it turns out we're right, we bring in the cops."

He walked briskly out the door of the café and she more slowly followed.

Four hours later they pulled off the highway and spent another twenty minutes on surface streets before Decker, who was using the GPS on his phone, directed Jamison to a many-decades-old, rundown neighborhood.

"The guy looks like he's fallen on hard times," noted Jamison.

Decker remained quiet, but his gaze moved steadily around, taking in everything.

"That's it, the third on the left with the black shutters. Pull past it."

Jamison drove on, and then Decker had her park at the curb on the opposite side of the street about a half dozen homes down from Sizemore's.

"Decker, Rabinowitz said that Sizemore had left the institute several years ago."

"That's right."

"I just thought of this. Could he really be Leopold? I mean, the guy really looked homeless and out of it. Could Sizemore go downhill that fast?"

"Yes," said Decker. "I did. And it didn't take me years."

She looked at him openmouthed for a moment and then slowly turned away before saying, "Oh. Okay."

Decker extricated himself from the back of the car and stepped out. When Jamison started to do the same he ducked his head back in and said, "You're staying in the car."

"What!"

"Anything bad goes down, drive away and call the cops."

"Decker, I'm not going to let you—"

"Yes you are." He closed the car door and set off toward the house.

He went down the sidewalk, his hands in his pockets, his head down, seemingly trying to avoid the stiff, chilly breeze.

But he kept gazing to the right, observing the house as he went. It was growing dark, but there were no lights on inside. No car in the driveway. Sizemore, if he still lived here, might not be home. He might be in Burlington planning his next murder.

He actually thought it improbable that Sizemore and Leopold were one and the same. Though it had been twenty years, and people could change, Decker felt like he would have recognized the man, even though he hadn't had that much interaction with Sizemore at the institute. But still, one couldn't be sure without digging further. And right now it was the only viable lead he had.

He crossed the street, stepped between two parked cars, one of which was up on cement blocks, and walked down the crumbling sidewalk. He passed by the house, went around the block, cut through an alley, and ended up behind the house's backyard. He struggled over the sagging chain-link fence and approached the house from the rear. There were no lights visible from here either.

He sidled up to the rear door, slipped one hand over the butt of his gun, and waited, listening intently. No footsteps. No sounds at all.

He looked left and right. He saw no one in the back-yards of the houses on either side. The night was too chilly for folks to be sitting outside.

He put his elbow through the glass, reached through, unlocked the door, and entered.

He was now in a small foyer. On his left were a washer and dryer. Up a short set of stairs was the kitchen. The smell of fried foods was in the air, along with the stale stink of cigarette smoke. He remembered that Sizemore had been a smoker. He'd seen him taking his smoke breaks, the pack of cigarettes in his hand, and it appeared the man had never kicked the habit. But Decker had sat in a bar with Leopold and the man had never lighted up. If you were a smoker, you were going to light up in a bar if you could, and it was legal in Burlington to do so. And Decker hadn't smelled smoke on Leopold's clothes. And he would have. This lead was starting to go sideways, but he had to follow it through.

He glided up the steps and looked around the small kitchen. There were some dishes in the sink. A newspaper was in the waste-basket. He checked the date. Two weeks ago. This was looking more and more squirrelly.

He left the kitchen and looked into each of the rooms on the main level. There was no evidence that anyone had been here recently. He walked up the short flight of stairs to the upper floor.

Then, growing impatient, he raced forward, kicking open doors as he went. He cleared the first room, the second, and then came to the third and last door.

He pushed it open and started taking deep breaths, not because he wanted to, but because it was the only way to deaden his sense of smell.

He walked over to the bed and looked down.

He wasn't sure whose corpse was lying on the sheets, because it was too badly decomposed. The height was about right. But the face was too far gone. From the state of decay, it looked like the body had been here for quite a while.

The body had commanded his attention. He had not looked anywhere else.

Now he did. His gaze drifted around the room and then held on one spot.

He walked over to that wall and stared dumbly at the writing there.

Wrong again. If he's rotted now, it took you long enough. Keep trying. Maybe you'll get there. Or maybe not. Xoxo, bro.

44

Agent Bogart said, "It's Chris Sizemore. They just confirmed the ID from prints and teeth."

Decker had called the police and then the FBI agent. The law had descended on the small rundown house like a hailstorm.

They were in Sizemore's house. Thankfully, the remains had long since been removed.

Alexandra Jamison was in her car with strict instructions not to write about a word of this.

Decker nodded. "Of course it is."

"Why?"

Decker pointed to the writing on the wall. "Because of that."

Bogart stood next to him. "Explain."

"They said I was wrong again. This is Sizemore's house. I would only have come here because I thought he was involved. He wasn't. He was just another victim."

"So they're playing you. Pulling your chain at every step."

Decker nodded. "Making like they're smarter than I am, and maybe they are."

"Well, let's hope to hell you're wrong about that."

"They've been a step ahead the whole way. 'If he's rotted now'? He was pretty decomposed by the time I figured it out."

"Well, they had a long time to plan this. You might just catch up. The tortoise and the hare. And you have the FBI behind you. It's not like you have to do this alone."

They walked outside; it was now the early hours of the morning.

"So 711 Duckton," said Bogart. "Your old stomping ground, you said."

"Yes."

"So if it's not Sizemore who had the grudge against you there, who could it be?"

"The other doctors and people working at the institute had no problem with me that I can recall."

Bogart sat down on the concrete stoop and sighed. "Okay. Anyone else? Because there has to be something. Otherwise, why point you to this place? How else would he even know about it if he wasn't a patient or a staffer there?"

Decker sat next to him. "It's not simply his being there. There has to be something I did, or that he perceived I did, that would have made him undertake something like this."

"To an unbalanced mind, pretty much anything

could be deemed to be a slight, Decker. You walked in a door ahead of him. You sneezed on him. You answered a question he wanted to answer. Who the hell knows?"

"*I* have to know. I'm the only one who can know."

"Well, you never forget anything, so I have to believe that it will come to you."

"That's the problem. If it hasn't come to me then it's not there." Decker tapped the side of his head. "I don't have things *come* to me. I go inside my head and retrieve them. There's a difference."

Bogart rose and looked down at him. "I guess there is, now that you explain it." He shoved his hands into his pockets. "Well, the ME estimates that Sizemore has been dead about two weeks. No telling where Leopold and his 'friend' were then. We're going to canvass the neighborhood, see if anything turns up."

"I doubt it will. I slipped in the backyard while it was still light and broke in. And big as I am, no one apparently saw anything."

"Well, we're still going to do it."

"Did Sizemore have a job?"

"We're checking that now. If he did, you'd think someone would have reported him missing when he didn't show up."

"Some jobs don't require you to show up anywhere."

"I'll let you know what we find."

Bogart left him and Decker rose and walked back over to Jamison's car and climbed in.

She looked sleepily at him from the driver's seat.

"You could have gone on to a motel," he said. "I'm sure I could have hitched a ride with one of Bogart's guys."

She shook her head and said, "No, I couldn't have slept anyway. So was it Sizemore?"

"It was. Dead about two weeks."

"When you came out of the house before, you said the message on the wall was another taunt?"

"That I had gotten it wrong but to keep trying. He also implied that maybe I wasn't as smart as I thought. And he called me 'bro' again."

"He's really playing mind games with you."

"Appears to be."

She stretched and yawned. "So what now?"

"We get some sleep. We both think about things. Maybe some ideas will come."

"You really think that will happen?"

"No, I don't."

He thought, *Because things don't come to me. There're already there. Or else they're not.*

45

They left the next day and began the long drive back to Burlington. Decker hardly spoke at all, and any questions posed to him by Jamison went largely ignored. She finally gave up and turned on the radio. They stopped to eat at a truckers' grill off the highway. Amid a sea of big rigs, Jamison pulled her minnow of a vehicle into an available slot and they climbed out.

Decker was moving stiffly. She noted this.

"Sorry about the cramped quarters," she said.

He rubbed his neck, straightened his back until he heard a little pop, and said, "I'm hungry."

The place was crowded and they were led to a corner table in the back adjacent to the pool hall where truckers smacked balls and bet on the outcomes. Next to that was a gift shop where the most popular items seemed to be lingerie and sex toys for the missus or girlfriend back home.

They ordered and Decker spooned sugar into his coffee while he stared at the laminated tabletop.

A Bonnie Raitt song started wafting over the room from a jukebox.

Jamison looked around at the beehive of activity, including one man wearing a Stetson who rode an electronic bucking bronco for a few seconds before being pitched off, to the delight of his buddies.

Decker scratched at his beard and lifted his gaze to her.

"You need to get on a plane and get as far away from me as you can. You understand that, don't you?"

"I thought we'd been through this and it was settled. Andy Jackson was—"

"He was your friend and mentor. And being your friend and mentor he would not want you to be murdered."

"I have my Mace and—"

"They could be here right now, you know. Watching us. Watching you."

"You're just trying to scare me."

"I don't have to try to scare you, Jamison. You're a smart woman, which means you're already scared."

Their food came and they ate in silence, each seemingly unwilling to meet the other's gaze. When the check came, Decker paid.

"You don't owe me anything," she said.

"I ate a lot more than you. Splitting the tab wouldn't be fair."

They walked back to the car. Decker, without seeming to, kept vigilant observation of their surroundings.

*

"Where do you want me to drop you?" asked Jamison as they drove along the city streets after having reached Burlington. "Your place, the school, the police department? Another life?"

"Are you going to be getting on that plane?"

She turned to look at him. "I don't know," she said quietly.

"I hear Florida is nice this time of year. Maybe Miami?"

"I don't like running away from trouble."

"This isn't trouble. It's something more than that. It's more about survival."

"And what about you? You're staying, right? You're not hopping on some plane and getting the hell out of Dodge."

"I'm staying," was all Decker would say. "And you can drop me off at my place."

She did. As he climbed out of the car Decker said, "Stay or go. Either way, let me know, okay?"

She nodded and then drove off.

Decker went to his room, took a shower, grabbed some sleep, and then headed back out, taking a crosstown bus to Mansfield.

He got off at the corner, looked up at the faded façade of the high school, and trudged inside.

Lancaster met him in the library. She looked thinner and paler, and her left hand was trembling so badly she stuck it in her pocket. They sat at the back and he filled her in on the events of the last two days.

"So you think Jamison will take your advice?" she asked.

He shrugged. "I hope so. I can't make her leave."

"Well, Chris Sizemore was out of town, and look what happened to him."

"They can't run everyone down, Mary. This is not some secret organization with unlimited resources. It's two people. Capable and methodical, but only two."

"That's not a fact. That's speculation on your part. Just like my speculation on 7-Eleven."

He considered this and nodded. "Actually, you're right. What's happened here, anything?"

She shook her head. "We've gotten lip service from the Army. Not that it's likely they could add much. Forensics has been a dead end. We know how the shooter got in, moved around, and left, but that doesn't really lead us where we need to go, Amos."

"The only proven point is my connection. It led me to Chicago and the institute. That lead was confirmed with the murder of Chris Sizemore. The only way they could possibly know about him, and the grievance he held against me, was if they were there, or had some inside knowledge of what went on there twenty years ago."

"And you remember nothing that could help us? From all the folks who went in and out of that place while you were there?"

Decker slumped back in his chair and looked around at the investigators at their various stations poring over details of the case. But he could see in their eyes and movements an ebbing energy, a malaise settling upon them. He had seen cases go sideways like this before. They were coming to believe that they were not going to solve this case. That they were not going to catch whoever had done this. It was draining everyone.

He looked back at Lancaster. "The only link right now is Leopold, but I know for a fact that he was not at the institute. The only person he could have been was Sizemore. And even that was a long shot, now disproved."

"Well, we've seen that these people can play with physical perceptions. They made a smaller person look massive. And we've had a BOLO out on him for a while now and nothing. Guy's just vanished."

"And no sign of our waitress from the bar?"

"None. Waitress or waiter, according to the barman."

"Physical perception again. The guy impersonated a woman. And he did it well. I was sold on it. And he served me a beer. Was inches from me and I never suspected anything."

"And you're convinced that the waitress was in on it?"

"The barman told the FBI that she vanished about five minutes before Leopold left, and never came back. Could be a coincidence, but I don't think so."

"Okay, but it's still not a fact. Not yet." She riffled through some papers. "But I have something here that *is* a fact."

He sat up. "What?"

"Six students and three adults were killed at the school. Five of the students were male."

"And Debbie Watson was the lone female."

"But the five males were all on the football team. Or three were, technically. One was a team manager, and one had gotten kicked off recently for some rule violation."

Decker sat up even straighter. "Beth Watson said that Jimmy Schikel was on the team. But I didn't make a connection with the others. Because of Debbie and the adults."

"And, Joe Kramer, while the gym teacher, was also the *football* coach."

"And the assistant principal?"

"Barry Dresden has no connection to the team that I could find. He has no kids at the school, so none of them could be on the team. And then there's Andy Jackson."

"But he was killed because he confronted the shooter. It might be that the others were targeted because of their connection to the football team."

"But Dresden had no such ties."

"But all of the male student victims plus the coach? That can't be a coincidence, Mary. The odds are way too long. There were lots of targets in each of those classrooms. He had to know who he was shooting. Wait a minute, were the victims all large? Did they look like football players?"

"Two did, the others were normal-sized. So I doubt he could have picked them solely on their physical appearance. They wear their game jerseys on Fridays before the football game, but the shooting didn't happen on a Friday. But he could have easily found out which ones were on the team. And he could have found their class schedules too. Or Debbie could have told him. And if so, maybe she knew what he was planning to do." She paused. "But anyway, I wanted you to know what I had found out."

He looked at her appreciatively. "That's good work, Mary. No one else saw that, including me."

She smiled wearily. "Well, I'm not used to getting somewhere before you, so it does feel good. But what does it mean, Amos?"

"I played on the football team here. They took all of my trophies. It could be just another way of getting back at me. Another facet of their vendetta." He lapsed into silence.

"What?"

"Dresden, the assistant principal, was targeted. The shooter went to the office to kill him. Debbie and Jackson can be explained away. But not Dresden. If he has no ties to the football team, then why was he killed?"

"You mean the reason might not be your playing football here? Despite their taking the trophies?"

"Yes. But if not that, what?"

"I have no idea," admitted Lancaster.

"Well, it won't do us any good beating our heads

against the wall on it until we find out more. But we do have someplace to go."

"Go? Go where?"

"The bar."

"You thirsty?"

"Yeah, but not for a beer."

46

A snowflake drifted down as Decker stood across the street from the bar, Lancaster at his side. The flake hit the sidewalk and then melted almost immediately.

Lancaster pulled out a handkerchief and blew her nose.

"If you don't want to go in, can we wait in the car at least?" she asked. "It's freezing and I feel the flu coming on."

Decker had taken in the city block grid by grid, and then his gaze started over and went through it again. He began to walk and Lancaster hurried after him. They covered both sides of the street for a block in either direction.

"No cameras," he noted.

"Burlington has surveillance cameras, just not every-where. I hear that London and New York have them on every street. But we don't have their tax base, do we?"

"There are private surveillance cameras," said Decker. "Banks, pawn shops, liquor stores. But none that I can see. Can you check on that? See if there are any on this block?"

"I'll put in a call." She did so while Decker continued to look around. A few more flakes were falling, and overhead the clouds had thickened with moisture. If the temperature continued to fall they might get some real accumulation.

Lancaster put her phone away. "They'll get back to me. Now what?"

Decker headed across the street to the bar and she followed.

It was full, with most tables occupied by couples, although there seemed to be a bachelor party going on in the back of the room. Lancaster eyed with disdain the stripper, who was in the process of shedding her skin-tight Catwoman costume.

"Amazes me what gets young men excited."

"It's the same thing that's always gotten them excited," said Decker absently. "Pretty women in the process of taking off their clothes." He worked his way to the bar and eyed the barman, the same guy he had talked to before. The man came over.

"What's your poison?" he asked.

"I'll take a Miller on draft." Decker looked at Lancaster.

"I'm officially on duty," she said in a low voice.

"And a Virgin Mary for my friend," said Decker.

When the man went off to fill this order, Decker turned around on his stool, leaned against the bar, and took in the room. Lancaster did the same.

"So Leopold led you to this bar where his partner

was allegedly masquerading as a waitress. You guys talked, and then, with the alleged aid of his alleged partner, he vanished."

"*Allegedly*, yes," said Decker irritably.

"How did he know you were going to follow him here?"

"How could I not? All charges dropped? He knew that I knew the police procedure. Processed out of his cell at central lockup and sent packing. He knew I'd be waiting outside. And if for some reason I wasn't, so what? No skin off his teeth. They'd find another way to lure me in."

"So you followed him here. What was his endgame?"

"Maybe he just wanted to see me again, up close. Size me up."

"But if we're reading this right, the person that really wanted to see you was the waitress. Maybe the one who was at the institute with you. The one you insulted somehow."

"I'm sure that was part of it too."

"It's a wonder he didn't kill you right then. Or at least try to."

"I haven't suffered enough, Mary."

"Haven't suffered enough! All these people dead, including your family? The story that Jamison wrote trashing you? Him taunting you the whole time?"

"Still not enough, Mary. Not for them."

"What do they want, Amos? I mean, what else could they possibly want from you?"

"More, Mary. I just don't know what that is yet."

But Decker did know what their real endgame was.

They want me.

The barman brought their drinks and said, "Hey, man, you cost me some business the other day. Cops all over the place. Scared away half my customers."

"You get paid the same, right?" said Lancaster bluntly.

"Tips, honey," said the barman. "I live on my tips." He put an electronic cigarette to his lips and took a puff. "You think the owners of this place pay an actual living wage? If you do, get your head examined."

Decker said, "I'm sure your waitresses rely on their tips too."

"They do."

"But maybe not the one who skipped out on you. Maybe she has another source of income."

"Maybe *it* does."

"You sure it was a guy?" asked Lancaster, watching him closely.

The barman eyed her. "What's your interest?"

She flashed her badge. He took another electronic puff and said, "I used to work as a grip off-Broadway. Lot of *its* around that world. I can tell guys from girls, although I have to admit this one was really good."

"So if it was a guy, why did you let *him* work?" asked Lancaster.

"I don't give a shit if a guy wants to dress up like a chick so long as he can serve the drinks without spilling. All I need is bodies. I don't count penises."

Decker said, "According to you, the waitress left before the guy I was talking to did."

"Well, I couldn't find her after you left. Had to serve drinks at the tables myself until I got a replacement in. So, yeah, it apparently skipped out."

"And you called the temp agency?" asked Decker.

"I did. And you were right about that. No record of her. Score one for you."

Decker's gaze drifted down to the man's waist. A key fob poked from the top of his front jeans pocket.

"What kind of car do you drive?"

The barman looked down in surprise and then back up at Decker. "Why? You need a ride somewhere?"

"No. Just curious."

"Nissan Leaf."

"That's an all-electric."

"I know it is. Great gas mileage since it doesn't run on gas. I just plug it in."

"Very quiet, I expect," said Decker.

"Too quiet sometimes. I've left it running more times than I can remember. Just walked off with the key in my pocket and the damn thing still on."

"Is that right? Where do you keep it parked?"

"Alley outside."

"Did you notice on the day I was in here that when you went out to the car it was in a slightly different location?"

The man thought for a moment and then said, "No, not that I remember. Why?"

"Because I looked in that alley when I was here that day and there was no car there."

"The hell you say," snapped the barman, his eyes wide in surprise. "But it was there when I left work."

"You always keep the car key on you?"

"Not always. Sometimes I hang it on a hook over there." He pointed to a wall behind the bar. "Have to move it sometimes when we're expecting a delivery. Beer truck can barely squeeze in that space. And it's a dead end so they have to back out. Sometimes I let one of the waitresses move it if I'm tied up."

"Well, I think the waitress in question drove it without your permission."

Decker dropped some dollars on the bar. "Tip included." He and Lancaster walked out.

47

The snow had begun to fall more heavily as Decker stared at the gray Nissan Leaf.

"Looks like he's charging it now," said Lancaster. She was staring at a power cable running from a port on the car to an electrical box next to the side door of the bar.

Decker didn't look at the cable; he was staring at the walls of the alley.

"Over there," he said.

Positioned up high and trained so that it would take in most of the alley was a video surveillance camera. Decker walked over to where the camera was mounted and then down at the door of the business.

"Pharmacy," he said. "This must be their delivery entrance."

"Lot of thefts from pharmacies around here," said Lancaster, who had come to stand next to him. "Not surprised they have a camera. Logical place to hit it from the rear. That's why the door's barred and locked."

"We need to get the footage from this camera, and we need it now."

They hurried around to the front. A clerk was

behind the cash register and there was an off-duty police officer near the entrance.

Lancaster flashed her badge at him. "I know you," she said. "Donovan, Fourth Precinct? Right?"

"Yes ma'am. What do you need, Detective Lancaster?"

She explained, and they walked together over to the cash register, where Donovan conveyed this to the cashier. He said, "I can pull it."

A few minutes later Lancaster and Decker were walking out of the drugstore with the DVD. They drove straight back to Mansfield, where Lancaster popped the disc into her computer and brought up the images.

There was a time stamp so Decker gave her the date to forward to. She worked the computer's controls until Decker said, "Stop it right there."

She did so and the frame on the screen froze.

He said, "Now roll it forward in slow-mo."

Lancaster hit the requisite buttons to accomplish this, and they watched as the waitress exited the bar, opened the door of the Leaf, and climbed in after disconnecting the charging cable. A few moments later she drove off.

Ten minutes later she drove back up again, got out, reconnected the cable, and reentered the bar.

"But the guy said she didn't come back," noted Lancaster.

"Just wait a minute," said Decker.

The woman came back out a few seconds later, turned, and walked off down the alley.

Decker looked at Lancaster. "She went back in to hang the keys on the hook. Bar guy probably never even saw her."

"Right."

"So she picked up Leopold and then dropped him off somewhere. Pretty smart to do it with someone else's car. No plate for us to run."

"But we can check the car for her prints. She wasn't wearing gloves."

While Lancaster put in a call, Decker was staring at the screen.

When she clicked off he said, "Okay, run it again but this time enlarge the image as much as you can."

Lancaster did so, several times, at Decker's request. From where the camera was angled they were watching from the rear of the car. They could see her slide into the driver's seat and later swing her long legs out to exit. Her short skirt rode up her thighs when she did so. But there was no direct shot on the face.

"She's got great legs," said Lancaster. "Gotta give her that."

"*He* does," corrected Decker. *At least I think it's a guy.*

"The barman was right, though."

"About what?"

Lancaster said, "He told us he'd seen lots of guys as girls when he worked off-Broadway. But he said this one was really good. And she—or he—is. I mean, those really look like a female's legs."

Decker slowly nodded and then looked back at the image. He ran it through two more times before shutting it down. But there was still never a clear image of the person's face.

"So?" said Lancaster. "Any mental breakthroughs?"

Decker shook his head. Only there *was* something. It seemed to be staring him right in the face, but he just couldn't make it out.

Lancaster yawned and stretched and then looked around at the activity going on in the library. "I wonder when Bogart will show back up?"

"He didn't tell me his travel plans," said Decker. "He came up to where Sizemore lived on a jet. I assumed he'd be returning the same way. He would have beaten me back in any case."

"Well, he hasn't checked in here."

"Probably not the only case he's working."

"Maybe not, but I hope Mansfield takes priority, even with the FBI."

"I wouldn't know," said Decker absently.

Lancaster checked her watch. "It's nearly eleven and I've been at this since five this morning. I have to get home. You need a ride? I doubt you should walk. It's starting to really come down out there."

She was staring out the window of the library, where, under the lights, the snow was falling rapidly.

"Okay. I guess I'm done here for now."

They walked to the exit.

She said encouragingly, "We have quite a few leads, Amos, we just have to run them down."

"They aren't leads, Mary. They're mostly fluff that will go nowhere. They've planned well."

"Well, you know what they say about the best-laid plans."

"I know the saying. Unfortunately, it's often wrong."

They climbed into her car and set off.

She glanced at him. "You seemed like you saw something on the security video."

"I did. I just don't know what."

"How did it feel to go back to that place? The institute?"

"I didn't. It had moved. I just spoke with one of the people who used to work there."

"Still a trip down memory lane."

"My whole life is one long memory lane."

"Is it that bad?"

"You ever want to get up from a movie?"

"Sure, lots of times."

"And if you couldn't turn it off? If you couldn't get up and leave it because it happens to be running inside your head?"

She gripped the steering wheel and stared ahead. "I guess I can see that."

The police radio mounted on the dash crackled. The address of a criminal incident was read out by the dispatcher.

Lancaster nearly ran the car off the road before righting it.

She stared horror-struck at Decker.

"That's my house," she screamed.

48

Mary Lancaster's house was a modest split-level rancher about thirty years old. Even though Earl Lancaster was in the construction business, the house needed painting and the roof required repairs, and there was rot in some of the wood. The asphalt driveway was cracked in numerous spots. The inside was in a bit better shape, but the rooms were small and dark and the air was musty.

The dark sky around the home was lit by the rack lights of the police vehicles.

Lancaster screeched her car to the curb, leapt out, flashed her badge at the two officers coming out the front door, and would have bolted past them if they hadn't stopped her.

One of them knew her.

"Detective Lancaster—"

She tried to push past him. He grabbed her.

"Wait!" he called out. "I'm trying to tell you—"

The cop struggled with her mightily, because though she was not big, the woman was completely out of control, enraged, screaming, spitting, and clawing. She was going in there.

Then she was snatched from them and held completely off the ground.

The cops looked up at Decker, who had her in a bear hug, her arms pinned to her sides.

She shrieked, "Let me go, Amos! I will kill you! I swear to God I will kill you, you son of a bitch. I . . . will . . . kill . . ."

She kept ranting and struggling, but he held her tight until she finally fell limp in his arms, her head down, her legs dangling. Exhausted. Her breaths came in ragged gasps.

The cop looked up at her. "I was trying to tell you that your family is okay."

"What!" she screamed. "Then why the hell are all these people here?"

Decker slowly set her on the ground.

The cop said, "Because there was an incident."

"I tried calling in to dispatch, but I couldn't get through," said Lancaster. "Where the hell is my family?"

"They've been taken into protective custody."

"What? Why?"

"Captain Miller's orders."

At that moment Miller walked out of the house.

"Captain, what the hell is going on?" asked Lancaster.

"Earl and Sandy are fine."

"What's the incident?" asked Decker.

"Some things left in the house."

427

"What things?" asked Decker, his gaze dead on Miller.

"Amos, you might want to sit this one out."

"That won't be happening unless you have some more officers on the scene." Decker glanced menacingly at the pair of uniforms who had tried to stop Lancaster.

"All right, then," said Miller, and he led the way inside.

They entered the kitchen. Decker eyed the beer bottles on the table and the overturned chair.

"I thought you said nothing happened!" cried out Lancaster.

"It's not what it seems to be," said Miller. "It's . . . it's all . . ." He couldn't finish.

Decker's gut took a jolt as the man struggled to find the words.

Miller led them into the adjoining room.

On the floor was a body. Well, it wasn't an actual body. It was a life-size inflatable male mannequin. Someone had colored its head brownish gray. But Decker's attention was riveted on the streak of red drawn across its neck.

"Was . . . was that supposed to be Earl?" said Lancaster.

"I think so," said Miller hesitantly, with a quick glance at Decker. "Sick bastard."

Decker also noted that an X had been drawn over each of the mannequin's eyes.

Everyone had seen mannequins before. They were

ubiquitous and thus innocuous. But this mannequin—it was the most sinister thing Decker had ever seen. It was like the threes marching in the dark at him. Pale, bloody, staring, silent, lifeless; the symbolism reeked of depravity.

Decker looked toward the stairs. And then he looked all around. He had been here several times in the past. But his mind, while obviously registering this fact, had now connected it to another fact.

This house was nearly an exact copy of Decker's. Not unusual in working-class cookie-cutter communities, where one builder used the same set of plans in constructing hundreds of houses that were essentially the same structures, but for a different color paint or some minor architectural differences.

"So there's another one of, what, Sandy?" said Lancaster. She put a hand out and snagged the back of a chair to steady herself.

"There's another mannequin up there, yes," said Miller, again nervously eyeing Decker.

In Decker's mind he thought back to when he had bolted up stairs very much like these at his house the night he had lost everything.

"So there's just one more of . . . of these things in my house," barked Lancaster.

Decker looked back at the mannequin with the "slit" throat and then his gaze settled on Miller. And something in those eyes, coupled with what he had just deduced, made Decker say, "No, there're two more there."

"Yes," said Miller miserably. "Two more."

"What the hell are you talking about?" said Lancaster. "There's just Earl and Sandy. Wait, is one supposed to be me?"

Decker was already heading for the stairs.

The first door they came to was partially open. Decker pushed it all the way open and they stepped inside.

A leg was sticking up on the other side of the bed, just as he knew it would be. He stepped to that side of the bed and looked down. As he knew it would be, this mannequin was a female dressed in a see-through nightgown. There was a blackened dot drawn in the center of its forehead to represent a bullet being fired into its head. Her eyes, too, had been marked with Xs.

Miller said to Decker, "I guess you know where the third victim is?"

Lancaster gaped as the truth struck her. "Oh my God, that's supposed to be . . . "

"Cassie," Decker finished for her.

Miller put an arm on Decker's shoulder. "Amos, why don't you go on back downstairs?"

Decker shook his head. "No."

"Amos, please."

"No!"

He bolted down the hall and opened the door to the bathroom. The others rushed after him.

On the toilet was the third mannequin, smaller, a child. They had even drawn in curly hair on the head, like Molly's. The robe belt held her upright. Ligature marks had been drawn in around her throat; Xs had been drawn over the eyes.

The killers had indeed replicated exactly what had happened at Decker's home, but fortunately substituting mannequins for real people.

But there was one difference, a significant one.

Above the toilet were words inked onto the wall:

This could so easily have been real. But ask yourself this. How much pain will you cause, bro? End it now. Do the right thing. Like you should have back then. Find the courage. Don't be a coward, bro. Not now. Or next time the blood will be real. Last chance.

Decker stared at the words for the longest time.

Then he turned and left the room, took the steps two at a time, and walked outside. Lancaster and Miller followed him. She caught up with him at the end of the driveway.

"Where are you going?" she demanded.

"I'm sorry for all this, Mary."

"You have nothing to be sorry for. My family is fine."

"They won't be next time. They'll be dead."

"No they won't. Look, this is not about you. It's about *them*."

"No, it's about me and them."

He set off down the street as snowflakes swirled around him.

49

Decker was sitting on the bed in his room at the Residence Inn. The snow continued to fall outside, but the ground was warm enough that most of it wasn't sticking. It was just slush. Just like his mind was.

My wonderfully perfect mind that remembers all.

But parts of his thoughts were crystal clear.

In his hand Decker held his pistol. A nice, serviceable weapon. He had carried it with him as a detective. And had brought it with him into civilian life.

This was also the pistol he had first stuck in his mouth and then placed against his head as he sat on the floor staring at his dead daughter.

He had not pulled the trigger that night and still didn't exactly know why. With a perfect memory did not come a perfect mind, or resolute decisions. Sometimes with perfection on one end of the equation, one was left with stark imprecision on the other. Perhaps it was nature's way of balancing things.

Regardless, he had not killed himself that night.

But tonight was a new night, wasn't it?

He racked the slide and heard a round fall neatly into

the chamber. He nudged off the safety and raised the weapon to his head, placing it against his right temple.

Find the courage. Don't be a coward, bro. End it now.

Decker thought that there must be both courage and cowardice in killing oneself. Did he have enough of both? Or was he totally lacking?

Yet he thought he did. Now, anyway.

He closed his eyes and let his finger drift to the trigger guard and then to the trigger. A couple foot-pounds of pressure and it would be over. It was the narrowest gap in the world, between the finger and the trigger. A simple movement, hook the digit and pull back. Folks did it every day, only not with a gun.

He tried to clear his mind, to just relax and let go of whatever it was that was tethering him to this world. It couldn't be much. What exactly did he have left?

The image of first Molly and then Cassie eased into his mind. Two frames of memory he could never let go, even if he could somehow release all the others.

He held on them. His DVR momentarily frozen.

The knock on the door caused him to open his eyes. He didn't move.

The knock came again.

"Amos? Amos, I know you're in there. Please open the door."

The images of Cassie and Molly held for an instant longer and then the frames rolled through and other visuals took their place.

Decker rose and opened the door.

Captain Miller stared back at him, the collar of his overcoat turned up against the cold, beaten-up old galoshes on his feet.

"I want to talk to you," said Miller. "Right now."

He didn't wait to be invited in. He strode past Decker into the small room. His gaze alighted on the pistol on the bed where Decker had dropped it. Miller glanced sharply at him.

"You do that, they win, you know."

"Do they?" Decker said.

Miller picked up the pistol, engaged the safety, and placed it on the bureau against the wall before sitting on the edge of the bed.

Decker closed the door and sat in a chair across from him.

"Of course they do," said Miller. "Since you're the only one who has a shot at taking them down. They get you to eliminate yourself, they have free rein to keep doing what they're doing."

"If their goal is to punish me, destroy me, then once they do, there's nothing more for them to do."

"Until they figure that someone *else* has disrespected them. And there's the small matter of letting this filth get away with killing all those people. I don't intend to let it happen. And I don't think you do either."

Decker glanced over at the gun and then back at Miller.

Miller said, "We can't bring any of them back. The only thing we can do is make this right by catching the people who killed them and make sure they never, ever hurt anyone else. That's it. May not sound like much, but in a civilized world it's all we've got."

"Civilized world?"

"Which always has parts that aren't civilized."

Decker shifted slightly in his seat and more dramatically in his thoughts. "Who called it in? The incident at Lancaster's house?"

"Earl Lancaster did. He was out with Sandy at a school function. They didn't get home until nearly eleven. That's when they found what they found and called 911."

"Anyone see or hear anything?"

"Still canvassing. Nothing yet. It was dark and messy. Easy enough to slip in. They could have brought the mannequins in deflated and then quickly inflated them." He rubbed his forehead. "Thank God they didn't opt for the real thing."

"Which is puzzling, since they've had no problem killing anyone."

Miller nodded thoughtfully. "You know, it's like these people can turn invisible."

"Not invisible. Innocuous."

"How do you mean?" asked Miller.

"Nonthreatening. Blend in. Someone so commonplace that no one notices them even though they're there. That makes them invisible because people don't remember them."

"Well, one of them dressed like a cop to snare Lafferty."

"Not a cop. A cop draws notice. They used that disguise specifically to get to Lafferty. No, I mean in a neighborhood someone that just blends in."

"Well, we'll have the canvassing reports at both places ready in about an hour. Why don't you come down to the precinct and go over them?"

Decker eyed his former commander. "Is this busy work?"

Miller rose. "Amos, you're a grown man. If you want to kill yourself you will. Nothing I can do to stop that. But while I have you alive and kicking I'd like to avail myself of your services. So let's go down to the precinct and see what we can see."

He turned and walked out the door.

Decker sat there for a few seconds, then rose, grabbed his gun, slipped it into his coat pocket, and followed.

50

Four cups of coffee and a stale breakfast burrito later, Decker pushed back from the table where he had been going over all aspects of the case and hit the john. When he came out, Alex Jamison was leaning against the wall, apparently waiting for him.

She looked up at him, her arms folded across her chest, her heel tapping against the dulled linoleum.

"I guess I missed my flight out of here," she said.

"There's always another one."

"Maybe. Maybe I'll go someplace warm. When we're all done here."

"This is not your fight. Or your concern."

"Don't even go there, Decker."

"What are you doing here?"

"I wanted to see you. Let you know that I was still working the case. And Miller called me. He knew I went with you to the institute and that I was with you when you found Sizemore."

"So?"

Miller appeared from around the corner. "So I thought another pair of fresh eyes on this sucker can't hurt. I'm not too proud to ask for help." He pointed at the two of them. "So why don't you get to it?"

"She's not on the force."

"Neither are you," shot back Jamison.

"Where's Lancaster?" asked Decker.

"Where she should be, with her family. Now go!"

Decker reluctantly led Jamison back to the room and they started going back over the statements given to the police. Both were from neighbors of the Lancasters.

An old woman and a dog.

And a dog. Nonthreatening. Something folks would just gloss over, not remember unless specifically asked.

He dialed up his DVR and went back over the canvassing reports from his neighborhood that the police had undertaken after the murders of his family.

No old woman with a dog. But there had been an old man seen out for a stroll. He had been described as slightly bent, feeble, supported by a cane and totally at odds with the violent slaughter that had occurred that night, no doubt perpetrated by a strong homicidal man in his prime.

Totally innocuous. Nobody gave him a second thought. Nobody wondered who he was. Or why he was there that night.

Including me.

There had been no forced entry at the Lancasters'. They'd apparently walked right in.

An old woman in disguise. An old man in disguise. His killer seemed to be a true chameleon.

Decker glanced back at the file on the Lancasters.

Walked right in.

He thought back to last night. The house had been neat and tidy. Mary had been working impossible hours. Earl, he knew, while a competent contractor, had his hands full with their daughter, Sandy. He didn't see the guy vacuuming, dusting, and doing the dishes every five minutes.

He rose from the table and headed out. He had questions that needed answers. He had apparently forgotten that Jamison was even there until she said, "Where are we going?"

"*I'm* going somewhere. I don't know where you're going."

"But I'm safer with you, right?"

Decker struggled to find a reply to this but then just gave up.

Jamison held up her keys. "And unlike you, *I* have a car."

"No, you have *half* a car."

Decker stalked out, with Jamison scurrying after him.

Against her wishes, Lancaster also had been placed in protective custody and was staying in a house rented by the FBI and guarded both by local Burlington cops and Bureau agents.

Decker cleared the security and entered the house with Jamison. Little Sandy had run forward and thrown her arms around Decker's legs. Not knowing what else to do, he had patted her on the head until she let go, stared straight up at him, and said, "You're Amos Decker!"

"I know I am. And you're Sandra Elizabeth Lancaster."

She had wagged a finger at him. "I know I am." Then she ran off, with her bedraggled father trying to keep up behind her.

Decker and Jamison had sat down opposite Lancaster, who eyed her suspiciously. "Why are you here?"

"Like Decker here, I'm a consultant on the case."

"I never knew a case to have so many consultants," said Lancaster. Then she settled her gaze on Decker. "How are you doing?"

"I'm doing," said Decker.

"Those heartless pricks. What they did at my house. Re-create *your* crime scene."

Jamison shot Decker a startled look.

"You didn't know?" asked Lancaster.

"No," said Jamison quietly.

"Fortunately for us, they used mannequins instead of real people," said Lancaster. She shivered, took out a pack of smokes, and then put them away again. Decker eyed her. She said, "I'm trying to quit. For Sandy's sake."

"Secondhand smoke?" said Jamison.

"No, I never smoke in the house or car. I meant I

wanted to be alive to see her grow up. Especially after . . . "

She reached into her pocket, pulled out a tissue, and dabbed at her eyes as she looked away, embarrassed.

She stuffed the tissue back into her pocket and said, "I don't want to be here. I want to be working the case. Those bastards came into my house and did that. I want them more than I've wanted anyone in my whole career."

"Did you or Earl hire a cleaning service for your house?" Decker asked.

She looked puzzled. "A cleaning service?"

"I know how security-conscious you are, especially with Sandy. How she got out of the house that one time and you didn't find her for hours."

"What is your point, Decker?" she snapped.

"No forced entry at your house. They just walked in, Mary. I wonder how that could be, unless someone had a key. Earl and Sandy had gone out. He locked up, right?"

"Yes, he always does. And you're right, Earl *did* hire a maid service, but they don't have a key to our house. We'd never have allowed that. Earl knew when they were coming and he let them in."

"But once in the house, could someone posing as a maid have gotten access to a key, made a copy of it, and used it to enter the house later?"

"But how would they know he'd even hired a maid?"

"If they were watching the house they could see the

car or van pull up. They usually have signs on them."

"But how could they impersonate a maid?"

"Call the service and ask them if someone posing as you or Earl called and canceled them coming on one of their workdays."

"Decker, do you really—"

"It's just a phone call, Mary. And it might be a break for us. You said you wanted to be working the case. So *work.*"

She slipped out her phone and called the maid service. From the words she spoke, Decker knew the answer before she hung up.

"You were right, Amos. They got a call saying not to come."

"So that's when the fake maid came and made an impression of the key. You keep your keys where?" said Decker.

"On hooks by the side door."

"I saw a calendar on your fridge. It has everybody's schedule?"

"Yes."

"So that's how they knew Earl and Sandy would be out that night."

"I can't believe the person who did all this was in my house," said Lancaster, staring at her hands. "I just can't believe it." She glanced up. "That means Earl has seen the killer. Maybe—"

Decker shook his head. "The person won't look

anything like Earl's description now. They're too smart for that, Mary."

Decker rose and looked down at her. Jamison followed suit. "Will you be okay here?" he asked.

"We'll be safe, if that's what you mean."

"Right now, that's what I mean."

"I'm lucky, Amos. My family is alive."

"This was a warning, Mary. A warning to me. I didn't do what they wanted me to do. There will be no more warnings. Which means I have to get to them, before they get to anyone else."

He turned to leave with Jamison.

"Where are you going now?" Lancaster stared at him like he was the last person left on earth except for her. If Decker could have felt sympathy, he would have been deeply moved.

"To look at a video one more time."

"What video?"

"Of someone getting out of a car."

51

Decker had watched the video on the laptop a dozen times, both at regular speed and in slow motion. Then he had sat back in his chair, closed his eyes.

She had come over.

The order given.

The beer delivered.

She had walked away.

He had seen her once more sauntering along the bar, slender hips twitching enticingly, before disappearing into the rear of the place.

Then he had seen her once more. Here. On the screen.

Getting out of the car. Over and over and over.

Everything he had seen replayed in his head. He went up and down her body over and over again. His mind focused on the little part of the face that he had seen.

And then it clicked. His DVR had finally come through for him.

He opened his eyes to see Agent Bogart standing there.

He and Jamison were in the library at Mansfield.

"You went to see Lancaster?" asked Bogart.

Decker nodded, his thoughts still on the images in his head.

"How's she doing?"

"Do you still have your jet handy?"

Bogart looked surprised by this. He perched on the edge of the table.

"Yes, why?"

"Can I get a ride on it?"

"If I say you can. What's up?"

Decker rose. "We need to get to Chicago."

"You were just there."

"I need to go again."

"You have a lead?" Bogart glanced at the laptop screen. His eagerness was palpable.

"I have a lead."

"Can I come too?" asked Jamison quickly.

Bogart looked at her and then at Decker. The latter shrugged.

Bogart said, "Okay, but keep in mind that the FBI is not running a freaking airline service. And not one word of anything gets printed."

"I quit my job at the paper."

"What?" said Decker. "Why?"

"I'm working this case full-time now. And I couldn't do my other reporting duties. And, quite frankly, it was time to move on."

She got up and snagged her bag. "So, let's go. Chop-chop."

She walked out of the room.

Bogart looked at Decker. "A real piece of work. What'd you do to deserve her?"

"I can't process that right now," said Decker.

The jet flew them to a private airstrip south of the Windy City and they took an SUV to the new head-quarters of the Cognitive Institute. It was in a three-story building in a campus-style office park about an hour outside of Chicago.

Bogart flashed his FBI credentials at the receptionist, which started a chain reaction that ended with their being escorted to a conference room in the back of the building outfitted in soothing earth colors.

A man in a dark three-piece suit with a pink shirt and yellow bow tie with green dots came in.

He looked at Bogart, who flashed his badge and introduced himself. Then Darren Marshall saw Decker.

"Amos Decker?"

Decker rose and shook his hand. "Dr. Marshall."

"It's been, what, twenty years?"

"Plus two months, nine days, and fourteen hours," said Decker automatically. The calculation came out of his head so fast he didn't even realize he was doing it. It didn't seem weird to him anymore. It just . . . was who he was now.

"Of course, I will take your word for it," said Marshall. He glanced at Bogart. "Amos was quite an exceptional case."

"I'm sure. But I know nothing about it."

Marshall next looked at Jamison. "And are you also with the FBI?"

"No. I'm just an interested citizen trying to help."

Marshall looked a bit startled by her comment.

"Exceptional case?" prompted Bogart.

Decker said tersely, "I suffered a head trauma. It changed how my mind worked. Made it more efficient in some ways." He paused. "A *manufactured* savant, as it were, unlike your brother."

Bogart nodded, studying him closely. "Okay. Right, I get that."

"Can you tell me what all this is about?" asked Marshall.

Decker explained the situation to Marshall, who slowly nodded before he was finished.

"I had heard about poor Sizemore of course, but I didn't know it was part of this . . . this awful event in Burlington."

"We had mentioned it to Dr. Rabinowitz," said Decker.

"So *that's* why he was calling," said Marshall. "I've been so busy I haven't called Harold back yet."

"It's connected to even more awful events," said Bogart. "None of which we need to get into at present." He glanced expectantly at Decker.

Decker said, "Our killer is almost certainly a male, a male who has partnered with someone calling himself Sebastian Leopold."

"Never heard of him. But you think it has a connection to the institute?"

"Considering that it was their carefully placed clues that led me back here, yes. And add the fact that Dr. Sizemore has been murdered."

"And you know they're connected for certain? I mean, Sizemore's death and the others?"

"Another message was left at his home. Again, for me."

Marshall slumped back in his chair looking highly unnerved. "My God, I can hardly believe it."

Decker said, "There was a woman in my group at the institute, Belinda Wyatt."

"Yes, I remember her."

"She was one of Dr. Sizemore's protégées."

"Well, we don't encourage such attachments here."

"But that doesn't mean they didn't happen. In fact is it correct to say that Dr. Sizemore was let go from here because he had formed an attachment with patients more recently? Perhaps female patients?"

"I really can't get into that."

Bogart leaned forward across the width of the table. "Dr. Marshall, we are hunting a killer who murdered more people than I care to mention, including a slew of high school students and one of my agents. This person has to be stopped before he kills again. So while I respect that you have confidences to maintain, any help you can give us will be much appreciated."

Marshall let out a long, uneven breath. "Well, I can

tell you that Sizemore had crossed the professional line with a female at the institute around the time that he was asked to leave. I really can't say more than that."

"Don't worry, he's not going to sue you," said Bogart. "He's lying in a morgue." He glanced at Decker. "Do you think Sizemore might have done the same thing with this Wyatt person?"

Decker ignored this query and said to Marshall, "What happened to her?"

"I would have to check the records."

"Will you do that?"

"This is very treacherous territory professionally speaking."

"Please, Dr. Marshall, just check the records."

Marshall rose and picked up the phone on the credenza and spoke into it. Five minutes later a woman entered carrying a bulky expandable file folder. She handed it to Dr. Marshall, turned, and left.

Marshall slipped on his glasses and said, "I'll need to look over the file."

Bogart said, "Go right ahead. Take your time."

Twenty minutes passed and then Marshall looked up. "Okay, what would you like to know?"

"What was her age then?" asked Decker.

"Sixteen."

"She was a hyper?"

"Yes, of extraordinary ability. Close to yours, in fact. But unlike you, she exhibited no signs of synesthesia."

"Which made my case more interesting to some here," said Decker. "The duality of it."

"And also how you came by it. Blunt-force trauma on the gridiron. Never had one before you. I seriously doubt we'll ever see another."

Bogart looked at Decker. "So that's how it happened?"

Jamison nodded at him. "Yes."

"She knows this but I don't?" said Bogart irritably.

Jamison explained, "We spent some long car rides together."

Decker said to Marshall, "How did Belinda come by hers? We had group sessions, but that fact was never revealed. Although some of the others here learned about my situation through the grapevine, I don't remember Belinda's ever being mentioned."

"Well, your background should not have been disclosed. And Belinda's was even more . . . complicated."

"How complicated?" asked Bogart. When Marshall said nothing, Bogart said, "I don't want to play hardball, but I can have a subpoena here in an hour. But in that time these people might kill again."

Marshall looked over at Decker. "Do you really think that this might be connected with all those deaths?"

"I *know* that it is."

Marshall took off his glasses and slid the file away. "Belinda Wyatt was a teenager living in rural Utah.

When she was sixteen she was, to put it bluntly, gang-raped, sodomized, brutally beaten, and left for dead."

Bogart glanced sharply at Decker, but the latter kept his gaze on Marshall.

"So she suffered a brain trauma from her injuries and she came out of it with hyperthymesia," said Decker.

"Yes. And she also suffered a great deal of emotional trauma, as you can imagine," added Marshall. "Enough that realistically a full recovery was never going to happen. She was permanently damaged from it, emotionally, and physically as well. With the physical damage done she would never be able to conceive a child, for instance."

"My God," commented Jamison.

Bogart said, "But, Decker, I'm not following this. Wyatt's a girl. She can't be our shooter. It's a guy."

"She *can* be our shooter. She *is* our shooter."

Bogart glanced at him sharply. "How do you figure that exactly?"

Decker looked at Marshall. "Belinda had issues, didn't she? Other than her being beaten and raped? Having to do with sexual orientation perhaps?"

Marshall said in amazement, "I really don't know how you possibly could have known that. To my knowledge that was never mentioned in any session."

"I can't exactly explain it other than in my head some things came together. The line of a jaw, the curve of a thigh, the hands. And mannerisms and movements. All jumbled together. Pieces of a puzzle."

"Your mind is truly extraordinary, Amos."

"So was that why she was raped and brutalized? I would guess twenty years ago in rural Utah someone like that would not be very popular."

"I was not privy to the exact details of the crime, but that could have been the case, yes. I'm not sure how far we've come as a society, actually. I would imagine that sort of condition would still provoke severe if totally misguided reactions."

"What exactly were her medical conditions?" asked Decker.

Marshall seemed about to protest, but then resignation swept over his features. "Twenty years ago Belinda Wyatt would have been classified as suffering from true hermaphroditism."

Jamison said, "You mean like a hermaphrodite?"

"Yes," said Marshall. "Now, that's an arcane term, no longer in use because it's more than a bit insensitive. Today we call such conditions intersex or DSD, which is an acronym for 'disorders of sexual development.' That's where there's a discrepancy between the external and internal genitalia, meaning testes and ovaries respectively, and also where you may have female chromosomes but male genitalia or vice versa. It has four known categories. Belinda technically belonged to a subset of the condition known as true gonadal intersex."

"Which means what exactly?" asked Decker.

"That the person has both ovarian and testicular tissue. Belinda also had both XX and XY chromosomes.

She also had one ovary and one testis. As you can imagine, it would be a difficult condition for anyone. The medical community has come a long way now in terms of helping the person to deal with the situation, to make choices, surgical and otherwise. Twenty years ago the decision was often made to have surgery immediately and to make the patient a woman in lieu of a man because the surgical procedures tended to be easier. Now we know there are many other factors involved. It's often better to wait and come to understand each person's unique situation and to allow the patient to have substantial input into the decision. I mean, it's their body and life after all."

"But twenty years ago?" said Decker.

"It was very different," said Marshall. "And people could be very ignorant. And extremely cruel. Wyatt was sixteen and in high school. That time period is perilous enough for many young people who do not have to deal with, well, being different biologically from other people their age."

Jamison said darkly, "So whoever gang-raped and beat her probably knew about her condition. And they were of the ignorant variety? And they decided to teach the girl a lesson?"

"Presumably, yes."

"And her parents?" asked Decker.

"Since she was not at the age of majority at the time, they had to give their authorization for her to come to the institute."

"Did they ever visit her?"

"No."

"Why not?"

"To put it delicately, I would number them among the ignorant."

"God, talk about being totally abandoned by your parents when you need them most," remarked Jamison.

"So they thought their daughter was what, a freak?" asked Decker.

"I spoke with them on the phone a few times. I don't think they cared what happened to her. Thoroughly unpleasant people."

Bogart said, "Why were you privy to all of this medical information on patients at the institute? I thought you just did research on cognitive issues."

"We approach things from a wider perspective. Yes, our primary focus is research into minds that are or have become extraordinary through various factors. But we also are medical doctors. The patients we saw, like Belinda and also Amos, had suffered serious trauma, which in turn caused enormous changes inside their minds. We needed to know their complete medical histories so that we could better understand what had caused the changes and also, we hoped, help them cope with what was essentially a new life." He looked at Decker. "I know we never did any follow-up with you, Amos. That was a gap in our procedures that we have since rectified. Simply because you leave us physically does not mean we cannot continue to support you."

"Your help was much appreciated," said Decker. "It enabled me to cope on my own."

"I'm so glad to hear you say that. Now, in Belinda's case it was quite evident to us that she was a special case even had she not suffered what she did. I had frank discussions with the doctor in Utah who had seen her and given the preliminary diagnosis of her condition. It's a total package, particularly when one is dealing with the mind, so we needed to understand everything. And her parents had no objection. I think they wanted to wash their hands of it," he added with a grimace.

"Did Belinda receive an operation that made her a man?" asked Decker.

"I don't know. She did not have such a procedure before or while she was here, that is for certain."

"Have you heard from her since she left here?"

"Not a word."

"Do you have an address for Belinda?" asked Decker.

"No."

"Her parents?"

"In the file, yes, but it's fifteen years old."

Decker said, "We'll take it."

52

Decker sat at the table, looking out the window. Jamison sat across from him, watching him nervously.

In an effort to lighten the mood, she said, "Okay, I have to admit, this beats my Suzuki."

"You mean your clown car," commented Decker, still peering out the window.

They were traveling at forty-one thousand feet and well over five hundred miles an hour in the Bureau's sleek tri-engine Falcon.

He looked up when Bogart placed cups of coffee in front of him and Jamison, then sat down across from him. The FBI agent unbuttoned his jacket and took a sip from his own cup.

Jamison looked around the plush interior. "Nice ride."

Bogart nodded. "The FBI pulls out all the stops for cases like this." He eyed Decker, who was still staring out the window.

"So you took a hit on the football field and it changed your life forever?"

"It changed my brain, and with it my life."

"And again, you don't want to talk about it?"

Decker said nothing.

"What do you think we'll find at the Wyatts' house in Colorado?" asked Jamison, peering anxiously between the two men.

Decker said, "Whatever we find will tell us something we didn't know before. And it will get us one step closer to Belinda Wyatt."

Bogart took another sip of coffee. "What made you look in Wyatt's direction? We were searching for a man and she's a woman, or she was when you knew her."

In answer Decker opened the laptop in front of him and spun it around so Bogart could see the screen. Then he ran the video.

Bogart looked at the frames and then turned back to Decker.

"Okay, it's a woman getting out of a car. The waitress from the bar. Leopold's accomplice. Maybe this Belinda Wyatt person. She certainly looks like a woman to me."

"Did you notice how the person got out of the car?"

Bogart glanced at the screen. "You said it was a guy masquerading as a woman. But now that we know Wyatt has this intersex condition, we don't really know what she is, male or female. So it could just be her being a woman because she *is* a woman. Maybe she never had the operation."

"That's right. She may be exactly what she was twenty years ago. We know Leopold couldn't have committed the murders. If Wyatt is involved with him, that leaves her. She's the shooter."

"Okay, but I'm not getting what you mean about her climbing out of the car. She swung her legs out and stood up. Like a girl or a guy would."

"No, not like a guy would. Nothing like a guy would."

"I'm not following."

"Turn to the side and stand up, like you're getting out of a car."

"What, now?"

"Yes, now."

"Decker!"

"Just do it."

Bogart looked put out, but he turned to his side and put his legs out into the aisle. He was about to stand when Decker stopped him.

"Look at your legs."

Bogart stared down at his splayed legs. "What about them? I swung them out into the aisle, which I have to do in order to stand up. The person on the screen did the exact same thing."

"Look at the distance between your thighs."

Bogart stared down at the large gap between his legs. "So what?"

"Look at the screen."

Bogart glanced at the screen. There the person's thighs were nearly touching.

"Look at the hand," added Decker.

Bogart looked at the person's hand. It was knifed into the narrow crevice between the thighs, edging the skirt down.

"Your legs were spread out and your hand was nowhere near your legs."

"Well, she's wearing a dress, I'm not."

"Doesn't matter. You're a guy and, wearing a dress or not, you wouldn't do it. You'd spread your legs and stand. And the person's in an alley. No one is there to catch a glimpse up the dress. So why keep the legs together? Why place your hand there for added security to prevent prying eyes?"

"I give up. Why?"

"It's the difference between being raised female and male. Women do that motion automatically. It's ingrained in them from an early age, as soon as they start wearing a jumper and tights, and then a dress or skirt. My wife taught our daughter that motion when she was just a little girl. Every mom does. But a guy would never think to do it. Never. Dress or no dress. Guys don't worry about people looking, because guys *are* always the ones who are looking."

Bogart stared down at his legs, and then at his hand, and lastly over at the screen where the frozen image showed explicitly everything that Decker had just explained. He looked at Jamison, who had been following this conversation closely. Before he could say anything, she swung her legs out into the aisle. She was wearing a skirt. Her knees were pressed together and her hand was in the same position as the person on the video.

"It *is* hammered into us, Agent Bogart," she noted. "Just like Decker said. It's just automatic, especially when one is wearing a skirt."

Bogart exclaimed, "So let me get this straight. Are you saying that our shooter *is* a woman, Decker?"

"I'm saying that if our shooter *is* Belinda Wyatt—and I believe she is—then she has retained the muscle memory from when she was raised as a girl. Whether she's now a man after having surgery, I don't know. Ironically enough, she may like that, after having been considered a freak for straddling genders, because she's now able to use it to her full advantage. She's a chameleon gender-wise. She can play both roles. It makes for very effective cover."

Bogart swung his legs back in and rested his elbows on the table. Jamison did the same.

"Why do you think she killed Sizemore?" asked Bogart.

"That's the other reason I started to focus on Wyatt. She was his favorite. He made that clear to me. He never told me about her background, but he spent a great deal of time with her."

"Okay, but why would she kill him, then?"

Decker gazed at Bogart with a look of disappointment. "It's pretty obvious, isn't it? He seduced her and had sex with her while she was at the institute."

Jamison and Bogart stared at him goggle-eyed.

"Damn," said Jamison. "That does make sense. Size-more *was* a slimeball. He got kicked out of the institute for doing that very same thing with another female patient."

Bogart said, "So he seduced this physically and emo-tionally battered teenager when she was at her most vulnerable just so he could get laid? Some favorite."

Decker said nothing to this. He had returned to gazing out the window.

"You don't miss much, do you?" noted Bogart.

"So long as I see it or hear it, then it's always with me."

Jamison said, "But what if someone tells you a lie? You remember it, but not necessarily as a lie, right?"

"Unless I'm told something else that doesn't align with the earlier statement. Then I can start to figure out what's true and what's not. Small things tend to lead to big results. People don't mess up on the big details. They fall down on the small ones."

"What about Leopold? How did those two hook up?"

Decker looked back out the window and watched the clouds pass by.

He had no answer to that question.

He might never have an answer to that question.

Belinda Wyatt and Sebastian Leopold. Two of the most unlikely partners ever. But like the two killers in Truman Capote's *In Cold Blood*, people paired together could do things unimaginable to each of them acting alone.

And he wondered what they were plotting right now.

53

The address in Colorado was at the foot of the Rocky Mountains, up a long paved road that had only a single house at the end that one reached through a motorized gate. But it was a substantial home, an estate really.

The SUVs slowly made their way up. An FBI team from Denver had met them at the private airport where the jet had landed. There were eight agents plus Bogart, Jamison, and Decker. Local law enforcement was down below keeping guard over the road.

"It's out of the way," said Bogart as the large two-story home came into view.

"Did you expect it not to be?" said Decker.

When they pulled to a stop Bogart looked at Jamison. "You stay put."

"Come on. Decker wouldn't let me go in Sizemore's place either. "

"Well, I'm pleased to be considered in the same league with Mr. Decker," retorted Bogart. "Until we get the all clear, you stay right here."

They climbed out of the SUVs and the team quickly surrounded the house. A large separate building that looked to be a four-car garage was set off to one side. There was a pool in the rear grounds, covered now for winter. There were no other buildings. And there were no cars visible either.

"Place looks abandoned," said Bogart. "For such a nice residence, the grounds are pretty let go."

"We'll see," replied Decker.

The air was cold and everyone's breath was visible.

Two agents went toward the garage while the others headed for the house. Three went to the rear, and the other half covered the front. With Decker next to him, Bogart knocked on the front door, identified himself, said that he had a search warrant, and asked to be let in. All he got in answer was silence.

He gave the countdown over his phone to the team in the rear.

Both doors were blown in by hydraulic battering rams.

The agents swarmed inside, clearing the rooms one by one until they came to the stairs. They headed up, cleared six bedrooms, and then stopped at the last one.

"Holy shit," said one of the agents, lowering his weapon.

Bogart and Decker entered the room and stared down at the two chairs situated in a sitting room off the main bedroom area.

There was a body in each chair, entirely wrapped in plastic that was compressed tightly around their figures.

The faces visible through the plastic were of a man and a woman.

"Mr. and Mrs. Wyatt, do you think?" asked Bogart.

"Anything is possible," replied Decker.

Eight hours later the forensic team and ME had finished their work. The bodies had been identified as Lane Wyatt and his wife, Ashby. Their time of death was hard to pin down because they had been embalmed.

"Damnedest thing," said the ME. "But it's well done. Whoever did it had some experience doing it."

"So all the blood removed and the fluid pumped into them?" said Bogart.

The man nodded. "And then they were wrapped in the plastic, and it looks like someone used a heat source to compress and then seal the plastic. Probably used a hair dryer. That and the embalming really preserved the body. No air could get in. The bodies are in remarkable shape."

"And they could have been here a long time or a short time?"

"I'll try to work up a TOD window for you, but it won't be easy."

Bogart said, "The cars in the garage are between two and four years old and the registrations are still current. And the food in the fridge, while expired, is not that old. And the house is in reasonably good shape. I don't think they've been dead for years, unless someone has been living here while they've been in their 'packages.'"

He looked at the ME. "Cause of death?"

"Not particularly evident. No visible wounds on the bodies. Could have been poison, but obvious signs would be long gone. There might be some trace of it in their tissue. And I might be able to get some blood out of them. There's usually some left even with embalming."

"Find what you can," urged Bogart.

The ME nodded and left.

Bogart turned his attention to Decker and Jamison, who were sitting at the kitchen table going over some papers they'd taken out of a shoebox. Bogart sat across from Decker.

"Well, at least there were no cryptic messages to you painted on the walls."

Decker nodded absently and said, "I doubt they expected us to get to here. Which is actually a good thing."

"Why?"

"It means they're fallible. And it means we're closing the gap. The tortoise and the hare? Remember?"

"But why leave the bodies like that? They must have assumed *someone* would find them."

Decker looked at him. "According to what your people found out, the Wyatts were retired. They had no family other than their daughter, and no friends. They kept to themselves."

"So folks might not have missed them," said Bogart. "At least for a while."

"We should check to see if they used a pool service company. The pool was probably only winterized a couple months ago. If they came up to do it, they might have seen the Wyatts."

"Good idea."

Decker said, "The Wyatts had money. This place is over ten thousand square feet. And there's a Range Rover, Audi A8, and Mercedes S500 in the garage."

"Money can't buy you happiness," remarked Jamison.

Bogart looked back down at the papers. "What do you have there?"

Jamison said, "Letters from Belinda to her parents when she was at the institute. Your team found them in that shoebox stuffed under some junk in a closet upstairs."

"What do they say?"

Decker said, "To sum it up, they're letters from a frightened young woman imploring her parents to come see her. To come take her home."

"Marshall said they never visited her."

"So her letters went unanswered."

"Marshall said they were part of the ignorant folks and really didn't care about her. I wonder why they kept the letters?"

"Because of this," said Decker.

He and Jamison laid the reverse side of all the letters out on the table side by side. Each page had a single capital letter written on the back. When read together and combined into words they spelled out something.

"'I WILL KILL THEM ALL,'" read Bogart. "So she will kill them all. Meaning her attackers?"

"Or people who dissed her," said Decker, glancing up at Jamison. "Or people associated with the one who dissed her."

"And you still don't know why Wyatt would think you did that to her?"

"No. But my wife and Special Agent Lafferty were both violated. Not raped, but sexually mutilated."

"But Belinda *was* raped. And Mrs. Wyatt wasn't mutilated."

"She wouldn't be. This didn't start with her. And she's not connected to me."

"Comes back to you again. Always you."

Jamison looked at Bogart. "Decker said you used to be an analyst at Quantico?"

"That's right."

"I have a friend at ViCAP."

"She has lots of friends," commented Decker dryly.

Bogart said, "Violent Criminal Apprehension Program. I was assigned there for two years."

Jamison said, "Then you must have seen things like this before."

Bogart nodded. "I've pretty much seen it all."

"Okay, so walk us through it. What would the mutilation symbolize?"

Bogart clasped his hands in front of him. "Actually,

mutilation of the female genitalia can have a lot of reasons behind it. It's like a cornucopia of psychoses. Freud would have had a field day with it. I've seen a number of cases, all serial killers, where it was employed."

"Then give us some examples of reasons," said Decker.

Bogart leaned in, and while his voice grew softer, it also grew firmer. "It can be symbolic of a hatred of women and what they represent—being mothers, giving birth. The female genitalia are the gates to the birth canal, to be a little crude about it. I've seen killers do that to women because their mothers abandoned them. Or let them be abused by others. Mothers are supposed to protect their children, always be there for them. When a mother doesn't do that it can lead to some really messed-up minds. The mutilation is a way of closing those gates, shutting off the birth canal permanently—not that murder didn't already do that. But in their minds they're actually doing something positive."

Decker said, "Meaning another child can't be born to that woman? And won't be abandoned or abused?"

"Exactly."

Jamison interjected, "Well, Belinda's parents *abandoned* her to her fate at the institute. They never visited her there. They ignored her pleas to come and get her. And could she have seen the rape and beating she endured as her mother's not protecting her?"

"Possibly," replied Bogart. "In fact, probably. Particularly if she wasn't supportive afterwards."

Decker said, "But then why was the message directed at me? Why target my family, people I know? Where do I fit in all this? I don't remember even speaking to her."

"We're talking about a sick mind, Decker. There's no way we can understand or make sense out of what went on in her head. This actually didn't start with you. This started with her being raped and nearly killed. And then her parents abandoning her afterward. And it started even before that, with her *condition*, and people's reaction to it. Her life was never going to be normal."

"And then there's Leopold," said Jamison. "Let's not forget about him!"

"And then there's Leopold," repeated Bogart. "Decker, you're still convinced he's Belinda's partner in all this? I mean, you haven't seen him since he left that bar. I know you told me about the waitress—supposedly Belinda—and her borrowing the barman's car, but you have no hard evidence that she actually picked up Leopold in it. She could have just used it to run an errand."

Decker shook his head. "She left the bar for good after she brought the car back. And the temp agency hadn't sent her. She was there to ferret Leopold away. *He* was the one who picked the bar. So I have no doubt that he's involved. He confessed to a crime he couldn't have committed. And he *knew* that he couldn't have committed. He played the role of a mentally unbalanced person well, but sitting in that bar he had moments of lucidity, not random, but intentional. He overplayed his hand. He knew exactly what he was doing."

"But why confess in the first place?"

"It was their opening salvo. After murdering my family. The confession got my attention. They knew I'd find out about it, investigate it. They lured me in. They wanted me to participate in their game."

"Some game," Bogart said disgustedly. "But they waited a long time in between killing your family and attacking the school."

"It all took time to plan out. They had to find the details of the passageway, among other things."

Jamison said, "But who's the leader of the pack? Wyatt or Leopold? Plus, how did they meet? Where does he come from? How did they hatch this whole thing?"

"All good questions," noted Decker. "For which we unfortunately have no answers."

Bogart said, "We've had no hit on the criminal databases. The guy has no record that we can find."

Decker jerked his head. "*Criminal* databases?"

"Yeah, that's where we typically look for *criminals*. We ran Leopold's prints through IAFIS, it's the largest criminal database in the world. I should know because the FBI runs it."

"But Belinda Wyatt wasn't a criminal. She was a

victim. Maybe Sebastian Leopold was too. Maybe that's how they hooked up."

Jamison gazed at Bogart. "So maybe you've been looking in the wrong databases."

54

They flew back to Burlington and Decker was driven to the Residence Inn. Decker looked at Bogart and then flicked his gaze to Jamison.

The FBI agent understood. He said, "Ms. Jamison, we request the pleasure of your company at our safe house."

She snapped, "What? No, I'll be—"

"Perfectly happy to accept or else I'll put you in a jail cell if I have to," interjected Bogart.

"On what charge?" she retorted.

"Publishing false information in a newspaper and inciting a riot against one Amos Decker."

Jamison started to say something but then sank back in her seat and said with a scowl, "Fine, have it your way."

As Decker was climbing out of the SUV Bogart hooked his arm.

"We pop anything on Leopold's prints and DNA in *noncriminal* databases, I'll call you right away."

"I'd also like you to send me whatever you can find on Belinda Wyatt's past."

Bogart nodded and then he drove off.

Decker headed up to his room and sat on his bed. He eyed the gun in his waistband and thought back to when Captain Miller had come knocking on his door. If he hadn't, would he have shot himself?

With the clarity that came after stepping back from a stressful situation, Decker knew that Miller was right. If he eliminated himself this pair would go on killing. If Decker had somehow dissed Belinda Wyatt, others could have too. Or maybe they would start on Leopold's list of "dissers" next.

He closed his eyes and thought back to two periods of time, one recent, the other much further in the past. He took the latter first, stopping at those frames in his mind.

Belinda Wyatt. Tall, blonde, thin, and androgynous-looking, scared all the time. Her personality had been so invisible as not to exist. Although her mind could do extraordinary things after what had happened to her, Decker recalled her as lacking confidence and even a shred of self-esteem. She barely talked in the group sessions. Decker had felt for her, to the extent he could with the new way his mind worked.

What had happened to him was brutal. But he had stepped out onto that field of his own free will with the knowledge that pro football was insanely violent, far more vicious than even the most die-hard fan could imagine.

Belinda Wyatt had been gang-raped, sodomized,

beaten, and left for dead. She had been horribly violated. There was nothing voluntary about that. She had had no say in it. She had been dealing with a difficult enough life situation as it was. With the discovery of her parents' bodies, it was clear that she was involved in all the other killings. And nothing in her past, no matter how horrific, would justify her doing what she had. But she was not the only one to blame for all this.

Next Decker's mind moved forward to the recent past.

He was sitting in the jail cell opposite Sebastian Leopold. He recalled down to the last detail the man's features and manner. The empty eyes, the utter calmness, the disregard for his personal safety since he had confessed to a triple murder. Of course, now Decker knew that Leopold was aware he would never be convicted of those crimes because he had a rock-hard alibi supplied by the *police*, of all people.

That had to mean that Belinda Wyatt had murdered his family. And she had to be the shooter at Mansfield too. Once again, Leopold had an alibi. Provided once more by the police.

Decker's mind ground to a halt at that point. *By the police?* Was that important? Significant? Imperative to understand? He didn't know, because he didn't have enough information.

The frames whirred back and forth in his head, going over every word of the conversation between him and

Leopold. Then the frames stopped whirring and Decker's eyes opened.

Is good.

Even though he had perfect recall, sometimes his mind, just like anyone else's, turned words into what it thought they should be instead of what they actually had been. He had done that here, mentally correcting Leopold when no correction was necessary. Decker had just assumed it was a contraction. *Is good* to *It's good*. He had modified the words that way because he thought he had just misheard. But he hadn't. He couldn't have. He was sitting right next to the man.

He picked up his phone and called Bogart.

"You need to expand your search to the international databases focusing on Europe. Interpol should be able to help. Germany should be at the top of the list, to start with."

"Why?" asked Bogart. "Why the international angle?"

"Because I remembered something wrong. And now I just remembered it right."

Decker put the phone away. *"I don't really drink. But it's good."* An American would say that all the time. But no American would say, *"I don't really drink. But is good."* In fact, Leopold might have actually said, *"Ist good."*

And the slight guttural undertones of the speech coupled with the sharp, angular bone structure of Leopold's face made Decker believe he was European, possibly German or Austrian. There was enough homo-geneity in those populations that the facial features were far more uniform over the generations than in melting pots like the U.S.

So it might be that Belinda Wyatt, undoubtedly a homegrown American girl perhaps turned boy, joined forces with an older European male. How do two such very different people meet? How do they come together to plan something like this? Decker felt sure if they could track down Leopold's true identity a lot of questions would start being answered.

As he thought about this another possibility entered his mind.

He said out loud, "7-Eleven."

That had undoubtedly been a clue. In her interview notes, Lancaster had instinctively interpreted it as a reference to the ubiquitous convenience stores. But was there more to it than that? Leopold had not wanted to come right out and say he was actually referring to 711 Duckton Avenue. But he had to know that Lancaster had misinterpreted his statement. She had actually asked him which 7-Eleven, and when Leopold had been non-committal she had just assumed it was the one closest to Decker's home. But Leopold had let that go. He would know that the police, that Decker more importantly, would check that out. That he would go to that store on DeSalle and see what he could see. And that meant—

He might be wrong. But he didn't think so. In fact, Decker thought he was absolutely right.

He left his room and headed back out into the night.

55

He spent ten minutes watching the store from across the street. He saw people go in and people go out. Cars came and went. And still he kept watching. He was watching to see if anyone was watching him. When Decker was satisfied that there was no one doing so, he hurried across the street and approached the door. He glanced through the glass and saw the same woman at the counter, once more counting packs of cigarettes and ticking them off on her sheets. He could see no other customers in the store.

He opened the door and the bell tinkled. The woman looked up. It took her a moment but she recognized Decker.

Because of his size and appearance he was hard to forget and harder to miss.

"You're back?" she said.

"I'm back," said Decker, his gaze darting around the corners of the store. His hand had slipped to his pocket where his gun sat.

She said, "I owe you change from when you were

here last. The coffee, pastry, and paper didn't add up to five dollars."

"Keep the change. You work long hours. Morning, night."

"I do work long hours, but I'm also on different shifts. Today I work the night shift."

"How's business?"

"Slow now. We sell a lot in the morning when people are going to work. Coffee, cigarettes, and sausage biscuits. And Red Bull by the gallon."

"The other person here when I came by the first time. Billy, right? Is he here?"

She shook her head. "No, he's not here."

"He doesn't work here anymore, does he?" Decker said.

She looked startled. "How did you know that?"

"When was he here last?"

"The day you came in the first time. I was pissed when he didn't show up for work after that. I had to do his job too."

"Do you have his employment file here?"

"Yes. In the back."

"Can I see it?"

"No. Company policy."

"Can you tell me his last name?"

"Why?"

"He might be the one I was looking for."

"I don't see how."

Decker held up his phone. "I can have the FBI here in

five minutes. And they'll take every file in this place." He eyed the woman steadily. "Are you an American citizen?"

She blanched. "No. But I have papers."

"I'm sure they're in perfect order. At least I hope they are. The FBI will check, of course. They check everything. Twice."

The woman slowly put a pack of cigarettes in the appropriate slot and made a check on her inventory sheet. He could tell she was stalling as she thought about how to respond to this.

"I might . . .. I mean, my work visa might be a little *overdue.*"

"That's unfortunate. With the government in gridlock over immigration reform, it's a touchy subject. I'm sure you can appreciate that."

"And if I let you see Billy's file?"

Decker put his phone away. "That might change things."

The woman went into the back office and came out a minute later with a file. "You can have this. I made a copy."

Decker went to the door, locked it, and turned the OPEN sign to CLOSED.

"What are you doing?" the woman cried out. Decker pulled out his phone again. "The FBI will be here in a few minutes. I'm afraid this store will be closed for quite a while."

"But I gave you the file."

"And I thank you for that. But one has nothing to do with the other."

"But what will the FBI do here?"

"They'll be looking for any trace of Billy. And don't worry. They won't care about your immigration status."

"But why is Billy so important? He just mops floors."

"He's important principally because he's not Billy. His name is Belinda."

Hours later Bogart walked out of the 7-Eleven and over to Decker, who was standing in the parking lot sipping 7-Eleven coffee while the snow slowly swirled around him.

Bogart said, "We got one usable print, seven points on a mop bucket in the storage room. We ran it but got no hits back yet. It may be Wyatt's or whoever else handled that bucket. And she might not be on any database. Or I guess she's a he now. This Billy guy."

"But she was gang-raped in Utah, according to Dr. Marshall. They must have a police file on her."

"You would think. But we checked with the police department where she grew up. They have no record of any rape of Belinda Wyatt."

Decker looked stunned. "But that can't be. She was raped and beaten and left for dead. It changed her brain. It's why she was sent to the institute. You heard Dr. Marshall. And he said he'd talked to the doctor from

Utah. She *had* been raped and beaten and left for dead."

"Well, maybe she was. But maybe she didn't file a police report, Decker. That's a possibility."

"But why wouldn't she?"

"Consider her personal situation. It being a small town where everybody knows everybody else's business? She might have made the decision not to report."

"Or her parents made that decision for her," retorted Decker.

"That's actually far more likely," conceded the FBI agent.

Decker finished his coffee and threw the cup into a trash can. "Belinda was very tall for a woman, about five-eleven, and skinny. Billy was that height and lean too, but he was wiry. Maybe a hundred and fifty pounds."

"And definitely a guy?"

"I think so, but he looked androgynous too. Belinda looked the same at the institute. I've already given your sketch artist a description. They're working on a finished drawing now."

"We can get that all over the place once it's done."

"I would just get it out to law enforcement for now. Don't go public. They may go underground if they discover we've gotten that far."

Bogart didn't look convinced but said, "Okay, we'll play it that way. For now." He put his hands in his pockets and studied the pavement. "We heard back from the pool service company the Wyatts used in Colorado.

They came and winterized the pool two months ago, but didn't see anyone. Their fees are on an automatic pay system. In fact, all their bills were on autopay. They didn't have to interact with anyone. Dead end. No pun intended."

"And Leopold?"

Bogart let out an extended breath. "Leopold, yes. I was getting to him. We finally got a hit."

"His real name?"

"Surprisingly enough, Sebastian Leopold. You were right. He's Austrian."

"And his story?"

"Still coming in. But the gist is his wife and daughter were murdered and the killer was never brought to justice."

"When did he come over here?"

"Hard to pin that down. The murder was eight years ago. So anytime after that, I guess. I doubt he's here legally. But then again, I don't think we're as picky with Europeans as we are with other folks."

"If he's only been here a few years he's worn his accent away relatively fast. He only had the one slip when I was talking with him. Can I see anything you have on him?"

"I'll arrange it. Where will you be?"

"Back at the library at Mansfield."

"You want a ride over there?"

"I need to make one stop first."

"Where?"

"To pick up my partner."

"Your partner? You don't mean Lancaster? After what almost happened to her family I don't think she's up to it."

"Mary *is* up to it."

"How do you know that?"

"Because I know Lancaster. She's tougher than you and me combined."

56

Lancaster and Jamison were sitting across from Decker in the school library. They were awaiting Leopold's files. Decker had filled Lancaster in on everything they had learned.

He said, "Bogart thinks that Belinda might not have filed a police report. He believes her parents might have discouraged her from doing so."

"Talk about scum," replied Lancaster fiercely.

"The thing is, her trauma left her with perfect recall. She would have remembered her attackers."

"If she knew them in the first place," said Jamison.

Decker replied, "Small-town Utah. Everybody probably knew everybody."

"At the institute did she ever talk?" asked Lancaster.

"Almost never. In the group sessions she never talked about what had happened to her. I didn't know until Dr. Marshall told me. And she was probably attacked because her assailants knew of her intersex condition," added Decker.

Lancaster shook her head. "I never heard the term until you told me. I can't imagine what that must have been like. You said Marshall told you she had one testis and one ovary?"

"Yes."

"The absolute shit she must have taken in school. In gym class, one of the other girls spots her private parts? Word spreads. It really must have been horrible."

Decker was staring down at the document in front of him. He had just seen one fact that did not align with another.

Lancaster was well used to this look. "What?"

He glanced at her. "Dr. Marshall said the address he had in the file for Belinda's parents was fifteen years old. But she was at the institute *twenty* years ago."

"Well, maybe they kept in touch for some reason. I doubt Belinda stayed there for five years. It must be a more recent address."

"But Marshall also said that the Wyatts never visited her at the institute. So why would he have had the later address in the first place? Were they corresponding?"

He pulled out his phone and made a call. Dr. Marshall was in a meeting but called back five minutes later.

"Yes, Amos, you're correct," he said. "The Wyatts did move, but we kept in touch, for about seven years after. And they sent me their new address so I could write to them from time to time."

"You didn't mention that when we questioned you."

"I know. I'm sorry. But I take patient confidentiality very seriously. I tried to be as helpful as I could while still respecting that professional duty."

"You said they never visited her at the institute. I assumed that meant they weren't interested in her care. In fact, you said you believed them to be ignorant people in regard to Belinda's condition."

"That's right."

"How did you come by that opinion? And how did she even come to be at the institute if her parents didn't care what had happened to her?"

"I don't think they initiated it."

"Who did, then?"

"I'm not sure. It might have been one of the doctors there who made the referral after it became clearer that her cognitive condition might be one that we should look into at the institute. Even twenty years ago we had a national reputation," he added proudly. "And we had enough funding to have paid for all of her expenses."

"Okay, but if the Wyatts had no involvement in sending her to you, why would they correspond with you?"

Decker thought he knew the answer but he wanted to hear it from Marshall.

"Well, because they were scared, Amos. They were scared of Belinda. At least that's what they told me. When she came back home to Utah she was a different person to them. And I don't mean for the better. Our work with her at the institute apparently did not help her. And she left home soon thereafter. But they would apparently get messages from her. Pretty frightening ones. And so they were scared."

"That she would, what, hurt them?"

"I don't like to speculate about that."

"Just give me your educated guess."

He could hear Marshall let out a long breath. "All right. I think they were terrified that she was going to murder them."

Well, they were spot on about that, thought Decker.

"Can I have their old address? The one in Utah? Do you have it?"

Marshall gave it to him from the file. Decker thanked him and clicked off.

He got on the computer and did a satellite search of the old address.

He spun the laptop around so that Lancaster and Jamison could see.

"Okay, ordinary house in an ordinary neighborhood," Lancaster said. "Looks like mine."

"And like mine," said Decker. "But the point is, the Wyatts' new house was five times the size with a pool and a separate four-car garage filled with luxury vehicles."

Lancaster's brows knitted together. "What did the Wyatts do for a living?"

"The info Bogart dug up says he was an assistant manager at the DMV. Mrs. Wyatt worked as a waitress in a diner."

Jamison said, "They were definitely not pulling

down big bucks. So how did they afford a house like that?"

"Well, you follow the money to answer that." Decker got on his phone again. He asked Bogart this question.

When he clicked off he looked at Lancaster. "He's going to check and get back to us."

"What do you think is going on, Amos?" asked Lancaster.

"I think we're getting close to finding out the motive behind all this, Mary. And once we do, it will all start to make sense."

"Good. Because up to this point nothing has made sense. Nothing."

"No, it's always made sense, to Wyatt and Leopold. It only doesn't make sense to us because we don't know enough."

"How can killing so many people ever make sense?" she said hotly.

"It doesn't have to make sense to us. Just to the ones who did it."

"I hate the world," said Lancaster, looking miserable.

"I don't hate the world," said Decker. "I only hate some of the people who unfortunately live in it."

57

They later grabbed dinner at a fast-food restaurant and brought it back with them to the library. After Decker finished eating he left Lancaster and Jamison and entered the cafeteria. From there he went through the door leading down into the tunnel and walked down the hall using a flashlight to illuminate the way.

They had been over and over this ground and the adjacent Army base but had found no new clues. The Army had gotten back to them with some information about the base and the tunnel connecting to the school, but it had shed no new light on the case.

Decker emerged on the other side and walked up into the bowels of the military facility. He sat on an old oil drum and let his mind wander back over past events.

Belinda Wyatt had been gang-raped, beaten, and left for dead. The motive was probably that her attackers had found out about her intersex condition. The trauma had changed her brain, turning her into what Decker also was.

I wonder if she remembers the rape and beating? Or if she's forgotten it like I did the hit on me? I wonder if she can never forget all the things she wants to forget?

He did not like feeling any sort of connection to someone who had ended the lives of so many innocent people, but part of him could not help it. They were bound by their conditions. They were connected by their histories, their paths crossing at a traumatic point in their lives.

Decker and Belinda had been at the institute together. Something he had done there had caused her to target him. At some point Belinda had become Billy. Billy had met up with Sebastian Leopold, an Austrian whose family had been killed and no one had been punished for the crime. Where had *their* paths crossed? A lot could happen in twenty years. Was it before or after she'd made the change to Billy? Had their meeting precipitated all the killings?

And what the hell did I do to Wyatt to deserve all this misery?

"I thought I might find you here."

Decker glanced over to see Bogart standing at the top of the steps leading from the tunnel. He held up a file.

"Information on the Wyatts' finances. And Sebastian Leopold's family."

They walked back to the library together and Bogart, Decker, Jamison, and Lancaster started to go over the files.

Twenty minutes later Lancaster held up a paper. "The Wyatts sold their house in Utah for forty thousand dollars about nineteen years ago. The new one they built, at a cost of nearly two million. And it came with twenty acres."

"And the source of the wealth?" asked Decker.

"We couldn't find one," said Bogart.

"How about a payoff?" said Decker.

Lancaster shot him a glance. "A payoff? You mean blackmail?"

"It would explain the absence of a police report on Belinda's rape. It would explain where the cash came from to buy the house. Far away in Colorado."

Bogart added, "And it might explain Belinda's outrage. That her parents could be bribed to not press the case."

"Abuse and abandonment?" said Decker, eyeing him.

Bogart nodded. "Hence the mutilation. And the murders of her parents."

Decker looked at the paper again. "With her parents dead, I wonder what happened to whatever money was in their accounts?"

"But if people didn't know they were dead?" said Jamison.

"These days money is accessible by computer. You just have to have logins and passwords," said Decker. "Which I'm sure Belinda, or Billy, could get."

"He would need something to live on, to fund travel," opined Bogart.

"He might need it for something else," said Decker.

"What?" asked Bogart and Lancaster together.

Decker stood. "We need to go to where the Wyatts lived when she was raped. And we need to find out who raped her, and how they got away with it. And we have to determine who paid all that money to the Wyatts."

"It's a twenty-year-old case, Decker," protested Bogart.

"There's another reason to go. An even more important one."

"What is it?" asked Bogart.

"Worth a ride in your private jet, for sure."

58

They landed near a small town in northern Utah.

"Mercy, Utah," said Lancaster, as they deplaned into heavy snow and saw the sign on a plane hangar.

"Okay, that's the height of irony," commented Jamison.

Bogart shivered and pulled his parka closer around him. "So what was the reason worth a tank of jet fuel?" he asked Decker.

Decker eyed the three SUVs sitting on the tarmac, engines running and heaters, he hoped, turned on full blast.

"I'll show you."

They drove to the address of Belinda Wyatt's former home. It was in a small community of post–World War II housing, each house nearly a carbon copy of its neighbor. The streets were frozen slush. The house was dark. No cars were in the driveway.

Decker sat in the backseat of the second SUV with Lancaster and Jamison next to him. Bogart was in front.

Decker looked out the window and said, "So it was recently sold?"

Bogart nodded. "Twenty months ago. Purchaser was a company."

"Around four months before my family was killed. They'd need a place to stay and plan it all out."

"You really think Wyatt bought her old house back?" said Lancaster. "And with it all those terrible memories?"

"This was *her* home. Not the behemoth where she killed her parents and wrapped them in plastic. Despite what happened to her, she might see it as a place of solace, of safety. And she probably used some of the bribe money to buy it. I'm sure she would have thought it fitting to use their blood money to buy back what they so desperately wanted to sell."

Jamison shot him a glance. "And what do you think we'll find inside?"

"Answers," said Decker. "I hope."

They went in through the front and rear while other agents manned the perimeter, to make sure no one inside could possibly escape. They cleared each of the rooms and then settled in the basement.

"Damn!" exclaimed Bogart, gazing around. "I guess I expected to see walls covered in index cards with strings attached, running to other cards, like a manual version of an air traffic control system."

But there was nothing like that down here. In fact, there was nothing but what one would expect to see in a basement: junk.

"I was hoping for the same thing," said Decker. He

looked all around, taking everything in, and started nodding as though the answer had occurred to him.

"Ironically, I overlooked one obvious but significant point. Wyatt has hyperthymesia. She doesn't need a wall of index cards. It's all in her head, every detail. And we don't know what Leopold is yet, except strange and a hell of an actor. He plays a clueless idiot better than anyone I've ever seen. But there's something else about him that I can't pinpoint."

Bogart said, "You told us he was inexplicable."

"He *is* inexplicable. Everyone has an agenda, whether altruistic or self-serving. So he has one too. I just don't know what it is yet."

Bogart said, "Should we call in the locals?"

Decker shook his head. "No."

"Why not? They get ticked when we don't at least inform them of what we're doing."

"Because it could be that the 'locals' are the reason behind this whole thing. So *we're* going to process what little there is down here."

He started poking around a plastic shelf with a few boxes of junk on them. Jamison started going through stuff in another corner. Lancaster and Bogart exchanged a glance and then did likewise.

Two hours later, Bogart said, "Okay, there is nothing here. Nothing!"

"No, there is," said Jamison. She held up a newspaper clipping.

"Where'd you get that?" asked Lancaster.

"It was stuffed in a box and under that table over there with rags on top."

"So what?" said Bogart. "It's junk, just like everything else here."

"No. When people save newspapers, they always save a *stack* of them. This was the only newspaper in this entire room. To a mind like Wyatt's I bet it was a particle of disorder. Which made me wonder why it was here. There had to be a reason."

Decker studied her curiously. "That's a good deduction, Jamison."

"Hey, I may not be a hyper-whatsis, but I have my moments. And I can smell newsprint from a mile away."

"What does it say?" asked Lancaster.

She held up the front page of the newspaper and pointed to the large headline.

Lancaster read, "'Giles Evers Gone Missing.'"

"Who the hell is Giles Evers?" said Bogart.

Jamison said, "He was a police officer. The news story also said he was the son of Mercy's most prominent citizen, Clyde Evers. Former mayor, made a lot of money in mining, gave a lot of it to his hometown. Typical big fish in a small pond."

"Why would Wyatt keep that clipping?" asked Bogart.

Decker answered. "Because Giles Evers raped her. And she made him disappear."

"Whoa, that's a helluva leap of logic, Amos," said Lancaster.

"No it's not. It would be the *only* reason this article would be here."

"When was the article from?" asked Lancaster.

Jamison said, "Nineteen months ago. Right about the time the house was sold to the company we think Wyatt is behind."

Bogart and Lancaster stared at Decker. "Okay, you're saying she was attacked by a police officer?" said Bogart in a skeptical tone.

"By police *officers*," said Decker. "It was a gang rape. And they did it because of her intersex condition, and Evers's old man paid off the Wyatts to keep it hush-hush. He got his son in the clear and saved the police department a ton of embarrassment and the rolling of heads. I can't imagine the Mercy Police Department is all that big. It might be that all the street cops were part of the rape. Hell of a hit for the men in blue to take. And the town. A town that maybe had no sympathy for someone like Belinda Wyatt."

"But we can't be sure of that," said Lancaster. "You're just speculating."

"We can confirm it," said Decker. "Let's go talk to some folks who were around back then."

59

The police chief from two decades ago had died six years before of a heart attack. There were two officers from that time who were still with the department. Neither of them knew anything about the Wyatt case, they had told Bogart when he and the others showed up at the single police station in town. The group was rapidly shown the door.

As they drove away Lancaster said, "They're lying. I could see it in their faces."

"Small town, small enough that everyone knows everyone else's business," said Decker. "I say we go to the top of the list."

"You mean Giles Evers's father?" said Jamison. "Clyde Evers?"

"If he's still alive."

Bogart was looking at his smartphone, on which he had been doing a search. "Apparently he is. And it looks like he still lives here."

The address they drove to turned out to be a small house on the edge of town. As they pulled up they could see lights on in the front windows. A porch ran along the front of the plank-sided house. Smoke curled upward from a chimneystack. The snow had started to fall once more.

The house was rundown. The lawn was lumpy, the trees and bushes diseased and mangled, and the single car in the driveway was an ancient Ford truck.

Lancaster muttered, "The town's patriarch, huh? Must've fallen on hard times."

"There might be a good reason for that," said Decker.

At their knock the front door opened and an old man, bloated and bent, stood there. His white beard reached to his chest, and his frayed pants were held up by knotted rope suspenders.

Bogart identified himself, flashed his badge, and said they needed to speak to him about his son. Evers nodded dumbly and led the four of them into a tiny room where a fire crackled in a soot-smeared stone-faced fireplace.

The inside of the house was dark and smelled both of mildew and mothballs and of whatever meal the man had microwaved that night.

Decker's gaze shot everywhere before coming to rest on the old man, who fell back into a recliner, his shoe-less feet off the floor. He scratched his cheek and looked at each of them in turn before his gaze returned to Decker.

"You don't look like FBI."

"That's because I'm not."

"Uh-huh," Evers said absently, as his gaze settled onto the fire. "So you're here to find my boy?" he said to the flames. "Didn't think they'd get the Federals involved. But so be it. All I got left is that boy. Not much, but that's it."

"You sacrificed a lot for him, didn't you?" said Decker. He looked around again. "Pretty much everything, right?"

Evers shot him a glance before looking back at the fire. "What the hell do you know about anything?"

"So you don't know where he is?" said Decker.

Evers turned a fierce gaze on him. "What are you saying? That I took my own damn son? Are you simple or what?"

"I'm saying that *Belinda Wyatt* took him. But you already knew that."

For a moment Evers looked like he might collapse to the floor. But then he regained his composure and even flung his flabby hand out dismissively. "Belinda Wyatt! Ghosts-of-the-past bullshit. What's she got to do with anything?"

Decker said, "She has to do with everything. She took Giles. And if we do find him, it'll just be his body, there can be no doubt of that. Something you also know, Mr. Evers. Your son is *dead*."

Bogart, Jamison, and Lancaster all stared in alarm at Decker because of this provocative statement. But Decker never took his gaze off Evers.

The old man's lips trembled and his breathing accelerated. He reached to a side table, picked up a cigarette and lighter, and ignited his smoke. He put it to his lips and inhaled. The nicotine seemed to calm him.

"You got his damn body?" he asked, blowing smoke out his nostrils. "Is that why you're really here?"

"I doubt we'll find it. Unless she wants us to."

Evers exploded, "Then why don't you go arrest that queer-ass bitch!"

Decker said, "That's why we're here. To get your help so we can do that."

Evers sat up straighter. "Why my help? I don't know anything. It's been over twenty years."

Decker continued. "And we came to you because your son and the other police officers who raped and nearly beat her to death apparently aren't around anymore. But *you* are."

Evers sat up straighter. "Nothing was ever proved. Hell, no case was ever even brought. My boy, not a mark on him. God's honest truth."

"Because you paid off the Wyatts and worked with the police chief back then to cover up the whole thing, including not filing a police report. They left her for dead. But she didn't die. She identified each one of them. Mercy may be extraordinarily misnamed, but it's a small town. Everybody knows everybody else. She knew who her assailants were. You're a prominent citizen here. She would have known your son. She would know he was with the police. But she was only sixteen.

She would have believed that the police would protect her even from other cops. She was probably always told that if you have a problem or feel threatened in any way, go to the police." He paused. "Because they'll help you." He paused again, keeping his gaze steady on the old man. "Well, they didn't help her. They raped her, nearly killed her, and then covered it up."

"No proof."

Bogart said, "We'll trace the money that was paid to the Wyatts by you, Mr. Evers."

"And we talked to the Wyatts," Decker added, drawing a quick glance from Bogart and Jamison. "They told us what you did. So you can stop with the denials. We're on a tight time frame. I'm actually surprised you're still alive. I would have thought they would have taken you at the same time they took your son."

The matter-of-fact tone employed by Decker seemed to deflate all the remaining fight in the old man. He jerked forward in the recliner so his feet touched the floor.

He pointed a stubby nicotine-stained finger at Decker. "Damned statute of limitations has run on all this."

"It probably has," conceded Decker. "So you can tell us everything without fear that you will go to prison for any of it, no matter how much you *should* go to prison for what you did. But murder has no statute of limitations, so we can still find and punish Wyatt. You can help us do that."

Evers stubbed out his cigarette and seemed to gather his thoughts for a few moments. "I think what you got to understand is that the girl was weird, asking for it, yes sir."

"Asking to be gang-raped and nearly beaten to death?" said Jamison, her mouth curved in disgust. "What woman would ask for that?"

"Well, not that, of course. But those boys got carried away is all. Boys being boys. Hell, you know."

"No, I really don't," said Lancaster, with even more disgust in her voice than Jamison's.

"And the 'boys' would include your son?" interjected Bogart.

Evers nodded curtly. "He was always in trouble. Got him to join the police force. Chief was a longtime buddy of mine. Owed me. Hell, the whole town owed me. Thought that would get him straight. Swear to God I did. Shows how wrong I was. Just gave him a gun and a chip on his shoulder and an attitude that what he wanted he just took."

"How did his attention get drawn to Wyatt?" asked Bogart.

"Well, see, there was talk over at the school about her. Like I said, weird shit. Never acted normal. Hell, like I said, she was queer-like. Disgusting crap. My boy's a red-blooded American man. He wasn't gonna brook none of that vileness. It's a sin."

"Actually, it's not," said Lancaster. "But keep going."

Evers lit another cigarette and puffed as he talked.

"Well, he and some others decided to go teach her a lesson."

"How'd they do that?" asked Decker.

Evers pointed a finger at Decker. "You don't have it exactly right. It wasn't a bunch of police officers. Just my boy. He was the only cop."

"I don't understand," said Decker, looking taken aback. "Belinda was gang-raped."

"She was. But my boy was the only one in uniform."

"Who were the others?" asked Lancaster.

"Oh, just some punks from the high school football team and—"

Decker interrupted, "And the coach?"

Lancaster hurriedly added, "And the assistant principal?"

Evers looked amazed. "That's right. How'd you know that?"

Lancaster looked at Decker. "Amos, *that's* how she chose her targets at Mansfield. That's how she chose the *location*."

Decker said, "How many football players were involved?"

Evers shrugged. "I don't know. Four, five."

"Try six."

"Hell, man, come on, how do you know that?" said Evers. "Even I can't remember. And I was *here*."

"Belinda Wyatt told us."

"But you said—"

"Just keep going. Where did the rape take place?"

"In the cafeteria, my son told me. Don't know why they picked that place. But that's where he said it happened. Did her up on a table, I believe," he added nonchalantly.

Bogart, Jamison, and Lancaster all exchanged glances.

"How did your son get a hold of Belinda?" asked Decker.

"He picked her up in his patrol car when he saw her walking on the street one night. Apparently she walked at night a lot. He'd seen her before. He told her he was going to look after her."

"What did he mean by that?" asked Bogart sharply.

"Like I said, she was a freak, and folks here made a point of telling her so to her face. No, they were none too kind. Me, I say the Lord makes 'em in lots of different ways. What will be will be. But not some others 'round here. So her life was pretty bad in Mercy. Giles knew that. So he used that to sort of lure her in."

"Why would he even care about her?" asked Decker.

"Hey, he played football at the high school. Went there with the coach, Howard Clarke, and Conner Wise, the assistant principal, when they were all younger, o' course." He lowered his voice. "And word at the school was that Wyatt was part man, part woman. Girls in gym class said she had *balls*. My God, can you believe that? I bet the Wyatts were into drugs and such. Maybe they were hippies. Get that in your body and have a kid, shit like that happens. A girl with balls."

"That is absolutely ridiculous," blurted out Bogart.

"So you say, don't make it true," countered Evers. "Anyway, some fellers on the football team, they dated some of these girls. So they got wind of it. They told Howard and my son and Conner. They all got together and figured they'd teach her a little lesson."

"By nearly killing her?" snapped Lancaster.

Evers got a thoughtful look on his face. "You know what? I think they were maybe trying to help her. You know, let the girl feel what it was like to have a man doing things to her. Get her back to normal. Make her see she was really a gal and all. And how good it was to be with a man."

Bogart said, "Don't try to spin this into something positive, Mr. Evers. The statute of limitations might have run out on the rape and assault, but if you try to obstruct justice, I'll have your ass in a prison cell faster than you can take another puff on that cigarette."

Evers stared at him for a moment and then hurried on with his story. "Well, I guess things got outta hand. She fought back real hard. So they had to, well, beat her up some. I guess one of 'em hit her so hard they thought they'd killed her. She was unconscious and bleeding and everything. And Giles told me she stopped breathing. So they got a little scared and they threw her in the Dumpster behind the school and then they all took off. But she come to and dragged herself outta there. She went to the cops and reported it. Like I said, the chief was my old buddy, owed me for things in the past. Called me. Her parents knew, of course. She told 'em. I scraped every dime I could get my hands on to keep it quiet." His face turned into a mask of fury. "The Wyatts sucked me dry. The bastards."

"Is that the way you saw it?" asked Bogart. "A negotiation?"

"It's the way *they* saw it. Look around. I live in this shitpile now. Wife long dead. It killed her. She knew. Killed her dead. Took every penny I got. Sold every property I had, all my assets, gone. The damn Wyatts probably built some mansion somewhere, hell, I don't know. And they were the ones brought that freak into this world. And I live here after busting my hump for sixty years. This is all I got to show for it." He looked around. "My fridge is twenty years old. Haven't had a new car in forever. One out there don't even run."

"Well, I'm sure it's been painful for you," said Bogart dryly.

Decker said, "But why do anything? Why pay any money? It was they-said, she-said. The whole town was against her. The cops could have gotten rid of the evidence. Protecting their own. And the chief was your buddy. The Wyatts suckered you."

Evers puffed on his cigarette and shook his head resignedly. "No sir, they weren't bluffing. They had evidence."

"How?" asked Bogart.

"Before Belinda Wyatt went home she walked herself on over to the damn hospital and they did a rape and assault kit. No question she'd been raped and beat up bad. Had my boy's evidence on it. And everybody else's. DNA, blood, and skin under her fingernails, all that shit. Dead to rights. Then, like I said, Belinda told her parents what happened."

"But they didn't call the cops," said Decker.

"No, they knew the lay of the land in Mercy. The Everses were at the top. Everybody else, not so much. No one here woulda given a damn, but the Wyatts played it smart. Had to hand it to them. They threatened to turn everything over to the *state* police, the FBI even. Well, I had to do something." He finished his cigarette and stared over at Decker. "Couldn't let my only son go down over messing up some piece of trash."

Decker said, "I thought you were of the mind to live and let live? The Lord makes 'em in lots of different ways? What will be will be?"

Evers looked at him cagily. "Yeah, well, the Lord wasn't going to get my boy off a rape charge if we let it get outsida Mercy, was he?"

"What were the circumstances of your son's disappearance?" asked Decker.

"Pretty damn simple. Went out drinking one night and never came back."

"Is he married, have any kids?"

"Divorced. Wife's gone and took the kids. Got his ass kicked off the police force. He lived here with me."

Well, *that's* some *justice*, thought Decker.

"Why all this interest now?" Evers wanted to know.

"Have you received anything that seemed off, weird,

inexplicable?" asked Decker, ignoring the old man's question.

Evers thought for a moment. "Well, there's that one thing."

"What thing?" said Decker quickly.

"Hell, I'll go fetch it." The old man struggled up and was gone for a minute.

Bogart looked at Decker. "Well, this explains why Wyatt is doing what she's doing. Revenge. She picked Mansfield because of what happened to her at the high school here."

Lancaster added, "And she picked her victims the same way. Mirrored the people who nearly killed her. Six football players, the coach, and the assistant principal."

Jamison looked at Decker. "But it still doesn't explain why she came after you."

Decker stared back at her. "No, it doesn't."

Evers returned with a single piece of paper. "Somebody slipped this under my door a few months back. Never could make heads nor tails of it."

He handed it to Decker. The others gathered around to look at it.

It was a printout of a Web page. Its title was "Justice Denied." Underneath was a list of names, and next to each was a crime: murder, rape, assault, kidnapping.

At the bottom of the page there was a declaration. "Each of these crimes was committed by a man in a police uniform. And every single one was covered up. But we will not forget. Justice will not be denied."

Decker quickly read down the list of names until he came to one that made him stop. "We just found how Belinda Wyatt and Leopold hooked up."

All three of them stared at the names: Caroline and Deidre Leopold. Next to their names was the crime committed against them.

Murder.

60

During the flight back to Burlington they all read over the case notes of the Leopolds' murders in a village twenty kilometers from Vienna. At the request of the FBI the Austrian police had also sent along information on Leopold's background.

"There is nothing in here about cops possibly killing Leopold's family," said Lancaster.

"Well, if it was true, I doubt they'd put that in the file," said Bogart.

Decker, who had been reading over the autopsy reports on the two victims, looked up at Bogart. "You have any string on this jet?"

"String?"

"Or rope."

They found some rope in an emergency kit stowed in a storage bin, and Bogart watched as Decker took lengths of rope and started forming knots out of them.

"What's that?" asked Bogart.

"It might be something or it might not," was all Decker would say.

Later he read down the "Justice Denied" paper that

someone had left at Clyde Evers's door. Then he looked at the knots he had formed with the rope and then at the page. He read over the Leopold murder file, again absorbing every bit of information. Finished, he closed his eyes and began putting the pieces together. His eyes were still closed when the jet touched down.

"Amos, time to go," said Lancaster.

As they drove away in the SUV, Bogart said, "My people will trace this website and see what we can find out."

Lancaster nodded and then glanced at Decker, who was staring out the window.

"What do you think, Amos?"

He was sitting in his seat still holding the knotted lengths of rope.

"I'm thinking that a lot of people are dead because of a bunch of ignorant folks."

"Wyatt and Leopold made choices, bad ones," said Bogart. "Horrible ones. They're responsible for this and no one else."

"And human beings have limits," said Decker. "And you can say all you want about the world being unfair and people rising above the atrocities done to them, but everyone is different. Some are hard as steel, but some are fragile, and you never know which one you're going to get."

"They killed your *family*, Decker," barked Bogart.

Lancaster and Jamison exchanged nervous glances.

Decker didn't look at the FBI agent. "Which is why

we're going to catch them and their lives will end either in prison or in a death chamber. But don't expect me to fully blame Wyatt for this. Because I can't, and I won't."

"I wonder where Giles Evers is," said Jamison.

"In hell, I hope," replied Decker.

Decker asked to be dropped off at the Residence Inn. He walked up the steps to the second floor and gazed back as the SUV rolled out of the parking lot. Jamison was staring out the window at him. She gave him a tiny wave.

He didn't return it.

He went into his room and sat on the bed, the springs sagging under his girth.

He closed his eyes and let his mind whir back to two images of the same person but in different situations and garb.

Billy the waitress at the bar.

Billy the mop boy at the 7-Eleven.

He had gotten a good look at Billy the mop boy's face, not so with Billy the waitress. He scrunched his eyes tighter as though refocusing a camera. The chin was the same on both. The line of the jaw. And the hands. People always forgot about the hands, but they could be as distinctive as a fingerprint if you knew what to look for.

Long, delicate fingers, short right pinky, no nail polish on the waitress, split nail on the left index, small wart on the right thumb. Same person absolutely.

He opened his eyes wide in surprise.

He had just seen Billy. In color. For the first time.

Gray.

For him, as for many folks, it was a confusing color. It lent itself to no particular interpretation. It was a color that could go one way or the other. People desperately wanted the world to be clear-cut in black and white. It made life so much easier: Tough decisions faded away; everything was nicely organized and cataloged. And so were people. But the world was not like that. And neither were the people who inhabited it. At least for those who bothered to explore its complexity.

Its grayness.

Now, for him, Leopold was yellow. Yellow was not ambivalent. Yellow was hostile, cunning. Sometimes colors were spot on. As clear-cut as numbers, actually.

The pieces were falling into place.

But why target me? What the hell did I ever do to you, Belinda/Billy? What?

Their only contact had been at the institute twenty years ago. His family had been killed more than sixteen months ago. Quite a gap. Why the wait? Because she had run into Sebastian Leopold during that time? And he had given her away to get back at Decker? Avenge herself? But for what?

The institute. Ground zero for them both. Interaction limited. Words spoken directly to each other? Exactly none.

He closed his eyes again. He had to get this right. He

had to be thorough. Wyatt had a reason for everything. She had been amazingly meticulous. The symmetry was spellbinding in its depravity. In its horror. So there had to be a reason for this too.

His DVR whirred back and forth. Images flashed past with astonishing speed, but he missed nothing. He saw everything that was there as though it was happening to him right then and at normal speed. No, in slow motion. Every word, every moment, everything moving at the pace of a snail.

In the group sessions he had spoken of his future. His hopes and dreams. But so had everyone else. Well, everyone except Belinda. She had been given the opportunity, but had not volunteered any information about her future plans. She apparently didn't have any future plans, at least not then.

Well, that changed.

Some knew of Decker's past, of his trauma, his near death on the playing field. He had not known of Belinda's plight, though perhaps she didn't know that. She might have thought that if she knew about him, he knew about her. But what did that matter, really?

He opened his eyes, his brow creasing with the failure of his mind—his extraordinary brain-traumatized, bastardized mind that had been born to him after his death and resurrection—to solve the one conundrum that would make all the other pieces fall into place.

He left because he could not stay here.

Thirty minutes later he walked into the Burlington

police station. Captain Miller was there. Bogart had already briefed him on the trip to Utah, Miller informed him.

"You don't look so good, Amos," Miller said.

"Should I?" Decker said back.

Miller tapped his head. "It's not coming?"

"It's there. I just can't make it tell me what I need to know."

"You have an exceptional mind, but it's still a lot to figure out."

"Well, someone has to. And if it's not me, it has to be someone else."

"You think they might pull up their tent and leave?"

"Not yet."

"What are they waiting for?" asked Miller.

"Me."

He went down to the evidence locker and filled out the necessary paperwork with Miller's authorization to step inside the locker and look through the evidence gathered thus far. Since he was no longer with the police, someone had to accompany him.

That person was Sally Brimmer, who explained, "It's not like I have a higher priority than this case, Decker."

They sat at a table as Decker went over every evidence bag, many of them twice. He finally came to his uniform the second time around.

"Technically, you should have turned in your badge," admonished Brimmer. "It's no good anymore anyway. The way they defaced it."

Decker picked up the bag and looked through the plastic at the badge with the X cut through it.

X-ing me out, he thought. *Like you did Giles Evers. He was wearing a uniform when he took you under false pretenses, Belinda.* In a sense they were all in uniform. The cop, the football players, the coach, even the assistant principal, cloaked in the authority of the school. *You were surrounded by people who should have protected you, but they didn't. Instead, they destroyed you. Starting with a cop. With a badge. Just like mine.*

He rubbed the metal through the plastic. Then he stopped. It was like rubbing a genie's lamp. He had made a silly wish, never thinking it would come true. But it just had.

The last piece had just fallen into place.

And Amos Decker finally understood what he had done to deserve all this.

61

He walked into the library at Mansfield High with the certain knowledge that he had to do this.

There were about a half dozen people working here, but Lancaster, Jamison, and Bogart were not among them. It was late. Perhaps they were catching some sleep. His phone buzzed. Surprisingly, it was Bogart. He had some information on the "Justice Denied" matter. And he also told Decker that the Wyatts had nearly $10 million in liquid assets but that monies had been funneled out of the accounts at the rate of $1 million per month for the last nine months. Decker listened to it all.

Bogart said, "What do you make of that?"

"That it all makes sense."

"What the hell does that mean?"

"Exactly what I said."

"Where are you?"

"In my room getting ready to go to sleep."

"I'll check back in the morning," said Bogart.

"Right," said Decker.

He sat down at one of the laptops and logged in

using the password he had previously been given. He went to the "Justice Denied" website. There was a program there to set up personal messaging accounts so that people could correspond privately with the organizers of the site. He set up a username and password, filled out a form, and made a request.

They had to monitor it, he thought. There was no way they could not. That might be why they had left the information about the site with Clyde Evers, just in case Decker made the connection and went to visit the old man. This was all a puzzle, and every piece fit in somewhere.

Thirty minutes went by. Then an hour. Then two hours. Decker just sat there, the color gray chief in his mind. Though he'd lived with this new mind for twenty years now, it still felt like he was existing in someone else's body. And that any minute, or after an odd synaptic fire, he would be back to his old self and his quite ordinary brain.

His phone buzzed again. It was Jamison. He didn't answer it.

At the three-hour mark the message popped up in his new account.

You finally got there, bro. Congratulations.

Decker also knew what the "bro" reference was to now. It was simple, really. They were all brothers, weren't they? All lumped together by Wyatt. By Leopold. It was unfair, of course. It was unjust, but still, he could understand it.

He typed in a request and sent it off. And waited.

Finally, the response came. *Why should we?*

He had not expected them to simply agree to what he had proposed. He typed in his answer. He hoped it was good enough. He doubted he would get another chance like this.

This needs to end sometime. Why not now? I'm the only one left.

Unless he was missing something really big, he *was* the only one left. And he didn't think he was missing anything. Not anymore. In fact, he might have discovered something that everyone else had missed. And he meant everyone, the two people on the other end of this digital line included.

They would suspect a trap, of course. They couldn't even know it was him. He was expecting a test. And it came with the next missive.

The number of Dwayne LeCroix's jersey.

They had definitely done their homework, or maybe Wyatt had heard something about him at the institute and dug that up.

The query said he had five seconds to answer. No looking up anything online. Google or YouTube was not going to be an option here. But he didn't need it. Even without his special talent he would forevermore remember those two digits, even if he hadn't seen them before the hit occurred.

He instantly typed in the answer and sent it off: *24.*

The response was immediate.

Instructions to follow in five minutes. Stand by.

He waited, his internal clock ticking away in his head. When three hundred and six seconds had passed, it came. He studied it.

It was smart, calculated. They were taking no chances. It was like traveling by stagecoach with way stations along the journey, allowing them ample opportunity to see if Decker was truly alone. He would get to one station and there would be a communication telling him where to go next.

They had obviously planned this out previously, as though they knew exactly how all of this was going to play out. And that, Decker had to concede, was more than a little unnerving.

He rose and left. He was back at his room in thirty minutes. It took him all of three minutes to pack up pretty much all he had.

It fit into a bag two feet square with room to spare.

As he hit the doorway he looked back. His home. The only one he had now, a rental, one room. Not really much of a home. So he felt absolutely nothing at leaving it.

If this turned out badly for him he would miss Lancaster, Miller, and Jamison. And maybe even Agent Bogart. But that was about it.

He closed the door and dropped the key off in the office slot.

He knew he would not be coming back.
That was just the way it had to be.
For a lot of reasons.

62

The bus took him to Crewe, three towns over from Burlington. The snow was picking up and the lights on the interstate illuminated a fat, wet precipitation that would add tonnage to this part of the country until it finally stopped falling. And then the highway department would spend days cleaning it up, only to see Mother Nature do it all over again.

He looked out the window of the bus, his phone in his hand. They hadn't told him how the next communication would come, but he wanted to be ready.

He alighted at Crewe along with only three others. Their possessions were nearly as meager as his, although one woman had a full suitcase and a pillow, and a small, sleepy child in tow.

He looked up and down the snowy underhang of the bus station platform. There were few people out and about, and all of them clearly of limited resources.

A man approached him. He was black, in his sixties, with a big belly, snow-caked boots, and a coat with rips down both sides. A flapped hat hung low over his head.

His glasses were fogged. He stopped in front of Decker and said, "Amos?"

Decker looked at him and nodded. "Who are you?"

"I'm nobody. But *somebody* gave me a hundred dollars to give you this, and so I am." He handed Decker a slip of paper.

"Who was it?"

"Didn't see 'em."

"How'd you know to look for me?"

"They said a really tall, fat, scary-lookin' white dude with a beard. You it."

The man lumbered off and Decker looked down at the instructions on the note.

He went in and bought another bus ticket. He had two hours to kill. He bought a coffee from the machine in the station. It was more warm than hot, but he didn't care. He spent his time looking at everyone in the waiting room. It was more crowded than he would have thought. Then he realized something.

Thanksgiving was nearly here. These folks were probably heading out to see family and carve up a big turkey.

He and Cassie had never celebrated Thanksgiving together, chiefly because one or the other had always been working the holiday shift. Decker had spent more than one turkey day chowing down at a diner or a fast-food place. Cassie had spent her share in the hospital dining hall. Whoever had Molly in a given year would eat out. They had enjoyed it and had never felt like they were missing much.

But looking around at these folks, Decker concluded that he had missed more than he had thought.

The next bus dropped him off at the Indiana border.

There was a compact car waiting in the station parking lot, its engine running. The note had said to walk toward it and tap on the driver's window. He knew this was also a test.

He went to the car and rapped on the window.

The woman inside rolled down the window and said, "Get in the back."

He did so. If the FBI had been tailing him, now would be the time to surround the vehicle. They didn't. Because they weren't tailing him.

He got in the back. The car was small so his knees were wedged behind the seat.

"You know my friends?" he asked.

"I don't have friends," she replied. Her hair was stringy and gray, her body odor strong and unpleasant, especially in the hot car—she had the heater on max and her craggy voice and the hazy cigarette smoke that hung in the air foretold a painful death from lung cancer.

"That's too bad," he said.

"Not from where I'm sitting."

"How much did they pay you to do this?"

"Enough."

"You meet them?"

"Nope."

"You know what this is about?"

"This is about six hundred bucks to yours truly. That's all I need to know."

She put the stick in gear and they sped off. They drove for so long that Decker found himself dozing off. That was remarkable when he woke and thought about it, since he was traveling to his death.

Or, more accurately, my murder.

They crossed over Interstate 74, reached nearly to Seymour, and then got onto Interstate 65 heading north toward Indianapolis. But they exited well before then. They sped west, passing Nashville, Indiana. Decker saw a sign for Bloomington to the south, but they didn't take it. He was thinking they might be driving all the way to Terre Haute near the Illinois border when the woman pulled off onto the shoulder at an exit a few miles before Interstate 70, running east to west, could be picked up.

She said, "Walk up this exit ramp. There's a rest stop. There'll be somebody there."

As Decker exited the car he thought again that all of this had been arranged well before he had contacted them through the website. They had clearly expected him to do this. Or at least hoped that he would.

And he had. Which meant they had read him right.

He hoped to have done the same for them.

He trudged through the snow to the rest stop with

his bag slung over his shoulder. The snowfall had slowed but his feet were soaked through. His belly was rumbling and his nose was running.

The white panel van was backed into the first parking space. The headlights blinked twice as Decker approached. The driver's window came down. It was another woman, with hollowed-out cheekbones. She looked like a druggie slipping in and out of withdrawal.

"You want me to drive?" said Decker, running his gaze up and down her skinny frame. "I want to get there in one piece."

She shook her head and jerked her thumb toward the back of the van.

"You sure you're good to go?"

In answer she put the van in drive and stared out the windshield.

Decker clambered into the back and slid the side door closed.

The woman drove off as Decker settled into the seat.

The gun placed against his right temple didn't unduly surprise him. After all, how many people could they engage to get him to this point? He had figured two max, and he'd been right.

His bag was taken from him and thrown out the back door. He was searched and he could tell the searcher was surprised that Decker was not armed. His phone was taken from him and hurled out the back as well.

The man tugged on his sleeve and tossed an orange

jumper over the seat and into Decker's lap. He held it up. "It looks a little small."

Neither of them spoke.

"Do you go by Billy now, Belinda?" Decker said to the driver. "Or was that just for the 7-Eleven gig?"

He watched as the wig came off. The eyes that flashed at him in the rearview were the same ones he'd seen at the convenience store. But they were very different from the eyes that he had remembered seeing at the institute, the pair that had belonged to the devastated teenage girl named Belinda Wyatt. She apparently was gone for good.

He said, "The disguise was good, but I have your hands memorized. Hard to change them unless you wear gloves."

She just kept staring at him, and in those eyes Decker could see the cumulative hatred of twenty years that was about to be unleashed.

On me.

Decker held up the jumper. "A little privacy, please?" The eyes looked away.

He started undressing, which was difficult in the confined space for someone so large. The person with the gun took his clothes and shoes and threw them out the back. Decker struggled into the jumper but could not zip it up in front because of his large gut.

He slumped back in the seat and turned to the man holding the gun and squatting in the back of the van.

"Hello, Sebastian."

He eyed the gun. It was an S&W .45 caliber. *The* .45. The weapon used to kill his wife and half the people at Mansfield. This gun had been the last thing his wife had seen before her life ended. Maybe it had been used to kill Giles Evers too, he didn't know for sure. Maybe a quick bullet wasn't in the cards for the cop turned rapist. But then again, he didn't give a damn about Giles Evers.

Leopold pressed the barrel tighter against Decker's cheekbone.

"I didn't know your situation, Belinda," said Decker. "When I stood up in the group session and said I wanted to go into law enforcement, that I wanted to be a cop. I didn't know that a bad cop had lured you into a gang rape and almost killed you."

The eyes flashed once more at him, but the driver said nothing.

Decker's mind whirred back to that day at the institute. His twenty-years-younger self stood in the middle of the group and proclaimed that his ambition now was to go into law enforcement, to be a good cop. That he wanted to protect others, keep them from harm. He had looked around at all the people, folks like him, with new and sometimes scary minds and personalities. His words had been met with admiring smiles by some and indifference by others. But one pair of eyes had been staring at him with something more than all the others combined. He could see that clearly now. Apparently his perfect mind had flaws, because this memory, while always there, had not made an impression on him. He had glossed right over it until he *hadn't* glossed right over it. It had struck him while he'd been rubbing his old badge through the plastic back at the Burlington police station.

My genie. My wish come true. Death.

Plastic badge, he had thought right before the epiphany had struck him. *A plastic cop. Not a real cop. A cop who hurt you. Giles Evers.*

And from my words, you lumped me right in with him. And maybe I can understand that, because right at that moment you probably were the most vulnerable you would ever be.

He recalled those eyes as the deepest, most shocked pair he had ever seen. But he hadn't registered it, because he had been very nervous standing up in front of strangers to talk about his future.

His mind stopped whirring and he returned to the present. He said to Wyatt, "That's why you singled me out, right? 'Bro'? Brotherhood of cops. Brotherhood of football players, because I was one of them too? Everyone at the institute knew about that. But not your bro, *their* bro. Giles Evers and his bunch? But I came here to tell you that I didn't know what had happened to you. If I had I wouldn't have said what I did. I'm sorry. I wanted to be a cop because I wanted to help people. Not hurt them like Evers did you."

They drove on. Neither one of them had spoken and Decker began to wonder why. He figured he would keep going until something he said drew a response.

They might be working up the nerve to do what they needed to do to him. But then again, the pair had killed so many people that he doubted they needed much preparation to put a bullet in him.

"I met Clyde Evers. He told me all about what happened at the high school in Utah. So now I know why you did what you did at Mansfield. But maybe you have something you want to add?" He looked at her expectantly.

The eyes flashed once more. But they weren't looking at him. They were looking at Leopold.

In his peripheral Decker saw the gun muzzle bob up and down ever so slightly. When you nod your head your hand sometimes moved in the same direction. So Leopold *was* calling the shots. That was telling. And maybe helpful for what Decker had come here to do.

Because these two weren't the only ones on a mission. So was Amos Decker. He hadn't come here to simply die, although that was a very real possibility.

Wyatt said, "I think it speaks for itself, don't you?"

Her voice was deeper than when she was a woman, and deeper than when she had spoken to him in the role of Billy the mop boy. It was amazing how she was able to modulate it. But the tone was far less important than the words. She didn't care. There was no remorse. There was nothing behind the eyes. She was thirty-six now. And he doubted she had had an easy, normal day in the last thirty of them. That couldn't help but change you. How could you respect or appreciate or care about a world and the people in that world when they loathed the fact that you shared *their* planet?

"Did you kill the people who raped you? I mean other than Giles Evers?"

"Well, that would have been a little obvious," said Wyatt. "So I chose symbolism over literalness."

Decker felt his face flush at these cruel words. His wife and daughter had been reduced to symbols of a warped mind seeking revenge?

Decker felt Leopold's breath on his cheek. He could smell garlic and stomach bile, but no alcohol. That was good. He didn't want a drunk holding a gun against his head. But the guy took drugs too. And you couldn't smell drugs on someone's breath.

He couldn't see the tattoo of the twin dolphins, because Leopold's sleeve covered it. But the tat was there; he knew that. It was real. It had all been in Leopold's file. All of it. Decker had memorized every word of that file. The crime against his family. Every detail. And the file on Evers and Mr. and Mrs. Wyatt. And the payoff from Evers. And the money that was there now. And the "Justice Denied" website. It had been interesting stuff. All very interesting.

"I guess I can see you taking that position. I mean, the victims at Mansfield were innocent, but to you, who is innocent, really, right? Nobody."

"I know you don't feel pity or sympathy or empathy anymore," said Wyatt. "Because I don't either. So don't even bother. I'm not stupid. I'm just like you."

The hell you are, Decker thought.

He said, "We found your mom and dad. They'll get a proper burial now. Not sure how you feel about that. But you made your point with them. ME said they'd been there a long time. So they'll be buried."

The muzzle pressed harder against Decker's skin.

Decker continued, "My daughter never lived to your age when you were raped. About six years shy."

"Six years, one month, and eighteen days," corrected Wyatt. "She died before her tenth birthday. Or, more accurately, I *killed* her three days before her tenth birthday."

Decker felt his anger edge up, which was the last thing he needed.

"Actually, three days, *four hours, and eleven minutes*," he corrected.

He locked gazes with Wyatt in the mirror. Without taking his eyes off her he said, "Are you a hyper too, Sebastian?"

"No, he's not," said Wyatt. "Just you and me are the freaks."

"You're not a freak. Neither am I."

"Oh, excuse me, I wasn't aware that you had ovaries. My mistake."

"You know what I mean."

"Dear Mom and Dad saw my rape as a way to get rich. You know what my father told me?"

"What?" asked Decker. He had not expected this outpouring from Wyatt. Especially not after her first terse words. But now he realized that she needed to talk. She needed to say things, get things out. Before she killed him. It was all part of a process. Her process.

And mine too.

"He said it was high time that I brought something positive into their lives. As though my *rape* was something *positive* in their lives. That's what he meant. And they took Clyde Evers's money and built themselves this castle in the sky. And they never let me step inside it. That was my home, you know. *I* bought it, not them."

"I can see that."

"They never even told me they had moved. They sent me away to a mental rehab facility. When I came home a week later they were gone. I was on my own. They just abandoned me."

"They were cruel, ignorant, and wrong, Belinda."

She looked away from the mirror. "Who cares? Now they're just dead."

"I died too. Not once but twice."

He saw the eyes flash at him in the mirror once more.

"On the football field. After the hit. They brought me back twice, maybe they shouldn't have bothered. Then I wouldn't have said what I did to you and all of those people would still be alive. One life to save all those others. Sounds like a good deal to me."

"Maybe it would have been," said Wyatt. "But you *didn't* die. Just like I didn't die. I climbed out of that Dumpster. Maybe I shouldn't have. Maybe I should have just died."

Her voice trailed off with this last part and Decker wasn't sure, but he wondered if that constituted remorse, or at least as close as Wyatt would ever get to it now.

"I see my family's murders in blue," said Decker, drawing another stare from Wyatt. "I know you don't suffer from synesthesia. It's odd seeing things in color that should have none. It's one of the things that scared the crap out of me when I woke up in the hospital and found out I was a different person."

"Well, I was two people to begin with," Wyatt shot back. "And after they raped and beat me nearly to death I became someone else entirely. So that makes *three*. A little crowded in someone my size." There was not a trace of mirth in her tone. She was being deadly serious. Decker would have expected nothing less.

"You chose male over female? Why?"

"Men are predators. Women are their prey. I chose never to be the prey again. I chose to be the predator. For that I needed a full set of balls and a tankful of testosterone. Now I've got them and all is right with my world."

Decker had figured that Leopold was calling the shots, but maybe he was wrong. If so, things were not going to work out so well for him. "Where are we going?"

"Somewhere."

This was Leopold. Decker had wondered when the man was going to assert himself. Maybe he wanted Decker to know that Wyatt was not running this.

Good, Sebastian, keep it up. I need you in my corner. Until I don't.

"Somewhere is good. Better than nowhere."

"Why are you here?" asked Leopold. "Why did you come?"

"Figured I'd save everyone the trouble. I knew you were targeting anyone associated with me. I didn't want anyone else to have to die because of me. I was surprised that you gave us a warning with the Lancaster family."

He glanced at the mirror to find Wyatt watching him again.

"You sure you have no empathy?" asked Decker. "You could have killed them."

"They weren't worth the trouble."

"Sandy has Down syndrome, but you knew that. Do you draw the line at killing kids like that?"

Wyatt focused back on the road.

Leopold said, "So you come so readily to the end of your life?"

The gent was downright talkative now. And his formal and somewhat clunky speech was another indicator that English was not his first language.

"We all have to die someday."

"And today is your day," said Leopold.

63

They drove for two more hours. Decker had no idea where he was, and it really didn't matter to him. Help was not coming.

The van finally pulled off the road and Decker was bumped up and down as the vehicle hit a rough patch but then kept going.

The van hung a sharp left and a few moments later skidded to a stop. Wyatt got out and Leopold motioned for Decker to do the same. His bare feet hit cold gravel and he winced as a sharp rock cut the bottom of his right foot.

There was an old outdoor light in a rusted metal cage over the door they were heading to. Decker could make out the faded, peeling remnants of a sign that had been painted in red on the white brick wall.

Ace Plumbing. Est. 1947.

It looked like flakes of blood resting on the pale skin of a corpse.

He looked to the right and left and saw nothing but trees. A leaning chain-link fence enclosed the abandoned property.

Leopold gave him a shove in the back and he staggered into the building behind Wyatt. Leopold closed and bolted the door after them.

Wyatt was dressed in jeans and a hooded windbreaker. With the wig gone the hair was short, blond, and receding. As Billy, Wyatt had been wearing another wig that had drastically changed his appearance; the same with the waitress gig. Decker figured Wyatt might go bald in a few more years.

If he had a few more years left to live. If any of them did.

A light dimly illuminated the space. It was all concrete, mostly bare, the floor and walls splotched with grease and other dirt. An old, leaning metal shelf at the far end held a couple of joint pipes. A wooden desk with a chair in the kneehole was set near the doorway to another room. A file cabinet sat behind the desk. Some wooden crates were stacked against one wall. The windows were barred and blacked out.

Wyatt pulled out the chair and rolled it across the room. It bumped crazily over the chipped concrete floor.

Leopold motioned with the gun for Decker to sit.

He did. Wyatt took duct tape and wound it around both Decker and the chair until the two were as one. Then Wyatt pulled a large box out from behind the desk, carried it over, and turned it upside down. Tumbling out of it and clattering to the floor were all of the trophies taken from Mansfield. All the ones with Amos Decker's name on them.

Wyatt picked one up and looked at it. "Football players and cops, my favorite people." He dropped the trophy.

The pair pulled up two of the old crates and sat on them staring at Decker.

Decker stared back, taking them both in, detail by detail. He could tell that Wyatt was doing the same to him.

Wyatt looked nothing like the teenage girl Decker had seen back at the institute. The twenty-year march of time had hollowed out her features, giving her a perpetually hungry, emaciated look. The mouth was jagged and cruel. There were no smile lines around the edges of the lips. What did Wyatt have to smile about? Ever? The long brow had worry lines that already had been forming back at the institute.

Decker glanced at Leopold. He had cleaned up some since their last meeting at the bar. His hair was combed and his clothes looked clean.

"Can you answer a couple of questions that have been bugging me?" Decker asked. When neither of them responded, he said, "The old man and old woman that were seen out and about in my neighborhood and then Lancaster's neighborhood. Was that you?"

Wyatt stood, pulled her hood over her head, bent over, mimicked gripping a cane, and walked slowly across the room. In a pitch-perfect impersonation of an elderly man's voice Wyatt said, "Can you help me find my little dog, Jasper? He's all I have left."

She pulled her hood back down and straightened.

"I can fool anyone," said Wyatt, staring dead at him. "Become anyone I want."

"Yes, you can," said Decker.

He wondered if Wyatt had always been able to transform like that. Stuck between two genders, a foot in each with an identity in neither, entrenched in limbo. When she had played the role of Billy, it had been a remarkable transformation. Happy-go-lucky, superficial, innocuous. As she had said, she could play any role.

Well, except for one. Herself.

He imagined Wyatt walking through the halls of Mansfield in the getup that made him look taller and far broader. This slip of a man—formerly a woman—transformed into a giant with guns, massacring people like they were bugs in the grass. Man as predator. Man that could never be hurt by another man. Like a woman could.

"Why did you stay in the freezer overnight? Why not just come in through the base side and meet Debbie in the shop class?"

"Because Debbie was with me in the freezer that night," said Wyatt. "She snuck out of her house. We did it right then and there. The first time." He grinned, though it didn't reach the eyes. "She thought it was so amazing! Sex in the freezer. In the dark. It brought back memories for me, you see. I was gang-raped in the school cafeteria. But now I was the guy doing the girl. Then she left. And in the morning I used the passageway to get to the other end of the school."

"And how much did she know about the plan?" said Decker. "We found the picture of you in cammies."

"I wore them sometimes when we were together. I told her I was former military. And now I was in military intelligence. She thought that was so cool. I told her I was here investigating a possible terrorist cell, and that she could help me. And of course I ended up seducing her. It wasn't hard. She knew nothing of the real plan. She just thought we were going to do it in the shop classroom smack in the middle of everybody. I suggested it, of course. It had to happen that way."

"And how did you find out that she might know something about the passageway?"

"I read an article years ago about bombproof shelters being put under schools. I figured with an Army base right next door there might be such a thing, and possibly more. So I searched the old Army base. It was easy to get inside. In a drawer in one of the rooms I found a duty roster with employee names on it. Simon Watson was on there. It said he was in engineering. Sebastian and I did some more digging and found out that the old man had lived with the Watsons and that Debbie went to Mansfield. I 'ran' into Debbie one day. It took time and I let my 'undercover' story out slowly, but it finally got around to her great-grandfather and things he had told her about the base. She knew about a passage and generally how it ran. She also knew that it connected to the base, she just didn't know exactly where. But that gave us what we needed. We started from the base end and worked our way toward the school. It all came together. And since she believed I was here on a secret mission she understood why no one could know about 'us.' She kept the secret. She was actually very useful."

"She called you *Jesus*, you know. You were the only positive in her life. She loved you very much, apparently. Right up to the second you blew her head off. Jesus."

Wyatt said nothing to this.

Decker glanced at Leopold. "Did you build the outfit that he wore in the school?"

"We did it together. We do everything together."

"And you found out the players on the football team and what classes they were in?"

"Debbie again. I told her I might have to recruit some of them in case I needed local muscle. It was stupid but she'd believe anything."

"And 'Justice Denied'? You left that paper at Evers's dump in Utah. So I guess you wanted us to know about it. It was how I was able to contact you."

"I'm not alone," said Wyatt. Decker glanced at her.

"Not alone?"

"There are lots of others like me. People like me can get justice too."

Decker nodded. "What name do you go by now? Or do you want me to just call you Wyatt?"

"You can call me Belinda. You're from that time. Not from this time. Not much longer, anyway."

"Okay, Belinda. And Leopold here introduced you to 'Justice Denied'?"

Wyatt now looked surprised. "How could you know that?"

"Well, for starters it's a foreign-based site. And Leopold is Austrian. His family was murdered. He actually started the site. Some of the word choices on there show that English was not the creator's first language."

Wyatt and Leopold exchanged a glance.

Decker shifted a bit in his seat. "You know, it would have been easier for you to just kill me," he said. "And leave my family alone."

"No one left me alone," said Wyatt. "No one." He drew a knife from his pocket and held it up. "I used this to kill Giles Evers. His father should be getting a package in the mail any day."

"He disappeared a long time ago. What have you been doing with him all this time?"

"Things," said Wyatt. "Just things." He looked like he wanted to smile, but it didn't seem that he could manage it.

"I don't think Clyde liked his son all that much. Giles sort of ruined his life."

Wyatt stood, walked across the room, and jammed the knife into Decker's thigh.

Decker screamed. When Wyatt worked the blade around he cried out more, cursing and twisting in the chair trying to free himself. Wyatt finally withdrew it and Decker slumped over and threw up from the shock of it.

"I didn't hit the femoral," Wyatt said calmly, retaking a seat on the crate. "I know where it is. Trust me. I read lots of medical books. And books on embalming," Wyatt added. He tapped his temple. "And as you know, we never forget. Anything."

Leopold said, "And you don't get off that easy."

He duct-taped the wound, though blood continued to bubble along the edges.

Ashen-faced, Decker lifted his head.

Wyatt was staring at him. "So you think *his* fucking life was ruined? Is that what you think?"

"Not as much as yours, no," gasped Decker, spitting vomit out of his mouth. Things were starting to accelerate now. He could afford no more mistakes. He eyed Leopold. "How many people like Belinda have you helped find justice?"

"Not enough."

Decker used his mind to compartmentalize, to will the effects of the pain away, for just a few minutes. He needed clarity of thought. He needed to be able to say what he needed to say. Otherwise, it was over.

"It was good that you were in jail when the murders happened. To my family and at the high school. The judge let you go because you had an ironclad alibi."

Leopold said, "My friend here wanted to do the honors. It was only right."

"So, contrary to what you said, you *don't* do everything together. Not when it comes to the actual crimes. We have evidence against Belinda, physical evidence, but nothing against you."

"You have nothing against me," said Wyatt sharply.

"Your parents were murdered. The doctor who attended you at the institute was murdered. I understand why you killed him. He took advantage of you. Another supposed protector who hurt you. And you left your handwriting at multiple places. And we got your print off the mop bucket at the 7-Eleven. And another from the bathroom at the bar where you were working as a waitress." Most of this was a lie, but it didn't matter. He looked at Leopold. "But nothing on this guy. But like he said, *you* wanted to do the honors while he stayed safely in the background."

Leopold stood and gazed at Wyatt. "I think it's time to end this."

Decker quickly said, "Clyde Evers paid your parents six million dollars to keep quiet about what his son did to you. The house in Colorado cost one-point-eight million. They didn't make any improvements to it. We checked their financial records. Their expense burn rate was only about twenty percent of the amounts thrown off by their investment portfolio. The rest just accumulated over time. Stocks did well. By the time you killed them they had over ten million in liquid assets. But someone got his hands on the authorization codes to start taking money out. About a million a month and counting over the last nine months. It's almost all gone now. Did you take it, Belinda?"

"That was bribe money to keep my parents quiet. And they told me if I said anything they would make sure the whole world knew I was a freak. They'd . . . they'd taken pictures of me down there. They said they would send it to the newspapers. So no, I didn't take the money. I didn't want that . . . that blood money. My blood!"

"So I wonder where that cash went? Maybe your buddy here knows."

Wyatt's gaze darted to Leopold and then back at Decker.

"I don't understand anything you're talking about," Wyatt said mechanically.

"Leopold has apparently helped lots of folks with 'Justice Denied.' And the folks he helps have two things happen to them. First, whatever money is around disappears. Second, the *friend* he's helping ends up dead."

Decker had no idea if this was true, but he suspected that it was. That outflow of cash from the Wyatts' account had to have gone somewhere. And he doubted that Leopold would want the "heir" around to find out. When he looked at Leopold the expression on the man's face told him that he was right.

Decker said, "And did he tell you that his family was murdered? Wife and daughter?"

"They *were* murdered," said Wyatt.

"Yes, they were."

"By cops."

"No, not by cops. *He* killed them."

Decker heard the hammer of the gun being pulled back.

"You're full of shit. You're lying!" screamed Wyatt.

Anger, lack of control, that's good. To a point.

Decker slowly shook his head. "I read the file. I looked at the pictures of the corpses. They were both strangled to death. By hanging. At the napes of their necks where the ligature compressed the life out of them they found a very unusual mark. It was nearly identical on both. The Austrian police didn't know what it was. They were baffled because the killer had cut the victims down and taken the rope with him. They were baffled because they never suspected Leopold. Lucky guy had another ironclad alibi provided by a couple of buddies who swore he was in Germany at the time. If they had suspected Leopold and done some digging they probably would have arrived at the truth behind the mark."

Decker felt the gun muzzle against his head.

Leopold said, "You said you've died twice? Well, they say the third time ist the charm."

Decker kept going. "I had seen that mark before. It was in a book I read and, of course, never forgot, because we can never forget anything, can we, Belinda? Like you said." He paused and studied her. When she seemed about to speak he said sharply, "It's called a double constrictor knot. It's like a clove hitch but with an overhand knot under two riding turns. I actually practiced tying it on the flight back from Utah. I discovered that it's nearly impossible to untie once the knot is set. In fact, it's one of the most effective binding knots in the world. Been around at least since the 1860s. It's also called the gunner's knot." He glanced at Leopold. "Every sailor worth his salt knows how to tie that knot. And before your friend here was on submarines, he grew up sailing with his father, who was a fisherman working in the Adriatic Sea six months out of the year." He looked at Wyatt. "I can keep going. As you know, it's all in my head. Every fact, every detail."

"Submarines?" said Leopold contemptuously. "Austria doesn't have a navy."

"No, but Russia does. Which is where you went to live when you were nineteen. You were kicked out of the Russian navy for stealing from your fellow sailors. It took me the longest time to pin down your accent. Because it's a blend. Austrian, Russian, with an overlay of English." He glanced sideways at Leopold. "*Ist* good, Herr Leopold? You said it at the bar. And you said it again just a minute ago. Maybe you didn't even realize?"

Leopold struck him on the side of the head with the gun.

Decker slumped over.

Now his leg and his head were hurting like a bitch. His tolerance for pain was greater than most. You didn't play football for as long as he had without being able to take pain. But a bullet to the head would not be painful. He would just be dead.

He looked up at Wyatt, who was looking at Leopold. Decker couldn't see Leopold's face, so he didn't know where he was looking. But the gun was now pressed against his temple.

"You see the lump on his neck, Belinda? I think the guy is terminal and doesn't give a shit what he does. He's also a druggie. And needs money for that. And I think he likes to make other people do things. I think he's a con man who likes to take people who are in desperate circumstances and screw with them. And if he makes millions in the process, like he did with you, so much the better."

"Sebastian?" said Wyatt weakly.

That was not what Decker wanted to hear. That was not going to cut it.

"He's full of shit," said Leopold.

That was also not going to cut it.

Decker barked, "*You* killed all those people, Belinda. But there were gaps. Nearly twenty years go by and then you kidnap Giles Evers. Then you come and kill my family. Who was next? Your parents? Chris Sizemore? Then a gap. Then Mansfield. And then Nora Lafferty."

"And now you," snarled Leopold.

"Why the gaps, Belinda? Why come after me twenty years later? Was it him? Was it this guy? 'Justice Denied'? Is that why all that time went by before you started killing? From the moment I said it twenty years ago I know you remembered that I wanted to be a cop. I recalled the stunned look on your face, the hurt you were feeling. But you did nothing with it. Not all that time. Until you ran into this guy. And you told him. And you told him about your parents' blackmail money. And he saw his chance. And in your mind he twisted what I said and made it into your absolute obsession, your total and complete vendetta. The one thing that you could do to make it all right. The only thing in life you cared about because otherwise you would have no life."

"Why would I do that?" said Leopold. "This was her revenge, not mine. She had to make it right. She came to me!"

"So it was her idea to make herself look like a big *man* with guns blazing, mowing down defenseless kids." He looked at Wyatt. "Are you telling me that's what you wanted, Belinda? Seducing a vulnerable young woman like Debbie Watson and then blowing her head off? You came up with that? She was almost your age when you were raped. She was just a scared kid with a screwed-up home life. Like you had! She wanted to have a better life. And you seduced her. Made her fall in love with you to such an extent that she called you Jesus, her savior. And then you just killed her? Like she was nothing? Like she didn't matter? Like *you* didn't matter? Like when people who you thought would protect you did just the opposite? Is that your idea of revenge, Belinda?

Because I'm not buying it. That's not you. I don't care how much you changed. You haven't changed that much!"

Wyatt said nothing. But Decker took it as a positive sign that Wyatt was not looking at him. She was staring at Leopold.

She rose from the crate. "Did you take my parents' money?"

"Why would I? Do you see me rolling in cash?"

Decker was not going to lose control of the situation. He barked out, "He does it for kicks, Belinda. He likes to manipulate. He must have loved what you did at the school. It was choreographed, like a play. And maybe he has the money socked away in a bank somewhere. But he killed his family, so why would he have founded 'Justice Denied'? The only justice denied with Leopold was his getting away with murdering his family."

Wyatt said, "Is this true?"

Decker expected more denials. He did not get them.

"Yes," said Leopold emphatically. "Do you feel better?"

He swiveled the gun away from Decker's head. At the same moment Decker launched himself sideways, pushing off mostly with his good leg and taking the chair with him.

The gun fired.

64

Decker catapulted headlong into Leopold, finally delivering the hit on the field during the kickoff denied to him for two decades. It felt good.

Leopold fell sideways with the brutal impact. Decker was sure the man had never been hit that hard in his life. Those who only watched pro football from the safety of their stadium seats or big-screen TVs could never imagine the devastating power of enormous men running at speed into other enormous men. It was like being in a car accident over and over. It didn't merely hurt; it stunned. It shocked the body in so many different ways that one could never be the same afterward. It pushed bone, muscle, ligaments, *and* brains to places they were never intended to go. It was no wonder that so many men who had played the game were now suffering the long-term debilitating effects of entertaining millions and making large sums of money for doing so.

Decker landed directly on top of Leopold, his full weight coming to rest on the much smaller man who was half his weight. A few seconds later Decker smelled the stench. He had hit Leopold so hard that the man's bowels had involuntarily released.

Leopold kicked at him. Then he tried to raise the gun to fire at him, but Decker, just as he had with Bogart, brought his weight down on top of the man and felt all the air leave him. His wide, heavy shoulder jammed down on Leopold's right arm, forcing it to remain straight out.

Leopold was trying with all his might to turn the gun back toward Decker so that he could fire, but the angle was impossible. With the barrel pointed that way, his finger couldn't reach the trigger. The weapon was useless. Which meant that it was man versus man here. And with the difference in size, there would only be one possible outcome.

Leopold seemed to understand this, because he smashed his knee against Decker's wound. Decker screamed in agony. But he closed his eyes and gritted his teeth and, little by little, managed to straighten his legs out from the sitting position he had been forced into by the chair and duct tape. He felt the tape lengthening, though it did not break. But inch-by-inch Decker pushed and stretched and pushed some more until he was finally flattened out and his three-hundred-and-fifty-plus pounds were lying directly on the much smaller man.

Leopold's breathing was ragged now. His body lurched up, trying to throw Decker off. But it was like an elephant on his chest.

And then Decker started to do something he never would have with Bogart, because he had never intended to end the life of the FBI agent. He very much intended to end the life of this man. Without the duct tape holding him back, he would already have killed Leopold. But he still would, he just needed to be patient.

So he began to inch his right shoulder in a new direction, a small measure at a time, while his other shoulder and upper arm remained jammed down on the limb holding the gun, keeping his opponent, in effect, weaponless.

The Smith and Wesson was not going to kill again.

Leopold kept kicking and pushing and bucking but the space for him to operate was now severely limited and growing ever smaller. Decker kept his eyes closed but the tears were running down his face with the pain. The bile rose to his throat and he threw up on Leopold.

The smaller man gagged and spit and cursed and heaved. He knew time was running out, and he was not going to go quietly.

Decker was in terrible pain; the wound was bleeding freely again. He felt his strength start to be sapped by the blood loss. But he didn't really need strength. He just needed his bulk concentrated on one spot in particular. So he kept working at it and his shoulder finally fell into the crevice that he had been striving so mightily for.

Under Leopold's chin and directly against the man's throat.

And then Decker let his weight bear down directly on this spot. His bare feet touched the concrete, gaining traction and leverage, and he thrust his pelvis forward and with it his huge shoulder, ramming it against the man's windpipe and compressing Leopold's chest so his lungs could not inflate. His big belly was sucking in and out through the opening of the jumpsuit with the effort of it all. Sweat dripped off him though the room was cold. He was not going to stop until this was done. His heart was hammering out of control. He felt dizzy and sick. His head felt ready to burst. But he didn't think about any of that. His one focused thought was to kill this man.

Decker let his bulk collapse, making himself as much dead weight as possible. He wished he weighed a ton. He kept driving and driving like he was slamming into a blocking sled over and over. He never had the talent of others on the gridiron, but his motor had never stopped. And no one, from the superstars down to the journeymen, ever worked harder than he did.

So this was his moment. This was his one play to end all plays.

He heard gasping, which wasn't enough.

He kept compressing. He was a gunner's knot. He was the constrictor. He was never going to stop until this was over. Never.

He heard gurgling, which still wasn't enough.

He pushed down harder. He was a whale on a minnow. It had never felt so damn good to be obese. He wanted to swallow this piece of shit whole. He wanted to make him disappear from the earth.

He heard a long, low exhalation, which would never be enough.

He rammed his body down with all his strength. In his mind his DVR whirled. Every victim, every face raced through his mind while he was slowly killing their killer.

Then his DVR slowed and two faces held steady. Cassie and Molly. That was all he could see in that enormous cavern his mind had become. It was the whole damn universe in there; it could hold so much and was ever-expanding. Yet still, right now, it held only their two faces. That was all. And it seemed more than fitting. More than right.

He smashed down one more time as he mumbled, "I love you, Cassie. I love you, Molly. I love you both so much."

Then he heard nothing. Nothing at all.

The lungs had not inflated because they no longer could.

And Leopold's body finally went limp and the gun fell to the concrete.

That was enough.

He lifted his head and stared down at the man.

There were few things in life that were certain.

There were many things in death that were.

He was staring at three of them.

Eyes wide open.

Pupils fixed.

Mouth involuntarily sagging.

Dead.

In Decker's mind the images of his wife and daughter slowly faded, like a movie ending.

And I miss you both so much. I will miss you forever.

He rolled off Leopold and then lay there panting for a few minutes. He had never felt so tired in all his life. His gut was clenching, his legs and head were throbbing. He could feel the swelling on his face from where Leopold had struck him with the gun. And with his heart racing, blood was now starting to flow more rapidly from his wounded leg.

But most of him—the most important parts of him, anyway—felt good. Felt terrific in fact.

It took him the better part of five minutes, but he finally managed to stand with the chair and the saggy, stretched-out duct tape still wrapped around him. He threw himself against the wall repeatedly until the chair fell away in pieces. Then he tugged and ripped until he was free of the tape, and stepped out of his prison.

He turned to look across the room.

He hadn't seen it before, during his struggles with Leopold, but, still, he had known.

She hadn't joined the fight after all, either on his side or Leopold's.

There had to be a reason for that.

Now he was looking at that reason.

He had been wrong. The Smith and Wesson *had* killed again. Or it was about to.

He staggered over to where Wyatt lay on the floor, blood still flowing out of her chest from where the shot had struck her.

He knelt down next to her. She looked far more male than female. But to him she would always be a woman. A sixteen-year-old girl, in fact, who'd suffered so much. Too much. More than anyone should.

Dr. Marshall had said that these days someone with Belinda's intersex condition was always involved in the decision as to what gender to become fully and finally. But someone should never feel compelled to choose to be a man simply because she was terrified of being a woman.

She was not dead yet but she soon would be. The pool of blood around her seemed to exceed what was left inside her. He had no way to stanch the bleeding.

And in truth, Decker also didn't have the desire.

He looked first at her hands. The hands that had strangled the life out of his daughter. Then at the finger that had pulled the trigger on the gun that had killed his wife. The hands that had slit throats and fired shotguns and wrapped a mother and father in plastic and stabbed an FBI agent in the heart.

Then he gazed down at the face. The eyes were starting to fix, the breathing to relax. The body's transition to death was commencing in earnest. The brain was telling the rest of the body that it was over and that everything would soon shut down. It was doing all this in as orderly a fashion as possible given that the cause was a hole in the chest driven there by violent means.

Decker had died before too. He didn't remember white lights, or a tunnel to brightness, or angels singing. For a man who could never forget anything, he could remember nothing of dying. He had no idea if that was comforting or not. He just wanted to be alive.

He sat down on his haunches next to her. Part of him wanted to take Leopold's gun and blow her brains out. Part of him wanted to use his huge hands to crush the remaining life out of her. To hurry her on to where she was inevitably going anyway.

But he didn't. Only once did her eyes flicker and seem to fix on his. There was a look there, just a glimpse, perhaps imagined, Decker didn't know, when he thought he was looking at the scared sixteen-year-old girl back at the institute.

He sighed and closed his eyes for a moment, but didn't even try to process what had become an unimaginable tragedy all around.

So he simply sat there and watched her die. And when she did, he closed her eyes. But he could close nothing that had come before. And Decker knew he never would.

And whether he wanted it or not, Amos Decker, Sebastian Leopold, and Belinda Wyatt, in life and now in death, were all bound together.

Forever.

But he was immeasurably relieved to be the one left standing.

65

A bench.

Christmas Eve.

A light snow was falling. It collected on top of the foot that had already fallen over the last three days. The stores were closed. The shopping was done. And after the cataclysmic events at Mansfield, everyone in Burlington was getting ready to sleep and then awake to a day of peace and quiet spent with family.

Well, almost everyone.

Amos Decker sat on the bench staring across at Mansfield High. But really he was staring at . . . nothing.

In deference to the weather he had on a new overcoat and a wool-lined flapped hat. His hands were gloved and he wore brand-new size-fourteen heavy-duty waterproof boots.

His thigh was nearly healed, though it would always carry a scar where the knife had struck and Belinda Wyatt had both symbolically and literally twisted the blade in him.

Decker had gotten in the van and driven to a shopping mall about thirty miles away, using the GPS on

Leopold's phone to direct him. He had called Bogart and given his location to the FBI agent. Bogart had ordered up a local medevac chopper, which had arrived surprisingly fast. They'd triaged him on the spot and then flown him to the nearest hospital. Before driving off in the van he'd done a tourniquet on his leg, but he'd still lost over two pints of blood by the time help arrived.

He had given Bogart the location of Leopold and Wyatt's hideout. The crime scene had been processed, but by far the two most important pieces of forensic evidence were the two bodies that lay barely six feet apart.

One shot by a .45 with a murderous trail attached to it.

The other literally suffocated to death by a fat guy.

Both deserved what they got. And only one of the people they'd killed had really deserved to die. They had never found Giles Evers's body. But, as Belinda Wyatt had promised, a package had arrived at his father's house.

Clyde Evers reportedly had dropped dead when he opened it.

Getting a severed head in the mail will do that.

Decker corrected himself: So maybe *two* people who deserved to die had.

And maybe four if you included Belinda's parents, who out of naked greed had turned against their fragile daughter when she needed them most.

He did not want to think about death on Christmas Eve. But he seemed so surrounded by it that it tended to crowd out all other things.

He had visited the graves of his wife and daughter. Lancaster had surprised him by showing up too and laying flowers on their graves. They had talked quietly for a few minutes, snatching some normalcy from what was undeniably abnormal.

Decker was sitting here because the Residence Inn had thrown a Christmas party for the guests staying there over the holidays. He had no impulse whatsoever to participate in *that*. Hence he had opted for a bench in the snow over unspiked eggnog and people seeking him out for lively but mindless conversation, which he could neither process nor appreciate.

The decision had been made to reopen Mansfield the following school year. All the blood would be scrubbed away by then, but all other stains would remain there, forever. The governor was planning to come and give a speech on the occasion of the school's reopening.

Decker did not plan to attend the ceremony.

The town had bricked over the entrance to the underground walkway leading from the cafeteria to the shop class. And the Army was officially cementing shut the connecting tunnel. Bulldozers were scheduled to arrive on January 2 to level the entire abandoned base and haul away the remnants to wherever old military bases went to die.

The national press had descended on the place when

the news had broken about the identity of the killers and their deaths. Bogart had managed to keep Decker's name out of everything. The FBI agent had turned out to be a good man who actually cared about things worth caring about.

Most folks would have wanted to be recognized as the one who stopped two killers in their tracks, risking his life to do so. These days money would have flowed from that: book and movie deals, endorsements, offers to join high-level investigative firms, opportunities to be wined and dined by the movers and shakers. Decker could have had millions of followers online riveted on his every tweet or Instagram posting.

Again, he would have opted for a bullet to the head over all *that*.

Yet he had allowed Bogart to buy him clothes and shoes to replace the ones he'd lost to Leopold and Wyatt. For a poor man any loss is a heavy one.

Bogart had pleaded with Decker to accept payment from the federal government for his work. Captain Miller had done the same on behalf of the Burlington Police Department.

"You were a *hired* consultant, Amos," he had said over and over until he just didn't have the strength to say it again.

Decker had refused it all.

He had not done so for noble reasons. He needed money to live. He wasn't shy about taking what was due him.

He had refused it out of guilt.

I stood up in front of Belinda Wyatt and said I wanted to be a cop. I said I wanted to be a cop because cops protect people. She never forgot that and twisted something innocuous into something sinister. And when Leopold came along to add fuel to that fire, building it into an inferno, the result was I unwittingly caused the deaths of so many people, including the two I can't really live without.

It didn't matter to him that it was done unwittingly. It clearly didn't matter to the dead that he hadn't intended it. But with anything, there was cause and effect.

And I was the cause.

And the effect was too terrible to even think about, though it seemed he could think of nothing else.

Decker could not afford to wallow in self-pity, contemplating this while gazing at his navel. He had to earn a living, and so at some point soon he would push off this bench and go in search of gainful employment. But now, right now, this evening, before Santa Claus came calling, he was just going to sit here and wallow in self-pity and at least pretend to gaze at his substantial navel.

But then again, maybe not.

The man sat down next to him and crossed his legs, shivering slightly from the cold.

Decker didn't look at him. "I thought you'd be back in D.C. by now."

Bogart shrugged. "I was, but I had some unfinished business here."

"It's Christmas Eve. Won't your family miss you?"

"What family?"

"You have a ring on your finger."

"I'm separated, Decker. Recent event."

"Sorry to hear that."

"She's not, and, in all honesty, neither am I."

"Kids?"

"She's a Hill staffer and works ungodly hours. So neither one of us ever found the time at the same time.

"Wyatt told you she had sex with Debbie Watson?"

"She was lying about that," replied Decker.

"How did you know? Because you're right: Autopsy revealed she hadn't transitioned entirely to a man. The *equipment* wasn't all there."

"The whole time she sat with her knees together. Tough for a guy to do. But more than that, I don't think she really wanted to be a man. What happened to her made that decision for Wyatt. But she couldn't go the whole way."

Both fell silent.

"Okay, cutting to the chase, I'd like you to come work with me."

Decker turned to look at him. "What does that mean exactly?"

"That means exactly, at the FBI."

Decker shook his head. "I couldn't pass the physical. I couldn't pass anything."

"You wouldn't be a special agent, of course. But I've been assigned to put together and head up a special task force made up of professionals from a wide range of occupations and disciplines, and that includes civilians. The goal is to catch really bad guys. And I can't think of anyone better suited to that than you."

"But I'm not a professional anything."

"You were a cop and then a detective. You have the experience and God knows you have the brains."

"You don't have to do this, Bogart. You bought me the boots and clothes."

"I'm not doing this for you. I'm doing this for *me*. I want to move up at the Bureau. My career is all I have left now. I'm pushing fifty. I've got to hit the turbos soon, or else I'm just wasting my time. And I figure with you on my side, my odds of cracking the really tough cases go way up. And then promotions will follow. I wouldn't mind one day running the place."

"So you mean leave Burlington?"

Bogart stared straight ahead. "Would that be a problem for you?"

"I didn't say that."

"So it *wouldn't* be a problem for you?"

"I didn't say that either."

Bogart looked at him. "Can I cut to the chase and up the ante?"

Decker said nothing but gave a small nod.

Bogart held up his cell phone and flashed the light. A minute later Decker could hear footsteps coming.

Alex Jamison came into the ring of light thrown by the street-lamp. She had on a long winter overcoat and calf boots, and a scarf was wrapped around her head. She stopped in front of the bench and looked down.

Decker looked at her and then at Bogart.

"What am I missing?" he said.

"I thought it would be obvious," said Bogart. "For a smart guy like you."

Decker looked back at Jamison.

"He made me the same offer, Decker, although I think it had a lot more to do with you than me."

Bogart said, "She made some good finds in the investigation. Showed some guts and intuition. I know she's a journalist by trade, but I'm just looking for talent, wherever I can find it."

"You'd leave Burlington?" Decker asked her.

"To tell the truth, I already have."

"What about being a reporter?"

"Andy Jackson taught me to find the truth. I figure that holds true for your line of work too. And maybe I can do more good working with Bogart than I can seeing my byline on a story."

Decker glanced at Bogart. "Does Captain Miller know you're making me this offer?"

"Yes. He's not thrilled about it, but he understands. And Lancaster is being promoted to his second in command. And in case you didn't know, she's taking meds for the tremor in her hand and it's working. And she's put on some weight now that she's stopped smoking."

Decker nodded to all this but didn't break his silence.

Bogart said, "So you'll think about it?"

"No."

"Decker," began Jamison in protest.

"I won't think about it, because . . . because I'm going to do it."

Bogart and Jamison exchanged surprised glances.

Decker looked at them both. "But tonight, I'd prefer to be . . . here. By myself."

Bogart got to his feet at the same time that Jamison said, "And we'll be back tomorrow. And you won't be by yourself ever again. I think you've been alone long enough."

They turned to walk off, but Jamison looked over her shoulder.

"Merry Christmas, *Amos*."

He acknowledged this with a tilt of his head, and they walked on and were soon out of sight.

Amos Decker closed his eyes. And with it his mind. If only for a little while. For just a little while.

ACKNOWLEDGMENTS

To Michelle, for always being there for me.

To Mitch Hoffman, for doing such a great editing job.

To Arnaud Nourry and Michael Pietsch, for handling an extremely difficult situation with grace and aplomb.

To Jamie Raab, Lindsey Rose, Sonya Cheuse, Karen Torres, Anthony Goff, Bob Castillo, Michele McGonigle, Andrew Duncan, Rick Cobban, Brian McLendon, Lukas Fauset, and everyone at Grand Central Publishing, for taking such good care of me.

To Aaron and Arleen Priest, Lucy Childs Baker, Lisa Erbach Vance, Frances Jalet-Miller, John Richmond, and Melissa Edwards, for rolling along with me for more than thirty books.

To Anthony Forbes Watson, Jeremy Trevathan, Maria Rejt, Trisha Jackson, Katie James, Natasha Harding, Sara Lloyd, Lee Dibble, Stuart Dwyer, Geoff Duffield, Jonathan Atkins, Stacey Hamilton, James Long, Anna Bond, Sarah Willcox, Leanne Williams, Sarah McLean, Charlotte Williams, and Neil Lang at Pan

Macmillan, for all your outstanding labors on my behalf.

To Praveen Naidoo and his team at Pan Macmillan in Australia, who have guided me to new heights "Down Under."

To Sandy Violette and Caspian Dennis, for always being so supportive.

To Ron McLarty and Orlagh Cassidy, for your outstanding audio performances. I love to listen to you both, even though I know how the story will end!

To Steven Maat and the entire Bruna team, for continuing to rock my career in Holland.

To Bob Schule, for rising above the pain and casting his eagle eye yet again.

To Roland Ottewell, for a great (and fast) copyediting job.

To Kristen and Natasha, for keeping Columbus Rose running smoothly.

King and Maxwell
DAVID BALDACCI

She's trained to kill. He's beaten the best.
This time all bets are off.

Former Secret Service Agents turned private investigators Sean King and Michelle Maxwell return in their most surprising, personal, and dangerous case to date.

King and Maxwell encounter teenager Tyler Wingo when he has just received the tragic news that his soldier father has been killed in Afghanistan. But then Tyler receives an email from his father . . . after his supposed death.

Sean and Michelle are hired to solve the mystery, and their investigation leads to deeper, even more troubling questions. Could Tyler's father really still be alive? Was his mission all that it seemed? Has Tyler's life been a lie, and could he be the next target?

It's clear that King and Maxwell have stumbled upon something even more sinister when those in power seem intent on removing them at any cost. Determined to help and protect Tyler, their search for the truth takes them on a perilous journey which not only puts their lives at risk but arrives at a frightening conclusion.

The Target
DAVID BALDACCI

**When revenge gets personal,
the stakes get higher . . .**

Government operatives Will Robie and Jessica Reel are faced with a lethal mission. An attack from North Korea looks likely as US involvement in an attempted coup is revealed, and a bond of trust has been broken at the very highest level.

Chung-Cha is a young woman who was raised in the infamous Yodok concentration camp. It's a place where honour, emotion, and compassion don't exist. Cold, calculating, and highly skilled, Chung-Cha has been trained to kill. And the task she has been given is to destroy the enemy at all costs.

A dangerous and deadly operation of cat and mouse plays out between East and West. But who will be the hunter and who will be the hunted when the true target is finally revealed?

The Escape
DAVID BALDACCI

Duty. Loyalty. Family.
The ultimate sacrifice.

Military CID investigator John Puller has returned from his latest case to learn that his brother, Robert, once a major in the United States Air Force, and an expert in nuclear weaponry and cyber-security, has escaped from the Army's most secure prison. Preliminary investigations show that Robert – convicted of treason – may have had help in his breakout. Now he's on the run, and he's the military's number one target.

John Puller has a dilemma. Which comes first: loyalty to his country, or to his brother? Blood is thicker than water, but Robert has state secrets that certain people will kill for. John does not know for certain the true nature of Robert's crimes, nor if he's even guilty. It quickly becomes clear, however, that his brother's responsibilities were powerful and far-reaching.

With the help of US intelligence officer Veronica Knox, both brothers move closer to the truth from their opposing directions. But as the case forces John Puller into a place he thought he'd never be – on the other side of the law – even his skills as an investigator, and his strength as a warrior, might not be enough to save him. Or his brother.

The Guilty
DAVID BALDACCI

When Special Agent Will Robie gets the call to make his first visit home since he was a teenager, it's because his father, the local judge, has been arrested for murdering a man who came before him in court.

The small, remote Bayou town hasn't changed and its residents remember Robie as a wild sports star and girl magnet. He left a lot of hearts broken, and a lot of people angry.

Will and his father, Dan, are estranged, and his mother left years ago. When he visits Dan in jail, he finds that time hasn't healed old wounds. There's too much bad blood between the men, and although Will feels no good will come of staying around, he is persuaded to confront his demons by fellow agent Jessica Reel.

But then another murder changes everything, and stone-cold killer Robie will finally have to come to grips with his toughest assignment of all. His family.

COMING SOON

extracts reading groups
competitions books new
discounts extracts
extracts
competitions discounts
books new events
new books
events extracts
extracts new title reading groups
interviews reading groups
events extracts extracts
books
discounts events
new books events interviews
events new events new extracts
discounts extracts discounts
www.panmacmillan.com
extracts events reading groups
competitions books extracts new